THE EVENTS IN THIS BOOK ARE REAL.

NAMES AND PLACES HAVE BEEN CHANGED
TO PROTECT THE LORIEN,
WHO REMAIN IN HIDING.

OTHER CIVILIZATIONS DO EXIST.

SOME OF THEM SEEK TO DESTROY YOU.

THE LORIEN ☐ LEGACIES

BY PITTACUS LORE

Novels

I AM NUMBER FOUR

THE POWER OF SIX

THE RISE OF NINE

THE FALL OF FIVE

THE REVENGE OF SEVEN

THE FATE OF TEN

The Lost Files Novellas

#1: SIX'S LEGACY

#2: NINE'S LEGACY

#3: THE FALLEN LEGACIES

#4: THE SEARCH FOR SAM

#5: THE LAST DAYS OF LORIEN

#6: THE FORGOTTEN ONES

#7: FIVE'S LEGACY

#8: RETURN TO PARADISE

#9: FIVE'S BETRAYAL

#10: THE FUGITIVE

#11: THE NAVIGATOR

#12: THE GUARD

#13: LEGACIES REBORN

The Lost Files Novella Collections

THE LEGACIES
(Contains novellas #1–#3)

SECRET HISTORIES
(Contains novellas #4–#6)

HIDDEN ENEMY
(Contains novellas #7–#9)

REBEL ALLIES
(Contains novellas #10–#12)

THE FATE OF TEN

OF TEN

BOOK SIX OF THE LORIEN LEGACIES

PITTACUS LORE

HARPER

An Imprint of HarperCollinsPublishers

Library of Congress Control Number: 2015938996
ISBN 978-0-06-219475-6 (hardcover)
ISBN 978-0-06-242751-9 (int'l ed.)
ISBN 978-0-06-242452-5 (special ed.)

Typography by Ray Shappell
15 16 17 18 19   CG/RRDC   10 9 8 7 6 5 4 3 2 1
❖
First Edition

THE FRONT DOOR STARTS SHAKING. IT'S ALWAYS done that whenever the metal security gate two flights down bangs closed, ever since they moved into the Harlem apartment three years ago. Between the front entrance and the paper-thin walls, they are always aware of the comings and goings of the entire building. They mute the television to listen, a fifteen-year-old girl and a fifty-seven-year-old man, daughter and stepfather who rarely see eye to eye, but who have put their many differences aside to watch the aliens invade. The man has spent much of the afternoon muttering prayers in Spanish, while the girl has watched the news coverage in awed silence. It seems like a movie to her, so much so that the fear hasn't truly sunk in. The girl wonders if the handsome blond-haired boy who tried to fight the monster is dead. The man wonders if the girl's mother, a waitress at a small restaurant downtown, survived the initial attack.

The man mutes the TV so they can listen to what's happening outside. One of their neighbors sprints up the stairs, past their floor, yelling the whole way. "They're on the block! They're on the block!"

The man sucks his teeth in disbelief. "Dude's losing it. Those pale freaks ain't gonna bother with Harlem. We're safe here," he reassures the girl.

He turns the volume back up. The girl isn't so sure he's right. She creeps toward the door and stares out the peephole. The hallway outside is dim and empty.

Like the Midtown block behind her, the reporter on TV looks trashed. She's got dirt and ash smudged all over her face, streaks of it through her blond hair. There's a spot of dried blood on her mouth where there should be lipstick. The reporter looks like she's barely keeping it together.

"To reiterate, the initial bombing seems to have tapered off," the reporter says shakily, the man listening raptly. "The—the—the Mogadorians, they have taken to the streets en masse and appear to be, ah, rounding up prisoners, although we have seen some further acts of violence at—at—the slightest provocation . . ."

The reporter chokes back a sob. Behind her, there are hundreds of pale aliens in dark uniforms marching through the streets. Some of them turn their heads and point their empty black eyes right at the camera.

"Jesus Christ," says the man.

"Again, to reiterate, we are being—uh, we are being allowed to broadcast. They—they—the invaders, they seem to *want* us here . . ."

Downstairs, the gate rattles again. There's a screech of metal tearing and a loud crash. Someone didn't have a key. Someone needed to knock the gate down entirely.

"It's them," the girl says.

"Shut up," the man replies. He turns down the TV again. "I mean, keep quiet. Damn."

They hear heavy footfalls coming up the stairs. The girl backs away from the peephole when she hears another door get kicked in. Their downstairs neighbors start to scream.

"Go hide," the man says to the girl. "Go on."

The man's grip tightens on the baseball bat that he retrieved from the hall closet when the alien mother ship first appeared in the sky. He inches closer to the shaking door, positions himself to one side of it, his back to the wall. They can hear noise from the hallway. A loud crash, their neighbor's apartment door being knocked off its hinges, harsh words in guttural English, screaming, and finally a sound like compressed lightning being uncorked. They've seen the aliens' guns on television, stared in awe at the sizzling bolts of blue energy they fire.

The footsteps resume, stopping outside their shaky door. The man's eyes are wide, his hands tight on the bat. He realizes that the girl hasn't moved. She's frozen.

"Wake up, stupid," he snaps. "*Go.*"

He nods toward the living room window. It's open, the fire escape waiting outside.

The girl hates when the man calls her stupid. Even so, for the first time she can remember, the girl does what her stepfather tells her. She climbs through the window the same way she's snuck out of this apartment so many times before. The girl knows she shouldn't go alone. Her stepfather should flee, too. She turns around on the fire escape to call to him, and so she's looking into the apartment when their front door is hammered down.

The aliens are much uglier in person than on television. Their otherness freezes the girl in her tracks. She stares at the deathly pale skin of the first one through the door, at his unblinking black eyes and bizarre tattoos. There are four aliens altogether, each of them armed. It's the first one that spots the girl on the fire escape. He stops in the doorway, his strange gun leveled in her direction.

"Surrender or die," the alien says.

A second later, the girl's stepfather hits the alien in the face with his bat. It's a powerful swing—the old man made his living as a mechanic, his forearms thick from twelve-hour days. It caves in the alien's head, the creature immediately disintegrating into ash.

Before her stepfather can get his bat back over his shoulder, the nearest alien shoots him in the chest.

The man is thrown backwards into the apartment, muscles seizing, his shirt burning. He crashes through the glass coffee table and rolls, ends up facing the window, where he locks eyes with the girl.

"Run!" her stepfather somehow finds the strength to shout. "Run, damn it!"

The girl bounds down the fire escape. When she gets to the ladder, she hears gunfire from her apartment. She tries not to think about what that means. A pale face pokes his head out of her window and takes aim at her with his weapon.

She lets go of the ladder, dropping into the alley below, right as the air around her sizzles. The hair on her arms stands up and the girl can tell there's electricity coursing through the metal of the fire escape. But she's unharmed. The alien missed her.

The girl jumps over some trash bags and runs to the mouth of the alley, peeking around the corner to see the street she grew up on. There's a fire hydrant gushing water into the air; it reminds the girl of summer block parties. She sees an overturned mail truck, its undercarriage smoking like it could explode at any minute. Farther down the block, parked in the middle of the street, the girl sees the aliens' small spacecraft, one of many she and her stepfather saw unleashed from the hulking ship that still looms over Manhattan. They played that clip over and over on the news. Almost as much as they played the video about the blond-haired boy.

John Smith. That's his name. The girl narrating the video said so.

Where is he now? the girl wonders. Probably not saving people in Harlem, that's for sure.

The girl knows she has to save herself.

She's about to run for it when she spots another group of aliens exiting an apartment building across the street. They have a dozen humans with them, some familiar faces from around the neighborhood, a couple of kids she recognizes from the grades below her. At gunpoint, they force the people onto their knees on the curb. A big alien freak walks down the line of people, clicking a small object in his hand, like a bouncer outside of a club. They're keeping a count. The girl isn't sure she wants to see what happens next.

Metal screeches behind her. The girl turns around to see one of the aliens from her apartment climbing down the fire escape.

She runs. The girl is fast and she knows these streets. The subway is only a few blocks from here. Once, on a dare, the girl climbed down from the platform and ventured into the tunnels. The darkness and rats didn't scare her nearly as much as these aliens. That's where she'll go. She can hide there, maybe even make it downtown, try to find her mother. The girl doesn't know how she's going to break the news about her stepfather. She doesn't even believe it herself. She keeps expecting to wake up.

The girl darts around a corner and three aliens stand in her path. Her instinct makes her try to turn back, but her ankle twists and her legs come out from under her. She falls, hitting the sidewalk hard. One of the aliens makes a short, harsh noise—the girl realizes he's laughing at her.

"Surrender or die," it says, and the girl knows this isn't really a choice. The aliens already have their guns raised and aimed, fingers nearly depressing the triggers.

Surrender *and* die. They're going to kill her no matter what she does next. The girl is certain of this.

The girl throws up her hands to defend herself. It's a reflex. She knows it won't do anything against their weapons.

Except it does.

The aliens' guns jerk upwards, out of their hands. They fly twenty yards down the block.

They look at the girl, stunned and uncertain. She doesn't understand what just happened either.

But she can feel something different inside her. Something new. It's as if she's a puppeteer, with strings connecting to every object on the block. All she needs to do is push and pull. The girl isn't sure how she knows this. It feels natural.

One of the aliens charges and the girl swipes her hand from right to left. He flies across the street, limbs flailing, and slams through the windshield of a parked car. The other two exchange a look and start to back away.

"Who's laughing now?" she asks them, standing up.

"Garde," one of them hisses in reply.

The girl doesn't know what this means. The way the alien says it makes the word sound like a curse. That makes the girl smile. She likes that these things ripping up her neighborhood are afraid of her now.

She can fight them.

She's going to kill them.

The girl throws one of her hands into the air and the result is one of the aliens lifting up from the ground. The girl brings her hand down just as quickly, smashing the airborne alien on top of his companion. She repeats this until they turn to dust.

When it's done, the girl looks down at her hands. She doesn't know where this power came from. She doesn't know what it means.

But she's going to use it.

CHAPTER ONE

WE RUN PAST THE BROKEN WING OF AN EXPLODED jet fighter, the jagged metal lodged in the middle of a city street like a shark's fin. How long ago was it that we watched the jets scream by overhead, a course set for uptown and the *Anubis*? It feels like days, but it must only be hours. Some of the people we're with—the survivors—they whooped and cheered when they saw the jets, like the tide was going to turn.

I knew better. Kept quiet. Only a few minutes later, we could hear the explosions as the *Anubis* blew those jets out of the sky, scattering pieces of Earth's most sophisticated military all over the island of Manhattan. They haven't sent any more jets in.

How many deaths is that? Hundreds. Thousands. Maybe more. And it's all my fault. Because I couldn't kill Setrákus Ra when I had the chance.

"On the left!" a voice shouts from somewhere behind

me. I whip my head around, charge up a fireball without thinking about it, and incinerate a Mog scout as he comes around a corner. Me, Sam, the couple dozen survivors we picked up along the way—we barely break stride. We're in lower Manhattan now. Ran here. Fought our way down. Block by block. Trying to put some distance between us and Midtown, where the Mogs are strongest, where we last saw the *Anubis*.

I'm exhausted.

I stumble. I can't even feel my feet anymore, they're so tired. I think I'm about to collapse. An arm goes around my shoulders and steadies me.

"John?" Sam asks, concerned. He's holding me up. It sounds like his voice is coming through a tunnel. I try to reply to him, but the words don't come. Sam turns his head and speaks to one of the other survivors. "We need to get off the streets for a while. He needs to rest."

Next thing I know, I slump back against the wall of an apartment building lobby. I must have gone out for a minute. I try to brace myself, try to pull myself together. I have to keep fighting.

But I can't do it—my body refuses to take any more punishment. I let myself slide down the wall so that I'm sitting on the floor. The carpet is covered in dust and broken glass that must've blown in from outside. There are about twenty-five of us huddled together here. These are all we could manage to save. Bloodstained and dirty, a few of them wounded, all of us tired.

How many injuries did I heal today? It was easy, at first. After so many, though, I could feel my healing Legacy draining my own energy. I must have hit my limit.

I remember the people not by name but by how I found them or what I healed. Broken-Arm and Pinned-Under-Car look concerned, scared.

A woman, Jumped-from-Window, puts her hand on my shoulder, checking on me. I nod to tell her I'm all right and she looks relieved.

Right in front of me, Sam talks with a uniformed cop in his fifties. The cop has dried blood all over one side of his face from a cut on top of his head that I healed. I forget his name or where we found him. Their voices sound far away, like they're echoing down a mile-long tunnel. I have to focus my hearing to understand the words, and even that takes a colossal effort. My head feels wrapped in cotton.

"Word came in over the radio that we've got a foothold on the Brooklyn Bridge," the cop says. "NYPD, National Guard, army . . . hell, everyone. They're holding the bridge. Evacuating survivors from there. It's only a few blocks away and they say the Mogs are concentrated uptown. We can make it."

"Then you should go," Sam answers. "Go now while the coast is clear, before another of their patrols comes through."

"You should come with us, kid."

"We can't," Sam replies. "One of our friends is still out there. We have to find him."

Nine. That's who we have to find. The last we saw him, he was battling Five in front of the United Nations. *Through* the United Nations. We have to find him before we can leave New York. We have to find him and save as many people as we can. I'm starting to come to my senses, but I'm still too exhausted to move. I open my mouth to speak, but all I manage to do is groan.

"He's had it," says the cop, and I know he's talking about me. "You two have done enough. Get out with us now, while you can."

"He'll be fine," Sam says. The doubt in his voice makes me grit my teeth and focus. I need to press on, to dig down and keep fighting.

"He passed out."

"He just needs to rest for a minute."

"*I'm fine,*" I mumble, but I don't think they hear me.

"You're gonna get killed if you stay, kid," the cop tells Sam, sternly shaking his head. "You can't keep this up. There's too many for just you two to fight. Leave it to the army, or . . ."

He trails off. We all know the army already made their attempt. Manhattan is lost.

"We'll get out as soon as we can," Sam replies.

"You hear me down there?" The cop is talking to

PITTACUS LORE

me now. Lecturing me in the same way Henri used to.
I wonder if he's got kids somewhere. "There's nothing
left for you to do here. You got us this far, let us do the
rest. We'll carry you to the bridge if we have to."

The survivors assembled around the cop nod, murmuring in agreement. Sam looks at me, his eyebrows
raised in question. His face is smeared with dirt and
ash. He looks hollowed out and weak, like he's barely
standing himself. A Mog blaster hangs from his hip,
hooked there by a chopped piece of electric cord, and
it's like Sam's entire body slumps in that direction, the
extra weight threatening to pull him over.

I force myself to stand up. My muscles are limp and
almost useless, though. I'm trying to show the police
officer and the others that I've got some fight left in
me but I can tell by the pitying way they're staring at
me that I don't look very inspiring. I can barely keep
my knees from shaking. For a moment, it feels like I'm
going to crash down to the floor. But then something
happens—I feel like a force is lifting and pulling me,
supporting some of my weight, straightening my back
and squaring my shoulders. I don't know how I'm doing
this, where I'm finding the strength. It's almost supernatural.

No, actually, it's not supernatural at all. It's Sam.
Telekinetic Sam, concentrating on me, making it look
like I've still got some gas left in the tank.

"We're staying," I say firmly, my voice scratchy. "There are more people to save."

The cop shakes his head in wonder. Behind him, a girl that I vaguely remember rescuing from a collapsing fire escape bursts into tears. I'm not sure if she's inspired or if I just look terrible. Sam remains completely focused on me, stone-faced, a fresh bead of sweat forming on his temple.

"Get to safety," I tell the survivors. "Then, help however you can. This is your planet. We're all going to save it together."

The cop strides forward to shake my hand. His grip is like a vise. "We won't forget you, John Smith," he says. "All of us, we owe you our lives."

"Give them hell," someone else says.

And then all at once the rest of the group of survivors are blurting out their good-byes and their gratitude. I grit my teeth in what I hope is a smile. The truth is, I'm too tired for this. The cop—he's their leader now, he'll keep them safe—he makes sure everyone keeps it quiet and quick, eventually hustling them out of the apartment building's lobby and onto the Brooklyn Bridge.

As soon as we're alone, Sam releases me from the telekinetic grip he was using to hold me upright and I slump backwards against the wall, struggling to keep my feet under me. He's out of breath and sweating from the exertion of keeping me standing. He's not Loric and he's had no proper training, yet somehow Sam has developed a Legacy and begun using it the best he can. Considering our situation, he's had no choice but to learn on the fly. Sam with a Legacy—if things weren't so chaotic and desperate, I'd be more excited. I'm not sure how or why this happened to him, but Sam's new-found powers are pretty much the only win we've had since coming to New York.

"Thanks," I say, the words coming easier now.

"No problem," Sam replies, panting. "You're the symbol of the Earth's resistance; we can't have you lay-ing around."

I try to push off from the wall, but my legs aren't ready yet to support my full weight. It's easier if I just lean against it and drag myself towards the nearest apartment door.

"Look at me. I'm not the symbol of anything," I grumble.

"Come on," he says. "You're exhausted."

Sam puts his arm around me, helping me along. He's dragging too, though, so I try not to put much weight on him. We've been through hell in the last few hours. The skin on my hands still tingles from how much I've had to use my Lumen, tossing fireballs at squad after squad of Mog attackers. I hope the nerve endings aren't per-manently singed or something. The thought of igniting my Lumen right now makes my knees nearly buckle.

"Resistance," I say bitterly. "Resistance is what happens after you lose a war, Sam."

"You know what I meant," he replies. I can tell by the way his voice shakes that it's a strain for Sam to stay optimistic after everything we've seen today. He's trying, though. "A lot of those people knew who you were. They said there was some video of you on the news. And everything that happened at the UN—you basically unmasked Setrákus Ra in front of an international audience. Everyone knows you've been fighting against the Mogadorians. That you tried to stop this."

"Then they know that I failed."

The door to the first-floor apartment is ajar. I shove it the rest of the way open and Sam closes and locks it behind us. I try the nearest light switch, surprised to find that the electricity is still on here. Power seems to be spotty throughout the city. I guess this neighborhood hasn't been badly hit yet. I turn the lights off just as quickly—in our current condition, we don't want to attract the attention of any Mogadorian patrols that might be in the area. As I stumble towards a nearby futon, Sam moves around the room closing curtains.

The apartment is a small one-room studio. There's a cramped kitchen cordoned off from the main living space by a granite counter, a single closet and a tiny bathroom. Whoever lives here definitely left in a hurry; there are clothes spilled across the floor from a hasty packing job, an overturned bowl of cereal on the counter and a cracked picture frame near the door that looks like it was crushed underfoot. In the picture, a couple in their twenties pose in front of a tropical beach, a small monkey perched on the guy's shoulder.

These people had a normal life. Even if they made it out of Manhattan and to safety, that's over now. Earth will never be the same. I used to imagine a peaceful life like this for Sarah and me once the Mogs were defeated. Not a tiny apartment in New York City, but something simple and calm. There's an explosion in the distance, the Mogs destroying something uptown. I realize now how naïve those life-after-war dreams were. Nothing will ever be normal after this.

Sarah. I hope she's okay. It was her face that I called to mind during the roughest parts of our block-by-block battle through Manhattan. Keep fighting and you'll get to see her again, that's what I kept telling myself. I wish I could talk to her. I *need* to talk to her. Not just Sarah, but Six too—I need to get in touch with the others, to find out what Sarah learned from Mark James and his mysterious contact, and to see what Six, Marina and Adam did in Mexico. That has to have something to do with why Sam suddenly developed a Legacy. What if he's not the only one? I need to know what's happening outside of New York City, but my satellite phone was destroyed when I fell into the East River and the regular cell phone networks are down. For now, it's just me and Sam. Surviving.

In the kitchen, Sam opens the fridge. He pauses and glances over to me.

"Is it wrong if we take some of this person's food?" he asks me.

"I'm sure they won't care," I reply.

I close my eyes for what feels like a second but must be longer, opening them only when a piece of bread bumps against my nose. With one hand extended theatrically like a comic book character, Sam telekinetically floats a peanut butter sandwich, a plastic container of applesauce and a spoon in front of my face. Even feeling down and out as I am, I can't help but smile at the effort.

"Sorry, I didn't mean to hit you with the sandwich," Sam says as I pluck the food out of the air. "I'm still getting used to this. Obviously."

"No worries. It's easy to shove and pull with telekinesis. Precision's the hardest part to learn."

"No kidding," he says.

"You're doing amazing for someone that's had telekinesis for all of four hours, man."

Sam sits down on the futon next to me with his own sandwich. "It helps if I imagine that I have, like, ghost hands. Does that make sense?"

I think back to how I trained my own telekinesis

with Henri. It seems like so long ago.

"I used to visualize whatever I focused on moving, and then will it to happen," I tell Sam. "We started small. Henri used to toss me baseballs in the backyard and I'd practice catching them with my mind."

"Yeah, well, I don't think playing catch is really an option for me right now," Sam says. "I'm finding other ways to practice."

Sam floats his sandwich up from his lap. He initially brings it too high for him to bite, but gets it at mouth level after a second more of concentration.

"Not bad," I say.

"It's easier when I'm not thinking about it."

"Like when we're fighting for our lives, for instance?"

"Yeah," Sam says, shaking his head in wonder. "Are we going to talk about how this happened to me, John? Or why it happened? Or . . . I don't know. What it means?"

"Garde develop Legacies in their teens," I say, shrugging. "Maybe you're just a late bloomer."

"Dude, have you forgotten that I'm not Loric?"

"Neither is Adam, but he's got Legacies," I reply.

"Yeah, his gross dad hooked him up to a dead Garde and . . ."

I hold up a hand to stop Sam. "All I'm saying is that it's not so cut-and-dry. I don't think Legacies work the way my people always assumed." I pause for a moment to think. "What's happened to you has to have something to do with what Six and the others did at the Sanctuary."

"Six did this . . . ," Sam says.

"They went down there to find Lorien on Earth; I think they did it. And then, maybe Lorien chose you."

Without even realizing it, I've already devoured the sandwich and applesauce. My stomach growls. I feel a little better, my strength starting to come back to me.

"Well, that's an honor," Sam says, looking down at his hands and thinking it over. Or, more likely, thinking about Six. "A terrifying honor."

"You did good out there. I couldn't have saved all those people without you," I reply, patting Sam on the back. "The truth is, I don't know what the hell is going on. I don't know how or why you suddenly developed a Legacy. I'm just glad you have it. I'm glad there's a little hope mixed into the death and destruction."

Sam stands up, pointlessly brushing some crumbs off his dirt-caked jeans. "Yeah, that's me, the great hope for humanity, currently dying for another sandwich. You want one?"

"I can get it," I tell Sam, but when I lean forward to get off the futon, I'm immediately woozy and have to sink back down.

"Take it easy," Sam says, playing it off like he didn't notice what a mess I am. "I got the sandwiches covered."

"We'll just hang here for a few more minutes," I say groggily. "Then we'll go track down Nine."

I close my eyes, listening to Sam clatter around in the kitchen, trying to spread peanut butter with a telekinetically held knife. In the background, always in the background now, I can hear the steady thunder of fighting somewhere else in Manhattan. Sam's right—we're the resistance. We should be out there resisting. If I can just rest for a few more minutes . . .

I don't open my eyes until Sam shakes me by the shoulder. Immediately, I can tell that I've dozed off. The light in the room is changed, the streetlights coming on outside, a warm yellow glow under the curtains. A plate stacked with sandwiches waits on the couch next to me. I'm tempted to dive right in and chow down. It's like all my urges are animal now—sleep, eat, fight.

"How long was I out for?" I ask Sam, sitting up, feeling a little better physically but also feeling guilty for sleeping when there are people dying all over New York.

"About an hour," Sam replies. "I was going to let you rest, but . . ."

In explanation, Sam gestures behind him, towards the small flat-screen television attached to the room's far wall. The local news is actually broadcasting. Sam's got the volume muted and the picture occasionally gives way to bursts of static, but there it is—New

York City burning. Grainy footage shows the looming hulk of the *Anubis* crawling across the skyline, its side-mounted cannons bombarding the uppermost floors of a skyscraper until there's nothing left but dust.

"I didn't even think to check if it was working until a few minutes ago," Sam says. "I figured the Mogs would've knocked out the TV stations for, you know, war reasons."

I haven't forgotten what Setrákus Ra said to me as I dangled from his ship over the East River. He wants me to watch Earth fall. Thinking even further back, to that vision of Washington, D.C., which I shared with Ella, I remember that city looking pretty busted up, but it wasn't completely razed. And there were survivors left over to serve Setrákus Ra. I think I'm beginning to understand.

"It's not an accident," I say to Sam, thinking out loud. "He must want the humans to be able to see the destruction he's bringing down. It's not like on Lorien where his fleet just wiped everyone out. That's why he tried putting on that big show at the UN, it's why he tried all that shadowy MogPro shit to bring Earth under his control peacefully. He's planning to live here afterwards. And if they're not going to worship him like the Mogs do, he at least wants his human subjects to fear him."

"Well, the fear thing is definitely working," Sam replies.

On-screen, the news has switched to a live shot of an anchor at her desk. The building that houses this channel has probably taken some damage from the fighting because it looks like they're barely keeping themselves on the air. Only half the lights are on in the studio and the camera is cockeyed, the picture not as sharp as it should be. The anchor is trying to keep up a professional face, but her hair is caked with dust and her eyes are red-rimmed from crying. She speaks directly into the camera for a few seconds, introducing the next piece of footage.

The anchor disappears, replaced by shaky video shot with a cellular phone. In the middle of a major intersection, a blurry figure spins round and round, like an Olympic discus thrower warming up. Except this guy's not holding a discus. With inhuman strength he's whipping around another person by the ankle. After a dozen spins, the guy lets go of the curled-up body, flinging it through the front window of a nearby movie theater. The video stays centered on the thrower as, shoulders heaving, he yells out what's probably a curse.

It's Nine.

"Sam! Turn it up!"

As Sam gropes for the remote, whoever's filmed Nine dives behind a car for cover. It's disorienting as hell, but the cameraman manages to keep recording by sticking one hand above the car's trunk. A group of Mogadorian warriors have appeared in the intersection, blasting away at Nine. I watch as he dances nimbly aside, then uses his telekinesis to fling a car in their direction.

". . . again, this is footage taken in Union Square just moments ago," the shaky-voiced anchor is saying as Sam turns up the volume. "We know this apparently superpowered, um, possibly alien teenager was at the UN scene with the other young man identified as John Smith. We see him here engaged in combat with the Mogadorians, doing things not humanly possible . . ."

"They know my name," I say, quietly.

"Look," Sam says, hitting my arm.

The camera has panned back to the movie theater, where a burly form slowly rises from the shattered window. I don't get a good look at him, but I immediately know exactly who Nine was throwing around. He flies up from the movie theater window, slashes through the few Mogs still in the intersection and then careens violently into Nine.

"Five," Sam says.

The camera loses track of Five and Nine as they plow through the grass of a small nearby park, churning up huge chunks of dirt as they go.

"They're killing each other," I say. "We have to get over there."

"A second extraterrestrial teenager is fighting the

first, at least when they're not fighting off the invaders," the anchor says, sounding baffled. "We . . . we don't know why. We don't have many answers at all at this point, I'm afraid. Just . . . stay safe, New York. Evacuation efforts are ongoing if you have a safe route to the Brooklyn Bridge. If you're near the fighting, keep inside and—"

I take the remote from Sam and turn off the TV. He watches me as I stand up, checking to make sure I'm all right. My muscles howl in protest and I'm dizzy for a second, but I can push through. I have to push through. Never has the expression "fight like there's no tomorrow" had more meaning. If I'm going to make this right—if we're going to save Earth from Setrákus Ra and the Mogadorians, then the first steps are finding Nine and surviving New York.

"She said Union Square," I say. "That's where we go."

CHAPTER TWO

THE WORLD HASN'T CHANGED. AT LEAST, NOT
that I can tell.

The jungle air is humid and sticky, a welcome change
from the cold dampness of the Sanctuary's subterranean
depths. I have to shield my eyes as we emerge into the late
afternoon sun, ducking one by one through a narrow stone
archway that's appeared in the Mayan temple's base.

"They couldn't have let us come in that way?" I
grumble, cracking my back and glancing over to the hundreds of fractured limestone steps we climbed earlier.
Once we were at the top of Calakmul, our pendants acti-
vated some kind of Loric doorway that teleported us to the
hidden Sanctuary beneath the centuries-old human-built
structure. We found ourselves in an otherworldly room
obviously created by the Elders on one of their visits to
Earth. I guess secrecy was a higher priority than ease of
access. Anyway, the way out wasn't such a hike and didn't

involve any disorienting teleportation—just a dizzying hundred yards of dusty spiral staircase and a simple door that, of course, wasn't there when we first entered.

Adam exits the Sanctuary behind me, his eyes narrowed to slits.

"What now?" he asks.

"I don't know," I tell him, looking up at the darkening sky. "I was sorta counting on the Sanctuary to answer that."

"I . . . I'm still not sure what we saw in there. Or what we accomplished," Adam says hesitantly. He pushes some loose strands of black hair out of his face as he watches me.

"Me neither," I tell him.

Truth be told, I'm not even sure how long we were beneath the earth. You lose track of time when you're deep in conversation with an otherworldly being made of pure Loric energy. We had scraped together as many pieces of our Inheritance as the Garde could spare—basically, anything that wasn't a weapon. Once inside the Sanctuary, we dumped all those unexplained stones and trinkets into a hidden well connected to a dormant Loralite energy source. I guess that was enough to wake up the Entity, the living embodiment of Lorien itself. We chatted.

Yeah. That happened.

But the Entity basically spoke in riddles and, at the end of our talk, the thing went supernova, its energy flooding out of the Sanctuary and into the world. Like Adam, I'm not sure what it all meant.

I'd expected to emerge from the Sanctuary and find . . . *something*. Maybe jagged bolts of Loric energy streaking through the skies, on their way to incinerate the nearest Mogadorian not named Adam? Maybe some more juice to my Legacies, putting me on a level where I'd be able to whip up a storm big enough to wipe out all our enemies? No such luck. As far as I know, the Mogadorian fleet is still closing in on Earth. John, Sam, Nine and the others could be rushing towards the front lines right now, and I'm not sure we've done anything to help them.

Marina is last through the temple's door. She hugs herself, her eyes wide and watery, blinking in the sunlight.

I know she's thinking about Eight.

Before the energy source went rocketing into the world, it somehow managed to resurrect him, if only for a few fleeting minutes. Long enough for Marina to say good-bye. Even now, already starting to sweat in the oppressive jungle heat, I get chills thinking about Eight returned to us, awash in the Loralite glow, smiling again. It was the kind of intensely beautiful moment I've hardened myself to over the years—this is war, and people are going to die. Friends are going to die. I've come to accept the pain, to take the ugliness for granted. So it can be a little stunning when something good actually happens.

Comforting as it was to see Eight again, it was still saying good-bye. I can't imagine what Marina's going through. She loved him and now he's gone. Again.

Marina stops and glances back at the temple, almost like she might go back inside. Next to me, Adam clears his throat.

"Is she going to be okay?" he asks me, his voice low.

Marina shut down on me once before, back in Florida, after Five betrayed us. After he killed Eight. This isn't the same—she isn't radiating a constant field of cold, and she doesn't look like she's on the verge of strangling whoever comes close. When she turns back to us, her expression is almost serene. She's remembering, storing that moment with Eight away and steeling herself for what's to come. I'm not worried about her.

I smile as Marina blinks her eyes and wipes a hand across her face.

"I can hear you," she replies to Adam. "I'm fine."

"Good," Adam says, awkwardly looking away. "I just wanted to say, about what happened in there, uh, that I . . ."

Adam trails off, both Marina and I looking at him expectantly. Being a Mog, I think he still finds it a little uncomfortable to get too personal with us. I know he was amazed by the Loric light show inside the Sanctuary, but I could also tell he felt like he didn't belong, like he wasn't worthy enough to be in the presence of the Entity.

When Adam's pause stretches on, I pat him on the back. "Let's save the heart-to-heart for the ride, okay?"

Adam seems relieved as we walk back towards our Skimmer, the ship parked alongside a dozen other Mog crafts on the nearby landing strip. The Mog encampment in front of the temple is exactly the way we left it—trashed. The Mogs that were trying to break into the Sanctuary had cleared jungle in a precise ring around the temple, getting as close to the temple as the Sanctuary's powerful force field would allow.

It isn't until we cross from the vine-strewn overgrowth of the land directly in front of the temple to the scorched brown soil of the Mog camp that I realize the force field is gone. The deadly barrier that protected the Sanctuary for years is no more.

"The force field must have shut down while we were inside," I say.

"Maybe it doesn't need protection anymore," Adam suggests.

"Or maybe the Entity diverted its power elsewhere," Marina replies. She pauses for a moment, thinking. "When I kissed Eight . . . I felt it. For a split second, I was part of the Entity's energy flow. It was spreading out *everywhere*, all through the Earth. Wherever the Loric energy went, now it's spread thin. Maybe it can't power its defenses here."

Adam gives me a look, like I should be able to explain what Marina just said.

"What do you mean it spread through the Earth?" I ask.

"I don't know how to explain it better than that," Marina says, gazing back at the temple, now cast half in shadow by the setting sun. "It was a feeling like I was one with Lorien. And we were everywhere."

"Interesting," Adam says, eyeing the temple and then the ground beneath his feet with a mixture of caution and awe. "Where do you think it went? Are your Legacies . . . ?"

"I don't feel any different," I tell him.

"Me neither," Marina says. "But something has changed. Lorien *is out there* now. On Earth."

It's definitely not the tangible result I was hoping for, but Marina seems so upbeat about it. I don't want to rain on her parade. "I guess we'll see if anything's changed back in civilization. Maybe the Entity's out there kicking ass."

Marina glances back at the temple. "Should we leave it this way? Without protection?"

"What's left to protect?" Adam asks.

"There's still at least some of the, uh, the *Entity* left in there," Marina replies. "Even now, I think the Sanctuary is still a way to . . . I don't know, exactly. Get in touch with Lorien?"

"We don't have a choice," I reply. "The others will need us."

"Wait a second," Adam says, looking around. "Where's Dust?"

With everything that happened inside the Sanctuary,

I completely forgot about the Chimæra we left outside the temple to stand guard. There's no sign of the wolf anywhere.

"Could he have gone into the jungle looking for that Mog woman?" Marina asks.

"Phiri Dun-Ra," Adam replies, naming the trueborn that survived our initial assault. "He wouldn't just go off on his own like that."

"Maybe the Sanctuary's light show scared him off," I suggest.

Adam frowns, then cups both his hands around his mouth. "Dust! Come on, Dust!"

He and Marina fan out, searching for any sign of the Chimæra. I climb onto our Skimmer to get a better look at the surrounding area. From up here, something catches my eye. A gray shape squirming out from beneath a rotten log at the edge of the jungle.

"What's that?" I yell, pointing the writhing form out to Adam. He races over, Marina right behind him. A moment later, Adam carries the small shape over to me, his face twisted with concern.

"It's Dust," Adam says. "I mean, I think it is."

Adam holds a gray bird in his hands. It's alive but its body is stiff and twisted, like it suffered from an electric shock and never recovered from the spasms. His wings jut out at odd angles and his beak is frozen half-open. Even though this is nothing like the powerful wolf we left behind just a short time ago, there's a quality that I immediately recognize. It's Dust, for sure. Bad as he looks, his black bird eyes dart around frantically. He's alive, and his mind is working, but his body isn't responding.

"What the hell happened to him?" I ask.

"I don't know," Adam says, and for a moment I think I see tears in his eyes. He steadies himself. "He looks . . . he looks like the other Chimæra did right after I rescued them from Plum Island. They were experimented on."

"It's okay, Dust, you're okay," Marina whispers. She gently smooths down the feathers on his head, trying to calm him. She uses her Legacy to heal most of the scratches that cover him, but it doesn't release Dust from the paralysis.

"We can't do anything more for him here," I say. I feel bad, but we need to keep moving. "If that Mog did this to him, she's long gone. Let's just get back to the others. Maybe they'll have ideas about what to do."

Adam brings Dust on board the Skimmer and wraps him in a blanket. He tries to make the paralyzed Chimæra as comfortable as possible before he sits down behind the ship's controls.

I want to get in touch with John, find out how things are going outside the Mexican jungle. I retrieve the satellite phone from my pack and settle into the seat next to Adam. While he begins powering up the ship, I call John.

The phone rings endlessly. After about a minute,

Marina leans forward to look at me.

"How worried should we be that he's not answering?" she asks.

"The normal amount of worried," I reply. I can't help but glance down at my ankle. No new scars—as if I wouldn't have felt the searing pain. "At least we know they're still alive."

"Something's not right," Adam says.

"We don't know that," I reply quickly. "Just because they can't answer right this second doesn't mean—"

"No. I mean with the ship."

When I take the phone away from my ear, I can hear the strange stuttering noise the Skimmer's engine is making. The lights on the console in front of me flicker erratically.

"I thought you knew how to work this thing," I say.

Adam scowls, then angrily flips down switches on the dashboard, powering the ship off. Beneath us, the engine rattles and clangs, like something's not catching.

"I do know how to work this thing, Six," he says. "It's not me."

"Sorry," I reply, watching as he waits for the engine to settle before powering the ship up again. The engine—Mogadorian technology that should be deathly silent—once again burps and spasms. "Maybe we should try something besides turning it off and on again."

"First Dust, and now this. It doesn't make sense," Adam grumbles. "The electronics are still working. Well, everything except for the automated diagnostic, which is exactly what would tell us what's wrong with the engine."

I reach over and hit the button that opens up the cockpit. The glass dome parts above our heads.

"Let's go have a look," I say, standing up from my seat.

We all climb back out of the Skimmer. Adam jumps down to inspect the ship's underside, but I remain atop the hood, next to the cockpit. I find myself gazing at the Sanctuary, the ancient limestone structure casting a long shadow thanks to the setting sun. Marina stands next to me, silently taking in the view.

"Do you think we're going to win?" I ask her, the question just popping out. I'm not even sure I want an answer.

Marina doesn't say anything at first. After a moment, she rests her head on my shoulder. "I think we're closer today than we were yesterday," she says.

"I wish I knew for sure that coming down here was worth it," I say, clutching the satellite phone, willing it to ring.

"You need to have faith," Marina replies. "I'm telling you, Six, the Entity did something . . ."

I try to trust in Marina's words, but all I can think about are the practicalities. I wonder if the flood of Loric energy from the Sanctuary was what screwed up our ride in the first place.

Or maybe there's a simpler explanation.

"Hey, guys?" Adam calls from beneath the ship. "You

better come take a look at this."

I hop down from the Skimmer, Marina right behind me. We find Adam wedged between the metal struts of the landing gear, a bent panel of the ship's armored underbelly in the dirt at his feet.

"Is that our problem?" I ask.

"That was already loose," Adam explains, kicking the dislodged piece. "And look at this . . ."

Adam motions me closer, so I slide in next to him, getting an intimate look at the inner workings of our ship. The Skimmer's engine could probably fit under the hood of a pickup truck, but it's a lot more complicated than anything built here on Earth. Instead of pistons or gears, the engine comprises a series of overlapping spheres. They spin fitfully when Adam pushes against them, ticking uselessly against the exposed ends of some thick cables that run deeper into the ship.

"See, the electrical systems are still intact," Adam says, flicking the cables. "That's why we still have some power. But that's not enough alone to get the antigravity propulsion going. These centrifugal rotors here?" He runs his hand over the overlapping spheres. "They're what gets us off the ground. Thing is, they aren't broken either."

"So you're telling me the Skimmer should work?" I ask, my eyes glazing over as I stare at the engine.

"It should," Adam says, but then he waves his hand in some empty space between the rotors and the wires.

"Except you see that?"

"I have no idea what the hell I'm looking at, dude," I tell him. "Is it broken?"

"There's a conduit missing," he explains. "It's what transfers the energy generated by the engines to the rest of the ship."

"And you're telling me it didn't just fall out."

"Obviously not."

I take a few steps out from underneath the Skimmer and scan the nearby tree line for any movement. We already killed every Mog that was trying to break into the Sanctuary. All except for one.

"Phiri Dun-Ra," I say, knowing that the Mog is still out there. We were too focused on getting into the Sanctuary to bother going after her earlier, and now . . .

"She sabotaged us," Adam says, reaching the same conclusion I have. Phiri Dun-Ra did a number on Adam when we arrived, beat him up pretty good and was about to try roasting his face on the Sanctuary's force field before we got the drop on her. He still sounds pretty bitter about it. "She took out Dust and then she stranded us here. We should've killed her."

"It's not too late," I reply, frowning. I don't see anything in the trees, but that doesn't mean Phiri Dun-Ra isn't out there watching us.

"Couldn't we replace the part with one from another ship?" Marina asks, motioning to the dozen or so Mog scout ships spaced out along the landing zone.

Adam grunts and shoves out from underneath our Skimmer. He strides towards the nearest ship, his left hand on the handle of a Mog blaster he took off one of the warriors we killed.

"I bet all these ships have engine panels that look just like ours," Adam grumbles. "I hope it at least hurt her messed-up hands."

I remember Phiri Dun-Ra's bandaged hands, scarred from coming into contact with the Sanctuary's force field. We should've known better than to leave one of them alive. Even before Adam reaches the nearest ship, I've got a sinking feeling.

Adam ducks underneath the other ship, examining it. He sighs and makes eye contact with me before gently elbowing the armored hull above his head. The engine panel falls away like there was nothing holding it in place.

"She's toying with us," he says, his voice low and gravelly. "She could've taken a shot at us when we left the Sanctuary. Instead, she wants to keep us here."

"She knows she can't take us by herself," I say, raising my voice a little, thinking maybe I can bait Phiri Dun-Ra out of hiding.

"She removed these parts, right?" Marina asks. "She didn't just destroy them?"

"No, it looks like she took them," Adam replies. "Probably doesn't want to be responsible for destroying a bunch of ships in addition to getting her squadron killed. Although, keeping us here long enough for reinforcements to capture and kill us would probably get her a pass from her Beloved Leader."

"No one's getting captured or killed," I say. "Except Phiri Dun-Ra."

"Is there any other way to get our ship moving?" Marina asks Adam. "Could you . . . I don't know? Rig something up?"

Adam scratches the back of his neck, looking around at the other ships. "I suppose it's possible," he says. "Depends what we can scrounge together. I can try, but I'm not a mechanic."

"That's one idea," I say, looking up at the sky to see how much daylight we have left. Not much. "Or, we could go out into that jungle, track down Phiri Dun-Ra and get our part back."

Adam nods. "I prefer that plan."

I look at Marina. "What about you?"

I don't even have to ask. The sweat on my arms tingles—she's radiating an aura of cold.

"Let's go hunting," Marina says.

CHAPTER
THREE

UNDER IDEAL CONDITIONS, THE WALK TO UNION Square should take about forty minutes. It's only a mile and a half. But these are far from ideal conditions. Sam and I are backtracking along the same blocks we spent the afternoon fighting through. Back to where the Mogadorian presence is heavier.

Hopefully, Nine and Five don't kill each other before we get there. We need them if we're going to have any shot at winning this war.

Both of them.

Sam and I stick to the shadows. Some blocks still have electricity, so the streetlights are on, shining like it's a normal evening in the big city, as if the roads aren't littered with overturned cars and broken chunks of pavement. We avoid those blocks, knowing it will be too easy for the Mogs to spot us.

We pass through what used to be Chinatown. It

looks like a tornado touched down here. The sidewalks are impassable on one side, an entire block's worth of buildings collapsed to rubble. There are hundreds of dead fish in the middle of the street. We have to pick our way carefully through the obstacles.

On our way down from the UN, there were still people on nearly every block. The NYPD were trying to manage an orderly evacuation, but most were fleeing haphazardly, just trying to stay ahead of the Mog squadrons that seemed equally likely to slaughter civilians as take them prisoners. Everyone was panicked and shell-shocked at their new horrific reality. Sam and I picked up the stragglers, the ones who didn't manage to leave quick enough, or whose groups got blown apart by Mog patrols. There were a lot of them. Now, after ten blocks, we haven't seen another living soul. Maybe most of the people in lower Manhattan made it to the evacuation point on the Brooklyn Bridge—if the Mogs haven't attacked it by now. Anyway, I figure that anyone who managed to survive the day is smart enough to spend the night in hiding.

As we sneak down the next desolated block, Sam and I skirting cautiously around an abandoned ambulance, I hear whispering from a nearby alley. I put my hand on Sam's arm and, when we stop walking, the noise cuts off. I can tell we're being watched.

"What is it?" Sam asks, his own voice low.

"There's someone out there."

Sam squints into the darkness. "Let's keep going," he says after a few seconds. "They don't want our help."

It's hard for me to leave anyone behind. But Sam's right—whoever's out there is doing perfectly fine in their hiding spot, and we'd only be putting them in more danger taking them with us.

Five minutes later, we turn a corner and see our first Mogadorian patrol of the night.

The Mogs are at the opposite end of the block, so we have the space to safely observe them. There are a dozen warriors, all carrying blasters. Above them, a Skimmer hums along, sweeping the street with a spotlight mounted on the ship's underbelly. The patrol moves methodically down the block, a group of four warriors periodically breaking off from the rest to enter darkened apartment buildings. I watch them go through this routine twice, and both times I breathe a sigh of relief when the warriors return without any human prisoners.

What would happen if these Mogs found a human in one of these buildings and pulled them screaming into the street? I couldn't just let that happen, right? I'd have to fight.

What about after Sam and I move on? They're predators. If we leave them alive, eventually they'll find prey.

As I'm considering this, Sam nudges me, pointing

towards a nearby alley that will let us avoid the Mogs. "Come on," he says quietly. "Before they get too close."

I stay rooted in place, considering our odds. There are only twelve of them, plus the ship. I've fought bigger groups before and won. Granted, I'm still fatigued from an afternoon spent battling nonstop, but we'd have the element of surprise on our side. I could take down the Skimmer before they even realize they're under attack, and the rest would fall easily.

"We can take them," I conclude.

"John, are you nuts?" Sam asks, grabbing my shoulder. "We can't fight every Mog in New York City."

"But we can fight these ones," I reply. "I'm feeling stronger now and if something goes wrong I'll just heal us after."

"Assuming we don't, you know, get shot in the face and killed outright. Battle to battle, healing us right after—how much of that can you take?"

"I don't know."

"There's too many of them. We have to pick our battles."

"You're right," I admit grudgingly.

We dart down the alley, hop a chain-link fence and emerge on the next block over, leaving the Mogadorian patrol to its hunting. Logically, I know Sam is right. I shouldn't be wasting my time with a dozen Mogs when there's a greater war to be won. After an exhausting day, I should be conserving my strength. I know all this is true. Even so, I can't help feeling like a coward for avoiding the fight.

Sam points up at a sign for First Street and Second Avenue. "Numbered streets. We're getting closer."

"They were fighting around Fourteenth Street, but that was at least an hour ago. The way they were going at it, they could've gone in any direction from there."

"So let's keep our ears open for explosions and creative cursing," Sam suggests.

We only make it a few more blocks uptown before crossing paths with another Mogadorian patrol. Sam and I huddle behind a delivery truck, abandoned carts of fresh-baked bread still sitting on the off-loading ramp. I poke my head around the front of the truck, taking a head count. Once again, there are twelve warriors with a Skimmer supporting them. This group behaves differently than the last one, though. The ship hovers in place, its spotlight fixed on the shattered front window of a bank. The Mogs outside all have their blasters pointed into the building. Something has them spooked.

I recount the pale heads glaring in the spotlight. Eleven. Only eleven where there were definitely twelve before. Did one of them just get ashed without me noticing?

"Come on," Sam says warily, probably thinking that

I'm spoiling for a fight again. "We should go while they're distracted."

"Hold up," I reply. "Something's happening here."

With the others covering them, two Mogs stalk towards the front of the bank. They stay low, weapons at the ready, looking for something beyond the reach of the Skimmer's spotlight.

When they reach the bank's threshold, both Mogs toss their blasters into the air. The entire squad pauses, frozen, stunned by this development.

It's telekinesis. Someone just disarmed those Mogs with a Legacy.

I give Sam a wide-eyed look. "Nine or Five," I say. "They're pinned down."

Spurred to action, the rest of the Mogs open fire on the darkness of the bank. The two disarmed warriors are lifted off their feet, again by telekinesis, and used as shields. They disintegrate in the flurry of their squad's blaster fire. Then a desk comes flying out from within the bank. Two Mogs are crushed by the airborne furniture, and the rest backpedal for better cover. Meanwhile, the Skimmer maneuvers closer to the street, its guns coming around, angling for a shot inside the bank.

"I'll take the ship, you take the warriors," I say.

"Let's do it," Sam replies, nodding once. "I just hope it's not Five holed up in there."

I spring out from behind the truck and run toward the action, firing up my Lumen as I go. The nerve endings in my hands feel fried. I can actually feel the heat from my own Lumen, like I'm waving my hand over a candle. The pain is bearable, an obvious side effect of overdoing it today. I push through, quickly tossing a fireball at the Skimmer. My first attack explodes their spotlight, darkening the street. The ship is knocked off course just as it unloads on the bank, the heavy blaster fire carving chunks off the brick side of the building. With the main gun distracted, I hope to see Nine charge out from the bank and join the fray.

No one comes out. Maybe whichever Garde is inside is injured. After a long day of fighting each other and the Mogs, they're probably more worn out than me.

I hear a sizzle of electricity behind me—Sam firing off his blaster—and watch as the two closest Mogs go up in clouds of ash. Seeing us coming from behind, another Mog tries to duck behind a parked car. Sam yanks him out of cover with his newfound telekinesis and lights him up.

One of the Mogs screams a burst of grating Mogadorian words into a communicator. Probably radioing for help.

Broadcasting our location—that's not good.

I bound up the hood of an SUV parked conveniently beneath the Skimmer. On my way, I lob a fireball at the

Mog with the communicator. He's engulfed by flames and is soon nothing more than ash pooled around some melted gear. Even so, the damage is done. They know we're here. We need to get out of here quick.

I leap from the roof of the SUV, putting a huge dent into the metal as I push off. At the same time, I hit the Skimmer with a telekinetic punch. I don't have the power to bring the ship down, but I hit it hard enough so that one side of the saucer-shaped craft dips low, towards me. I land right on top of the thing, two Mogadorian pilots staring at me in shock.

A few weeks ago, it might've felt good to see the Mogs recoil in fear. I might've even said something funny, borrowed some quip from Nine's playbook before killing them. But now—after the terror they've unleashed on New York—I don't waste the breath.

I tear the cockpit door loose from its hinges and send it flying into the night. The Mogs try to unbuckle from their seats, groping for their blasters. Before they can do anything, I unleash a funnel of white-hot fire. The Skimmer immediately begins to careen out of control. I leap free of the ship, landing hard on the sidewalk below, my tired legs barely supporting me. The Skimmer smashes into a storefront across the street and explodes, black smoke rising out of the store's shattered window.

Sam runs up next to me, his blaster pointed at the

ground. The rest of the area is clear of Mogs. For the moment.

"Twelve down, like a hundred thousand left to go," Sam says dryly.

"One of them got off a distress call. We gotta go," I tell Sam, but even as I say this, I feel the same light-headedness from earlier creeping on. The rush of battle gone, my fatigue is now back. I have to support myself on Sam's shoulder for a minute, until I get my bearings.

"No one's come out of the bank," Sam says. "I don't think it's Nine in there. Unless he's hurt, it's way too quiet."

"Five," I growl, moving cautiously towards the bank's busted entrance. I'm not sure I can handle a fight with him at this point. My only hope is that Nine's done a good job of softening him up.

"There," Sam says, pointing into the darkened lobby. Someone's moving around. Whoever it is, they appear to have spent the battle hiding behind a sofa.

"Hey, it's all clear out here," I call into the bank, gritting my teeth as I shine my Lumen inside. "Nine? Five?"

It isn't one of the Garde who cautiously steps into my beam of light. It's a girl. She's probably about our age, only a couple of inches shorter than me, with a lean sprinter's body. Her hair is pulled back in tight rows of braids. Her clothes are scuffed up either from the fight or the general chaos, but otherwise she looks unhurt. Tossed over the girl's left shoulder is a heavy-looking duffel bag. She looks from Sam to me with wide brown eyes, eventually focusing on the light shining from the palm of my hand.

"You're him," the girl says, inching forward. "You're the guy from TV."

Now that the girl is close enough to see, I shut off my Lumen. Don't want to be lighting up our location for the Mog reinforcements that are on their way.

"I'm John," I tell her.

"John Smith. Yeah, I know," the girl says, nodding eagerly. "I'm Daniela. You really killed the hell out of those aliens."

"Uh, thanks."

"Was there someone else in there with you?" Sam cuts in, craning his neck to look past her. "A dude with anger issues and a habit of taking off his shirt? A gross one-eyed guy?"

Daniela cocks her head at Sam, eyebrows raised. "No. What? Why?"

"We thought we saw someone attack those Mogs with telekinesis," I say, looking Daniela over again, feeling equal parts curious and cautious. We've been tricked before by potential allies.

"You mean this?" Daniela reaches out her hand and one of the dead Mogs' blasters floats to her. She plucks it out of the air, resting it against the shoulder not supporting her duffel bag. "Uh-huh. That's a new development for me."

"I'm not the only one," Sam breathes, looking at me with wide eyes.

My mind is cycling through possibilities so quickly that I'm struck speechless. I might not have understood the why of it, but Sam getting Legacies made sense to me on a gut level. He's spent so much time around us Garde, done so much to help us—if any human was going to suddenly develop Legacies, it would be him. The hours since the invasion have been so crazy that I didn't really have time to think about it. Didn't need to, really. Sam with Legacies just seemed logical. When I imagined other humans besides Sam getting Legacies, I'd been thinking of people we know, people who have helped us. I was thinking of Sarah, mostly. Definitely not some random girl. This girl, though, Daniela, her having Legacies means something bigger than I imagined has happened.

Who is she? Why does she have powers? How many more like her are out there?

Meanwhile, Daniela is staring at me with that starstruck look again. "So, um, can I ask why you picked me?"

"Picked you?"

"Yeah, to turn into a mutant," Daniela explains. "I

couldn't do this shit until today when you and the pale guys—"

"Mogadorians," Sam clarifies.

"I couldn't move stuff with my mind until you and the Moga-dork-ians showed up," Daniela finishes. "What's the deal, man? None of the other people I've seen out here have powers."

Sam clears his throat and raises his hand, but Daniela ignores him. She's on a roll now.

"Am I radioactive? What else can I do? You got those flashlight hands going on. Am I gonna be able to do that? Why me? Answer the last one first."

"I—" I rub the back of my neck, overwhelmed. "I have no idea why you."

"Oh." Daniela frowns, looking down at the ground.

"John, shouldn't we get moving?"

I nod when Sam reminds me of the impending Mogadorian reinforcements. We've already stood here talking for way too long. Standing in front of me—and next to me, for that matter—are . . . what exactly? New members of the Garde? Humans. It's like nothing I've ever contemplated. I need to wrap my head around the new status quo quickly, because if there are more human Garde out there, they're going to be looking for guidance. And with all the Cêpan dead . . .

Well, that leaves us. The Loric.

First things first, I need to make sure Daniela stays

with us. I need time to talk with her, to try figuring out what exactly triggered her Legacies.

"It's not safe here, you should come with us," I tell her.

Daniela looks around at the destruction that surrounds us. "Is it gonna be safe wherever you're going?"

"No. Obviously not."

"What John means is that this particular block is going to be crawling with Mogs any minute now," Sam explains. He starts walking away from the bank, trying to lead by example. Daniela doesn't follow and so I don't either.

"Your sidekick's nervous," Daniela observes.

"My name's Sam."

"You're a nervous guy, Sam," Daniela replies, one hand on her cocked hip. She's staring at me again, sizing me up. "If more of those aliens come, won't you just blow their asses away?"

"I . . ." I find myself having to recycle the pick-your-battles logic that made me bristle so much when Sam used it on me. "There are too many to keep fighting. It might not feel like it now because you've just started using them, but our Legacies aren't a limitless resource. We can push too hard, get tired, and then we're no good to anyone."

"Good advice," Daniela says. She remains rooted in place. "Too bad you couldn't answer any of my other questions."

"Look, I don't know why you have Legacies, but it's an amazing thing. A good thing. It's destiny, maybe. You can help us win this war."

Daniela snorts. "Seriously? I'm not fighting any war, John Smith from Mars. I'm trying to survive out here. This is America, yo. The army will take care of these weak-ass dust aliens. They got the drop on us, that's all."

I shake my head in disbelief. There's seriously no time to explain to Daniela everything she needs to know about the Mogadorians—their superior technology, their infiltration of Earth's governments, their endless amounts of disposable vatborn warriors and monsters. I never had to explain those things to the other members of the Garde. We always knew the stakes, we were raised understanding our mission on Earth. But Daniela and the other newly minted Garde who might be wandering around . . . what if they aren't ready to fight? Or don't want to?

An explosion shakes the ground under our feet. It emanates from a few blocks away, but is still powerful enough to set off car alarms and rattle my teeth. Thick smoke darker than the night sky floats into view from the north. It sounds like a building just collapsed.

"Seriously," Sam says. "Something's headed our way."

Another explosion, closer, confirms Sam's suspicion. I turn desperately to Daniela.

"We can help each other. We have to, or we won't

survive," I say, thinking not just of the three of us, but of humans and Loric. "We're looking for our friend. Once we find him, we're going to get out of Manhattan. We heard the government's established a safe zone around the Brooklyn Bridge. We'll go there and—"

Daniela waves off my whole plan, stepping towards me. Her voice is raised, and I feel her telekinesis buffet my chest, like a jabbing index finger.

"My stepdad got roasted by those pale scumbags and now I'm out here looking for my mom, alien guy. She worked down here. You saying I should drop all that and join your army of two, running around my city that you played a part in getting blown up? You saying the friend you're looking for is more important than my mom?"

Another explosion. Closer, still. I have no idea what to say to Daniela. That yes, saving Earth is more important than saving her mom? Is that my recruitment speech? Would I have listened to that if someone said it about Henri or Sarah?

"Oh my God," Sam says, exasperated. "Could we at least agree to all run in the same direction?"

And that's when the reinforcements come into view. It isn't a squadron of Skimmers or warriors come to kill us.

It's the *Anubis*.

CHAPTER FOUR

THE MASSIVE WARSHIP, BIGGER THAN AN AIR-
craft carrier, becomes visible in the night sky when it's
still five or so blocks away. It pushes slowly through the
acrid smoke its recent bombings kicked up. Sam and I
had been able to stay ahead of the *Anubis* earlier that
afternoon, fighting our way south as it slowly prowled
the skyline to the east. But now, here it is, looming up
the avenue, right in the direction of Union Square.

I clench my fists. Setrákus Ra and Ella are on board
the *Anubis*. If I could just get on there, maybe I could
fight my way to the Mogadorian leader. Maybe I could
kill him this time.

Sam stands at my side. "Whatever you're thinking,
it's a bad idea. We need to run, John."

And as if to punctuate Sam's declaration, a sizzling ball of electric energy gathers in the barrel of
the *Anubis*'s huge hull-mounted cannon. It's like a

miniature sun building up within the barrel, and for a moment it lights the surrounding blocks in a ghostly blue. Then, with a sound like a thousand Mog blasters going off at once, the energy erupts forth from the cannon, shearing through the façade of a nearby office building, the twenty-story structure almost immediately collapsing inwards.

A wave of dust rolls down the street towards us. Coughing, the three of us have to shield our eyes. The dust might give us some cover, but that doesn't really matter when the warship has a gun that can demolish whole buildings. The *Anubis* lumbers closer, already prepping for another shot. I'm not sure if Setrákus Ra is aiming at heat signatures in the buildings or if he's just destroying things at random, hoping to hit us. It doesn't matter. The *Anubis* is like a force of nature and it's headed in our direction.

"Hell with this," I hear Daniela say, and then she takes off.

Sam follows her and so do I, the three of us retreating the way Sam and I just came from. We'll have to find another way to track down Nine. If he's still in the area, I hope he manages to ride out this bombing.

"Do you know where you're going?" Sam yells to Daniela.

"What? You guys are following *me* now?"

"You know the city, don't you?"

Another building explodes behind us. The dust is thicker this time, choking, and my back gets pelted by small chunks of plaster and cement. The explosions are too close. We might not be able to outrun the next one.

"We need to get off the street!" I shout.

"This way!" Daniela yells, hooking a sharp left that momentarily takes us out of the deluge of building debris that funnels down the avenue.

When Daniela turns, something slips loose from under the broken zipper on her duffel bag. For a split second, my eyes track a hundred-dollar bill as it floats through the air and is quickly swallowed by the billowing cloud of debris. Weird what you notice when you're running for your life.

Wait. What exactly was she doing in that bank when the Mogs pinned her down?

There's no time to ask. Another explosion rocks the area, this one deafeningly close and strong enough that it knocks Sam off his feet. I drag him back up and we scramble onwards, both of us covered in the clinging, choking dust of the destroyed buildings. Even though Daniela is just a few yards ahead, she's only visible as a silhouette.

"In here!" she yells back to us.

I try to shine my Lumen ahead but it doesn't do much good in the swirling building fragments. I have no idea where Daniela's leading us, not until the ground disappears from beneath my feet and I fall headfirst into a hole in the ground.

"Oof!" Sam yelps as he hits the concrete floor next to me. Daniela is on her feet a few yards away. My hands and knees are scraped from the landing, but otherwise I'm unhurt. I glance over my shoulder, seeing a darkened staircase that's rapidly filling in with debris from above.

We're in a subway station.

"A little warning would've been good," I snap at Daniela.

"You said off the street," she replies. "This is off the street."

"You okay?" I ask Sam, helping him up. He nods, catching his breath.

The subway station begins to vibrate. The metal turnstiles rattle and more dust filters down from the ceiling. Even through the barrier of concrete, I hear the mighty growl of the warship's engines. The *Anubis* must be right above us. Electric-blue light pours into the station from outside.

"Go!" I yell, shoving Sam, Daniela already hopping a turnstile. "Into the tunnels!"

The cannon unloads with a high-pitched shriek. Even shielded by layers of concrete, I tingle from the electricity, my body fizzing down to its bones. The subway station shakes and, above us, a building lets out a mournful groan as its steel girding twists and collapses. I turn and run, jumping onto the tracks after Sam and Daniela. I look over my shoulder as the ceiling starts to cave in, first sealing off the stairs we just fell down, then spreading farther into the station. It isn't going to hold.

"Run!" I yell again, straining to be heard over the crumbling architecture.

Into the darkness of the subway tunnel we sprint. I fire up my Lumen so that we can see, my light glinting off the steel tracks on either side of us. I sense movement at my side and it takes a moment to realize that there's a herd of rats running alongside us, also fleeing the collapse. Somewhere down here, a pipe must have burst, because I'm running through ankle-deep water.

With my enhanced hearing, I listen to the stonework that surrounds us grinding and tearing. Whatever the *Anubis* destroyed on the street level, it caused major damage to the foundation of the city. I glance at the ceiling just in time to see a jagged crack spread through the cement, breaking off into tributaries that spread down the mold-covered walls. It's like we're trying to outrun the structural damage.

We can't win this race. The tunnel's going to collapse.

I'm about to yell out a warning when the tunnel gives way above Daniela. She only has time to look up and scream as a dislodged chunk of cement plummets towards her.

I put everything into my telekinesis and shove upwards.

It holds. I manage to stave off the cave-in centimeters from Daniela's head. I exert so much counterforce to support the massive weight overhead that I'm pushed down to my knees. I feel the veins in my neck protruding, fresh sweat dampening my back. It's like carrying a tremendous weight when you're already exhausted. And meanwhile, new cracks are spiderwebbing out from the broken piece of ceiling. It's physics—the weight has to go somewhere. And that somewhere is going to be right on top of us.

I can't hold this. Not for long.

I taste blood in my mouth and realize I'm biting my lip. I can't even yell to the others for help. If I shift even a tiny bit of focus away from my telekinesis, the weight will become too much.

Luckily, Sam realizes what's happening.

"We have to hold up the ceiling!" he shouts at Daniela. "We have to help him!"

Sam stands next to me and throws his hands up. I feel his telekinetic strength join mine and it alleviates some of the pressure. I'm able to get up from my knees.

Out of the corner of my eye, I see Daniela hesitate. The truth is, if she ran now, with Sam and me supporting the tunnel, she could probably make it to safety. We'd be screwed, but she'd make it.

Daniela doesn't run. She stands on the other side of me and pushes up. The cement in the ceiling groans and more cracks erupt in the tunnel walls. It's a delicate balance—our telekinesis just forces the weight from the broken stonework to shift elsewhere. No matter what we do, eventually, this tunnel is going to collapse.

Enough of the weight's been taken off that I can speak again. I ignore the burning agony in my muscles, the heaviness sinking into my shoulders. Sam and Daniela are holding, waiting for my instructions.

"Walk . . . walk backwards," I manage to grunt. "Let it go . . . slowly."

Shoulder to shoulder, the three of us march slowly backwards down the tunnel. We keep the telekinetic pressure on directly above us, gradually letting go of the sections of ceiling that we've safely passed under. It rumbles and collapses in our wake. At one point, I see a couple of cars fall into the tunnel, quickly swallowed by more debris. The street above is collapsing, but the three of us manage to hold it at bay.

"How long?" Sam asks through gritted teeth.

"Don't know," I reply. "Keep going."

"Shit," Daniela repeats over and over, her voice a hoarse whisper. I can see her arms shaking. Both she and Sam are raw, not used to telekinesis. I've never supported this much weight before, and I certainly didn't come close to it on my first day with Legacies. I can feel their strength waning, beginning to slip.

They just need to hold on a little bit longer. If they don't, we're dead.

"We're going to make it," I growl. "Keep going!"

I can feel the subway tunnel gradually sloping downwards under my feet. The deeper we get, the sturdier the ceiling is above us. Step by step, the telekinetic counterpressure we need to exert lessens, until finally we reach a section of tunnel where the ceiling is stable.

"Let go," I groan. "It's okay, let go."

As one, we release our hold on the ceiling. Ten yards away, the last bit of ceiling we'd been supporting crashes into the tunnel, blocking off the way we came. Above us, the tunnel creaks and holds. All three of us collapse into the filthy water that fills the bottom of the tunnel. I feel as if an actual weight has been lifted from my shoulders. I hear a retching noise next to me and realize that Daniela's throwing up. I try to stand up to help her, but my body doesn't cooperate. I fall face-first into the water.

A second later, Sam's hands are under my arms, lifting me up. His face is pale and strained, like he doesn't have much left to give.

"Oh man, is he dying?" Daniela asks Sam.

"However much ceiling we were holding, he was

probably carrying four times as much," Sam replies. "Help me with him."

Daniela slides underneath my other arm. She and Sam lift me up, dragging me down the tunnel.

"He just saved my life," Daniela says, still breathless.

"Yeah, he does that kinda thing a lot." Sam turns his head, speaking into my ear. "John? Can you hear me? You can shut off the lights. We can make it in the dark for a bit."

That's when I realize that I'm still illuminating the tunnel with my Lumen. Running on fumes, and still I'm instinctually keeping the lights on. It takes a conscious effort on my part to let my Lumen go out, to not fight against my own exhaustion, to allow myself to be carried.

I let go. Trust in Sam.

And then I can no longer feel Sam's and Daniela's arms around me. I can't feel my feet dragging through the thick slop of the subway tunnels. All my aches and pains melt away until I'm peacefully floating through darkness.

A girl's voice interrupts my rest.

"John . . ."

A cold hand slips inside mine. It's slender and girlish, fragile, but it squeezes with enough force to bring me back to my senses.

"Open your eyes, John."

I do as she says and find myself stretched out on an operating table in an austere room, an array of ominous-looking surgical machinery spread out around me. Right next to my head is a machine that looks almost like a vacuum cleaner—a suction tube with scalpel-sharp teeth at its end is attached to a barrel filled with a viscous, writhing black substance. The ooze floating through the machine reminds me of the stuff I cleansed from the secretary of defense's veins. Just looking at it makes my skin crawl. It's inherently unnatural and Mogadorian.

This isn't right. Where am I? Were we captured while I was unconscious?

I can't feel my arms or my legs. And yet, strangely, I don't panic. For some reason, I don't feel like I'm in any real danger. I've had this kind of out-of-body experience before.

I'm in a dream, I realize. But not my own dream. Someone else is controlling this.

With some effort, I manage to turn my head to the left. There isn't anything in that direction except more bizarre-looking equipment—a mixture of stainless-steel medical tools and complicated machinery like the stuff we found inside Ashwood Estates. On the far wall, though, there's a window. A porthole, really. We're in the air, the sky dark outside, lit only by the fires in the city below.

I'm on board the *Anubis*, floating above New York City.

Trying to take in every detail, I turn my head to the right. A team of Mogadorians dressed in lab coats and wearing sterilized gloves huddle around a metal table exactly like the one I'm laid out on. There's a small body on the table. One of the Mogs holds the tube from another of those ooze machines, in the process of pressing it into the sternum of the young girl on the table.

Ella.

She doesn't cry out when the blades on the hose pierce her chest. I'm powerless to do anything as the black Mogadorian goo is slowly pumped into her.

I want to scream. Before I can, Ella turns her head and locks eyes with me.

"John," she says, her voice totally calm despite the gruesome surgery being performed on her. "Get up. We don't have much time."

CHAPTER
FIVE

"WE CAN DO THIS, BUT FIRST YOU NEED TO understand how Phiri Dun-Ra thinks," Adam whispers.

"You are the expert on Mog psychology," I reply, watching as Adam uses a broken branch to draw a square in the dirt. "Enlighten us."

The three of us crouch next to our lifeless Skimmer on the dirt strip the Mogs were using as a runway. It's dark now, but the Mogs had plenty of handheld electric lanterns on hand to illuminate their round-the-clock attempts to break into the Sanctuary. I guess Phiri didn't have the foresight to steal all the batteries, so at least we've got light. There are also some huge floodlights positioned around the temple's perimeter, but we've left those off. No need to make spying on us any easier for her.

The jungle around us seems louder now that the sun's gone down, the chirping of tropical birds replaced by the shrill buzzing of billions of mosquitos. I slap the back of my neck as one of them tries to bite me.

"There's no doubt in my mind that she's out there right now, watching us," Adam says. "Every Mog warrior of her class is trained in surveillance."

"Yeah, we know," I reply, glancing out into the darkness. "You guys have been stalking us all our lives, remember?"

Adam continues, ignoring me. "She's probably capable of going at least three days with no sleep. And she won't remain in one place, she'll stay mobile. There won't be a campsite to find or anything like that. If we go in there after her, she'll move, stay ahead of us. She's got a lot of jungle to hide in. That said, it'll be her instinct to stay close. She'll want to keep tabs on us."

Marina frowns at Adam, watching as he draws some squiggly lines in the dirt around his square. I realize that he's drawing Sanctuary and the surrounding jungle.

"So we have to draw her out," Marina says.

"You know a good way to do that?" I ask Adam.

"We give her something no Mog can resist," Adam replies, and he draws an "M" in the western part of the jungle. Then, he gives Marina a pointed look. "A vulnerable Garde."

Immediately, I feel the air around us get a little colder. Marina leans forward, getting close to Adam, her eyes narrowed threateningly.

"Do I seem vulnerable to you, Adam?"

"Of course not. We just want you to appear that way."

"A trap," I say, trying to mediate. "Marina, chill out."

Marina gives me a look, but I feel her icy aura dissipate.

"So," Adam continues, "first, we split up."

"Split up?" Marina repeats. "You're kidding."

"That's always the worst idea," I say.

"We can just go out there and hunt her down," Marina says. "Six can make us invisible. She won't have a chance."

"That could take all night," Adam says. "Maybe longer."

"And it's not exactly easy moving through a dark-ass jungle," I remind Marina, thinking back to our journey through the Everglades.

"We split up *because* it's a dumb move," Adam explains. "We make it look like we're trying to find her, like we're trying to cover more ground. Phiri Dun-Ra will see it as an opportunity . . ."

Adam draws three lines moving away from the temple, fanning out into the jungle.

"Six, you'll go east, I'll go south and, Marina, you'll go west." Adam looks at me. "When you get two hundred paces into the jungle, Six, you turn invisible. She won't be watching you at that point."

"What makes you think she won't attack me?" I ask. "I can be vulnerable."

Marina snorts.

Adam shakes his head. "She'll go after our healer first. I know it."

"Because it's what you would do?" Marina asks.

Adam meets her eyes. "Yeah."

Marina and I exchange a look. At least Adam's being straight up about how he'd hunt us down. I'm glad he's on our side.

"I guess it makes sense," Marina says, examining the drawings in the dirt. Suddenly, she looks back up at Adam. "Wait. You're saying the Mogs know I'm a healer?"

"Of course," he replies. "Any Legacies they've observed in the field have become part of your dossiers. And all Mogs study those. It's like their second-favorite leisure activity after the Great Book."

"Fun," I say.

Marina considers this. "They wouldn't know about my night vision. It's not something they could observe."

Adam looks up from his battle plan. "You have night vision?"

Marina nods. "If you're right and Phiri does attack me, I might actually see her coming first."

"Huh," Adam replies. "Well, that's a bonus."

"So what do I do after I turn invisible?" I ask.

"You find me, we go invisible, and then we double back and follow Marina. Back her up for when Phiri Dun-Ra attacks."

"And if she attacks me before you guys get there?" Marina asks.

Adam smirks. "I guess try not to kill her until you've gotten back the conduits."

"Do you think she's going to just hand them over?" Marina asks, cocking her head at Adam.

"Hopefully, she's carrying them on her," he replies.

"And if she's not?"

"I . . ." Adam looks from Marina to me, trying to gauge our reactions. "There are ways to make people talk. Even Mogadorians."

"We don't torture," Marina says emphatically. Even after everything she's been through, even after losing Eight—she's still the moral compass. She looks over at me for support. "Right, Six?"

"We'll figure it out," I reply, not wanting to take a position at the moment. "First things first. Let's get the bitch."

The three of us make a big show of separating, each of us carrying one of the electric lanterns into the forbidding jungle. As I duck through the thick vines and clawlike branches in the dense brush, I focus my hearing as much as possible. I'm hoping maybe I'll stumble upon Phiri, shorten this whole plan Adam hatched, but no such luck. I'm only successful in amplifying the ceaseless sounds of the jungle. On my left, something dark and furry shrieks out a warning as I move through its territory. There's so much movement and noise out here—Adam was right, it'd be next to impossible to track Phiri Dun-Ra.

I push aside a branch with more force than necessary. It snaps back and slaps my shoulder. I grit my teeth and wonder if I could just call a hurricane down on this whole stupid jungle and pick up Phiri Dun-Ra.

One Mog. We're out here chasing one stupid Mog. This must be exactly what Phiri Dun-Ra wanted, to take us out of the game while who the hell knows what happens back in New York. A full-scale invasion could be under way. I imagine John and Nine trying to fight off hordes of Mogadorians, Sam running for his life, the entire world engulfed in flames.

Yeah. We need to hurry this up.

Before splitting up and heading into the jungle, we turned on the large halogen work lights around the Sanctuary's perimeter so we'd be able to find our way back. Once I've gone far enough that I can barely see the lights through the trees, I turn invisible. Just in case Phiri Dun-Ra is watching me instead of Marina, I use my telekinesis to float my lantern ahead of me. I wait a few seconds to see if any shadowy forms detach from the surrounding jungle to pursue my ghostly lantern and, when none do, I hook the lantern to a low-hanging branch and leave it behind.

I'm comfortable with my own invisibility, having developed a good sense of spatial awareness after years of practice. Still, it isn't easy navigating without my light. At least I've got some experience from back in Florida. I take it slow, glancing often at muddy ground in front of me, ducking low to go under branches. At one point, I have to carefully step over a striped rattlesnake, the thing not even shifting as I pass by.

Before long, I spot Adam's lantern bobbing through the jungle. He's moving purposely slow, waiting for me to catch up to him. He doesn't hear me coming. When I slip my hand into his, in the moment before I turn him invisible, I hear his breath catch and shoulders tense.

"Scare you?" I whisper to him. I pluck the lantern out of his other hand with my telekinesis, going through the same routine that I did with my own.

"Surprised me, that's all," he replies quietly. "Let's go."

We start picking our way through the jungle towards where Marina should be. I'm careful not to go too fast at first, but Adam has good balance and seems to be keeping up just fine. His hand is surprisingly cool and dry despite the humid jungle air—he's steady, this whole situation isn't weird to him at all. I can't help but breathe out a little laugh.

"What?" he asks me, his voice a whisper in the darkness.

"Just never imagined reaching a point in my life where I'd be holding hands with a Mogadorian," I reply.

"We're allies," Adam responds. "It's for the mission."

"Yeah, thanks for clearing that up. Still, it isn't weird for you?"

Adam pauses. "Not really."

Adam doesn't say anything more. I remember something he said back on the flight to the Sanctuary.

"Who do I remind you of?" I ask him as we carefully climb over a fallen log.

"What?"

"Back in the Skimmer, you said I reminded you of someone."

"You want to talk about that *now*?" he whispers back.

"I'm curious," I reply, keeping an eye out for the telltale glow of Marina's lantern. We don't see it yet.

Adam is quiet for long enough that I start to think he's just done talking, like his silence is a reprimand for not staying on mission. I'm about to tell him that I can successfully track one Mogadorian while also carrying on small talk, thank you very much, when he finally answers me.

"Number One," he says. "That's who you remind me of."

"One? The Garde you took your Legacies from?"

His hand tenses up in mine, like he has to stop himself from yanking away.

"She *gave* her Legacy to me," Adam snaps. "I didn't take anything."

"All right," I reply. "Sorry. Poor choice of words. I didn't realize that you actually got to know her."

"We had a . . . complex relationship."

"Like, you were in charge of the Mogs stalking her or something?"

Adam sighs. "No. After she was killed, One's consciousness

was implanted in my brain alongside my own. For a while, basically, we shared a body. I guess that's why I'm not concerned with holding hands or whatever juvenile thing has been making you uncomfortable for the last five minutes. I've been really, really close to Garde before."

Now it's my turn to fall silent. I never even met Number One. She remains a complete mystery to me, more like a concept. The unlucky one. First up to bat. The first one to get killed. And yet Adam has all this intimate knowledge of her. It's weird to think that a Mogadorian has given more thought to Number One than I ever did. Not just that, but it sounds like he actually cared about her. Our world just gets stranger and stranger.

"There she is," I whisper, sparing us any further awkward conversation as Marina's lantern comes into view.

"Good," Adam says, sounding relieved. "Now we follow along and wait for Phiri Dun-Ra to take the bai—"

Adam's interrupted by cobalt-blue blaster fire sizzling through the air, aimed right for Marina's lantern. Even with all the jungle noise, I can hear Marina scream.

"Shit! Go!"

I release Adam's hand and sprint through the jungle, using my telekinesis to shove aside the tangled branches and dense blockades of leaves. I'm sure I pick up a few scratches along the way, but that doesn't matter. The creature sounds around me become loud with panic as I trample through their territories. I'm distantly aware of

Adam running behind me, taking advantage of the path I'm clearing.

Up ahead, I can tell that Marina's lantern has fallen to the ground by the way it throws crooked beams of light through the twisted tree limbs.

Running full throttle, it takes me less than a minute to knife my way through the jungle. I burst into the small clearing where Marina's lantern is on the ground, just in time to see Marina running her hand over a blaster burn on her upper arm. She glances up at me as she heals the blistered flesh.

"Plan worked," Marina says casually.

"You're hurt," I reply.

"This? Lucky shot."

I breathe a sigh of relief, then look to Marina's left where Phiri Dun-Ra glares at us from her knees. There's a fresh trail of blood dripping through her mess of Mog tattoos and severely pulled-back braids, probably from where Marina clocked her. Phiri's blaster is in the dirt next to her, out of reach and crumpled beyond use by a telekinetic attack. Her hands and ankles are bound in what I quickly realize to be shackles made from solid ice. Looks like Marina's getting pretty good with her new Legacy.

Adam arrives in the clearing a few seconds after me. Phiri Dun-Ra's look of hatred only intensifies when he shows up.

"You got her," Adam says, and Marina nods, even

smiles a little. "You're all right?"

"I'm good," Marina replies. "Now what should we do with her?"

"You should kill me," Phiri Dun-Ra growls, spitting into the dirt in front of her. "The sight of a trueborn consorting with you Loric trash so offends my eyes, I no longer wish to live."

"Hello to you too, Phiri," Adam says, rolling his eyes. "What did you do to my Chimæra?"

Phiri Dun-Ra's eyes light up. "A little trick I learned from the Plum Island scientists with blaster frequencies. Did your pet die? I didn't have time to check its body."

"He survived. Unlike you."

"We aren't going to kill you—," I start to say, but Phiri thrashes in the dirt, interrupting me.

"Because you're cowards," she hisses. "Do you want to rehabilitate me like this one? Make me into another Mogadorian pet? It won't happen."

"You didn't let me finish," I say, stepping closer to her. "We're not going to kill you *yet*."

"Did you search her?" Adam asks Marina.

"She was only carrying the blaster," Marina replies. The rest of Phiri's outfit is the standard sleek body armor of a Mog warrior. There's no room to hide a bunch of ship parts.

"Where are the conduits?" I ask her. "Give them back and I'll at least make your death quick."

Marina shoots me a quick look, her eyebrows upraised. I put off answering these questions before—what do we do with a captured Mogadorian and how far do we go to get what we need? Torture. The thought gives me a chill of revulsion, especially thinking back to my time spent being one of their captives. It feels like crossing a line, like something they would do to us. It's different from killing them in battle, when they're fighting back and trying to kill us too. Phiri Dun-Ra is helpless, our prisoner. But one Mog prisoner is useless and we need to get the hell out of this jungle. I know we shouldn't sink to their level, but our situation is desperate. *How far will threats take us?* I wonder.

"Die a slow death, Loric scum," Phiri spits back at me.

So, she isn't going to make this easy.

Before I can decide what to do, Adam darts past me and strikes Phiri across the face with the back of his hand. She cries out and topples over onto her side. Phiri is stunned, I realize. She wasn't expecting the blow. Maybe she was banking on the fact that Marina and I wouldn't have the stomach for torture. Adam, on the other hand . . .

"You forget who you're dealing with, Phiri Dun-Ra," Adam says through clenched teeth. He slides onto his knees in the dirt next to her and grabs her by the front of her shirt, yanking her partially upright. "Do you think because I've spent time with the Garde that I've forgotten our ways? You know who my father was. Much to his disappointment, my marks were always highest in the non-combat-related subjects. But still . . . the General found ways to focus my training. Interrogation. Anatomy. Imagine how rigorously the General trained his heir. I remember well."

Adam reaches one of his hands around Phiri's head, digging his thumb into the space behind her ear. She screams out, her legs thrashing. Marina takes a step towards the two Mogs, giving me another look. I swallow hard and shake my head, stopping her.

I'm going to let this play out. Wherever it leads.

"I might not share your ideology, Phiri Dun-Ra," Adam says, raising his voice to be heard over her screaming, "but I do share your biology. I know where your nerves are, where to hurt you best. I will spend the rest of the night picking you apart until you beg for disintegration."

Adam releases his grip on Phiri, letting her fall back into the dirt. She's panting, struggling to get in a deep breath.

"Or you can tell us where you hid the conduits," Adam says calmly. "Now."

"I'll never—" Phiri is cut off, flinching as Adam stands up. He's suddenly lost interest in her.

He saw the same thing I did. The way Phiri Dun-Ra's eyes flicked towards a moss-covered log at the edge of the clearing. Adam walks over to the log while she squirms around in the dirt, trying to keep her eyes on him. On closer inspection, the log is rotten, hollowed out by termites. Adam plunges his hand inside and tugs out a small duffel bag. Phiri must have shoved the bag in there before attacking Marina.

"Aha," he says, giving the bag a good shake. Inside, metal parts clang together. "Thanks for your help."

Marina and I exchange a relieved look, even as Phiri screeches out her latest taunt.

"It doesn't matter, traitor," she says. "Nothing you do matters anymore!"

That gets my attention. I give Phiri a not-so-gentle kick in the back to make her roll over and look at me.

"What does that mean?" I ask her. "What're you saying?"

"War came and went," Phiri replies, laughing at me. "Earth is already ours."

My stomach drops at the thought, but I don't let it show. We have to get out of Mexico and see for ourselves.

"Are the parts intact?" I ask Adam.

"She's lying to you, Six. It's what she does," he reassures me, maybe detecting a tremor of nervousness in my voice. He tosses down the duffel bag and crouches over it.

"What should we do with her?" Marina asks me. She focuses on Phiri Dun-Ra for a second, reinforcing the ice shackles that have begun to melt.

I'm considering my answer when Adam grunts, yanking on the zipper that appears to be stuck on something. When the zipper comes loose, something inside the duffel bag clicks, like a timer being armed.

"Watch out!" Adam screams as he shoves the bag away from him. Everything happens so fast. I see the ground rise up in front of the duffel bag and realize that Adam is using his seismic Legacy to try shielding us. With an orange flash of light and a loud pop, the bomb inside the bag detonates right in front of him. Chunks of dirt and deadly shrapnel fly through the clearing. I'm thrown to the ground from the concussion blast. I can feel fresh pain in my leg—a jagged piece of metal, probably ship parts, is lodged in my thigh.

Above the ringing in my ears, I can hear Phiri laughing hysterically.

CHAPTER
SIX

A HEAVY WEIGHT FALLS ACROSS MY LEGS, DRIV-
ing the shrapnel sticking out of my thigh even deeper. It's
Phiri Dun-Ra. She has fresh lacerations on her face and
arms, the results of her own improvised bomb. Her wrists
and ankles are still bound by the ice manacles, but that
hasn't stopped her from throwing herself on top of me. I'm
still stunned from the blast, so I don't react as quickly as
I should. Phiri headbutts me in the sternum as she worms
her way across my body.

"Now you die, Loric trash," she says maniacally, still
giddy over the success of her booby trap.

I'm not sure what her plan is here—maybe to bite me to
death or smother me with her body, but I'm not so out of
sorts that either of those things is going to happen. With
a quick burst of telekinesis, I swipe Phiri Dun-Ra off me.
She tumbles through the dirt, rolling across glowing bits
of scorched duffel bag. She tries to get herself onto her feet,
screaming in frustration as her bonds get in the way.

She's silenced when I kick her across the face as hard as I can. Phiri flops to the ground unconscious.

"Stay with me!"

It's Marina's voice that snaps me out of my rage or I'd probably kill Phiri right there. I spin around and see her bent over Adam.

"Is he . . . ?!"

I limp across the clearing, forgetting that there's a six-inch piece of jagged steel protruding from my thigh. I ignore the pain. Adam's in much worse shape than I am.

I stagger around the small hill of earth Adam was able to construct in the few seconds before the explosion. It absorbed a lot of the shrapnel, but not enough. The bomb still basically detonated right in front of him, so Adam took the brunt of the blast. He's on his back now, Marina leaning over him, and I cringe at the amount of damage he's taken. His entire midsection is blown open, like he's been scooped out. He should've dived out of the way instead of standing there like a human shield. Stupid Mog, trying to be a hero.

Amazingly, Adam's still conscious. He can't speak; all the strength he can muster seems to be going into breathing. His eyes are wide and scared as he sucks in wet, rattling breaths. His hands, soaked with his blood, are curled into tight fists.

"I can do this, I can do this . . . ," Marina repeats to herself, not hesitating at all as she lays her hands on Adam's grisly wound. Looking over her shoulder, helpless, I realize how sadly familiar this situation must be for Marina. It's like Eight all over again.

As Adam's breathing becomes more and more ragged, I watch as his insides begin to knit themselves back together under Marina's touch. And then something disturbing happens—there's a crackle and hiss, like a fire starting, and a piece of Adam's midsection briefly sparks before dis-integrating into that familiar Mogadorian death ash.

Marina cries out in surprise, pulling her hands away.

"What the hell was that?" I ask, eyes wide.

"I don't know!" Marina yells. "Something's fighting me, Six. I'm afraid I'm hurting him."

The second Marina's healing stops, Adam's still-open wound begins bleeding again. He's getting pale. More pale than usual, even. His hand scrabbles through the dirt and gropes for Marina.

"Don't . . . agh, don't stop," Adam manages to gurgle, and when he does I can see that there's dark blood in his mouth. "Whatever happens . . . don't stop."

Steeling herself, Marina again presses down on Adam's injury. She squeezes her eyes shut and concentrates, fresh sweat dripping down the sides of her dirt-smudged face. I've seen Marina heal a lot of injuries before, but this is definitely the most effort I've seen her expend. Adam's body slowly begins to regenerate, until another section of his insides sparks and disintegrates, looking like the fuse of a bomb burning up inside him. When that's over, though, the rest of him heals normally.

It takes a couple of minutes, but Marina finally gets Adam closed up. She falls backwards onto her butt, breathing like she's just finished sprinting, her hands shaking. Adam remains on his back, running his fingers over the skin of his abdomen that minutes ago wasn't there. Finally, he props himself up on an elbow and looks at Marina.

"Thank you," he says, locking eyes with her, his face a mixture of amazement and gratitude.

"Don't mention it," Marina replies, catching her breath.

"Um, Marina . . . would you mind?" I gesture to the piece of metal still sticking out of my leg.

Marina groans from the exertion, but nods, maneuvering around so she's on her knees in front of me. "Do you want me to pull it out or . . . ?"

Before she can finish, I yank the jagged piece of shrapnel out of my thigh. A fresh spurt of blood trickles down my leg. The pain is bad, but Marina quickly numbs it with a blast of cold before using her healing Legacy to close me up. Compared to putting Adam back together, it takes no time at all.

When she's finished with me, Marina immediately looks back at Adam. "What was that when I was healing you? Why was it so hard?"

"I . . . I don't know, exactly," Adam replies, staring into the distance.

"You started to disintegrate a little," I say. "Like you were dying."

"I *was* dying," Adam says. "But that shouldn't happen to me. The vatborn warriors you've faced turn to ash because they're made entirely from Setrákus Ra's genetic experimentation. Some trueborn, like me, receive modifications that would cause them to disintegrate when they die. I haven't received anything like that, though. At least . . ."

"Not that you know of," I finish the thought for him.

"Yeah," Adam replies, looking down at himself like he suddenly doesn't trust his own body. "I was in a coma for years. It's possible my father might have done something to me. I don't know what, though."

"Whatever it was, I think my healing burned it out of you," Marina says.

"I hope so," Adam replies.

All three of us fall silent. With the medical emergencies averted, it becomes clear just how badly we've screwed up. I walk over to the scorched patch of dirt where Phiri Dun-Ra's explosive went off, kicking around tattered bits of duffel bag and misshapen hunks of metal. The bag was probably filled with conduits, but I don't find anything even slightly salvageable.

We are now totally stranded here.

When I turn around, I find that Adam has picked himself up and is now standing over Phiri's unconscious body.

"We should kill her," he says coldly. "There's no reason to keep her alive."

"We don't do that," Marina answers, her voice gentle, reasonable. "She can't hurt us if she's tied up."

Adam opens his mouth to respond, but seems to decide against it. Marina just saved his life, so I guess he feels like he should listen to her. I actually find myself agreeing with both of them—Phiri Dun-Ra is nothing but trouble, and holding on to her is just begging for her to screw us over again. But killing her when she's unconscious seems wrong.

"We'll at least wait for her to wake up," I say diplomatically. "Figure out what to do with her then."

The others nod in silent, glum agreement. We head back to the Sanctuary. I use telekinesis to float Phiri's unconscious body along with us. Once we're back, Marina keeps the ice shackles nice and thick until we've used an electric cable to safely secure the Mog trueborn to the wheel of one of the many broken-down ships. At this point, I'm pretty sure she's playing possum. Let her. Marina's right—she can't hurt us while she's tied up, and if she gets free, well, I'll make sure Adam gets his wish.

Not sure what else to do, I try the satellite phone again. Still no answer from John. That makes me think of Phiri Dun-Ra telling us that the war had already come and gone. I don't have any new scars, which means John and Nine are still very much alive, but that doesn't mean everything is copacetic back in New York.

"Adam, can we key into the Mog communications from one of these ships?" I ask. "I want to know what's happening."

"Of course," he replies, jumping at the opportunity to do something productive.

The three of us climb on board our old Skimmer, Adam settling into the pilot's seat. He successfully powers on the ship's electric systems, although the lights flicker spastically and something in the Skimmer's core groans at the effort. Adam begins turning a dial on the dashboard, picking up nothing but intermittent bursts of static.

"I just need to find the right frequency," he says.

I sigh. "It's fine. Not like we're going anywhere."

Next to me, Marina gazes at the Sanctuary through the Skimmer's window. Because we left the floodlights on, the entire temple is lit up, the ancient limestone practically glowing.

"Don't lose hope, Six," Marina says quietly. "We'll figure this out."

When Adam turns the dial again, the static is replaced by a guttural Mogadorian voice. The Mog speaks in a clipped, no-nonsense way, like he's reading items off a list. Of course, I can't understand a word of what he's saying.

I elbow Adam. "You going to translate?"

"I . . ." Adam, staring at the radio like it's possessed, doesn't know what to say. I quickly realize that he doesn't want to tell me what news is coming in over the radio.

"How bad?" I ask, keeping my voice level. "Just tell me how bad."

Adam clears his throat and shakily begins to translate. "Moscow, moderate resistance. Cairo, no resistance. Tokyo, no resistance. London, moderate resistance. New Delhi, moderate resistance. Washington, D.C., no resistance. Beijing, high resistance, preservation protocols lifted—"

"What are these?" I cut him off, losing patience with the droning. "Their attack plans?"

"They're status reports, Six," Adam says, his voice low. "Warships are reporting in on how the invasion is progressing. Each of those cities has one of the huge warships backing up an occupation effort, and they aren't the only ones . . ."

"It's happening?" Marina asks, sitting forward. "I thought we had more time."

"The fleet is on Earth," Adam replies, his face blank.

"What did that thing mean about preservation protocols?" I ask. "You said they were lifted in Beijing."

"Preservation protocols are Setrákus Ra's way of keeping Earth intact for long-term occupation. If they're lifted in Beijing, it means they're destroying the city," Adam says. "Using it to send a message to other cities that might cause trouble."

"My God . . . ," Marina whispers.

"One warship alone could destroy a city in a few hours," Adam continues. "If they . . ."

He trails off, some new status on the radio getting his attention. He swallows and turns the dial hard, lowering the volume on reports of Mogadorian success.

I grab him by the shoulder. "What is it? What did you hear?"

"New York . . . ," he begins grimly, pinching the bridge of his nose. "New York, Garde-assisted resistance . . ."

"That's us! That's John!"

Adam shakes his head, finishing the translation. "Garde-assisted resistance *overcome*. Incursion successful."

"What does that mean?" Marina asks.

"It means they've won," Adam replies darkly. "They've conquered New York City."

They've won. The phrase repeats itself in my mind.

They're taking over and we're stranded down here.

Because I don't have a better target it for it, I punch the console where the dull buzz of Mogadorian progress drones on. Sparks erupt from the dashboard and Adam leaps out of the pilot's chair, startled. Marina gets onto her feet and tries to wrap her arms around me, but I shrug her off.

"Six!" she yells after me as I jump out of the cockpit. "It isn't over!"

I stand atop our Skimmer feeling rage burning inside me, but having nowhere to channel it. I look at the Sanctuary, bathed in light. This place was supposed to be our salvation. Our trip down here hasn't changed anything, though. It almost got us killed and now we're out of the war. How many people are dying because we're not there to help John save New York?

I feel an itch on the back of my neck. Someone's watching me. I turn around, my gaze drifting to the runway and the other ships. Phiri Dun-Ra is awake, tied up right where we left her.

She grins at me.

CHAPTER
SEVEN

WHEN ELLA SPEAKS, A JOLT PASSES THROUGH me. Suddenly, I can move again. I leap up from my operating table and try to shove the Mogadorian doctors surrounding Ella.

My hands pass right through them, like they're ghosts. They're frozen in space now, unmoving, the moment a snapshot before me. I need to remind myself that this is all happening inside my head, or Ella's head, or somewhere in between. In our dreams.

"Don't worry about them," Ella says. She sits up, passing through the ooze machine that's attached to her chest, and then the Mogs as she hops down from her table. "I can't even feel what they're doing to me."

"Ella . . ." I don't even know where to begin. *Sorry for letting you be kidnapped back in Chicago, sorry for not saving you in New York . . .*

She hugs me, her small face pressed into my chest.

That much feels real, at least.

"It's okay, John," she says. Her voice is almost serene, like someone who has accepted her fate. "It isn't your fault."

There's the Ella I'm hugging and then there's the Ella frozen in time, still pinned down to the operating table beneath the Mogadorian machines, surrounded by enemies. I can't help looking past the Ella in my arms and staring at the horrific results of her Mogadorian imprisonment. She looks pale and drained, streaks of gray running through her auburn hair. There are already black veins visible beneath her skin. A chill runs through me and I force myself to look away, squeezing Ella a little tighter.

The hug ends and Ella peers up at me. This version of her looks almost as I remember—wide-eyed and innocent—although there's a tiredness around her eyes, a kind of weary wisdom, that wasn't there the last time I saw her. I can't imagine what she's been through.

"What are they doing to you?" I ask, my voice quiet.

"Setrákus Ra calls it his Gift," Ella says, her lips curling in disgust. She looks over her shoulder, watching herself get experimented upon, and hugs herself. "The stuff he's putting into me, I'm not sure where it comes from. It's the same weirdo genetic crap he grows the vatborn warriors from. It's the stuff he used to augment some of the humans—you know about that?"

I nod, thinking of Secretary of Defense Sanderson and the cancerous resistance I felt in his body when I healed him.

"He's doing it to you. His own—" I still hesitate to say this part out loud. "His own flesh and blood."

Ella nods sadly. "For the second time."

I remember how out of it Ella seemed during the battle at the United Nations. "He did it to you before the big public appearance," I say, putting the pieces together. "Drugged you up so you couldn't ruin his moment."

"It was punishment for trying to escape with Five. The Gift . . . it makes it hard for me to focus, at least when I'm awake. I'm not sure how, but he uses it to control me. It could be related to one of his Legacies. I tried to figure out everything he can do, John, I tried to stop him, but . . ."

Ella's shoulders slump. I place my hand gently on the back of her neck.

"You did everything you could," I tell her.

She snorts. "Uh-huh."

I take a long look at the machine Ella's hooked up to, trying to memorize the details. Maybe if we ever manage to hook back up with Adam, he can shed some light on how exactly this thing works.

"He's not controlling you now," I say, gesturing around to the frozen-in-time Mogadorian operating theater. "You're doing this. You're still fighting him."

"I've been able to hide that I'm telepathic," Ella replies, straightening up a bit. "Whenever he hurts me, I hide inside my own mind. I practice. My Legacies are getting stronger. I could sense you down there from on board the *Anubis*. I was able to pull you into my, um . . . my dream? Whatever this is."

"Just like in Chicago," I muse, trying to work this out. "Only, you needed to touch me that time."

"Not anymore. I guess I'm getting stronger."

I give Ella's shoulder a squeeze. This should be a proud moment, her coming into her own, learning to master such a powerful Legacy when she's still so young. But our situation is too dire for any real congratulations.

I look across the medical bay towards the door, then back at Ella.

"Can you show me around?" I ask. "Is that even possible?"

Ella manages a shaky smile. "You want the tour?"

"It might come in handy to know what the ship's like. For when I get up here and rescue you."

Ella lets out a mirthless laugh, looking away from me. I hope that she hasn't given up hope. The odds might seem bad now, but I won't let her stay Setrákus Ra's pet grandchild forever. I will find a way. Before I can tell her all that, Ella nods.

"I can show you around. I've been all over this ship.

If I've seen it, then it's stored up here," Ella says, tapping her temple.

We step out of the medical bay and into the hallway. It's all stainless metal walls lit by dull red lighting, a cold and economical place. Ella leads me through the *Anubis*, showing me the observation deck, the control room, the barracks, all these areas completely empty. I try to commit every detail to memory so that I can draw a map when I wake up.

"Where are all the Mogs?" I ask her.

"Most of them are down in the city. The *Anubis* only has a skeleton crew now."

"Good to know."

Deep down in the ship, we pause in front of a glass window that looks into another laboratory. Inside, the floor is completely taken up by a vat of viscous black liquid. There are two catwalks crisscrossing over the vat, each one equipped with a variety of control panels, monitoring equipment and, oddly enough, heavy-duty mounted blasters. Growing out of the liquid is an oblong shape that vaguely resembles an egg, except it's covered in dark purple mold and throbbing black veins.

I press my hand to the laboratory glass and turn to Ella. "What the hell is this place?"

"I don't know," she replies. "He doesn't let me in there. But . . ."

Ella knuckles her forehead and appears to strain for

a moment. Inside the laboratory, figures suddenly manifest. A half-dozen Mogs wearing gas masks stand on the catwalks, silently operating the strange machines. Standing among them is Setrákus Ra himself. Seeing him there causes me to flinch towards the glass. I have to resist the urge to attack him, reminding myself that this isn't exactly real.

"Is this . . . is this a memory?" I ask Ella.

"Something I saw, yeah," she answers. "I think—I don't know. It might be important."

As we watch, Setrákus Ra lifts his stolen Loric pendants over his head. He holds them in his thick hands for a moment, considering the blue Loralite jewels. He's got several of them—three from the Garde he killed and the rest were probably taken from the Garde he captured at one point or another. He seems almost nostalgic for a moment as he gazes upon his trophies.

Then, he drops them into the vat. Four tiny little mouths open up on the egg and suck in the pendants, smothering their glow.

"What was that?" I ask Ella, feeling like I might be sick even in this dream state. "When did this happen? What's he doing?"

Setrákus Ra's gaze suddenly shoots towards us and he shouts something. A second later, he and the rest of the Mogs disappear back into thin air.

"That's when he caught me spying," Ella explains,

biting her lip. "I don't know what he was doing, John. I'm sorry. Everything's a bit . . . fuzzy."

We move on. Eventually, Ella brings me to the docking bay. It's a huge area with high ceilings, filled by row after row of Skimmers. It's from here that the squadrons of Mogs currently terrorizing New York City first took flight.

"They're always coming and going from here," Ella says, waving at the big metal doors at the end of the docking bay. "You might be able to get in through there, if they're open. It's where Five and I tried to escape from."

I make a note of the docking bay doors. We'd just have to figure out a way to make the Mogs open them up. It'd be pretty easy to get on board if we had someone who could fly us up there.

"About Five . . . ," I say, hesitating, not sure how much Ella has heard. "Do you know what he did?"

Ella bites her lip, looking down at the floor. "He murdered Eight."

"But he also tried to help you escape," I say, feeling her out. "Is he . . . ?"

"You're trying to figure out how evil he is?"

"I'm looking for him right now. I'm trying to figure out, when I find him, if I should kill him."

Ella frowns and walks away from me, looking at a dented spot on the floor. I assume it's from when she and Five tried to escape.

"He's confused," she says after a moment. "I don't know . . . I don't know *what* he'll do. Don't trust him, John. But don't kill him."

I remember the last time Ella sucked me into one of these dream states, back when her Legacy was first manifesting and out of control. It was back in Chicago. That time, she didn't bring me to her present location. Instead, we were trapped in a vision of the future, watching Setrákus Ra lord over the people of Washington in a world where the Mogadorians had won the war.

"Don't we know what he does, though?" I ask, my fists clenching on reflex. "You showed it to me. Five goes back to Setrákus Ra. He works for the enemy. He captures Six and Sam . . ."

I trail off, not wanting to further dredge up the memory of witnessing my friends' execution. I don't want to remember that doomed prophecy of how we're going to lose. Ella shakes her head. She opens her mouth, and suddenly I realize that there's something big she isn't telling me.

"That future doesn't exist anymore, John," she says after a lengthy pause. "My visions . . . they aren't like the nightmares Setrákus Ra used to give you guys. And they aren't prophecies. We aren't locked into them, like Eight thought. They're premonitions. Possibilities."

"How do you know that?"

Ella thinks for a moment. "I'm not sure. How do you know how to make fireballs? You just do. It's instinct."

I take a step towards her. "So that vision of D.C., where everyone was dead and you were . . . ?"

"I can't see it anymore. Something in the present changed what will happen."

"If it's a Legacy like my Lumen . . ." My eyes widen as I consider the possibilities. "Can you control the visions now? Can you look into the future at will?"

Ella's eyebrows are scrunched, like she's not sure how to describe what she's seen. "I can't control it exactly. The visions . . . they aren't reliable. I don't know if that's because of me, because I'm just learning or if it's because the future is so unstable. Either way, I've spent a lot of time searching through them . . ."

Now I know why Ella looks so exhausted even in this dream space, why she's suddenly so wise beyond her years. She mentioned before how much time she's spent hiding in the safety of her own mind. I wonder how much of that time was spent wrestling with visions of the future. It must be agonizing to sift through all those possibilities.

"What have you been searching for?" I ask her.

Ella hesitates, avoiding my eyes. "I wanted . . . I wanted to see if there was a future where I die."

"Ella, no," I say, my voice sharp. Five told me about

the twisted Loric Charm that Setrákus Ra used on himself and Ella, the one that binds them together so we'll have to kill her to get at him. "We'll figure out a way to break the charm. There's gotta be a weakness."

Ella shakes her head, not believing me. Or maybe already knowing that I'm wrong.

"I'm not putting myself before the whole world, John. I wanted to see a future where Setrákus Ra is killed, no matter the consequences." Now she looks right at me, fire in her eyes. "I wanted to see a future where *someone* has the guts to do what needs to be done."

I swallow hard. I'm not sure if I really want to know the details of Ella's visions, but I can't stop myself from asking.

"What . . . what did you see?"

"Lots of things," Ella says, calming down. She gets a distant look in her eyes as she tries to explain what seeing the future is like. "The visions start out as blurry possibilities. There are millions of them, I think. Some of them are more solid than others—those are the ones I can see. The ones that seem . . . I dunno. Likely? But even that's not a guarantee. You remember that future we saw in Chicago. It felt real, impossible to escape, clear as day. It's gone completely now. The future has changed too much. And it keeps changing."

My head hurts. I feel half crazy just listening to Ella. We need a Cêpan, someone who could help her get control of these mental Legacies before they drive her insane. At least we've avoided the bleak future I witnessed. But what did we trade it for?

"Ella, did you see yourself die?"

She hesitates, and a knot of dread tightens in my stomach.

"Yes," she says. Her body shakes and I realize it's from holding in a sob. I crouch down in front of her and put my hands on her shoulders.

"It won't happen," I insist, my voice as firm as I can make it. "We'll change the future."

"But we *win*, John."

Ella grabs my hands. Tears stream freely down her cheeks. I realize something, the way she's looking at me, the way she's squeezing my hands. Ella's not feeling sorry for herself.

She's feeling sorry for me.

"It's going to hurt you so much, John," she says, her voice cracking. "You have to be strong."

"It's me?" I don't believe it. "Am I the one that—?"

I can't even finish the question. I yank my hands away from Ella. I'd never hurt her, not even if it meant ending this war.

"There has to be another way," I say. "Use your Legacy and find us a better future."

Ella shakes her head. "You don't understand—"

In the blink of an eye, Ella is changed. She looks like

the girl stretched out on the operating table, black ooze worming its way beneath her skin. She struggles to focus on me. The docking bay around us gets weirdly hazy and starts melting away.

"Ella? What's happening?"

"The *Anubis* is moving out of range," she says, narrowing her eyes, trying to strengthen our telepathic connection. "I'm going to lose you. Quick! There's one more thing you have to see!"

Ella snatches my hand and then we're running towards the docking bay entrance. We step through it and—

Dirt crunches beneath my feet. Hot sun beams down on the back of my neck, the air sticky and humid. It's disorienting to be suddenly transported from the sterile gloom of the *Anubis* into the heat of the jungle, vivid green on all sides, tropical birds loudly chirping. I'm standing on what looks to be an airstrip carved into the jungle. The black-armored hulls of a handful of Mogadorian Skimmers reflect the bright afternoon sun.

My eyes are drawn to the limestone pyramid that stands a few yards away from the airstrip, all the Mog gear seemingly positioned at a safe distance from the ancient structure. I instinctually recognize the temple, even though I've never actually seen it before. Maybe it's just my imagination, but it feels as if something buried within the centuries-old Mayan architecture is calling out to me. I feel safe here.

"This is the Sanctuary," I say, my voice quiet and reverent.

"Yeah," Ella says, and I notice that she's also admiring the temple.

"Six, Marina and Adam . . ." I pause, realizing that Ella's never met our Mogadorian ally. "Adam is a—"

"I know who he is," Ella says, her tone giving nothing away. "We meet soon."

"Okay, well, they were just here," I continue, looking around for signs of our friends. "They're probably headed back by now. Are you going to show me what they did to give the humans Legacies?"

"This isn't the past or present, John. We're in the future. One that I can see very, very clearly."

I should've known that since the sun is out. I turn to face Ella, sensing that she hasn't brought me here to deliver good news.

"Why are you showing me this?"

"Because of *that*."

Ella points into the sky to the north of the Sanctuary. There, like a storm cloud rolling across the otherwise blue and cloudless sky, is the *Anubis*, slowly floating towards the temple. My legs jerk, reflexes still keyed to run for cover after I narrowly survived the bombardment in New York. I force myself to stay put and watch the warship approach.

"When?" I ask Ella. "When does this happen?"

Before Ella can answer, her form contorts, again turning pale and black-veined. The scenery flashes, the jungle suddenly overlapping with the *Anubis* operating room and also with what looks to be the inside of a subway car—all three places existing simultaneously, like three transparent pictures laid on top of one another. For a second, it's impossible for me to focus on any particular detail, everything blending to the point where I feel unmoored from reality. But then Ella cries out, either from frustration or pain or both, and the jungle and the Sanctuary solidify once again.

"You're pushing yourself," I say, watching as dark circles form around her eyes. "We're getting too far apart."

"Don't worry about me," she replies hurriedly. "Doesn't matter. This is where we're going *now*, John. The *Anubis* is leaving for the Sanctuary right this second."

"So Setrákus Ra will get there . . ."

"He'll get there at sunset," Ella says. "He stops in West Virginia to gather reinforcements after leaving so many warriors behind in New York, and then . . ."

Ella waves towards the *Anubis*. It's closer now, the warship's long shadow falling across the stones of the Sanctuary.

"What does he want?"

"He wants what's inside!" Ella shouts. And yet, even though her voice is raised, she's beginning to sound farther away. "I think it's what he always wanted! They opened the door to the Sanctuary! It isn't protected anymore!"

"What do—?"

She cuts me off, grabbing my arm. "John, listen! Six, the others, you have to warn them! Tell them—"

Ella's hands pass through me. I see it all again—the Sanctuary and the *Anubis*, Ella squirming on the operating table, the darkened subway car—and then all the colors blend together, nothing solid to grab on to. Ella screams something at me, but she's too far away. The words don't reach me.

Then, darkness.

CHAPTER EIGHT

I SNAP AWAKE ON A HARD PLASTIC BENCH, MY legs dangling off the end. I know I'm back in my body, no longer in Ella's dreamworld because of the intense ache that immediately soaks through my every muscle. I'm on my side, facing the orange and yellow seatbacks of the subway bench. I've never been on one of these cars before, but I've seen enough movies and TV shows to recognize them immediately. On the wall above my head is a poster reading IF YOU SEE SOMETHING, SAY SOMETHING.

With a groan, I prop myself up on an elbow. Sam is slumped on the two-seater adjacent to my bench with his head propped against the window, snoring gently. Outside the window, I can see only darkness. This train is stalled underground somewhere, inside the tunnel. The passengers must have abandoned it early on during the attack. The train car is dead, unmoving and powerless, the panels of overhead lights completely dark.

And yet, there's light coming from somewhere.

I sit up and look around, immediately spotting a row of cell phones spread throughout the train's main aisle. With their flashlight apps turned on, the phones function like battery-powered candles. On the bench opposite from me, awake and watching, sits Daniela. Her feet are propped up on the duffel bag she carried out of that bank, the thing presumably filled with stolen money.

"You're alive," she says, keeping her voice low so as not to wake Sam. I do the same, even though Sam's snoring like he could sleep through another *Anubis* bombing.

"How long have I been out?" I ask.

"It's morning according to the phones," Daniela replies. "About six hours, I guess."

Morning already. I shake my head. An entire night wasted. We couldn't find Nine and Five, and who knows which part of New York they've fought their way to by now. To make matters worse, I know where Setrákus Ra and the *Anubis* are heading—right to the last known location of the rest of the Garde. Because I lost contact with Ella at the last minute, I'm not sure what to do with that information, even if I could get in contact with Six and the others. Should they be getting ready to turn around and head back to the Sanctuary? Or does Ella want me to keep them as far from there as possible?

I need to move, to do something productive. But my body still doesn't feel one hundred percent and Sam is out like a light.

"We're still in the subway?" I ask Daniela, knowing the answer, but wanting to get a better grip on our situation before I make any decisions.

"Yeah. Obviously. We dragged you in here after you fainted."

"Fainted," I repeat with a grimace. "I passed out from exhaustion."

"Same diff. Anyway, we were all pretty wiped after that cave-in stunt," Daniela continues, maybe sensing my annoyance. "I fell asleep pretty much as soon as we got here." Daniela glances at Sam, a faint smile on her face. "Your boy Sam was gonna stand guard, but I guess that didn't go so hot. No big deal. Not like anyone is looking for us down here."

"Not yet, at least," I reply, thinking about the Mogadorians on the surface and wondering how their occupation of New York City is progressing.

One of the phones winks out. Daniela crouches over it, pressing a few buttons, but the battery is dead.

"People slept in front of the store for these things," she says, holding up the dead phone for me to inspect.

"Shit goes down, though . . . lot of people drop everything and run. What's that make you think about humanity, alien guy?"

"That they've got their priorities straight," I reply, glancing again at the duffel bag full of money.

"Yeah. I guess," Daniela says, then casually tosses the phone to the other end of the train car, where it hits the floor and breaks apart. Even the phone shattering doesn't disturb Sam. "That felt surprisingly good," Daniela tells me, smirking in my direction. "You should try it."

"Where'd you get all the phones?" I ask Daniela, watching her closely as she sits back down.

I still don't know what to make of her. She's a human *with* Legacies, which we don't even have a word for. But she seems to think this entire situation is one big joke. I can't tell if she's unhinged like Five or hiding behind a massive defense mechanism. She mentioned before that the Mogs killed her stepfather and that her mom is missing. I know what it's like—to lose people, to not know what's happening to your loved ones. I could tell her that, except I don't really think Daniela's the type to open up easily. I wish Six were here. I have a feeling they'd get along great.

"I woke up first," she says, gesturing around the train. "Went through all the cars. People left a lot of shit behind."

"Back at the bank, did somebody leave all that cash behind, too?" I ask, jerking my chin at her duffel bag.

"Oh yeah, that," Daniela says, looking to the side with feigned guilt, but unable to keep the smile off her face. "Wondered if you noticed."

"I noticed."

"Thing's heavier than you'd think," she says, nudging the bag with her filthy sneaker toe.

I rub my hand across my face, trying to figure out how I should approach this. It's not like I haven't stolen before. I always did it out of necessity, though, and never right in the middle of a full-scale invasion.

"Weird you had time to rob a bank while you were searching for your mom."

"First of all, I didn't steal it. I mean, not technically. There were some dudes hiding from the Mogs in that bank. They were the ones robbing it. I just ended up taking cover in there. They got blasted, then you showed up. I figure, why waste a perfectly good duffel bag?"

I frown, shaking my head. I have no idea if what Daniela's telling me is the truth. I'm not sure if it even matters how she got the money. I'm more concerned with figuring out if this new Garde is someone we can trust. Someone we can rely on.

"Second of all," she continues, leaning toward me, "my mom would be *pissed* if she found out I missed an opportunity like that."

She tries to keep her voice cavalier, but a tremor sneaks in when she mentions her mom. Maybe this attitude is all a front, a way to cope with how screwed up her world has gotten in the last twenty-four hours. I get that. My expression must be too sympathetic, though, or maybe she noticed me noticing her voice shaking, because Daniela raises her voice and keeps going, more heated than before. It occurs to me that as much as I'm trying to figure her out, she's also trying to figure out me.

"Third, I didn't sign up for these superpowers that you don't even know why I have. And I damn sure didn't sign up to fight in your alien war. Neither did my family."

"You think there was an alien invasion sign-up sheet getting passed around?" I ask sharply, trying and failing to keep my temper from flaring. "No one asked for this. The Loric, my people, we didn't ask for the Mogs to destroy our home world. It happened anyway."

Daniela holds up her hands defensively. "All right, so you know what this is like. All I'm saying is that you shouldn't be judging how I choose to spend my alien invasion. Shit is nuts."

"I was too young to fight back when they attacked Lorien," I tell her. "But you . . ."

"Oh shit, here it comes. The recruitment speech." Daniela starts to do an impression, her voice suddenly higher pitched, her words theatrically enunciated. "Look outside your window," she recites. "The Mogadorians are here. The Garde will fight them. Will you stand for Earth?"

I shake my head, confused. "What's that?"

"It's from *your* video, dude. The whole *support the Garde* thing. They played it on the news."

I shake my head. "I don't even know what you're talking about."

Daniela studies my face for a moment, and eventually seems satisfied with my bafflement. "Huh. You really don't. Guess you probably haven't been watching much TV. Me? I was glued to it when those ships first started appearing. It's like, all of a sudden we're living in one of those alien invasion movies. Was pretty cool until, well . . ."

Daniela waves her hand, encompassing not just our current situation of hiding out underground, but the citywide destruction we both lived through. I notice her hand trembles a little. She quickly hides this, folding her arms tightly across her chest

"Sam and I helped a group of people get out of Manhattan yesterday," I tell her. "I wondered how some of them knew my name, but it was too chaotic to ask. Was it on the news? Did they show me fighting at the UN?"

Daniela nods. "They showed some of that. Except when that Clooney-looking creep turned into a genuine alien monster, people really started to freak out and the cameras got all shaky. You were featuring pretty heavy on the news before that, though."

I tilt my head, not understanding. "How do you mean?"

"There was this, like, YouTube video. It got posted on some stupid conspiracy website first—"

"Wait—was it 'They Walk Among Us'?"

Daniela shrugs. "'Nerds Walk Among Us,' I dunno, sure. It starts off with a picture of Earth that they totally snagged from Google images and this girl's narrating like—'This is our planet, but we are not alone in the galaxy, blah blah blah.' She's trying to sound all professional like it's a nature documentary or something, but you can tell she's our age. Why are you making that stupid face?"

While Daniela's speaking, I can't help a dumb smile from crossing my face.

I try to keep my expression neutral as I lean forward. "What else happens?"

"So, they show some pictures of Mogadorians and say they've come to enslave humanity. These pale aliens look like they could be guys in corny monster makeup or something. Nobody would've taken this shit seriously if, you know, there weren't a ton of UFOs menacing cities. And then, she starts talking about you. There's video of you jumping out of a burning house that shouldn't be possible, and then there's footage of you healing this FBI agent's burned-up face and . . . well, it's pretty grainy but the special effects would have to be mad good for it to be fake."

"What . . . what does she say about me?"

Daniela smirks, eyeing me. "She says your name is John Smith. That you're a Garde. That you've been sent to our planet to fight these aliens. And now, you need our help."

That's what Daniela was quoting before. Her terrible impression was supposed to be Sarah. I sit back, thinking about the video that Sarah and Mark made, their contribution from the sideline. Even though she's mocking it, the video seems to have made an impression on Daniela. She could quote it from memory. Hell, the survivors we came across in the street had certainly seen it. They trusted me. They were ready to stand and fight. But was it all too little too late?

I grimace involuntarily, thinking out loud. "I've spent my whole life hiding from the Mogadorians that were hunting me here on Earth. Getting stronger. Training. The war was always being fought in secret. We were starting to get our allies together, though, starting to figure things out. I wonder if we'd only gone public sooner, how many lives could we have saved if New York was ready for an attack like this?"

"Nah," Daniela says, dismissing this notion with a

wave of her hand. "Nobody would've believed that shit even a week ago. Not without people on CNN shouting about spaceships appearing over New York. I mean, you needed that whole UN fight for it to really sink in. Before that, the news people were debating whether it was a hoax, a viral stunt for a movie, whatever. I saw one lady on TV saying you were an angel. Pretty funny."

I chuckle dryly, not really feeling in the mood. "Yeah. Hilarious."

I realize that Daniela's trying to comfort me in her caustic way. I'll never know what would have happened if we'd spent the last few months trying to make our war with the Mogadorians public. There were humans at high levels involved with MogPro that would've made any attempt at exposing the Mogs extremely difficult, if not impossible. I know all this, logically. And yet I can't help feeling that yesterday's colossal loss of life is on me. I should've done more.

"How old are you, anyway?" Daniela asks.

"Sixteen," I tell her.

"Yeah." Daniela nods, like she already knew this. "You're like the girl that narrates the video. You got that whole wise-beyond-your-years thing going, that's true. And you look like you've been through some shit. But take a closer look . . ." She trails off, clicking her tongue in thought. "You should be finishing high school, man. Not saving the world."

I can't let what happened in New York bury me under guilt. I need to make sure nothing like it ever happens again. I need to find my friends and figure out a way to kill Setrákus Ra, once and for all.

I square my shoulders and smile at Daniela, affecting a nonchalant shrug. "Somebody's gotta do it."

Daniela smiles back for a second, then catches herself and looks away. For a second there, I thought she might volunteer to join the fight. I can't make her stick with us after we get out of the subway. I just have to trust that she, and the other humans out there, have developed their Legacies for a reason.

"We need to get moving," I say.

I shake Sam's shoulder and he snorts awake. His eyes are bleary for a moment, adjusting slowly to the bluish LCD lighting of the subway car.

"So it wasn't a bad dream," he sighs, standing up slowly and stretching out his back. His gaze drifts over to Daniela. "You decided to hang around, huh?"

Daniela shrugs, like the question embarrasses her. "You mentioned getting some people out of New York . . . ," she says to me.

"Yeah. The army and the police have secured the Brooklyn Bridge. They're evacuating people from there. At least, they were last night."

"I'd like to go there," Daniela replies, standing up. She straightens her dust-covered and blood-spattered

T-shirt. "Maybe see if my mom made it."

"All right," I say. I don't want to push her on joining forces. If it's going to happen, she's the one who has to make the decision. That doesn't mean we shouldn't stick together for the time being. "We should head that way too."

Sam rubs his eyes, still working moisture into his mouth. "You think Nine and Five battled their way to the evacuation point?"

"Doubt it," I reply. "But Nine's a big boy, he can handle himself for a little longer. Priorities have changed. I really need to get in touch with Six. If anywhere has working phones, I think it'll be the evacuation point." I turn to Daniela. "Can you lead us out of here?"

Daniela nods. "Only one way to go with the uptown tracks caved in. We follow the tracks for a few more stops, we should just about make it to the bridge."

"Wait. How did priorities change while we were sleeping down here?" Sam asks.

I tell Sam how Ella reached out to me telepathically from her prison aboard the *Anubis*, explaining that Setrákus Ra is headed for the Sanctuary. Daniela listens in, her eyes wide and locked on me, mouth slightly opened. When I'm finished describing the dreamscape, prophecies and endangered Lorien historical sites, she shakes her head in total mystification.

"My life has gotten so effing weird," she says,

walking down the train car towards the exit.

"Hey," Sam calls after her. "You forgot your bag!"

Daniela glances over her shoulder. Then, she looks at me. I don't know if she wants permission or if she's challenging me to stop her. When I don't say anything, she doubles back and lifts the heavy bag with a grunt.

"Use your telekinesis," I say casually. "It's good practice."

Daniela eyes me for a moment, then nods and grins. She concentrates and floats the bag out in front of her.

"What's in there, anyway?" Sam asks.

"My college fund," she replies.

Sam gives me a look. I just shrug.

When Daniela reaches the end of the car, she levitates the bag aside and yanks the metal door open with a sharp clatter. She steps onto the gangway that connects to the next car. Sam and I follow a few feet behind her.

"Whoa, whoa," Daniela says, her words not directed to us. Her duffel bag rockets back into our subway car, Sam and I both having to jump out of the way. Daniela telekinetically slides the bag under a bench, like she's trying to hide it. A second later, she steps backwards through the door, her hands raised in surrender. Immediately, my muscles tense. I thought we were safe down here in the tunnels.

But we aren't alone.

A machine-gun barrel with a flashlight attachment is leveled inches from Daniela's face. A shadowy form, covered in bulky equipment and body armor, inches cautiously into our train car, backing Daniela down. Too late, I notice flashlight beams in the next car over—at least a dozen of them, maybe more. A second halogen beam shines right into my eyes, a second gunman boarding our car. Without thinking about it, I ignite my Lumen, fire slithering across my fists.

"Wait," Sam warns. "They aren't Mogs."

I hear the telltale click of a round being chambered, probably in response to my channeling a fireball. The subway car aisle is narrow, Daniela is in the way and the light in my face makes it difficult to see. Definitely not ideal conditions. I could probably disarm them with my telekinesis, but I don't want to risk them getting off a burst of automatic fire at such close quarters. Better to wait and see how this plays out.

I let my Lumen wink out, and at the same time the soldier in front lowers his flashlight beam out of my face, pointing his gun at the floor. He's wearing a helmet, fatigues and night-vision goggles. Despite all that, I can tell he's only a few years older than me.

"You're him," the soldier says, a bit of awe in his voice. "John Smith."

I'm still not used to this whole being-recognized thing, so it takes me a moment to answer. "That's right."

The soldier snaps a walkie-talkie off his belt and speaks into it. "We've got him," he says, not taking his eyes off me.

Daniela edges towards Sam and me, glancing between us and the soldiers, more of whom are now filtering into our train car, fanning out, making the whole area even tighter. "Friends of yours?"

"Not sure," I reply quietly.

"Sometimes the government likes us, other times not so much," Sam explains.

"Great," Daniela replies. "For a second there, I thought they were here to arrest *me*."

The soldier's walkie-talkie crackles to life, a familiar woman's voice filling the train car. "Ask them nicely, but bring them in," the woman commands.

The soldier clears his throat uncomfortably, staring at us.

"Please come with us," he says. "Agent Walker would like a word."

CHAPTER
NINE

THE SOLDIERS RUSH US THROUGH THE SUBWAY
tunnels, out through the nearest station and finally
into daylight. They're constantly in a tight knot around
us, a human shield, treating us like the Secret Service
does the president. I let myself be hustled along, knowing that I can easily shove through them at the first
sign of trouble. We don't encounter any Mogadorian
patrols on the way back to their armored Humvees, and
pretty soon we're rumbling through streets filled with
broken chunks of building, the wreckage the result of
last night's *Anubis* bombardment.

We reach the Brooklyn Bridge quickly and without
incident. On the Manhattan side, the army has set up a
heavily armed checkpoint—soldiers packing mounted
machine guns watch the streets from behind a block-
ade of sandbags. Behind them, three rows of tanks are
parked six across on the bridge, their turrets armed

with surface-to-air missiles and aimed at the sky. Helicopters laden with more missiles patrol the skies and some muscular-looking boats sit ready in the river. If the Mogadorians try to push into Brooklyn, they'll definitely encounter some resistance.

"Have you had to fight many off?" I ask the soldier driving our Humvee as we're waved through the security checkpoint and begin slowly weaving through the choke points on the bridge.

"None whatsoever, sir," he replies. "The hostiles have stuck to Manhattan so far. That big ship flew right over us this morning and didn't engage. You ask me, they don't want a piece of us army boys."

"Sir," Daniela repeats, raising an eyebrow at me and snickering.

"They're holding Manhattan," I say, leaning back and frowning, not understanding why the Mogs haven't pressed their attack.

"It's like Setrákus Ra is sending a message," Sam says quietly. "Look at what I can do."

"If they come at us, we'll be ready," the soldier says, overhearing. Looking out the window, I make out snipers hidden among the bridge's high struts, watching the Manhattan side of the bridge through their scopes.

I exchange a doubtful look with Sam. I want to believe in this show of force by the army and echo the soldier's confidence, but I've seen what kind of destruction the Mogs are capable of. The only reason this Brooklyn camp is still standing is because Setrákus Ra allowed it.

The soldier parks our Humvee in the middle of a city block that's been converted into a staging area for the military. There are tents nearby, more Humvees and a lot of anxious-looking soldiers with guns. There's also a long line of civilians, many of them filthy and superficially injured, clutching their scant possessions as they wait in a haggard line. At the front of the line, some Red Cross volunteers with clipboards take down the exhausted people's information before waving them onto commandeered city buses.

Our escort notices me watching the slow procession of refugees. "Red Cross is trying to keep track of the displaced," the soldier explains. "Then we're evacuating them to Long Island, New Jersey, wherever. Getting them away from the fighting until we can retake New York."

The soldier sizes up Sam and Daniela, then looks at me again. It suddenly occurs to me that this guy is looking to me for orders.

"Do you want these two evacuated?" the soldier asks, referring to my companions.

"They're with me," I tell him, and he nods, accepting that without further question.

Daniela watches the aid workers check in an

elderly couple and help them onto a bus. "They have a list or something I could check? I'm . . . looking for someone."

The soldier shrugs like this isn't his area of expertise. "Sure. You could ask."

Daniela turns to me. "I'm gonna—"

"Go," I say, nodding. "I hope you find her."

Daniela smiles at Sam, then me, and starts to turn away. "Um, about that whole saving-the-world thing," she says, hesitating.

"When you're ready, come find me," I tell her.

"You're assuming I'll ever be ready," Daniela replies. She hasn't mentioned her duffel bag of stolen money since it got left behind on the subway.

"Yeah. I am."

Daniela lingers for a second longer, eyes locked with mine. Then, nodding to herself, she turns and jogs over to hassle the Red Cross. Sam looks at me like I'm crazy.

"You're just letting her go? One of the only . . ." Sam glances at the soldier who's still patiently standing nearby, not sure how much he should say.

"I can't force her to join us, Sam," I reply. "But what happened to her—what happened to *you* . . . there has to be a reason. I have faith it won't be for nothing."

"Agent Walker is this way, sir," the soldier says, motioning Sam and me to follow.

"Are cell phones working yet?" I ask him as we walk

through the busy camp. "I need to make a call. It's important."

"Traditional methods are still down, sir. The hostiles saw to that. We've probably got something you can use in the communications center, though," the soldier says, gesturing to a nearby tent bustling with activity. "I'm supposed to bring you directly to Agent Walker, though. If you'll allow it."

"If I'll allow it?"

"We were briefed on your history of . . . difficulty with authority," the soldier says, sheepishly examining the handle of his rifle. "We were told not to engage in combat or force you to do anything. Mission parameters are limited to, uh, gently prodding."

I shake my head in disbelief. It wasn't too long ago that I was considered an enemy of the state. Now, I'm being treated like a foreign dignitary by the army.

"All right," I say, deciding not to make life difficult for our escort. "Point me in the direction of Agent Walker and then help my friend Sam get his hands on a satellite phone."

Moments later, I walk along the concrete pier overlooking the East River and Manhattan. The air is crisp and cool, although still tinged with the acrid, burned smell that blows in from Manhattan. From here, I have a clear view of the destruction the Mogadorians wreaked on the city. Pillars of dark smoke rise into the bright blue sky, fires still burning. There are gaps in the city's skyline, spaces where I know buildings should be, simply erased by the powerful energy weapons of the *Anubis*. Occasionally, I can make out a Skimmer zipping between buildings, the Mogs patrolling the streets.

Agent Walker stands alone at the railing, staring out at the city.

"How'd you find me?" I ask by way of greeting as I approach.

The FBI agent who once tried to have me imprisoned actually smiles at me.

"Some survivors trickling in mentioned seeing you," Walker answers. "We sent teams out to the general area. Figured we'd start looking where the alpha warship was dropping heavy ordnance."

"Good call," I reply.

"Glad you're alive," she says brusquely.

Walker's gray-streaked red hair is pulled back in a tight ponytail. She looks exhausted, heavy bags under both of her eyes. At some point she traded in her customary FBI Windbreaker and pantsuit for a Kevlar vest and fatigues, probably borrowed from the large army contingent securing this area. Her left arm is in a sling, and there's a hastily bandaged gash on her forehead.

"Do you want me to heal those?" I ask.

In response, Walker takes a look around. The two of

us are alone for the moment, standing in the small park tucked under the Brooklyn Bridge. Or rather, alone as one can get in what's basically become a refugee camp overnight. The hilly lawn behind us is cluttered with makeshift tents, wounded and frightened New Yorkers packed in tight. I guess these are the people who refused to be evacuated by the Red Cross, or else are too injured to make the trip. The tents spread out into the surrounding blocks, and I'm sure there are people squatting in the fancy riverfront apartment buildings nearby. Interspersed throughout the survivors, keeping order and tending to the wounded, are soldiers, cops and a few medics, just a small part of the force of thousands I saw gathered closer to the bridge. It's essentially organized chaos.

"Those powers of yours have limits?" Walker asks, watching as a woman sprawled in the park's grass has her severely burned arm treated by a harried doctor.

"Yeah. I hit them pretty hard yesterday," I reply, rubbing the back of my neck. "Why do you ask?"

"Because much as I appreciate the offer, we've got thousands of injured here, John, with more trickling in every hour. You want to spend your whole day patching people up?"

I stare out over the rows of people in the park, many of them resting on nothing more than grass. A lot of them are watching me. I'm still not comfortable with this, being the face of the Garde. I turn back to Walker.

"I could," I say. "It would save some lives."

Walker shakes her head and gives me a level look. "The badly injured are in the triage tent. We can stop by later if you want to do the whole Mother Teresa thing. But you and I both know there are better ways to be spending your time."

I don't reply, but I don't press the issue any further. Walker grunts and walks along the pier, heading towards a collection of army tents set up in a nearby plaza. I take another quick look around the park. Crossing over the bridge, things looked pretty secure. Back here, though, it's absolute madness. Injured people, soldiers, military officials—I don't even know where to begin. I might be in over my head.

"So, you're in charge here?" I ask Walker, attempting to get my bearings.

She snorts. "You're kidding, right? There are five-star generals on the scene planning counteroperations. The CIA and the NSA are here, coordinating with people in Washington, trying to make sense of the intel that's coming in from around the world. They had the president on video conference earlier this afternoon from whatever bunker the Secret Service spirited him off to. I'm just an FBI agent, very much not in charge."

"Okay, if that's the case, why did they bring me to you, Walker? Why are we talking?"

Walker stops and turns to me, her hands on her hips.

"Because of our history, our relationship—"

"That's what you're calling it?"

"I've been named your liaison, John. Your point of contact. Anything you can tell us about the Mogadorians, their tactics, this invasion—that goes through me. Likewise for any requests you might have of the U.S. armed forces."

I let out a sharp, humorless laugh. I wonder where the generals are set up. I scan the nearby tents, looking for one that appears more important than the others.

"No offense, Walker, but I don't need you as a go-between."

"Not up to you," she replies, resuming her walk along the pier. "You have to understand that the people in charge, the president, his generals, what's left of his cabinet—they weren't MogPro people. When the Mogs made contact, we almost had a glorified coup on our hands with the MogPro scum advocating surrender. Luckily, with Sanderson out of the picture—"

"Hold up. What happened to him?" I ask. I lost track of the secretary of defense during the battle with Setrákus Ra.

"He didn't make it," Walker replies grimly. "I had enough people in Washington to get rid of most of the bad apples. The ones we knew about, at least."

"So you're saying MogPro is mostly gone and we're left with . . ."

"A fractured government that's been kept totally in

the dark. This invasion, the idea of aliens from outer space attacking us, it's all new to them. They accept that you're fighting on our side. But you're still an extraterrestrial."

"They don't trust me," I say, unable to keep the bitterness out of my voice.

"Most of them don't even trust each other anymore. And anyway, *you* shouldn't trust *them*," Walker replies emphatically. "The known members of MogPro have all been arrested, killed or gone underground. But that doesn't mean we got them all."

I give Walker a look, rolling my eyes. "So better for me to stick with the devil I know, huh?"

She opens her arms, obviously not really expecting me to hug her. "That's right."

"All right, here's my first request, liaison," I say. "The *Anubis*—that's the warship that left New York this morning—it's carrying Setrákus Ra and is on its way to Mexico—"

"Oh, good," Walker interrupts. "They'll like that. One less threat in U.S. airspace."

"They need to scramble jets, fighters, drones, whatever they've got," I continue. "It's headed to a place of great power, a Loric place. I'm not sure what Setrákus Ra wants there, but I know it's bad if he gets it. We need to take the fight to him."

Walker's expression darkens the more I talk. I can

already tell that I'm not going to like whatever she's got to tell me. She leads me off the pier, across some matted grass and stops in front of a canvas tent slightly isolated from the others.

"A direct attack isn't going to happen," she says.

"Why the hell not?"

"My headquarters," she says, pushing open the entrance flap. "Let's talk inside."

Inside Walker's tent is an unused cot, a cluttered table and a laptop computer. There's a map of New York City with red lines crisscrossing it—if I had to guess, I'd bet that line represents the path the *Anubis* took during yesterday's attack. Walker pulls a second map from beneath the New York one, this one of the entire world. There are ominous black X's drawn over a bunch of major cities—New York, Washington, Los Angeles and faraway places like London, Moscow and Beijing. There are more than twenty cities marked in this way. Walker taps her fingers on the map.

"This is the situation, John," she says. "Every marking is one of their warships. You know how to bring one of those things down?"

I shake my head. "Not yet. But I haven't tried."

"The air force tried yesterday. It didn't go well."

I frown. "I saw them flying in. I know they didn't make it."

"They had some success against the smaller ships,

but they didn't even get close to the *Anubis*. The air force was considering another strike when the Chinese went all in."

"What does that mean?"

"A couple hours after the attack on New York, they got trigger-happy. Were probably worried they might be attacked next. They threw everything short of a nuke at the warship over Beijing."

"And?"

"Casualties in the tens of thousands," Walker answers. "The warship still in the air. They're shielded somehow. Chinese scientists say it's some kind of electromagnetic field. They got tired of crashing jets up against it, so they tried parachuting a small force directly onto the warship. Those guys didn't survive contact with the field."

I'm reminded of the force field surrounding the Mogadorian base in West Virginia. The shock I received from touching it was enough to knock me out and make me sick for days.

"I've run into their force fields before," I tell Walker. "Literally."

"How'd you break them down?"

"Never did."

Walker gives me a deadpan look. "And here I was getting my hopes up."

I look back at Walker's map and shake my head.

Every black X looks to me like a fight I don't know how to win.

"Twenty-five cities under attack. You have any good news, Agent Walker?"

"That's just it," she says. "This *is* the good news."

I raise an eyebrow at her.

"Some places, like London and Moscow, sent troops out to fight the Mogs. But the response is nothing like here or Beijing. No bombardment, no rampaging monsters. It's like the Mogs are taking it easy on them. And then there are the places like Paris and Tokyo that didn't put up any fight at all. Those cities aren't actually under attack. The warships and scout ships are controlling the airspace, but other than that there aren't any Mogs on the ground. And then, this morning, that warship flies right over us, like we're nothing. It's got some people thinking maybe they don't want to fight. Maybe it's all just a big misunderstanding with the aliens, that we shouldn't have attacked them first."

"We didn't," I snap.

"I know that. But around the world, what they saw—"

"Setrákus Ra is sending a message," I say. "Even though he's got the advantage, he doesn't want a protracted fight. He wants to frighten humanity into submission. He wants us to give in."

Walker nods and walks over to her laptop. She

enters a series of passwords, no easy task considering she's typing one-handed, before finally pulling up an encrypted video.

"You're more right than you know," Walker says. "It's not clear how he got access, but this video appeared via secure channels in the president's private inbox. Other world leaders we've talked to have reported receiving the same thing."

Walker clicks the play button and an HD-quality image of Setrákus Ra's face appears on the screen. My blood runs cold at the sight of his pale skin and empty black eyes, at the dark-purple scar that encircles his neck, at the smug way he smiles into the camera. It's the exact same smile he wore right before chucking me into the East River. Setrákus Ra is seated in the ornate commander's chair on the *Anubis*—I remember seeing it when Ella showed me around the ship. Over his shoulder, New York City is visible through a massive floor-to-ceiling window. The sun is rising, the city still in flames. There's no doubt in my mind he chose this background on purpose.

"Respected leaders of Earth," Setrákus Ra begins, these polite words issued in a scratchy rumble, "I pray that this message finds you open-minded after the unfortunate events in New York and Beijing. It was with great reluctance, and only after an attempted assassination by alien terrorists, that I used a fraction of the available Mogadorian force against your people."

"You're the alien terrorists, by the way," Walker says.

"Yeah. I got that."

Setrákus Ra continues. "Despite these regrettable circumstances, my offer to embrace humanity and show it the way of Mogadorian Progress still stands. I am nothing if not forgiving. While my forces will continue to hold New York City and Beijing as a reminder of what happens when inconsiderate beasts bite a gently guiding hand, the other cities where my warships are positioned have nothing to fear. Assuming, that is, my generals receive unconditional surrender from these governments within the next forty-eight hours."

My head whips around to Walker. "They're not actually buying this shit, are they?"

She points at the screen. "There's more."

"In addition," Setrákus Ra intones, "I believe the United States government is currently harboring the Loric terrorists known as the Garde. To continue assisting these twisted souls will be considered an act of open war. They are to be turned over to me at the time of surrender, in the interest of avoiding the costly and painful process of rooting them out. It is also my understanding that some humans may have suffered a mutation at the hands of the Garde wherein they will manifest certain unnatural abilities. These humans are to be turned over to me for treatment."

"What does he mean about mutations?" Walker asks me. "More bullshit?"

I don't reply. Instead, I back away from the laptop while Setrákus Ra is still talking, my gaze shifting towards Agent Walker.

"You have forty-eight hours to surrender, or I will have no choice but to relieve humanity of your foolish leadership and liberate your cities by force . . ."

The clip stops and Walker turns to face me. When she does, I've already got a small fireball prepared, hovering it above the palm of my hand.

"Oh, Jesus Christ, John," she groans, leaning away from the heat.

"Is that why you brought me here?" I snap at her, backing up. I'm half expecting a group of soldiers to burst in and try to restrain me, so I keep one eye on the tent's exit as I move towards it. "Are my friends safe?"

"Do you think I showed you that as prelude to an ambush? Calm down. You're safe."

I stare at Walker for another couple of seconds. At this point, I don't really have much choice but to trust her, especially considering the alternative is fighting my way through an army. If the government wanted to trade me to Setrákus Ra as a gesture of goodwill, it probably would've already happened. I extinguish my fireball and frown at Walker.

"So, is it true?" Walker presses. "What Setrákus Ra

said about humans manifesting unnatural abilities? Does he mean that humans are getting Legacies?"

"I . . ."

I'm not sure how much to share with Walker. She tells me I'm safe, but it wasn't too long ago that she was chasing me across the country. Even though she claims MogPro have been driven underground, there are still humans out there working against us. Hell, she just told me not to trust the government. What if there are new Garde all over the world, and what if a sellout like Secretary of Defense Sanderson gets to them before we can? And could I really out Sam and Daniela to Walker? I can't tell her anything. Not until I've figured it out myself.

"I don't know what the hell he's talking about, Walker," I say after a moment. "He'll say anything to get what he's after."

I think she can tell I'm holding out on her. "I know it's hard to accept considering our history, but I'm on your side," Walker says. "For now, so is the United States."

"For now? What does that mean?"

"It means, no one's real eager to surrender to the alien maniac that just blew up New York. But if he starts torching more cities and we haven't figured out a way to successfully fight back? Things might change. That's why your request for a military operation in Mexico isn't going to happen. For one, it's a losing proposition against the warship. And two, prevailing wisdom right now is that we shouldn't openly aid you."

"They're hedging their bets," I say, unable to keep a sneer off my face. "In case they decide to surrender."

"Word from the president is that all options are currently open, yes."

"Giving up isn't an option. I've seen—" I stop myself from referencing Ella's vision of the future, figuring Legacy-powered prophecies won't carry much weight with the hyperpractical Walker. "It won't end well for humanity."

"Yeah, you and I know that, John. But when Setrákus Ra starts killing civilians and all he wants in trade is you and the other Garde? That's a course of action the president will be forced to consider."

I turn away, opening up the tent flap to look outside, wondering where Sam is with that satellite phone. I also want to hide my face from Walker, feeling a choking panic coming on. I don't know what to do. If Setrákus Ra's deadline passes and he starts bombing another city, am I supposed to just let that happen? Do I turn myself in? Meanwhile, what do I do about his impending attack on the Sanctuary? And what about Nine and Five, who are still unaccounted for? It's too much to handle.

"John?"

Slowly, I face Walker, making sure my expression is neutral. Even so, she must detect something there, because she crosses the tent and stands right in front of me. She grabs my shoulder with her good arm and I'm so surprised that I let it happen. There's fear in Walker's eyes, mixed with a kind of suicidal determination. I've seen that look before worn by my friends, right before they threw themselves into battle against impossible odds.

"You need to tell me how to do this," Walker says to me, her voice low and shaky. "Tell me how to win this war in less than forty-eight hours."

CHAPTER
TEN

"HOW'S IT GOING?"

Adam jumps when I put my hand on his shoulder and lean in to check on his progress. He hunches over a workbench where the Mogs tweaked their weapons before pointless attempts to bring down the Sanctuary's force field. Adam has swept all the Mog crap that was cluttering the bench onto the ground and replaced it with an assortment of mechanical parts. The mismatched pieces come from the disabled Skimmers collecting dust on the airstrip, some from within the guts of the engines, others from behind the touch-screen dashboards. Among the ship parts are other odds and ends—the battery from one of the halogen lamps, a broken-down Mog blaster and the casing of a laptop. All these things have been bent, warped or hammered by Adam as he tries to replace our ship's destroyed conduit using spare parts.

"How does it *look* like it's going?" he replies, glumly

setting down the blowtorch he was about to ignite. "I'm not an engineer, Six. This is strictly trial and error. So far, one hundred percent error."

The sun is only now climbing above the jungle's tree line to scorch the landing strip, no reprieve from the sticky heat out here. Adam has already sweated through his shirt, the pale skin on the back of his neck turning pinkish. I leave my hand on his shoulder until he sighs and turns to face me. His dark eyes are bleary and a little wild, gray circles forming around them.

"You didn't sleep," I say, knowing this for a fact. He worked through the entire night, his hammering and cursing often interrupting the fitful hours of rest I managed while curled up in the Skimmer's cockpit. The only breaks he took were to check on Dust, whose paralyzed condition hadn't changed. "Maybe I'm not up on my Mogadorian biology, but I was pretty sure you guys needed to do that."

Adam brushes some hair out of his eyes, trying to focus on me. "Yeah, Six, we sleep. When it's convenient."

"You're going to push yourself to exhaustion and then what'll you be good for?" I ask.

Adam frowns at me. "Same thing I'm good for now," he says, glancing at the collection of trashed parts in front of him. "I hear you, Six. I'm fine. Let me keep working."

In truth, I'm glad Adam is so devoted to his work. As much as I don't want to see him hurt himself, we desperately need to get out of Mexico. There's still no word from John. I'm afraid we're missing the war.

"At least eat," I tell him, yanking a light green banana off the bunch I just picked from a nearby tree and shoving it into Adam's hand.

He considers the banana for a moment. I can actually hear Adam's stomach growl as he begins to peel it. Food wasn't something we thought to pack—we didn't know what to expect when we came to the Sanctuary, but we definitely weren't planning to get stranded. We didn't bring the necessary supplies for an extended stay.

"You know, Nine had these stones in his Chest that, if you sucked on them, they'd give you all the nutrients of a meal," I tell Adam, peeling my own banana. "Kinda gross, especially after you thought about where they'd been and how many times Nine probably reused them. But right now, I really wish we hadn't tossed them down that well in the Sanctuary."

Adam smirks, glancing over at the temple. "Maybe you should go back in and ask real nice. I'm sure that energy-thing doesn't want Nine's spit-stones."

"Maybe I should ask it for a new engine while I'm at it."

"Couldn't hurt," Adam replies, and swallows the rest of his banana in a hurry. "I'm going to get us out of here, Six. Don't worry."

I leave a second banana on the table and let Adam get back to work. I cut across the airstrip, heading to where

Marina sits cross-legged in the grass, facing the Sanctuary. I'm not sure if she's meditating or praying or what, but she was in that spot when I woke up this morning and hasn't moved in the time that I've been out scrounging the jungle for food.

I'd like to think it's an accident that my route to Marina takes me by the Skimmer strut where Phiri Dun-Ra is tied, but I know it's not. We've got her tied up securely in the middle of camp and have all been keeping an eye on her. I want the Mogadorian to say something, to give me an excuse. She doesn't disappoint.

"He's going to fail, you know."

"Did you say something?" I ask, stopping and turning slowly to face her. I heard Phiri Dun-Ra perfectly.

Our Mogadorian prisoner smiles gruesomely at me, her teeth outlined with dried blood. Her right eye is swollen shut. I did that to her last night. After learning about the Mogadorian invasion, I got real tired real quick of her incessant cackling. So, I clocked her. Not my proudest moment, punching out a tied-up Mogadorian, but it felt good. In truth, I probably would've done more if Marina hadn't dragged me away. As I stare at Phiri Dun-Ra, her good eye narrows in amusement. My fist clenches again. I want to hit something. All I need is a reason.

"You heard me, little girl," she replies, jerking her chin towards Adam. Phiri Dun-Ra projects her voice enough that I'm sure he can hear, too. "Adamus Sutekh will fail, as he always does. You see, I have known him much longer than you. I know what a perpetual disappointment he was to his father. To our people. It's no wonder he turned traitor."

I glance over my shoulder at Adam. He's pretending not to hear Phiri Dun-Ra, but his hands have stopped working and his shoulders are bunched up.

"You want to get knocked out again?" I ask Phiri Dun-Ra, taking a step towards her.

She looks thoughtful for a moment, then continues on. "Although, hmm . . . something only now occurs to me. I remember hearing of young Adamus's technical prowess. He was something of a prodigy with machines as a young trueborn. It is odd, then, that he's been unable to fix one of these ships, especially with all that equipment at his disposal."

I glance again at Adam. He's turned now, a confused expression on his face, staring at Phiri Dun-Ra.

"I wonder if he is stalling on purpose," Phiri Dun-Ra muses. "Perhaps, now that Mogadorian Progress has proven inevitable, he thinks keeping you here will earn him favor with our Beloved Leader, so that he might come crawling back to his real people . . . Or perhaps he is simply too much of a coward to face the losing battles to come."

Adam is past me in a blur. He crouches down in front of Phiri Dun-Ra and yanks her head back. She tries to bite him, but Adam is too quick.

"Death is coming for you, Adamus Sutekh! For all of you!" she manages to shriek, before Adam shoves a rag into her mouth. Next, he tears loose a piece of duct tape and slaps it across Phiri Dun-Ra's face. Her breath now comes in furious and forceful bursts from her nose, the Mogadorian glaring venomously at Adam. Over on the grass in front of the Sanctuary, Marina has stood up to watch this scene play out, a small frown on her face.

Adam stands over Phiri Dun-Ra, his teeth bared, dark lines creasing his face. It's a murderous look, one I've seen on the face of many Mogadorians, usually right before they tried to kill me.

"Adam . . . ," I say warningly.

Adam whips around to face me, trying to get control of himself. He takes a deep breath.

"Everything she said is a lie, Six," he says. "Everything."

"I know that," I reply. "We should've gagged her sooner."

Adam grunts and returns to his workbench, his eyes downcast as he walks by me. Phiri Dun-Ra definitely knows how to get a rise out of him. Out of all of us, really. Well, except for Marina. I know she's trying to drive a wedge between our group, but it isn't going to work. How stupid does she think I am? I'll always take the word of a Mogadorian that was allowed to walk through the Sanctuary's force field over one that tried to blow us up with a grenade.

With the skirmish over, Marina sits back down in the grass before the Sanctuary. I join her, watching brightly colored birds fly playful loops around the ancient temple.

"Would you have stopped him if he tried to kill her?" Marina asks me, after a moment.

I shrug. "She's a Mogadorian," I reply. "One of the shittiest ones I've ever met, too. And that's saying something."

"In the heat of battle is one thing," Marina says. "But when she is tied up . . . she is not like the warriors we've faced so many times. She's like Adam, a trueborn. When I used my healing on him, prevented him from disintegrating, I could . . . I could feel the life there, not so different from ours. I fear what we might become as this war goes on."

Maybe I'm overtired, and I'm definitely beyond stressed with our current situation, but Marina's moral-compass thing is beginning to wear thin. When I reply, there's more harshness in my voice than I'd like.

"So what? You're a pacifist now? A few days ago, you stabbed out Five's eye with an icicle," I remind her. "He's a lot more like us than Phiri Dun-Ra is, and *they both* have bad shit coming to them."

"Yes, I did that," Marina replies, running her hand over the sharp tips of the grass. "I regret it. Or, actually, I regret how little regret I feel. Do you see what I mean, Six? We have to be careful not to turn into *them*."

"Five deserved it," I reply, softening my voice a little.

"Maybe," Marina admits, and finally looks at me. "I wonder what will be left of us when this is over, Six. What we will be like."

"*If* there's anything left of us," I reply. "Big if, at this point."

Marina smiles sadly. She turns her gaze back to the Sanctuary. "I went inside the temple early this morning, before the sun was up," she says. "I went back to the well, to where the Loric energy came from."

I study Marina. While I was sleeping, she was climbing down those twisting stairs back into the Sanctuary's underground chamber. The stone well where the Entity erupted from, the glowing maps of the universe on the walls. I wish we'd gotten more answers from that place.

"Find anything useful?"

She shrugs. "It's still there. The Entity. I can feel it, spreading out from within the Sanctuary, although I don't know for what purpose. I can still see the glow, deep down in the well. But . . ."

"You were hoping for some advice?"

Marina nods, chuckling softly. "I'd hoped it might guide us. Tell us what we should do next."

I'm not surprised that the Entity living inside the Sanctuary, apparently the source of our power, didn't poke its head out for another visit with Marina. When we first encountered the Entity, it seemed almost amused with us—happy to be awoken, sure, but in no rush to help us win the war against the Mogadorians. I remember something it said during our conversation; that it bestows its gifts on a species, it doesn't judge or take sides, not even in its own defense. I think we've already gotten as much help from the Entity as we're going to get. I keep this thought to myself, not wanting to discourage Marina or shake her faith, which seems to be mostly keeping her together, even if it does lead her to some morbid ethical questions that I frankly don't feel like thinking about.

"I've been sitting out here praying on our situation," Marina continues. "I suppose it's silly to hope for some kind of sign. I don't know what else to do with myself, though."

Before I can respond, a shrill buzzing sounds from behind us. At first, I think it's only Adam's latest attempt to create a new conduit. The noise is too close. It's coming from practically right on top of us. Marina's grinning at me, her eyes wide and excited. My heart starts to beat harder as I realize what's happening. Maybe Marina's prayers actually worked.

"Six? Aren't you going to answer it?"

The thing's been annoyingly silent for so long, I'd forgotten what the ringer on the satellite phone sounds like. I jump up, yanking the phone out of the back of my pants. Marina stands with me, leaning her head in close to listen, and Adam jogs over to join us. I can feel Phiri Dun-Ra watching us, but I ignore her.

"John?"

There's a burst of static as the satellite phone establishes a connection, a familiar voice coming through between squeals of interference.

"Six? It's Sam!"

A wide smile spreads across my face. I can hear the relief in Sam's voice that I answered.

"Sam!" My own voice breaks a little. I hope he doesn't hear it over our crackly connection. Actually, I don't care. Marina grabs my arm, grinning wider. "You're okay?" I ask Sam, the words coming out half question and half exclamation.

"I'm okay!" he shouts.

"And John?"

"John, too. We're at a military encampment in Brooklyn. They loaned us a pair of satellite phones and John's talking to Sarah on the other one."

I snort and can't help rolling my eyes a little. "Of course he is."

"Where *are* you guys? Is everyone all right?" Sam asks. "Things have gotten nuts."

"Everyone's fine, but—"

Before I can tell Sam about our predicament, he interrupts. "Did anything happen down there, Six? While you were at the Sanctuary? Like, for instance, did you push a button for Legacies or something?"

"There weren't any buttons," I say, exchanging a look with Marina. "We met, I don't know—"

"Lorien itself," Marina says.

"We met an *Entity*," I tell Sam. "It said some cryptic stuff, thanked us for waking it up and then, um . . ."

"Spread out into the Earth," Marina finishes for me.

"Oh, hi, Marina," Sam says distractedly. "Listen, I think this Entity of yours might have, uh, spread out into me."

"What the hell does that mean, Sam?"

"I've got Legacies," Sam replies. There's such a strong mixture of excitement and pride in his voice that it's impossible for me not to imagine Sam puffing out his chest a bit, looking like he did right after we kissed for the first time. "Well, just telekinesis. That's always the first one, isn't it?"

"You've got Legacies?" I exclaim, looking wide-eyed at the others. Marina's hand tightens on my arm, and she turns to look at the Sanctuary. Meanwhile, Adam's expression turns thoughtful as he looks down at his own hands, maybe wondering what this development says about his own Legacies.

"And I'm not the only one," Sam continues. "We met another girl in New York by chance who had gotten powers, too. Who knows how many new Garde are out there?"

I shake my head, trying to digest all this information. I find myself staring at the Sanctuary too, thinking about the Entity hidden within.

"It worked," I say quietly. "It actually worked."

Marina faces me, tears in her eyes. "We're home, Six," she says. "We've brought Lorien here. We've changed the world."

It all sounds great, but I'm not ready to celebrate just yet. We're still stranded in Mexico. The war isn't suddenly over.

"That Entity didn't give you a list of new Garde, did it?" Sam asks. "Some way for us to find them?"

"No list," I reply. "I can't say for sure, but judging by my conversation with the Entity, it all seems pretty random. What's happening there?" I ask Sam, steering the conversation towards the battles we've been missing. "We heard about the attack on New York . . ."

"It's bad, Six," Sam says, grimness creeping into his voice. "Manhattan is, like, on fire. We don't know where Nine is; he's still out there somewhere. Where are you guys? We could really use your help."

I realize that I never finished telling Sam about our current situation. "There were Mogs guarding the Sanctuary," I tell him. "We got all of them but one. While we were inside the temple, she wrecked all the ships. We're stuck here. You think you could get your new friends in the military to send a jet? We need to be picked up."

"Wait, you're still in Mexico? At the Sanctuary?"

I don't like the fear in Sam's voice. Something's not right.

"What's wrong, Sam?"

"You need to get out of there," Sam says. "Setrákus Ra and his big-ass warship are heading right for you."

CHAPTER
ELEVEN

A FEW MINUTES AFTER AGENT WALKER TELLS ME I've got forty-eight hours to win a war, a pair of soldiers in full body armor and a middle-aged civilian carrying a tablet device arrive at her tent. They want to deliver some kind of urgent report related to a recording the civilian made on his tablet that morning. I'm not paying much attention—my ears are ringing, heart pounding. I can feel the new arrivals stealing looks at me, like I'm a cross between a celebrity and a unicorn. That doesn't help my feeling that the tent walls are slowly closing in.

I think I might be having a panic attack.

Agent Walker takes one look at me and holds up her hand, stopping the soldiers from saying anything more. "Let's take a walk, gentlemen," she says. "I need the fresh air."

Walker ushers the three men out of her tent and follows them, pausing at the exit. She looks back at me, grimacing like she's in pain. I know she probably wants to say something comforting or encouraging, and I also know that Agent Walker simply isn't equipped for that.

"Take a few minutes," she says gently, and that's probably the most empathy I've ever seen from her.

"I'm fine," I reply sharply, although I don't feel fine. Not at all. I'm rooted in place and struggling to keep my breathing even.

"Of course, I know that," Walker says. "Just—I don't know, you've had a rough twenty-four hours. Take a breath. I'll be back in a few minutes."

As soon as Walker's gone, I immediately collapse into the chair in front of her laptop. I shouldn't be taking a minute. There's too much to do. My body isn't cooperating, though. This isn't like the exhaustion I was pushing through yesterday—it's something else. My hands are shaking, and I can hear my heartbeat thumping loud in my head. It reminds me of yesterday's explosions—the screams, the dead. Running for my life, passing by the corpses of people I wasn't good enough to save. And more of that to come.

Unless I can do the impossible.

I feel like I'm going to throw up.

Needing something to focus on, something to pull me out of this funk, I turn on Walker's laptop. I know what I'm hoping to find, what I need to hear. In addition to the video she showed me of Setrákus Ra's threat,

Walker has a few other files open on her desktop. I'm not at all surprised to see the video I'm looking for there, already open.

FIGHT FOR EARTH—SUPPORT THE LORIC

I turn the volume up and click play.

"This is our planet, but we are not alone."

Daniela was right: Sarah does sound like she's trying to come off as older and more professional than she actually is, like a newscaster or documentarian. It makes me smile, all the same. I close my eyes and listen to her voice. I don't even necessarily listen to the words—although it's definitely nice to hear your girlfriend describe you as a hero to the human race. Hearing Sarah's voice starts to settle my nerves, but it also creates a feeling of longing that I've been too panicked to indulge over the last couple of days. I imagine us back in Paradise, way more innocent, hanging out in my bedroom while Henri's out running errands . . .

I'm not sure how many times I've replayed the clip before Sam enters Walker's tent. He clears his throat to get my attention and holds up a satellite phone in each hand.

"Mission accomplished," Sam says. He cranes his neck to see the laptop screen. "What're you watching?"

"The, um, the video that Sarah made," I reply, feeling embarrassed. Of course, Sam doesn't know that I've just played the video a dozen times, that I'm listening to my girlfriend's voice to try to attain some kind of zen state. I sit up straight and try to look like the strong leader the video portrays me as.

"Is it awesome?" Sam asks, coming over. He sets one of the phones down next to me.

"It's . . ." I trail off, not sure what to say about the video. "It's pretty corny, actually. But, right now, it's also kind of the greatest thing ever."

Sam nods and pats my shoulder, understanding. "Why don't you just call her?"

"Sarah?"

"Yeah. I'll call Six and check in with Team Sanctuary," he says, sounding eager. "Find out where they are. Maybe they've already made it back to Ashwood Estates. I'll let them know what's up with us and we'll figure out a place to meet. I should probably call my dad, too. Let him know I'm alive."

I realize Sam is looking at me the same way that Walker did, like I'm suddenly fragile. I shake my head and start to stand up, but Sam puts a hand on my shoulder.

"Seriously, dude," he says. "Call your girlfriend. She's got to be worried sick."

I let Sam push me back into the chair. "All right," I say. "But if anything's happened to Six and the others, or you can't reach them—"

"I'll come get you right away," Sam says as he heads

towards the exit. "I'll give you some privacy until the next crisis."

When Sam's gone, I push both my hands through my hair and leave them there, squeezing my head, like I'm literally trying to keep it together. After a moment of composing myself, I reach for the phone Sam left behind and punch in the number that I've committed to memory.

Sarah answers on the third ring, breathless and hopeful. "John?"

"You have no idea how badly I needed to hear your voice," I reply, glancing sidelong at Walker's laptop screen and finally closing it. I press the phone tight to my ear, shut my eyes and imagine Sarah is sitting next to me.

"I was so worried, John. I saw—we all saw what happened in New York."

I have to bite the inside of my cheek. The image of Sarah I was calling up in my mind's eye is replaced by one of buildings crumbling under the bombardment of the *Anubis*.

"It was—I don't know what to say about it," I tell her. "I feel lucky to have made it out."

I don't mention the guilt I've been feeling, or how hard it has been to keep going. I don't want Sarah to know that about me. I want to be the heroic guy from her video.

Sarah doesn't say anything for a few seconds. I can hear her breathing, slow and shaky, the way it gets when she's trying to keep her emotions from bubbling out. When she finally speaks, her voice is a quiet and desperate whisper, coming from far away.

"It was so horrible, John. All those poor people. They're dying, the world's basically ending, and all—all I could think about was what might have happened to you, why you weren't calling. I don't—I don't have a charm on my ankle to keep track of you. I didn't know if . . ."

I realize that Sarah's relief at hearing my voice is the angry kind, the kind that comes when you've spent sleepless nights worrying about a person. I remember how it felt when the Mogadorians had taken her, how it felt like a piece of me was missing. I also remember how much simpler things were then—avoid the Mogs, rescue Sarah, there weren't millions of lives hanging in the balance. Crazy to think that used to seem like a crisis.

"My sat phone got destroyed or I would've called sooner. We made it to Brooklyn where the army has set up. I'm fine," I reassure her, knowing that I'm partly trying to convince myself.

"I've felt like a ghost these last couple days," Sarah says quietly. "Mark and me, we've been hitting the internet hard, working on projects to help, you know, win hearts and minds. And we finally met GUARD in person, which—oh my God, John, I have so much to tell you. But I need you to know first that during all this keeping busy, I've felt like I'm just going through the motions. Like I'm out of body. Because all I could think about was you getting blown up with those people in New York."

I should ask Sarah about the identity of the mysterious hacker she and Mark have been working with. I should find out the details of what she and Mark have been doing. I know I should. Except in that moment, all I can think about is how much I miss her.

"I know part of the reason you went to find Mark was because you didn't want to be a distraction," I say, trying to sound more reasonable than desperate. "Not being able to talk to you, to see you, to touch you—that might be a bigger distraction than anything. You've been helping so much, but . . ."

"I miss you too," Sarah replies, and I can tell when she speaks that she's trying to find her resolve, to be tough like she was when I dropped her off at the bus station in Baltimore. "We made the right decision, though. It's better this way."

"It was a stupid decision," I reply.

"John . . ."

"I don't know how I let you talk me into this," I continue. "We should've never separated. After everything that happened in New York, everything I had to see—"

My breath catches for a moment as I remember the fires, the destruction, the wounded and the dead. I realize that I'm shaking again, and definitely not from exhaustion. I feel like I might have hit my limit, like there's only so much brutality my brain can endure. I try to focus on Sarah and on getting my words out, on making sense and not sounding too desperate.

"I need you with me, Sarah," I manage to finish. "I feel like these are the last battles we're ever going to fight. After New York, I—I've seen how quickly it can all be taken away. I don't want us to be apart if something happens, if this is the end."

Sarah gathers a deep breath. When she speaks next, her voice is firm.

"This is *not* the end, John."

I realize how I must sound to her. Weak and scared, not at all like the alien hero she portrayed in that video. I'm embarrassed by how I'm acting. Alone for the first time since the attack in New York, without constant skirmishes to distract me, with things finally slowed down enough for me to think—the result is me breaking down while on the phone with my girlfriend. We've been in bad situations before, fought some brutal battles and seen friends die. But, until now, I've never felt hopeless.

When I'm silent for a few moments, Sarah continues, her voice gentle. "I can't imagine what it was like to be in New York during . . . that. I can't imagine what you're going through—"

"It was my fault it happened," I tell her quietly, glancing to the tent flap in case someone outside might overhear. "I could've killed Setrákus Ra at the UN. I had time to prepare for this invasion. And I failed."

"Oh, John. You cannot possibly blame yourself for New York," Sarah replies, her tone understanding but insistent. "You are *not* responsible for the murderous rampage of an alien psycho, okay? You were trying to stop him."

"But I didn't."

"Yeah, and neither did anyone else. So either all of us are equally to blame, or maybe it's the evil Mogadorian's fault and we can leave it at that. Your guilt isn't going to bring anyone back, John. But you can avenge them. You can stop Setrákus Ra from doing it again."

I laugh bitterly. "That's just it. I don't know how to stop him. It's too much."

"We'll find a way," Sarah replies, and her certainty almost convinces me. "We'll do this together. All of us."

I rub my hands over my face, trying to get myself together. Sarah's telling me exactly what I need to hear. As usual, I know she's right, at least on a logical level. But that doesn't loosen the knot of guilt tying up my guts, or make the future seem any less overwhelming.

"They look at me like a hero," I say, scoffing. "I

walk around this camp and the soldiers, the survivors, everyone looks at me like I'm some kind of superman. They don't know—"

"I guess my video really worked," Sarah quips, trying to lighten the mood. "They look at you that way because you are a hero, John."

I shake my head. "They don't know that I have no idea what I'm doing. I don't know how to fight a battle on this scale. Nine's missing, Ella's taken and basically getting tortured, I don't know what's taking Six and the others so long to get back from the Sanctuary, but when they do we might have to go back anyway because that's right where Setrákus Ra is headed. Meanwhile, there are twenty-five warships over twenty-five different cities. I don't know how to deal with this, Sarah."

"Well," Sarah replies, her voice calm and collected, like I haven't just dropped an insurmountable pile of problems at her feet. "It's a good thing you've got friends. Now let's take this one thing at a time. Let me tell you about GUARD."

CHAPTER TWELVE

SARAH TELLS ME EVERYTHING ABOUT HER TIME with Mark, and I really can't believe what she says about GUARD. After all these years, it's incredible. I try to keep my voice down, though, to hide this amazing news from Agent Walker and her friends in the government, at least for the time being. After Sarah's filled me in, I tell her everything that's happened to me, and everything that we're still facing. She doesn't falter. She tells me that we can do this. She tells me we can win.

She makes me believe.

When I finally come out of Walker's tent, I'm not shaking anymore. Unburdening myself to Sarah, hearing her voice, remembering what I'm fighting for—all this is enough to get me on my feet, moving, ready to charge back into battle. I still don't have all the answers, but I'm no longer afraid to confront the questions.

Outside the tent, Sam is still on the phone. He's pacing back and forth, gesturing emphatically with his free hand.

"Six, that's crazy," he insists. Obviously, Six is alive and well. And of course Sam is already trying to talk her out of something. "You haven't seen the *size* of this thing. It tore through whole city blocks like they were made out of paper."

Sam spots me, then widens his eyes like Six is saying something crazy in response.

"Here's John," Sam says sharply into the phone. "Maybe he can talk some sense into you."

Sam holds out the phone to me.

"They're okay?" I ask Sam, accepting the phone.

"Yeah. They released the spirit of Lorien on Earth, which is probably why I have Legacies, but now they're stranded in Mexico, and Six is talking about fighting the *Anubis* when it shows up at the Sanctuary," Sam says breathlessly. I stare at him, trying to wrap my mind around all that as I lift the phone to my ear.

"John? Sam?" There's Six's familiar voice, sounding annoyed. "Someone talk to me."

"Hey, Six," I say. "Good to hear your voice."

"You, too," she replies, her smile audible. "Want me to catch you up on the details? Or should we get to the part where you try talking me out of fighting Setrákus Ra and his warship?"

I can't help grinning at her bluster. Between talking to Sarah and now Six, things no longer feel so massively overwhelming. We're definitely up against it, but at least I'm not up against it alone.

"I want you to catch me up," I tell Six. "But first, I really need to talk to Adam."

"Oh," Six replies, sounding surprised. "Sure. Hang on a second."

Sam fixes me with a look, like I should've immediately told Six and the others to flee the Sanctuary. I'm not sure that's the right move yet. We know Setrákus Ra is heading there, but he doesn't know that we know. That gives us a rare advantage. Ella showed me the Sanctuary in her vision. She told me to warn Six and the others. Maybe it's there that the final battle against Setrákus Ra will be fought. If that's the case, at least it'll be fought in the middle of nowhere. Civilians won't be in danger.

Adam gets on the phone, sounding weary. "How can I help?"

"Your warships—I mean, the Mog warships, they're protected by force fields. Tell me how to bring them down."

Adam snorts. "You're kidding, right?"

"I need to give the government something," I tell Adam. "Setrákus Ra has set a deadline for their surrender and if they don't see a way to defeat his armada they aren't going to help us."

"John, those warships were designed before the invasion of Lorien," Adam replies. "The shields are meant to sustain attacks from a planet full of Garde. There's no weapon on Earth short of a nuclear bomb that could even *potentially* break through them and attempting such an attack over a major population center would be catastrophic." Adam pauses, and I can hear dirt crunching. He's moving towards something. "Although . . ."

"What? I'll take anything you can give me, Adam."

"Maybe brute force isn't the answer. I'm staring at an airstrip of disabled Skimmers," he says. "It occurs to me that there are a hundred or so assigned to each warship. They act as scouts and transport squads of ground troops. They come and go from the warships quite a bit, which makes lowering the warship's force field each time impractical. So, the Skimmers are outfitted with an electromagnetic field generator that masks them from the warship's shield, allowing them to pass through unharmed."

I should've thought of that. Now that Adam's jogged my memory, I realize that I saw this technology at work back at the West Virginia mountain base. When Setrákus Ra first arrived on Earth, his ship moved through the base's force field like it wasn't even there. When I tried to chase him down, the shield totally fried me.

"Would it be possible to strip that technology out

of the Skimmers and put it into something else?" I ask Adam. "Like, for instance, a fighter jet?"

Adam considers this. "Possible, yes. But while it wouldn't have to worry about the warship's shields, it would still be targeted by the cannons."

I remember what Ella showed me during our shared dream—the docking bay where she and Five tried to escape. Maybe we can use the Mogs' own technology against them.

"We could get like ten people onto one of those Skimmers, right?" I ask next, considering a new plan of attack.

"Twelve, plus two pilots," Adam answers quickly. "You're considering a less obvious assault."

"Yeah. If we could board one of those warships, how many people do you think we'd need to overtake it?"

There's a bit of excitement in Adam's voice now. "That would depend on how many of those people had Legacies. Have I mentioned, John, that when I was a child I dreamed about flying one of those warships?"

I smirk at that. "You might just get your chance, Adam. Thanks for the info. Can you put Six back on?"

Adam says good-bye and hands the phone back to Six.

"You think we should try boarding the *Anubis*?" Six asks me. "Sam was just encouraging me and the others to run as fast and as far from that thing as possible."

"I'm not sure what we should do yet, but I want to know our options," I reply. I look at Sam and can't help frowning. He's not going to like what I have to say next. "Stay put, Six. Help is on the way."

A short time later, Sam and I walk along the pier, looking for Agent Walker. Wherever she went with those two army guys and their civilian, it's taking longer than expected. Up ahead, there's a large military presence on the concrete dock that juts into the East River. When we arrive, a small group of soldiers are hard at work pulling empty kayaks from the water and dumping them in a pile out of the way so that the military ships have a clear place to dock. This place wasn't exactly designed for battleships. In the last twenty-four hours, it's been turned into something of a staging area, with a bunch of navy destroyers floating ominously in the narrow waterway, their guns pointed at the smoking remains of downtown Manhattan.

"How's Malcolm doing?" I ask Sam. He made a short call to his dad after we got off the phone with Six.

"Mostly relieved that we're alive. And very excited about my new . . . thing," Sam replies, glancing around to make sure no one's listening. "He and the FBI agents Walker left behind got scooped up by the government during the evacuation of Washington. I guess he's getting the VIP bunker treatment. They've got him in the same underground complex as the president."

"Maybe he could put a good word in for us."

"I told him," Sam says. "Right now, he says they think he's some crazy scientist that specializes in aliens with a lot of pets."

"The Chimærae."

"Dad thinks it's best if they pass as normal animals for now. I know we've decided to trust Agent Walker's little group of rebels, but there's more than just her crew in Washington. Some of the scientists down there, well, Dad thinks they might be a little too curious about alien biology."

I think about how Adam rescued the Chimærae from Mogadorian experimentation. Much as I want to trust that the U.S. government is better than that, I don't. "That's smart," I reply. "Keep them from getting dissected or something until we need them. In the meantime, they can look after your dad."

"Yeah . . ." Sam trails off. I can tell there's something else he'd rather be talking about, mostly because he hasn't let up since we got off the phone with Six. "John, I still can't believe you told them to stay down there."

I'm planning to call Six back once I figure out how much support I can drum up from Walker and the government. At least until then, they're staying put at the Sanctuary. They've got some time until Setrákus Ra shows up. "You honestly think Six would've retreated if I told her to?" I reply. "I don't like putting them in danger either, Sam, but . . ."

"John, come on. The *Anubis* almost killed us yesterday! We were like ants against that thing. Not even there. What chance do they have?"

"Ella told me Setrákus Ra wants what's inside the Sanctuary, which I'm assuming is this Loric Entity Six told us about. We can't just let him go there unopposed. Nothing good can come of him getting what he wants."

"But how are they going to fight him off? What good is going to come of them staying down there?" Sam asks, raising his voice. "They can't even hurt him. Not without—"

"I know what the situation is, Sam," I snap, losing my cool. "We're going to find a way to get down there and help them, all right? Ella *showed* me—she showed me the Sanctuary, she told me to warn Six and the others and she also told me that we can win. That she's seen a way. It all starts there."

I leave out the parts where Ella told me that there would be sacrifices and where she implied that I might be the one to kill her. That part of her prophecy I'm going to be working my ass off to change. I know Sam is only pressing me because he's worried about the others and Six in particular. I'm worried about them, too. But I also trust Six to keep her head and make her own decisions.

Before Sam can put together a rebuttal, I spot Walker ahead of us and pick up my pace. The FBI agent is surrounded by a huddle of high-ranking military officials. I have to nudge my way through a crowd of soldiers to get close. I get some disgruntled looks at first, dressed as I am like a civilian who just survived a natural disaster. When they start to realize who I am, a path clears real quick. I'm not so surprised by this treatment anymore, and I try not to let it make me feel uncomfortable. One of the soldiers even salutes me, although his buddy standing beside him elbows him hard and rolls his eyes.

Walker sees me coming and breaks away from the military brass. I notice them noticing me, but it seems like Walker was right about the higher-ups wanting to avoid direct contact with us dangerous Loric rebels. They move away and gather again farther down the pier, many of the soldiers going along with them. Once there, they start pointing towards the East River and exchanging words. Something about the water's definitely alarming them. I start to amp up my hearing to eavesdrop on what's got them so spooked, but Walker is already right in front of me and talking.

"Good, you're here. I was just coming back to get you," Walker says. She's holding the tablet computer belonging to the civilian who showed up at her tent earlier, although that guy's no longer anywhere to be seen. Walker must have commandeered his tablet and sent him on his way.

"I know the weakness of the warship shields. I know how we can beat them," I tell Walker, cutting to the chase.

Her eyebrows shoot up. "Damn, John. That was quick. That's definitely something the army boys will be interested in."

"Good." I make a pointed glance at the officers gathered down the pier. "I need to get to Mexico, Walker. We're talking in the next couple hours. There's going to be a battle down there that I can't miss. I need whatever support they're willing to give me."

"Is there an 'or else' you're waiting to drop on me?" Walker asks, her expression darkening. "I'll do what I can, but I already told you the military's position. That comes direct from the commander in chief."

"Yeah, well, tell them the parts they need to beat the shields? They're sitting on a runway in Mexico. So they better scramble some damn jets and get me down there."

Walker holds up her hand, letting me know she's heard me. "All right, all right. I'll do my best. But we've got other crap to deal with before we go jetting off to your special Loric safe zone or whatever the hell it is."

"Whoa," Sam says. He's wandered closer to the

railing and is staring into the water. "They've got a submarine out there."

"Yeah," Walker replies. "Before you go anywhere. John, I want you to take a look at this."

She slides up next to me and clicks play on the tablet, starting a video. It's shaky footage from earlier this morning, when the *Anubis* left Manhattan and glided over the Brooklyn Bridge. The camerawork is jittery and the audio is convoluted with screams and soldiers shouting orders to each other. Eventually, the sinister warship passes out of sight.

"What am I supposed to be looking for, Walker?"

"That's what I said. I missed it the first time, too," Walker replies, running the footage back again. "Apparently, the thousands of highly trained military personnel didn't notice this happen in real time either. Watch the river now."

Sam leans in next to us, squinting at the video. "Something falls off the ship," he states flatly, pointing at the screen.

He's right. A round object about the size of Setrákus Ra's pearl-shaped getaway ship drops from the warship's belly. It hits the East River with a large splash and immediately sinks out of view.

"Ever seen anything like that before?" Walker asks.

I shake my head. "I'd never even seen one of the warships until the *Anubis* attacked New York."

Walkers sighs. "So we're still in the dark."

"Are they sending that sub down to look for whatever that was?" Sam asks.

Walker nods. "The river's only about a hundred feet deep, but they don't want to risk sending divers down in case it's some kind of weapon or trap."

"What else could it possibly be?" I ask Walker, putting my hands on my hips and turning towards the river. Add this mysterious object to the long list of things I've got to worry about.

"The higher-ups are hoping it was an accidental drop, that something fell off the warship that we could potentially study or use against the Mogadorians, get a better understanding of what we're up against."

"Setrákus Ra doesn't do anything by accident."

"So you're saying we shouldn't send anyone down there?" Walker asks, one eyebrow raised. "You aren't curious, John?"

Before I can reply, there's a screech of tires from the end of the pier. One of the army jeeps comes in fast and has to slam on the brakes when it reaches the knot of soldiers milling around. Two soldiers, a driver and her passenger, jump out of the car. The driver throws off her helmet, revealing a sweaty shock of dark black hair. She yanks open the back door and the other soldier comes around the car to help her lift a third soldier out of the car. He looks wounded, although I can't tell how badly from this distance. Other military personnel gather around, trying to help these new arrivals.

"Where are they?" shouts the woman. "Where's the alien? Where's that FBI bitch?"

A lump forms in my throat. Setrákus Ra put out a bounty on me and the rest of the Garde. Maybe these soldiers have decided it's time to collect. All the same, I step forward. I'm not going to hide. The soldiers clustered at the end of the pier are pointing in my direction, anyway. There's nowhere to go. I glance over my shoulder and see the high-ranking old men, the colonels and generals and whatever the hell else, they've all turned to watch this scene play out. They don't seem all that interested in intervening should this turn dangerous.

Or maybe I'm just being paranoid. Maybe sensing that I've tensed up, Walker puts a hand on my arm.

"Let me handle this," she says.

"We don't even know what this is," I tell her, striding forward to meet the soldiers.

"He's all messed up," Sam says, eyeing the soldier now being carried by the driver and her spooked-looking partner. The front of the injured soldier's fatigues are soaked through with blood. He's barely conscious and has to be held up by the others. The male soldier supporting him doesn't look injured, but still looks almost dead on his feet. Shell-shocked. Only the driver seems at all with it, and she's glaring daggers at Agent Walker.

"What happened, soldier?" Walker asks as the trio

stops a few feet in front of us. I can see the last name embroidered on the driver's shirt is Schaffer.

"We were doing what *you* said. Out looking for him and his friends," Schaffer replies, jerking her chin in my direction. So there were other units in the city besides the one that pulled us out of the subway station. "We thought we'd found a survivor, but we got attacked."

"Mogadorians did this?" I ask, taking a step towards the injured soldier. The front of his shirt is slashed open and so is the bulletproof vest underneath it. That happened while he was out trying to help me. "Hold him steady. Let me heal him."

With Schaffer and the other soldier holding their injured partner up, I start to carefully peel off his shredded shirt and bulletproof vest. All the while, Schaffer glares at me.

"You're not listening," Schaffer snaps. "We found a kid, looked like he was made of metal. Thought he was one of you Garde freaks, so we told him we'd bring him back here to you. He came at us with a blade. He *flew* at us. Moved faster than anything should. Took our weapons, and did *that* to Roosevelt."

I swallow hard. Only now do I notice that the soldier hasn't just been slashed up. A message is carved into him.

5

"Where is he?" I ask, my voice like ice.

"He sent us back here to tell you," Schaffer replies. "He said he'll be at the Statue of Liberty at sunset. Wants you to meet him."

"Was there anyone with him?" Sam asks.

"Big, dark-haired guy. Unconscious," Schaffer says. She turns back to me. "He said to tell you what will happen if you don't come. I don't know what this crazy crap's supposed to mean—he said meet him at sunset or he'll give you a new scar."

CHAPTER
THIRTEEN

WE STAND AT THE EDGE OF THE GRASS IN FRONT of the Sanctuary, side by side, our backs to the temple. Together, we look out at the horizon, to the north. That's the direction Setrákus Ra's warship will be coming from. We've got until sunset.

The three of us are the last line of defense.

The day has only gotten hotter. At least that lets me pretend the sweat dampening the back of my shirt is all from the heat.

I point towards the tree line. "The Mogs did us a favor cutting down all that jungle," I say as I cock my head, trying to gauge the distance. "We should be able to see the ship coming from at least a mile out."

"They'll see us, too," Adam replies, his voice somber. "I don't know, Six. This seems like madness."

I'd been waiting for Adam to say something like that. I knew from the look on his face during our conversation with John and Sam that he wasn't on board with us staying to fight Setrákus Ra and his warship.

"Setrákus Ra cannot be allowed to enter the Sanctuary," Marina says, before I can reply. "That is a Loric place. A sacred place. He would defile it. Whatever he wants, we must stop him from getting it."

I glance from Marina to Adam, and shrug at the Mogadorian. "You heard her."

Adam shakes his head, growing more frustrated. "Look, I understand this place is special to you, but it's not worth trading our lives for."

"I disagree," Marina replies curtly. She's definitely already made up her mind. There's no way she's leaving the Sanctuary now, not after all that's happened here.

"We accomplished what we needed to here," Adam argues. "Some of the humans have Legacies now. There's nothing Setrákus Ra can do to change that. He's too late."

"We don't know that," I reply, glancing over my shoulder at the Sanctuary. "If he got in there he could . . . I don't know. Reverse what we've done, maybe. Or do something to hurt the Entity."

Adam frowns. "He's controlled your home planet for more than a decade and never been able to take away your Legacies. Not permanently, anyway."

"Because Lorien was *here*," Marina replies emphatically. "It's been hiding here and now he's found it. We can't let him touch the Entity. The consequences could be catastrophic."

Adam throws up his hands. "You're not listening to reason!"

I glance away from Adam, towards the landing strip cluttered with disabled Skimmers. Of course, my eyes find their way to Phiri Dun-Ra. Still gagged and tied to a wheel strut, she's made an effort to sit up straighter, probably trying to listen in to our conversation. I can tell by the way that her face crinkles around the duct tape that she's smiling at me. I remember what she said earlier this morning, when she was trying to convince me that Adam was secretly out to get us.

"You don't think we can win, so you're afraid to fight," I say bluntly, regretting the words almost as soon as they're out of my mouth.

Adam whips around to look at me, then follows my gaze to Phiri. He must make the connection between my statement and her earlier rant. He disgustedly shakes his head and walks a few steps away from me.

Marina nudges me, whispering, "Six . . ."

"I'm sorry, Adam," I say quickly. "Seriously. That was a low blow."

"No, you're right, Six," Adam replies dryly, shrugging. "I'm a coward because I don't want to die today. I'm a coward because, as a boy, I watched from the deck of one of those warships as *your* home planet was obliterated. I'm a coward because I think we should find a better way. A smarter way."

"All right, Adam," I say, feeling a tightness in my chest

at his casual mention of Lorien's destruction. "We hear you."

"It might not be smart," Marina adds. "But it's what's right."

Adam rounds on us, his tone acidic. "In that case, which one of you is going to do it?"

"Do what?" I ask.

"Kill Ella," he replies. "We all heard what John said. Setrákus Ra has her bound with his own version of your old Loric charm. You can't hurt him without first hurting her. I've never even met the girl and I can tell you right now, *I'm* not going to do it. So tell me, which one of you is going to kill your friend?"

"No one," I say resolutely, locking eyes with Adam. "We're going to figure out a way to stop Setrákus Ra without hurting her."

Adam glances up at the sun, as if trying to figure out how much daylight we've got left.

"Great," Adam says. "Fantastic. Our resources are some broken-down ships and whatever the hell we can find in the jungle. Tell me how the hell you're going to stop Setrákus Ra in our situation, Six."

"John said there'd be backup coming, the military—"

"He said he'd *try*," Adam practically shouts at me. "Look, I trust John, but he's thousands of miles away. Help is thousands of miles away. Right here? It's just us. We're it."

"Help is right behind us," Marina says. Her voice is still calm, but there's a strain there. What Adam's been saying has gotten under her skin. "The Sanctuary will give us a way to fight."

Adam takes this in for a moment before rolling his eyes. "A miracle. That's what the two of you are hoping for? A miracle! I get that you woke that thing in there up, and I know it let you talk to your . . . your friend one last time. But that's *all* it's going to do, okay? It is *done* helping us. Don't believe me? Maybe we could ask some of the Loric how much that Entity helped during the last Mogadorian invasion. If they weren't all dead."

The air around me gets cold. At first, it feels pretty good in this overbearing jungle heat, until I realize that it's Marina fuming in her own special way. She takes a step towards Adam, her fists clenched, the whole serene-sister-of-the-Sanctuary thing dropped in a hurry.

"Don't talk about what you don't know, you monster!" she yells, jabbing her finger in the air at him. An icicle shoots from Marina's index finger and stabs into the dirt at Adam's feet. Immediately, it begins to melt. Adam takes a surprised step back, staring at Marina.

"Enough," I say, stepping in between the two of them. "This isn't getting us anywhere."

From the airstrip, Phiri Dun-Ra makes a series of muffled gagging noises. I realize that she's laughing at us. I tune her out, turn around and take Marina by the shoulders. Her skin is cold to the touch.

"Much as I love the air conditioning right now, you need to walk away for a minute," I tell her.

Marina gives me a look of disbelief, like she can't believe I'm siding with Adam against her. I shake my head gently and raise my eyebrows, letting her know that's not what this is. She sighs, pushes a hand through her hair and walks towards the Sanctuary.

I turn to glare at Adam. At first, he doesn't look at me. He's too busy watching the icicle Marina fired at him turn to water.

"Lucky she didn't take your eye out," I say, only half joking.

"I know," he replies, finally looking up at me. "Six, look, I'm sorry. I shouldn't have brought up Lorien. That's not—that's not my place."

"You bet your ass it isn't," I say, taking a step closer to him. "It's all right, you're freaking out a little, I'm gonna chalk it up to that. But yeah, don't talk about our dead families and massacred planet again, okay? Because I seriously wanted to punch you in the face."

Adam nods. "Understood."

"I'm still not sure you do," I reply, lowering my voice and getting even closer. "Let me make it perfectly clear for you, Adam. I've got no intention of dying out here today. You think I don't get that the odds are against us? Dude, I don't need that explained to me. But you didn't magically fix one of those Skimmers while I wasn't looking, did you?"

He frowns at me. "You know I didn't, Six."

"Then we're stuck here until reinforcements arrive. And if we're stuck here, we're going to fight. You get me?"

"We could run," Adam replies, pointing to the jungle. "We don't need a Skimmer to escape."

"Look at it this way. Booking it into the jungle is never going to stop being an option," I admit to him. "If the *Anubis* gets here and things don't go our way, we'll run."

"Will we?" Adam asks, his gaze sliding off me and towards Marina. "All of us?"

I turn my head to subtly watch Marina. Her back is to us as she takes deep breaths, calming herself. She's staring at the Sanctuary again, like she's been doing most of the day. Marina's developed an almost religious devotion to the old temple. I understand why—our experience with the Entity was pretty heavy, maybe more so for a girl who was raised around a bunch of nuns. Not to mention, the guy she loved is buried in there. The Sanctuary's become both a religious symbol and a gravesite to her.

"I'll drag her away if I have to," I tell Adam, meaning it.

Adam seems satisfied with that answer. The frantic look he had when he berated us is gone, replaced by cold Mogadorian calculation. I never thought I'd actually be happy to see those features on someone's face.

"I can start removing the force field cloaking modules for John and keep trying to repair the Skimmer, but neither of those things is going to help us defend this place or survive an attack by the *Anubis*." He looks at me, eyebrows raised. "So, what's our plan for not dying?"

Good question.

I take a look around. The plan aspect of this whole thing is something I'm still working out. How can we stop Setrákus Ra from doing whatever he wants to the Sanctuary? How can we even hurt him without endangering Ella? Once again, my gaze drifts towards Phiri Dun-Ra. She isn't laughing at us anymore, instead she's watching us like a hawk. I think of her hands, currently tied to the wheel strut behind her back, and the way they were bandaged up, the dirt-stained dressings covering electrical burns she suffered from the Sanctuary's force field. The Mogs spent years out here, trying to force their way into the Sanctuary to earn favor with their Beloved Leader. It's too bad we didn't see a fuse box or control panel inside the Sanctuary to turn that force field back on.

"At least we know where he's going," I say out loud, still thinking. "Setrákus Ra wants inside the Sanctuary, he's gotta come down from his big bad warship. That gives us a chance."

"A chance to do what?" Adam asks.

"We can't hurt Setrákus Ra without hurting Ella, which means we can't really stop him from muscling into the Sanctuary. But if he's got Ella and the Sanctuary, well, maybe we should take something of his."

Adam catches on quickly. "Are you thinking . . . ?"

"You did mention you always wanted to fly one of those warships. Whatever Setrákus Ra wants in the Sanctuary, he won't be able to take it anywhere," I say, feeling the beginnings of a plan starting to take shape. "Because we're going to rescue Ella and steal his ship."

Our preparations begin mostly in silence, tension still in the air between Marina and Adam. We start by going through the equipment that the Mogadorians left behind. There are crates piled in one of the larger tents, a veritable arsenal of weaponry and tools that the Mogs shipped down here only to have it all break against the Sanctuary's force field. There's a whole array of Mogadorian blasters, but the rest of the gear appears to have been manufactured here on Earth. There are crates of weapons stamped as property of the U.S. military, mining equipment shipped from Australia and what Adam tells me are experimental EMPs covered in Chinese lettering. Adam went through this stuff earlier when he was looking for spare Skimmer parts, so he knows how it's organized.

"We want explosives," I tell him. "What have they got?"

Carefully, Adam moves some crates around before opening up one packed with blocks of a beige substance that reminds me of clay.

"Plastic explosives," he says. "C-4, I think."

"You know how to work with that stuff?"

"A little bit," Adam replies, and starts gently pushing aside objects in the crate. Besides the C-4, there are also some wires and cylinders that I assume have some role in detonation. After a quick search, Adam smirks and holds up a small paper booklet. "There's instructions."

"Perfect," Marina mutters.

"How many bombs total?" I ask.

Adam does a quick count of the clay bricks. "Twelve. But I can break them up, make them smaller if you want. The smaller the brick, the smaller the explosion, though. And we've only got the dozen blasting caps, so the smaller ones would need to be wired together."

Before replying to Adam, I poke my head out of the tent and do a quick count of Skimmers parked on the landing strip. Sixteen of them, including the one Adam's been working on and the one Phiri Dun-Ra's tied to.

"We should be good with twelve," I tell Adam. "Don't blow yourself up, okay?"

"I'll try my best."

"Great. Come on, Marina."

I grab an empty burlap sack from the Mog supply tent before setting out towards the landing strip. Marina follows next to me.

"What exactly are we wiring to explode, Six?" she asks.

"Hold that thought," I say, approaching the Skimmer where Phiri Dun-Ra is restrained. She watches me approach, eyes hot and angry, not smiling through her duct tape anymore. I think she knows what's coming. She struggles a bit against her bonds but can't do much to stop me from pulling that burlap sack over her head.

"Sick of looking at her?" Marina asks.

"Yeah, that. And I don't want her to see what we're up to." I lead Marina away from our prisoner, towards the other Skimmers on the airstrip. "We're going to wire the ships. I figure Setrákus Ra's not coming alone, he'll have other Mogs with him. We don't have the force field to keep them out of the Sanctuary, but we can damn sure blow them up if they get close."

Thanks to Phiri Dun-Ra, none of the Skimmers are in condition to move on their own. One by one, Marina and I use our telekinesis to push the ships into position. With the two of us working in tandem, the weight isn't that bad, at least once we get the wheels rolling. We space the Skimmers about thirty yards apart in a semicircle in front of the Sanctuary's entrance. The ships end up on almost the exact same line as the Sanctuary's force field.

Now that we've moved most of the Skimmers, there's a big empty space on the landing strip. "Let's hope Setrákus Ra parks his big-ass warship in the most obvious place possible," I say, tracing my finger through the air from the landing strip and towards the Sanctuary's entrance. "There's only one way into the Sanctuary, so his people will have to walk right through the ships, which is where we're going to hide the bombs."

"That will at least eliminate his first wave," Marina says.

"Yeah, and hopefully it'll get them nice and confused and looking for an attack, so that Adam and I can sneak in behind them and board the *Anubis*."

Marina frowns at me. "Wait. Where am I in all this?"

Before I can answer, Adam emerges from the Mogadorian armory with a duffel bag filled with plastic explosives. He takes a look at what we've done so far and nods approvingly. Then, he walks over to us, sets the duffel bag down and produces a large remote control.

"Check this out," Adam says. "I guess the Mogs were trying to use sequenced explosions to take down the force field, maybe thinking timed detonations at multiple angles would bring the thing down."

He hands me the remote control. It's got a row of twenty switches, each with a corresponding red and green light. Twelve of the red bulbs are currently lit up. Adam comes up next to me, explaining how the device works.

"The blasting caps all have remote detonators," he says, and flicks the left-most switch on the controller one notch up. The little light above the switch changes from red to green. "I just armed the first bomb."

I glance to the duffel bag at our feet, presently filled with a ton of plastic explosives, then back to the controller. There's a little metal tooth that you need to guide the switch around for it to reach its third notch, probably to keep anyone's finger from slipping. Still, I'm a little nervous about this demonstration. "Uh, okay . . ."

"Safety first." Adam flicks the switch back into its original position, the red light coming back on. "If you were to press the switch all the way up, the blasting cap would get the signal to fire its charge, and the bomb would detonate."

I nod once, then hand the remote control over to Marina. "You get all that?"

"Yes, but . . ." Her brow furrows as she accepts the controller.

"You asked where you're going to be," I say. "You're going to be hiding in the jungle, controlling the Sanctuary's defenses."

Marina considers this for a moment, a smile slowly spreading across her face. "It will be my pleasure."

Adam walks down the line of ships, sticking lunchbox-sized parcels of plastic explosives on the underbelly of each Skimmer. A cautious Mogadorian might notice them, yeah, but not before it would already be too late.

Meanwhile, Marina and I maneuver the last two Skimmers past the ones we've wired to explode. These we position on opposite sides of the Sanctuary, both at the very edge of the jungle, and both pointing towards the Sanctuary's entrance.

"We can create a cross fire here," I say, opening up the

cockpit on one of the Skimmers. "If your telekinesis is strong enough to work the controls . . ."

"It will have to be," Marina replies.

Adam comes over, powers on the Skimmers' weapon systems and explains to Marina which buttons she would need to press to discharge the cannons. Marina spends a long time studying the controls, memorizing them, committing them to her mind's eye. Then, she walks slowly away from the Skimmers, and heads to a patch of jungle far away from the wired-up ships but close enough to have a clear view of the entire battlefield. It's from this hidden spot that she'll defend the Sanctuary.

Marina concentrates. She reaches one hand out towards the Skimmer.

"Ugh," she says, after a moment, rubbing the bridge of her nose. "I don't know, Six. It's hard to use my telekinesis on something I can't see."

We try a different tactic. Adam and I walk around the edge of the jungle, propping up Mogadorian blasters in the overgrown grass and trees. We camouflage them with loose branches and leaves, well enough that a Mog warrior wouldn't notice them right off, but not so hidden that Marina can't see them. From her spot, she tests each one, telekinetically pulling the trigger so that a burst of blaster fire sizzles into the clearing in front of the Sanctuary.

"Nice," I say. "You don't even have to hit anyone,

Marina. You just have to make them think the attack is coming from all sides."

Now that we're finished, there are only two Skimmers left on the runway: the one we came down here in that Adam's been trying to repair, and the one that's got Phiri Dun-Ra tied to it. I'm satisfied with our setup so far. It feels good to be doing *something*, at least.

"This is good, Six," Marina says, her arms crossed, looking at the Mogadorian ships now arranged like guards in front of the Sanctuary. "Perfect if Setrákus Ra sends in his warriors. But what if he's out there on the front line himself? Hurting him would mean hurting Ella. We can't risk that."

"You're right," I reply. "We'll have to figure out a way to at least slow him down."

I start towards the passageway that leads into the Sanctuary and pretend not to notice when Adam lags behind, touching Marina gently on the elbow as he does. They slow but only walk a few steps behind me. With my enhanced hearing, it's pretty much impossible for me not to eavesdrop.

"I'm sorry about before," Adam says to her quietly. "I got carried away."

"It's all right," Marina replies kindly. "I shouldn't have called you a monster. It just slipped out. I don't really think that."

Adam laughs once, self-deprecatingly. "No, you know,

I've wondered a lot over the years if that—if that's not a good word for us."

Marina makes a noise, about to say something more, but Adam cuts her off.

"It's okay—I'm sorry again, about everything. I know what it's like to lose someone you care about. I shouldn't . . . I won't be so cavalier about leaving this place again. I get why it's so important. What it means."

"Thank you, Adam."

I turn around, pretending not to have been listening to their entire conversation. We're in front of what used to be the Sanctuary's hidden door. It's a narrow stone archway leading to stairs that run all the way down to the hidden chamber beneath the temple.

"So," I say, hands on my hips. "How do we stall the most powerful Mogadorian in the universe without hurting him, while at the same time stealing his warship out from under him?"

Adam raises his hand. "I have a question."

I can see the wheels turning in his head. "Shoot."

"This entire plan is predicated on chance—Setrákus Ra going for the door, Setrákus Ra sending out warriors, Marina being able to distract them with some bombs and ghost weapons." I open my mouth to respond, worried he's getting freaked out again, but Adam keeps rolling. "It's the best option we've got. I agree with you. But, assuming it works, assuming we do manage to steal the *Anubis* while

Setrákus Ra sits down here. What then? What do we do next? We still can't kill him."

"But he won't be able to kill us either," I reply. I know it's not exactly the brilliant strategic gem Adam's hoping for, but I honestly haven't thought that far ahead. I've been too focused on our immediate survival.

"Perhaps we could negotiate," Marina suggests half-heartedly. "For Ella, or the Sanctuary . . ."

"Despite how fervently he would tell you otherwise, Setrákus Ra has no honor," Adam says. "There can be no negotiating."

"Then it'll be a stalemate," I say. "And that's better than losing, right?"

Adam considers my words, digging his heel into the dirt in front of the archway.

"All right," Adam says. "Then I suggest we dig a hole."

"A hole?"

"A pit," Adam continues. "In front of the door. A large one. Then, we cover it up and let Setrákus Ra fall into it."

I push my toe into the dirt. Thanks to the shadows of the Sanctuary and the nearby plant growth, it's soft and a little damp, not like the hard-packed and sunbaked dirt of the runway. All our Legacies, that stockpile of Mog weapons, a bunch of C-4—and now we're talking about digging a hole. "Well, he's exactly the kind of asshole who doesn't watch where he's going, especially if he's sporting a major boner to get into the Sanctuary."

"There's an image," Adam replies.

"Once he's down there I can ice over the top from my hiding spot," Marina says, getting on board. "That could slow him down further."

"Well, at least it'll be hilarious to watch him fall in a hole," I add optimistically.

"It'll have to be pretty big," Adam says, rubbing his chin thoughtfully. "He can change sizes."

"Good thing we've got Legacies to help with the digging," I reply. "Even if it only buys us a few minutes, that might be enough to get us on board the *Anubis*."

"One more thing, and you might not like this idea," Adam says to Marina, before gesturing towards the Sanctuary's door. "But maybe we should cave that in. It'll be one more thing to get in Setrákus Ra's way."

It's a good idea, but I look over at Marina before saying anything. She thinks about it for a moment and then shrugs. "They're only stones," she says. "What's important is that we protect what's inside."

"Should I get some of the C-4?" Adam asks.

"I think I can handle it," I reply, already tapping into my Legacy and channeling a small storm. The air gets heavy as I pull together a dark cloud above our heads, a small pattering of raindrops falling loose from it. With a downward motion of my hand, four bolts of lightning slice down at an angle Mother Nature couldn't hope to duplicate. The strikes arc into the Sanctuary's doorway and explode into the decrepit limestone, collapsing the passage in on itself with a burst of musty air.

I step up and take a look at my handiwork. The doorway is now filled with rubble, with some of the interior wall obviously collapsed as well. It won't keep an army of Mogs out forever and Setrákus Ra will definitely be able to dislodge the rubble with his telekinesis. Still, it's better than nothing.

Meanwhile, with a thoughtful look on her face, Marina takes measured steps around the entrance to the Sanctuary, keeping count. When she's walked a near-perfect square in front of the entrance, Marina looks over at me.

"About thirty feet on each side, do you think?" she asks me. "For the pit?"

"I think that'd do it."

"Let me try something," Marina says, and then begins to concentrate.

She walks a thirty-foot line away from the Sanctuary's entrance, her hands fanning the air as she goes. A wall of ice begins to take shape along Marina's line, although its bottom edge doesn't make contact with the ground.

"Help me hold it in place, would you?" Marina asks, glancing at me.

I'm not quite sure where this is going, but I play along. Using my telekinesis, I hold up Marina's growing sheet of ice. I notice that the ice is thicker at the top and narrows to a lethally sharp edge at the bottom, almost like a guillotine blade. She walks the same lines as a second ago, this time generating ice as she goes. After a couple of minutes, Marina has created a hollow cube of ice, roughly thirty feet by thirty feet, with no top or bottom. The ice hovers above the ground, dripping water, and Marina has to continually use her Legacy to keep it from melting.

"What happens now?" Adam asks, looking on.

"We lift it up," Marina says, referring to the two of us. "And then we slam it down with as much force as we can muster. Ready, Six?"

I do as instructed, using my telekinesis to levitate Marina's ice sculpture about twenty feet above the ground.

"Ready?" she asks, looking at me. "Now!"

Together, we drive the ice into the ground. There's a thudding sound as the sharpened edges drive into the dirt, followed by the sound of glass breaking as cracks form rapidly in the ice and begin to spread. All in all, the ice doesn't get driven very far into the earth, about four feet at most. Marina seems pleased with the result, though.

"Okay, okay! Hold on a second!"

She races around the box of ice, its four walls now embedded in the ground, and begins to reinforce the walls, thickening and hardening the ice as she touches it. When the cracks in the ice are sealed up and the broken chunks filled in, Marina kneels down at one of the corners and puts her hands on the ice, as close to the ground as possible.

"All right, I'm not sure if this part will actually work," she says. "Here goes."

Marina closes her eyes and concentrates. Adam and I exchange a look, both of us pretty confused. Still, we stay quiet for what ends up being more than five minutes, watching Marina work her Legacy. I want to put my forehead on the cold ice, but I worry that might screw up whatever she's doing.

"I think I got it," Marina says at last, standing up and rolling her neck. "Six, let's lift the ice back up."

"Now you want it *out* of the ground?" I ask.

Marina nods excitedly. "Quick! Before it melts too much."

So, we concentrate on the cube again. It feels much heavier this time and as we lift it, I realize why. Marina spread the ice under the ground, connecting the four walls of her cube. When we lift the ice, it comes up with a ripping and crunching sound, as the remaining roots of the grass are torn apart. The ice cube floats up on our telekinesis and, inside it, sits a four-foot deep cross section of the earth, perfectly maintained.

"Gently now," Marina says, as we transport the ice and earth off to the side. "I got in there pretty deep, but it could still break apart."

"Brilliant," Adam says, grinning at the floating mound. "We won't have to cover the hole with, like, really big branches. Once we've dug it the rest of the way, we can just lay that piece back on top. It'll look normal when Setrákus Ra steps on it, but you should be able to cave it in from a distance with your telekinesis."

Marina nods. "That was my thinking."

We lower the immaculately shaped box of dirt and grass to the ground with a gentle thump. Without Marina constantly augmenting it with her Legacy, the ice soon begins to melt away. The edges of our pit's lid get a little muddy, but that'll dry quickly considering the heat.

Adam strides forward, kneeling in front of the thirty-by-thirty hole in the ground.

"My turn," he says.

He places his hands right into the dirt and a second later I can feel vibrations flowing out from him. The seismic ripples are focused primarily in front of him, but his control isn't precise enough to keep them from fanning out. For a moment, I feel a little bit queasy as the ground shifts beneath my feet, but I'm able to quickly get a grip. The soil in front of Adam begins to loosen and shift, the packed-down layers beginning to break apart into sizable chunks.

Adam looks over his shoulder at me. "How's that?"

I use my telekinesis to lift a crumbly section of dirt and stone up from the pit, then chuck it into the jungle. It'll be easier to dig through now that Adam's broken up the dirt, but it's still going to be a pain in the ass. I give him an approving nod.

"It's a start," I tell him.

He stands up. "I'm going to go look for . . . a shovel."

Adam can barely finish his thought, his eyes suddenly pinned to the sky behind me. I whip around, hearing the sound of an engine.

No. It can't be. It's too soon. We aren't ready.

"Six?" Marina asks, her voice catching. "What is that?"

It's a ship. Sleek and silver, without the hard angles and guns like the other crafts I've seen the Mogs flying. It's like nothing I've ever seen before, yet it's also oddly familiar.

The ship's coming in fast, and it's headed right for us.

CHAPTER
FOURTEEN

"SCOUTS?" MARINA ASKS ME. I CAN FEEL HER ice Legacy kicking back on, in case we need to fight this new arrival.

"That's not a Mog ship," Adam says, stepping up beside me.

"No," I reply, because I've already figured that out. I put my hand on Marina's arm. "It's okay. Don't you . . . don't you recognize it?"

"I . . ." Marina trails off as she takes a closer look at the incoming ship. The spaceship zips in over the trees and pivots effortlessly in the air, cutting its speed with a flourish over the recently cleared Mogadorian runway. Although it's dented and scuffed, and even has a bit of rust on the edges, the ship still shines a glittering silver, its armored paneling made from materials not found on this world. It hovers for a moment, the sun glinting off the cockpit's tinted windows, and then gently lands.

"That's one of ours," I say. "Like the one that brought us here. To Earth, I mean."

"How is that possible?" Adam replies.

"Are these our reinforcements?" Marina asks, not taking her eyes off the ship. "Did John mention anything about this?"

"He said he was sending Sarah, Mark and something else . . ." I answer them both dazedly. "Something we'd have to see to believe." Who could be piloting a Loric ship? Where did it come from? I take a halting step forward.

A metal ramp unfurls from the back of the ship and I tense up. I have a hazy memory of running up a ramp like that as a child, Katarina at my side, explosions and screaming in the background. Here we are again, in the middle of a second Mogadorian invasion, and once again there's a Loric ship in front of me. Only this time, I don't know whether I should be running towards it or away from it. Even though John told me help was coming, I can't shake the feeling this could be a trap. My paranoia has gotten me this far, no reason to ignore it now.

"Get ready for anything," I tell the others. "We don't know what's coming out of there."

And then a familiar beagle bounds down the ramp.

Bernie Kosar, tongue hanging out of his mouth, leaps onto me first, his front paws braced against my legs. His tail is a blur as he greets Marina next and then even jumps onto Adam. I hear an unfamiliar sound and quickly realize that it's the Mogadorian laughing.

When I look back to the ship, Sarah Hart now stands at the top of the ramp, her arms open in greeting and a smile on her face.

"Hey, guys," Sarah says casually. "Look what we found."

Marina lets out a laugh of delighted surprise and jogs forward, meeting Sarah at the bottom of the ramp and immediately wrapping her in a tight hug. It's been a while since we've seen Sarah—she'd already gone off on her secret ex-boyfriend mission when Marina and I returned from Florida. She has her blond hair pulled back in a tight ponytail and her smile is bright, but there are some lines under her eyes, which I notice are a little red-rimmed the closer I get. Sarah's also sporting some fresh scrapes and bruises that her big smile can't hide. Yeah, she's happy to see us, but she's also tired, stressed and a little beat-up. Regardless, she looks better than we do—filthy from a couple of days in the jungle, sunburned and exhausted. But I don't hold it against her.

"You're here," I say to Sarah, hugging her, too. In truth, I'm a little distracted. I still can't take my eyes off the ship.

"It's good to see you, Six," Sarah replies, squeezing me despite the sweat and grit. "John said you could use some help and a lift. We brought both."

Who exactly the "we" is becomes apparent a second later. The Mark James who exits the ship behind Sarah is a hell of a lot different from the guy I briefly fought alongside in Paradise. He's retired the whole gel-haired-jock thing. Mark's dark hair is longer and scruffier. I think he may have lost some weight, his muscles leaner now than I remember. He's got an overtired look on his face and squinty eyes that suggest he's not used to so much sunshine.

"Whoa, shit," Mark says, stopping halfway down the ramp. "You've got one of them behind you."

"That's Adam," Sarah replies. "I thought I told you about him."

"Yeah, I guess you did," Mark says, shielding his eyes while he openly stares at Adam. "It's just spooky to see one of them, you know, hanging around like a normal. Sorry, bro," Mark adds, nodding to Adam.

"It's all right," Adam replies diplomatically. He gestures over his shoulder to where Phiri Dun-Ra is hooded and tied to a Skimmer. "I'm not the only Mog here, as you can see. But I am the friendliest."

"Noted," Mark replies.

Sarah starts to make the necessary introductions. I cut her off before she can really get started.

"I'm sorry, but where did you get this ship?" I ask, walking by her and up the ramp.

"Yeah, about that," Sarah replies, motioning me onwards like I should keep exploring. "You'll probably want to talk to *her*."

"Who?"

Sarah gives me a look like I should quit asking questions and just go, so I do. This exchange raises Marina's eyebrows too. She follows me up the ramp into the ship. A few steps inside, and I'm hit with major déjà vu. We're in the passenger area. It's a wide-open space, completely devoid of any furniture. The walls give off a gentle light indicating that the ship is still powered on. I have a vague memory of being lined up in here alongside the other Garde, our Cêpan pushing us through aerobic exercises and some light martial arts training.

I walk over to the closest wall and trace my fingers across the surface. The soft plastic material responds, shining brighter, the trail from my fingers lit up. The walls act as one big touch screen. I pull a command from my memory, quickly drawing a Loric symbol on the wall. The symbol flashes once to show it's been accepted and then, with a hydraulic hiss, the floor opens up and a couple dozen cots rise into view. Marina has to hop backwards as one opens up right where she was standing.

"Six, is this . . . ?"

"It's our ship," I say. "The same one that brought us to Earth."

"I always assumed that it was destroyed or . . ." Marina trails off, shaking her head in wonderment. She traces her fingers across the opposite wall, inputting another command. The entire wall turns into a big high-definition screen displaying a picture of a happy-looking beagle chasing down a tennis ball.

"In English, *dog*," says a recorded voice with a noticeable Loric accent. "Dog. The dog runs. En español, *perro*. El perro corre . . ."

Earth language training. How many times did we have to sit through this video as we flew towards our new planet? I'd forgotten about it, or blocked it out, but all the boredom of my childhood came rushing back. A whole claustrophobic year spent in here, watching that dog run through a bright green field.

"Oof, turn it off," I say to Marina.

"You don't want to see what the dog does next?" she asks with a little smile. She swipes her hand across the wall and the program stops.

I walk over to one of the cots and crouch down next to it. The sheets smell musty and a little like the greasy inner workings of the ship. They've probably been stowed down there for the last decade. I push aside the blankets and the thin matress, inspecting the frame.

"Ha, look at this," I say.

Marina leans in over my shoulder. There, carved into the metal frame by a bored little girl, is the number six.

"Vandal," Marina laughs.

The low hum of the ship's engine slowly decreases to silence and the touch-screen walls flicker and turn off. Someone has just powered down the ship.

"Just like you left it, right?"

Marina and I both turn in the direction of the voice and wind up facing a woman as she slowly emerges from the ship's cockpit. My first reaction is that she's breathtakingly beautiful. Her skin is a dark shade of brown, her cheekbones high and pronounced, hair dark and buzzed short. Even though she's dressed in a baggy mechanic's jumpsuit complete with fresh grease stains, the woman looks like she belongs on the cover of a fashion magazine. I quickly come to realize that what's so stunning about her isn't purely looks. It's an indistinct quality most people on Earth wouldn't be able to put their finger on but which I notice immediately.

This woman is Loric.

She looks almost nervous to see me and Marina. That's probably why she took such a long time to power down the ship. Even now, the woman lingers in the cabin doorway, as uncertain of us as we are of her. There's a jumpiness about her, like at any moment she might retreat into the cockpit and lock the door. I can tell she's trying to psych herself up to keep talking to us.

"You must be Six and Seven," she says after a moment of getting nothing but stunned looks from the two of us.

"You—you can call me Marina."

"Noted, Marina," the woman says with a gentle smile.

"Who are you?" I ask, finding my voice at last.

"My name is Lexa," the woman answers. "I've been helping out your friend Mark under the name GUARD."

"Are you one of our Cêpan?"

Lexa finally moves out of the doorway and takes a seat on one of the cots. Marina and I sit down across from her. "No, I'm not a Cêpan. My brother was Garde but he didn't make it through training at the Lorien Defence Academy. I was enrolled there too, as an engineering student, when he . . . when he died. After that I kind of, ah, fell off the grid. As much as you could on Lorien. I didn't exactly fit into one of their prescribed roles. I worked with computers a lot, sometimes not so legally. I was nobody special, basically."

"But you ended up here," Marina says, her head tilted.

"Yeah. Eventually, I got hired to retrofit an antique ship for a museum . . ."

That detail clicks for me. "You flew the second ship to Earth," I say.

"Yes. I came here with Crayton and my friend Zophie. You probably know this by now, but we weren't part of the Elders' plan. We managed to escape Lorien because of Crayton—well, because Crayton worked for Ella's father, and because we had access to that old ship. Ella's father, he knew what was coming. That's why he hired me to fix it up. I wasn't even really a pilot. I had to learn, well . . . on the fly."

I snort at Lexa's bad joke and smile at her, but my mind is racing. There are more of us. Maybe the Loric aren't as extinct as we thought. I should be excited about this, but instead I feel suspicious. I'm probably just being paranoid after what happened with Five. Still, I think of Crayton and how he raised Ella while secretly hunting for the rest of the Garde. He never mentioned that he came here with two other Loric. My eyes narrow a fraction.

"Crayton never told us about you," I say, trying to make it sound not too much like an accusation. Crayton did withhold a lot from us, after all. Ella's real origin didn't even come out until after he died.

"I guess he wouldn't have," Lexa replies, frowning slightly. "His only concern was keeping Ella alive. We agreed not to have contact with each other. It was safer for everyone if we kept our distance. You know how the Mogs are. They can't torture any information out of you if you don't actually know anything."

"What about your friend? Zophie? Where's she?"

Lexa shakes her head. "She didn't make it. Her brother was the pilot of this ship. *Your ship.* Zophie went looking for him, actually thought she'd found him through the internet, but . . ."

Marina fills in the blank. "Mogs."

Lexa nods sadly. "After that, I was alone."

"You weren't alone, though," I say. "We were out there. A lot of us—hell, all of us, we lost our Cêpan. Some of us pretty damn quick. We could've used some guidance. Why did you wait so long? Why didn't you try to find us?"

"You know why, Six. For the same reasons that your Cêpan didn't try to find each other. It was dangerous to try making contact. Every internet search risked exposure. I did what I could from afar. I funneled money and intel to groups that were working on exposing the Mogadorians. I started a website called 'Aliens Anonymous' to try spreading the word, to maybe expose what they were up to with MogPro. That's how I met up with Mark."

I think about what it must've been like for her, a stranger in a strange land, with no one to rely on. Actually, I don't have to imagine what she went through. I lived it myself. I knew the dangers and I never stopped looking for the others. I can't keep the bitterness out of my voice. "Dangerous for us? Or dangerous for you?"

"For all of us, Six," Lexa replies. I can tell that my words stung her. "I know it's not even a fraction of the responsibility the Elders hung on the nine of you but . . . I didn't ask for this either. I took a cake job in a museum and next thing I know I'm flying an antique ship to a planet in a completely different solar system with one of the last living Garde as cargo. I lost my brother, my best friend, my whole life."

She takes a breath. Marina and I are both silent.

"I told myself that helping you all from afar was enough. So, I did what I could from a distance. I erased whatever information I found about you all online. I tried to make you invisible, not just to the world, but to me. Maybe it was cowardice. Or shame. I don't know. I knew deep down that I should be doing more. I always intended to get this ship, though, and contact you, once you were old enough and once I . . ."

"You're here now," Marina says gently. "That's what matters."

"I couldn't stay away any longer. I'd already fled one planet during an invasion. I decided it was time to stop running."

That hits home for me. In a way, after spending years hiding from the Mogadorians, we've all decided it's time to stop running. I only hope it isn't too late.

"Would it be okay if I gave you a hug now?" Marina asks Lexa.

The pilot is taken by surprise, but she nods. Marina wraps her up in a big hug, burying her face in the woman's shoulder. Lexa sees me watching and gives me a tight, almost embarrassed smile before closing her eyes and letting herself be squeezed. She sighs, and maybe I'm just imagining this, but some invisible weight seems to lift from Lexa's shoulders. I don't join in. The group-hug thing isn't really for me.

"Thanks for coming," I say after a moment. "Welcome to the Sanctuary."

With that, I lead the two of them out from the ship. I take one last lingering look at the passenger area before tamping down that memory of fleeing Lorien. I'm not a child anymore. This invasion is going to play out differently.

Outside, Adam and Mark are in the middle of a

discussion. Sarah stands a few feet away from them, closer to the ship, obviously waiting for us. She raises her eyebrows questioningly when she sees me and I let out a deep breath in response.

"Crazy who you run into in Mexico," I say, trying to play off the shock and mixed feelings of encountering Lexa.

Together, we walk over to Mark and Adam. Mark, already sweating through his T-shirt, looks like he's having trouble wrapping his mind around something.

"A hole," he says flatly. "You're going to kill Setrákus Ra with a hole in the ground."

Adam sighs, pointing to the sections of the jungle where we've hidden Mog artillery. "You're really stuck on the hole aspect of the plan. I told you, we've got guns, bombs—"

"But for Setrákus Ra, you've got a hole."

"I realize it's low-tech, but our options are seriously limited," Adam replies. "And we aren't trying to kill him. That's not even a possibility considering any damage we do to him will be reflected onto Ella. We just want to slow him down and buy ourselves some time."

"Time to do what?" Mark asks.

Adam glances at me. "To rescue Ella, steal the *Anubis* out from under Setrákus Ra's nose or both."

"Why don't we just bail?" Mark asks, thumbing towards the newly arrived Loric ship. "I get that all these booby traps might've been a good idea when you were, like, stranded. But we can leave now."

"That's not an option," Marina replies. "The Sanctuary must be defended at all costs."

"At *all* costs?" Mark repeats, glancing back to the ship, then over to the temple. "What the hell is so special about this place?"

I notice that Lexa's been awfully quiet during this discussion. Her eyes are locked on the Sanctuary, her face blank, sort of like how Marina looks when she goes into one of her reverent trances. Lexa must sense me watching her, because she abruptly shakes her head and meets my gaze.

"This place . . ." She searches for the right words. "There's something special about it."

"It's a Loric place," Marina replies. "*The* Loric place now, actually. The source of our Legacies resides inside."

"We just sealed the entrance or I'd give you the tour," I put in. "Could've introduced you to the creature living in there. Pretty nice for an Entity made out of pure Loric energy."

Lexa flashes me a quick smirk before replying. "I can feel it . . . whatever's in there. I can feel it in my bones. I understand why you'd want to protect this place."

"Thank you," Marina replies.

"That said . . ." And now Lexa glances in my direction. "Keep in mind that my ship—*our* ship—is ready. If you need it. It has outrun their warships before."

I nod subtly and exchange a quick look with Adam.

Marina might not want to admit we need one, but we've got an exit strategy all the same, and it's now a lot better than running into the jungle.

"Man, so whatever's inside there, it's like in charge of the Legacies?" Mark asks, looking at the Sanctuary with his hands on his hips.

"We think so," I reply.

"So, that's what decided that nerdy Sam Goode should get superpowers and that I . . ." Mark trails off, grimacing. "Shit. I should've been nicer in high school."

I try not to laugh. John must have filled Sarah and Mark in on humans getting Legacies thanks to our messing around in the Sanctuary. I don't know how the Entity decided who would get Legacies, but I wouldn't really expect a guy like Mark to make the cut, even if he's been risking his ass for us over the last couple of months. Sarah, on the other hand . . .

"What about you?" I say, facing her.

Sarah shrugs and looks down at her hands, like she's expecting rays of light to shoot out of them at any moment.

"Nothing yet," she says, frowning. "Still just a regular old human."

Sarah tries to play this off, but I can tell it's bothering her. After all she's done for us, for John in particular, it does strike me as a major oversight on the Entity's part to pass her over when choosing which humans receive Legacies.

"The way John told it, Sam only discovered he had

Legacies when a piken was bearing down on them," I say. "Maybe you just haven't been in a situation where they've developed."

"Yes," Marina says, jumping in. "Speaking from experience, Legacies have a habit of manifesting when you really need them."

"Oh, great," Mark says. "So, if we hang around here to face certain death, maybe there's a chance I'll at least die with superpowers."

"Yep. Maybe," I reply to him.

"Or maybe the Entity didn't *choose* anyone," Adam says. "Maybe it's all just random."

"Says the Mogadorian with Legacies," replies Mark.

"Whatever, it's okay," Sarah says, clearly trying to change the subject. "I'm not counting on it happening. So, whatever. That doesn't mean we can't help in other ways. I just got off the phone with John before we landed."

"Is he on his way?" I ask. "He's supposed to be bringing the big guns with him when he comes down here."

"I don't know if that's going to happen," Sarah replies, her face creased by a frown that I know means bad news is coming. "The government isn't exactly cooperating. Like, they want to fight, but they don't want to *lose*."

"What the hell does that mean?"

"They're being little bitches," Mark explains helpfully.

"They don't want to throw themselves into a conflict against Setrákus Ra unless they *know* they can win. So, they'll support us, but they won't fight him directly. Not yet, anyway."

"Pathetic," I say.

Sarah looks at Adam. "John still wants you to get those cloaking devices out of the Skimmers."

"So he can turn that technology over to the army that won't help us?" Adam asks, an eyebrow raised.

"Pretty much."

"Already taken care of. I took them out before we wired the ships to explode," Adam replies, glancing at me. "Whether or not we turn them over? We can decide that later."

"Why the hell would we if they aren't going to help us fight?" I ask Sarah. This whole deal sounds an awful lot like what Agent Walker described to us back at Ashwood Estates. MogPro. Even now, with their biggest city practically a smoking crater, the government is still playing angles and trying to scam cool swag from the friendly aliens.

"Because diplomacy?" Sarah replies, shrugging like the situation is out of her control. Which it obviously is. As usual, we're on our own. "John thinks they'll be more inclined to help us once he can show them a way to beat the Mogs."

"When's he getting here?" Marina asks.

Sarah's face falls. "More bad news there. Five has taken Nine hostage in New York."

I hear a crackle of frost as Marina's fists clench tight. "What?"

"Yeah, not good," Sarah replies. "John and Sam are trying to track him down and stop him from doing—well, whatever the hell that psycho has planned."

"I should've killed him," Marina mutters. I shoot a quick look in her direction. She's been peaceful while we've been at the Sanctuary, so much like the old Marina, all nonviolent and serene. One mention of Five, though, and the darkness comes rushing back.

Sarah continues, not hearing Marina. "Once they've got that sorted out, John will be on his way, but . . ."

I look towards the jungle's tree line. The sun is already starting to get low.

"He won't make it in time," I say, feeling it in my stomach. "It's just going to be us."

"He's going to try," Sarah insists, and I can tell she's hoping to see her boyfriend appear on the horizon like some conquering hero, he and Sam backed by the full might of the U.S. armed forces. I don't hold on to any such delusions.

"We need to get back to it," I say. "We need to get ready."

"Or we could bail," Mark says, raising his hand. When that earns him a dirty look from Marina, he backs down. "All right, all right. Show me where I need to dig."

We get to work.

First, Adam moves Dust's twisted body onto Lexa's ship. The Chimæra seems a bit more alert now, like the tension is going out of his muscles, but he still can't change forms and is nowhere near fighting shape. He's just going to have to sit this one out.

Lexa wants to see the cloaking devices we stripped out of the Skimmers, so then Adam and I show her where we piled them in the ammunition tent. Each one is a solid black box about the size of a laptop.

"They were hooked in to the Skimmer consoles, behind the piloting controls," Adam says, fingering the ports and cords on the back of one of the devices. "I tried to keep them as intact as possible."

We gather them up in a duffel bag and bring them onto Lexa's ship, ready to be delivered to our generous friends in the government, who, in trade, will be giving us a whole lot of nothing.

Of course, that's all assuming we get out of Mexico alive.

"Will it work?" I ask her.

"I think so," Lexa replies. She strips the rubber off a cable and then connects the exposed wire to the cloaking device's power port. "I guess we won't know for sure until we try flying through their warships' shielding."

Careening towards a massive warship while on board a refurbished Loric vessel that may or may not be able to pass through the impenetrable force field surrounding it. There's a situation I'm not looking forward to.

"If it doesn't work . . ."

"We'd explode," she says, before I can even finish the question. "Let's not rush trying it out, okay?"

While Adam and Lexa continue to patch the cloaking device into the Loric systems, the rest of us get to work on the pit in front of the Sanctuary's entrance. Adam did manage to find a few shovels buried among the Mogadorian equipment—apparently, they gave up trying to dig their way under the force field pretty early on. Mark seems a little too happy to take off his shirt and start tossing shovelfuls of dirt over his shoulder. Bernie Kosar gleefully jumps in, too, the Chimæra morphing into a large mole-like creature. With his three-toed claws, Bernie Kosar sends funnels of dirt raining messily out of the pit. It seems like he's having a blast. Mark, on the other hand, doesn't last too long. The jungle heat quickly takes a toll. "This sucks," I overhear him complain to Sarah, wiping sweat off his forehead.

"Wait until the Mogs show up and start shooting at us," Sarah replies. "You'll be wishing we had more manual labor."

Pretty soon we reach a layer of earth that's just too rocky to get through by hand. It's easiest if Adam comes over and uses a quick seismic burst to break up the ground, and then Marina and I use our telekinesis to lift the big chunks free of the pit and hide the displaced dirt in the jungle.

Eventually we've got an honest-to-goodness pit dug. Now that we're finished, Marina and I carefully use our telekinesis to lift our surgically removed dirt cube back into place. It's suspended over the pit pretty precariously and it sags a little in the middle, but it looks natural enough if you don't know the difference. I'm pretty sure it'll cave in as soon as Setrákus Ra reaches the middle, and drop him down about thirty feet, so he won't be able to jump right out. Hopefully, between this and our other traps, we distract him enough to get on board the *Anubis*.

Back in beagle form, Bernie Kosar sniffs around the pit's now-hidden edge, wagging his tail. He seems to approve.

"What's next?" Mark asks, dusting off his hands. "We going to set up some trip wires that trigger hidden crossbows or something?"

"I haven't seen any crossbows lying around," Adam replies, rubbing his chin. "However, we might be able to fashion some spears from the tree branches. How are you at whittling?"

Either Adam doesn't quite get that Mark's being sarcastic, or he really likes setting traps.

"Yeah, let's table that for now," Mark replies, inching away.

Sarah and company actually had the foresight to pack some supplies. Everyone takes a break, passing around bottles of water and food. We all do a pretty good job of pretending not to be scared as hell of what's coming.

I stand a little ways away from the rest of the gang, eating my sandwich and considering the Loric ship parked on the runway. Something's nagging at me, but I can't figure out what it is. It's like there's a little voice shouting a warning in the back of my mind and I can't quite make out the words. Seeing me locked in a staring contest with her ship, Lexa approaches me.

"You think this will work?" she asks me, inclining her head towards our defenses.

"Are you asking me if we're going to win the war today thanks to a big hole in the ground and some guns hidden in the jungle?" I shake my head solemnly. "No way. But maybe we can screw up Setrákus Ra's plans somehow."

"I know this probably doesn't mean much coming from me," Lexa begins hesitantly, clearly uncomfortable. "But you're a good leader, Six. You're holding it together. Your Cêpan would be proud. Hell, all of Lorien would be proud of the fight you guys are putting up."

I can tell Lexa doesn't mean just today, she means all our time on Earth, surviving against the Mogadorians. I watch her out of the corner of my eye. I recognize in Lexa a similar quality to one I've always strived for myself. She's a survivor. I wonder if she's what I'll become if this war goes on for long; a person who avoids making connections because she's already experienced too much pain. Maybe I'm already a little too much like that.

"Yeah," I reply awkwardly. "Thanks."

Lexa seems satisfied with this short exchange. She probably gets me in the same way I get her and understands I don't want some big mushy moment. With one hand, she gestures towards the western expanse of jungle.

"When we were landing, I spotted a small clearing about a mile off. I'm going to move our ship over there, away from the Sanctuary. I'll drive it under the canopy, so they won't be able to see it."

"Good thinking," I reply. "Don't want to give away to Setrákus Ra that we're here."

"Yeah. There's a good chance he'll think you retreated."

"Element of surprise is pretty much the only thing we've got going for us."

"Sometimes that's all it takes," Lexa replies, and then leaves me, striding off towards her ship. *Our* ship, she called it.

I watch her go. There's still that little voice shouting in the back of my mind, louder now, but still unintelligible. I don't know what it's trying to tell me.

"Six? Do you hear that?"

It's Marina, walking up next to me with one hand pressed to her temple like something is giving her a migraine.

"Hear what?" I ask her.

"It's like—it's like a voice." She swallows. "Oh God, maybe I'm losing my mind."

And that's when I realize what's nagging at me isn't the voice of my conscience or some other mental warning system gone haywire. It's literally a voice in my head. One that doesn't belong there and is desperately trying to be heard.

"You're not crazy. I hear it, too."

I focus on the shrill buzzing and, at that moment, it becomes perfectly clear, if still distant, like it's coming through a tunnel.

Six! Marina! Six! Marina! Can you hear me?

Marina and I lock eyes. That little telepathic voice belongs to Ella. John mentioned that her Legacies had gotten stronger, but her telepathy must be seriously juiced up if she's able to broadcast to both me and Marina like this. With every second that passes, her voice becomes clearer in my head.

That can only mean she's getting closer.

"Ella!" I say these words out loud, not really used to communicating telepathically. "Where are you? What's happ—?"

She cuts me off with a telepathic shout. *What are you guys doing there? I told John! He was supposed to warn you.*

"He did warn us," Marina says. "We're here to try to help you. And to protect the Sanctuary."

NO! No no no. Ella sounds a little deranged and definitely panicked. *He was supposed to warn you.*

"Warn us about what?" I ask.

Warn you to run! Ella screams. *You have to run! RUN OR YOU DIE!*

CHAPTER
FIFTEEN

MARINA AND I STARE AT EACH OTHER, BOTH OF us frozen.

That's the thing about death prophecies delivered over telepathic group chat. It's not exactly clear who they apply to. Is Ella talking about me? Marina? Both of us? Everyone here?

Hell, I don't believe the future is set in stone. I don't believe in fate. We're not running now. Not without first trying to execute our plan. After a moment of uncertainty, I see a flare of determination light in Marina's eyes.

"I'm not running," she says.

"Me neither," I reply, already regretting these last few seconds we spent standing still. "Go! Get the others into position!"

Marina runs towards Sarah and the others. I bolt in the opposite direction, across the landing strip, trying to chase down Lexa. She hears the commotion and turns around at the top of the ramp, an eyebrow raised at me.

"He's early," I tell her.

"Shit."

"Fly low so they won't see you. I'm not sure how close they are."

CLOSE! Ella screams in my brain. I flinch at the loudness.

"You know I've got some weapons on this thing, right?" Lexa asks, pointing her thumb towards her ship. "I can help fight them off."

"No. It's our only escape plan. We can't risk the ship getting damaged."

"You got it, Six," Lexa replies. "I'll get it hidden and be right back."

"No," I say, shaking my head. "Don't come back. We can't risk our pilot getting clipped either. Get the ship parked and hidden, then wait. If things go bad here, I want you to be ready to get us the hell out. We might need to run."

"All right," Lexa says, keeping her cool. She points into the jungle to the south, where broken stone pieces of an ancient causeway are still visible. "I'll be a mile in that way, Six. A straight line from here. Mark's got a radio for the cockpit if you need to get in touch."

"Got it."

"Good luck," Lexa replies. What she really means is *survive.*

Lexa gets our ship in the air and flies it low enough that the tops of the trees brush against its underbelly. As soon as she's out of sight, I glance first towards the horizon— no *Anubis* yet—and then run towards the jungle on the eastern side of the Sanctuary. It's where the others have gathered, a good place to hide out—there's plenty of dense foliage and an overturned log we can use for cover. From there, we can see both the front of the temple and the side door. It's the perfect place to trigger our traps. We'll also be able to see the *Anubis* coming in when it does, which can't be long now.

"Ella?" It feels weird to be speaking her name out loud, but I can't get down this whole talking-inside-my-head thing. I wonder if Marina is still looped into the telepathic conversation. "What the hell? You told John sunset!"

Setrákus Ra didn't stop for reinforcements. He's too . . . excited to get here.

Well, that's good news at least. Setrákus Ra didn't replenish his troops after leaving New York. That means we won't have to deal with so many. Even so, I'm still more than a little freaked out by Ella's first dire announcement.

"What did you mean before? Who's going to die?"

I . . . I don't know. It was a vision. Not entirely clear. But I saw blood. So much blood. And I'm not worth it, Six! You could leave now, escape and . . .

I sense that Ella is holding something back, not being totally honest about what she knows. John told me that her

Legacies were amped up, but that her clairvoyance wasn't foolproof. I'm not about to change our plan based on her vision of a future that we might still be able to change.

"We're staying," I say firmly, hoping she can detect the resoluteness in my mind. "We're getting you off that ship. Do you hear me?"

Yes.

"We could use your help. How close are you? What do you see?"

Five minutes, Six. We're five minutes out.

Five minutes. Holy shit.

"What's he sending against us?"

He's coming down personally. One hundred warriors, ready to go. And I'll be there. I won't be able to help you, Six. I can't . . . my body doesn't work anymore.

One hundred. That's a lot. We can handle them, though. At least if we catch a good chunk of them when we blow up the Skimmers.

"There's gotta be something we can do, Ella. Just tell me how to help you."

You can't, her voice comes back, sad and resigned. *Don't worry about me. Do what you need to do.*

Adam joins me as I run towards the edge of the jungle where the others have already hidden. Instead of immediately running to our hiding spot, he took a detour into the Skimmer we flew down here and collected the vicious Mogadorian sword that once belonged to his father. The sword looks heavy strapped across Adam's back, but he keeps up with me.

"Almost forgot it," he says, catching me looking at the sword.

"Isn't there an expression about bringing a knife to a gunfight?" I ask.

He shrugs. "You never know when a big sharp thing might come in handy."

We skid to a stop at the edge of the jungle, where the rest of our group is already hunkered down behind a fallen tree. Adam turns around and watches the sky, his mouth a tight line, arms crossed. Mark is holding the detonator control for our bombs that Adam showed him how to use earlier. With Mark acting as our demolitions expert, Marina is freed up to focus on telekinetically firing the blasters we've hidden throughout the jungle. Sarah stands next to them, a blaster held in one hand, her other hand pressed to her temple, pale and frowning.

"I don't accept that," Marina says as I slide in next to her. I realize that she's having a conversation with Ella, too.

"Accept what?" Mark asks, confused. Sarah shushes him. Taking another look at her, I realize that Sarah is also tuned in to Ella's telepathic channel. She knows death might be coming.

"We're going to steal his ship right out from under him. We're going to rescue you." I say these things out loud, steel in my voice, knowing that Ella can hear me.

I'm sorry. That won't happen, Ella says telepathically. I can tell by the way her eyes well up with tears that Marina can hear her, too. Sarah covers her mouth and swallows hard, looking at me questioningly.

"Bullshit," I say.

"Don't you dare give up hope," Marina practically yells into the empty space in front of her. "Ella? Do you hear me?"

Ella doesn't respond. I can still feel her there, almost like a tickle in the back of my mind. I know she's listening in. She just isn't answering us anymore.

"I don't care what she says or how many Mogs we have to go through," I say, addressing Marina now. "If we do one thing today, we're getting Ella away from Setrákus Ra. Get hold of her and get her back to Lexa's ship."

"Agreed," Marina says.

"Maybe that'll work," Sarah adds, that look of shock gone from her face, replaced by a thoughtful look. Like Marina and me, she isn't backing down from the threat of death. "I mean, wasn't there something with your guys' old Loric charm that broke it when you got together?"

"Yeah," I reply. "So?"

"So, maybe Setrákus Ra's messed-up version works in the opposite way," Sarah explains. "Maybe that's why he's been taking Ella with him everywhere he goes. He's got to keep her close for it to work."

"Makes sense to me," Mark says, shrugging. "Not that I'm, like, an authority on this shit."

It's definitely a possibility worth testing out, especially since we planned to rescue Ella anyway.

I turn to Adam. The plan was for the two of us to go invisible and board the *Anubis* while the others provided the distraction. "What do you think? Go for the warship or go for Ella?"

"Your call," he replies.

"You might have to get right under his nose to get to Ella," Sarah says.

"Which means he could turn off your invisibility," Marina adds.

"Shit," I say, mind racing. "All right. Maybe we can get them separated when we spring our traps. If we see an opportunity, let's go for Ella. Otherwise, we stick to the plan and take the *Anubis*." I point south. "There's some old stonework that way. If you head south from there, that's where Lexa hid our ship. If things get bad out here, if the Mogs figure out your position, I want you three to make a break for it."

"And leave you behind?" Marina asks.

"We'll be invisible, at least," I reply, looking between her and Sarah. "Just stay alive. That's what's important now."

Sarah nods grimly and Marina turns away, looking towards the Sanctuary. Even after Ella's warning, I doubt she has any intention of retreating.

Before I can say anything else, Adam grabs my arm and points towards the landing strip.

"Damn it! Six, we forgot about our friend."

I look to where Adam points and see Phiri Dun-Ra squirming wildly against her bonds. In our rush to get into position, I completely forgot about our Mogadorian prisoner. Even though she's hooded, Phiri Dun-Ra must have heard the commotion and knows we're distracted. She's going nuts on her restraints, doing anything she can to get loose. We tied her to that wheel strut pretty tightly, so I don't think she's going to break free. All the same, it's probably not a good idea to leave her out there when the *Anubis* shows up.

"Setrákus Ra will know something's up if he sees her," Adam says, reading my mind.

Mark lifts up his blaster and looks down the sights, the barrel aimed in Phiri Dun-Ra's direction. "Want me to take her out? I think I can make the shot."

Marina puts a hand on his blaster and makes him lower it. "If we wanted to execute her, Mark, don't you think we would've done it already?"

Adam gives me a look, like maybe it's not a bad idea to finally put Phiri Dun-Ra out of *our* misery. He's wanted to kill her all day, though. And I can understand why.

"Should've stuck her in the pit," Sarah says regretfully.

"We have to get her out of sight," I say.

I reach out with my telekinesis and undo Phiri Dun-Ra's bonds. It takes me a few seconds—like Marina firing off the hidden blasters, such a precise task is not easy to accomplish at this distance. Phiri Dun-Ra must think she's done this on her own. She rips off her hood and gag, then springs to her feet, stumbling, surprised to have the ropes suddenly give way. The trueborn rubs her wrists for a moment, looks around and then takes off running towards the jungle opposite of us. She's headed right towards where we've hidden some of the Mog blasters.

"Six?" Marina asks, a note of warning in her voice. "Do you know what you're doing?"

I do. Before Phiri Dun-Ra can make it far, I use the ropes we'd tied her up with to telekinetically lasso her feet. She falls forward hard, pretty much landing on her face. Then, I drag her towards us, dust and dirt scrabbled up as she claws at the ground and tries to escape. Her frustrated screams are loud enough to scare up some birds from the nearby trees.

"We need to shut her up," Adam says.

"Marina, reel her in," I reply.

As Marina takes over the telekinesis, I focus on the clouds rolling in on the evening sky. I don't want to create a full-fledged storm—not with the *Anubis* and Setrákus Ra so close. Luckily, I don't need one. There's a dark cloud up there with just enough charge to generate a small lightning bolt. I send this arcing down into Phiri Dun-Ra, zapping her good. I guess there's a chance this could kill her, but I don't really have time to worry about that. The Mog spasms as the electricity shoots through her, then stops struggling against Marina's telekinesis. She doesn't disintegrate, so I guess she's still alive.

When Marina's dragged Phiri Dun-Ra over to the tree line, Adam grabs her under the arms and pulls her the rest of the way. He shoves her behind the log we're hiding behind and begins retying her wrists and ankles.

"So, you guys are taking prisoners now?" Mark asks.

"She might come in handy," I reply, shrugging.

"We can't keep dragging her around," Adam says as he finishes tightening the knots.

"We'll leave her here. She mentioned loving the jungle, right?" I say, with a smile on my face. We've got bigger things to worry about than the fate of Phiri Dun-Ra.

"Let's not jinx our chance at survival by making lots of plans," Mark says.

Before anyone can reply, the jungle around us gets strangely quiet. I'd gotten so used to the incessant squawking of tropical birds that it's absolutely jarring when it's gone. Even the bug noises taper off. Across the clearing that the Mogs made around the Sanctuary, to the north, a whole flock of birds flies out from the trees and scatters.

The *Anubis* is here.

I hold out my hands and arms. "Grab on," I tell

everyone. "I'll keep us all invisible until we're ready to attack."

Marina takes one of my hands and Sarah takes the other. Mark, detonator at the ready, gets hold of my shoulder. Adam is last. He gives me a nod, probably remembering when I told him how strange it was to hold hands with a Mogadorian. Until this is over, the two of us will be attached at the hip. I nod back, over it, and he squeezes in next to Marina, his hand on my upper arm. Only Bernie Kosar doesn't get close to me. Instead, our Chimæra transforms into a toucan and flies into a nearby tree.

It's sort of funny, the five of us crowded together like this. It almost looks like we're posing for a picture.

I turn us invisible just as the *Anubis* glides into view. The warship is bigger than I even imagined. The whole ship is made from overlapping panels of a metallic gray alloy that almost look like scales. It's shaped like one of those Egyptian bugs—a scarab—except with a whole ton of guns, the massive cannon jutting off the front of its hull particularly catching my eye.

"God," Sarah whispers.

"Holy shit," Mark says, a little louder. His hand tightens on my shoulder. As the *Anubis* lumbers closer, the entire clearing and the Sanctuary itself are stuck in its shadow.

"Easy now," I say, trying to keep from freaking out myself. "Stay still and stay close. They can't see us."

The enormous ship comes to a stop so that it's hovering

above the Mog encampment. Even considering the large swath of jungle the Mogs cleared, the warship is so big that it won't have room to land.

Adam must realize that the *Anubis* hovering above the battlefield kind of screws up our plans. "We're going to need to find a way up there."

"If he lands any ground troops, we can pick them off and fly their own Skimmers back up there," I reply. It's exactly the tactic John and the absent U.S. military want to employ against the Mog warships, so who better than us to be the guinea pigs.

"What's he doing?" Sarah wonders. "What are they waiting for?"

Ella stopped telepathically broadcasting to us a few minutes ago, and now I'm wondering if it's just my imagination that I can still feel her presence lingering in the back of my mind. If she's still there, though, if she can hear me, we could definitely use the help.

"Ella?" I ask, feeling stupid saying her name out loud like this. "Can you hear me? What's going on up there?"

There's no response.

"Marina? Sarah? Is she . . . ?"

"Nothing, Six," Sarah answers, one disembodied voice talking about another.

"I think she's gone," Marina adds.

But then it happens. A whisper in the back of my mind. Ella's voice, forlorn and hopeless.

You should've run.

In the air above us, a humming sound begins to emanate from the *Anubis*. It's noticeable because of how amazingly silent the warship is otherwise. It starts low but builds up quickly. Pretty soon, my teeth are vibrating because of it. I scan the underbelly of the warship, expecting to see Setrákus Ra's soldiers descending in Skimmers, but the skies are clear.

"What the hell is that?" I ask, hoping Adam will answer.

"It's . . . it's powering up," Adam replies. His voice is shaky and I feel his hand get looser on my arm, like he's stunned and forgetting that he needs to hold on to me to remain invisible.

"Powering up what?" I ask.

"The main weapon," he answers. "The cannon."

I can see it. The dark hollow of the cannon's barrel begins to glow as energy coalesces there. The humming gets louder as the cannon fills with pure energy, like a Mogadorian blaster overcharging. In seconds, the Sanctuary and the jungle around it are all bathed in the azure light. I want to shield my eyes, but Marina and Sarah are gripping my hands tight.

"This is bad," Mark says. "Really bad."

"Adam?" I shout to be heard over the charging weapon. "How powerful is that thing?"

As a group, we all shuffle backwards. I'm barely able to

keep track of everyone and maintain our invisibility.

"We need to move," Adam replies, the awe gone from his voice, replaced by terror. "We need to get back!"

Everyone's already backing up, leaving only Phiri Dun-Ra hidden behind the overturned log. Marina tugs against my grip. She's not moving.

"Marina!" I yell. "Come on!"

"We said we wouldn't run!" she shouts back.

"But—!"

The hum reaches a crescendo and the energy built up in the warship's cannon discharges with a deafening shriek. A solid arc of electricity the size of ten thousand lightning bolts shears directly into the Sanctuary and slices right through it, the ancient limestone glowing red-hot. The cannon's blast cuts through the temple, top to bottom, like it was nothing. I have only a moment to consider the Sanctuary, still standing but cut down the middle. I can see light through the cracks in the once-solid wall.

A second later, the condensed energy from the cannon expands outwards in a bright surge of light.

The Sanctuary explodes.

"NO!" Marina screams.

We screwed up. Setrákus Ra didn't come here to claim the Sanctuary. He came here to destroy it.

I don't have time to think about what that means or what happens next. Adam yanks me backwards and we go staggering into the jungle, just as chunks of the temple begin to rain down around us. I lose my grip on Marina and she pops back into visibility. Mark's hand falls off my shoulder and he reappears as well. Only Sarah and Adam keep holding on to me.

Marina actually goes running forward, like she's going to be able to fight against that warship.

"Stop!" I yell. "Marina! Stop!"

Mark reacts quickly, his football reflexes coming naturally. He lunges towards her, wraps his arms around Marina's waist and tackles her.

"Get off me!" Marina screams at Mark. She shoves him away, icy handprints forming on his chest.

Then, something else explodes. One of the Skimmers we wired with C-4. It must've taken a direct hit from a piece of the Sanctuary and triggered the bomb. Shrapnel whizzes by all around us, sizzling-hot pieces of bent metal tearing through the leaves of the trees.

Mark sucks in a breath and topples over. There's a jagged piece of thick cockpit glass jutting out of his chest.

"Mark!" Sarah screams, wrestling free from me and running towards him.

Marina sees Mark's injury and gasps. She turns her back on the Sanctuary and falls to her knees beside him, yanking out the glass and immediately starting to heal him.

Branches break above my head and I look up in time to see a basketball-sized chunk of limestone hurtling towards me. On reflex, I use my telekinesis and catch it in midair, tossing it aside.

I don't catch the next one.

It hits me on top of the head. Before I even realize what's happened, there's something sticky and warm coating the side of my face. Adam grabs me under the arms as I fall to my knees. We're both visible now. Must have lost my concentration. I try to get my legs under me, to refocus on my invisibility, but I can't do either. My head swims and I have to blink blood out of my eyes.

"Help!" Adam yells to Marina. "Six is hurt!"

I try to hold on to consciousness, but it's hard. The world is going black, even as everything we've fought for goes up in flames. Ella warned us there would be death. Feeling almost detached from my body, I wonder if this is it.

As I slip away, I hear Ella's voice in my head.

I'm sorry, she says.

CHAPTER
SIXTEEN

I DON'T HAVE TIME FOR THIS SHIT.

Five wants to meet me at sunset at the Statue of Liberty. It sounds like the plan of some supervillain. He's holding Nine hostage and plans to kill him if I don't show up. I don't know what he wants from me. At the United Nations, it seemed like he was trying to help us in his own psychotic way. At the very least, he stopped me from unintentionally hurting Ella. Of course, he can't possibly know that I'm on the clock here, that every minute wasted on his screwed-up games is a minute not spent helping Sarah, Six and the others. If he did know, would he even care?

I sent Sarah and Mark to Mexico with the newly discovered Loric hacker-turned-pilot who I'm dying to meet. I sent them there because they're literally the only support I could drum up for Six and the rest of the Garde who are in for a major fight.

At least they can escape now. They aren't stranded. Six and Sarah are smart enough to cut their losses and get out of there. This is what I keep telling myself.

I do a quick mental calculation. Even if Agent Walker could somehow convince the military to loan me one of their fastest fighter jets, I still won't be able to make it to Mexico ahead of Setrákus Ra. Not at this point.

That doesn't mean I'm not going to try.

"Can you at least get me a boat?" I ask Walker. Having left the chaos of the docks behind, we're back in the FBI agent's tent.

"To take you to the Statue of Liberty?" Walker nods. "Yeah, I can arrange that."

"Right now, though," I reply. "I want it right now."

"Five said sunset. That's still almost an hour away," Sam adds grimly. I know he's been doing the same mental calculations that I have. He knows we won't make it to the Sanctuary. Not unless we leave Nine to whatever fate Five has in store for him, and neither one of us is willing to go down that road.

"I'm not waiting. We aren't on Five's time. He's probably sitting there right now, setting up a trap or something. Whatever the hell he does. We're going early. If he's not there, then we'll be waiting for the bastard."

"Good idea," Sam says, nodding. "Let's do it."

"Make it happen," I tell Walker, and step outside her tent.

From here, in Brooklyn Bridge Park, we can see Liberty Island. The green outline of the famous statue is visible against the smoky sky. It won't take us long to get there. From this distance, I can't discern any details. If Five is there or if he's set up some kind of trap for us, I can't tell. It doesn't really matter. Whatever we find, we're going to face head-on.

Sam follows me outside. "What're we going to do?" he asks me. "I mean, with Five."

"Whatever we have to," I reply.

He falls silent and crosses his arms, also gazing out across the water at the statue.

"You know, I always wanted to see the Statue of Liberty," is all he can think to say.

Inside the tent, I can hear Walker doing a lot of yelling into her walkie-talkie. Eventually, she succeeds in commandeering us one of the coast guard's speedboats. It doesn't have the artillery of one of the navy boats I spotted in the harbor, but it'll get us to Liberty Island in a hurry. Walker also puts the call out to her trusted agents, assembling a crew of three guys who I recognize from the anti-MogPro task force that helped us go after the secretary of defense. I guess they're the ones who survived the battle with Setrákus Ra at the United Nations. One of them is the guy I healed during that first skirmish in Midtown, the one who costars in the video Sarah posted all over the internet. He looks almost embarrassed when he shakes my hand.

"Agent Murray," he introduces himself. "Never got a chance to say thank you. For the other day."

"Don't worry about it," I tell him, then turn to Agent Walker. "We don't need the backup. Just the boat."

"Sorry, John. Can't let you two go out there alone. You're government assets now."

I snort. "Oh, we are?"

"You are."

I'm not going to waste time arguing about this. They can come if they want. I start towards the docks, Sam next to me, and Walker and her agents fanned out around us like bodyguards. As usual, I get a lot of stares from the soldiers milling around. Some of them look like they want to help, but I'm sure they're under orders not to get involved with us. Agent Walker and what's left of her splinter group of ex-MogPro agents are all the help the government's willing to grant us at this point. At least they upgraded their weapons, the agents having traded in their usual standard-issue handguns for some heavy-duty assault rifles.

"Hey! John Smith from Mars! Wait up!"

I turn in time to see Daniela squeeze her gangly body through a group of soldiers and trot towards us. The agents surrounding us immediately raise their rifles and, seeing this, Daniela skids to a stop a few yards away and puts her hands up. She eyes the FBI agents with a cocky grin.

"It's all right, calm down," I tell Walker and her bunch, waving Daniela over. "She's one of us."

Walker raises an eyebrow. "You mean . . . ?"

"A human Garde," I say, keeping my voice low. "One of the people Setrákus Ra wants turned over to him."

Walker sizes up Daniela. "Great," she says dryly.

Daniela just amps up the wattage on that smirk. "You guys heading off on an adventure or something? Can I come?"

I frown at how lightly she's taking this and exchange a look with Sam.

"Did you find your mom?" Sam asks her, and Daniela's smile falters a bit.

"She's not here, and she never checked in with the Red Cross," Daniela replies, shrugging like it's no big deal. Even though she tries to keep her tone light, her voice is shaky and I can tell she expects the worst. "Probably got out of the city some other way. I'm sure she's all right."

"Yeah, definitely," Sam replies, forcing a smile.

"We're on our way to confront a rogue Garde," I tell her bluntly. Walker gives me a look, but I see no reason to lie. All hands on deck.

"Whoa. You guys, like, go rogue?"

I think about Five and how he turned on us and I think about Setrákus Ra and the uncountable horrible acts he's committed. He used to be a Garde too, maybe even something higher than that, if Crayton's letter to

Ella can be believed. Then, I look at Daniela and consider her and the other humans with new Legacies who
we haven't met yet. Will they all fight for good? Or will
some of them turn out like Five and Setrákus Ra?

"We're people, just like anyone else," I tell her.

"Except with awesome powers," Sam adds.

"Like anyone else," I continue, "we can go bad without the proper guidance."

Daniela turns on that sly smile again. It's almost
infuriating, but I'm starting to realize it's just a defense
mechanism. Whenever she feels uncomfortable, she
tries really hard to return the favor. "Yeah. Got it. You
going to be my guide, John Smith? My sensei?"

"We called them Cêpan, actually. Our trainers. But
they're gone. Now, we pretty much figure stuff out for
ourselves."

Agent Walker clears her throat. I think she wants
me to get rid of Daniela, but I'm not turning away any
help. No way.

"You can come with us," I say. "But you should know,
the guy we're going after is extremely dangerous."

"Unhinged," Sam adds.

"He's already killed one of us," I continue. "And I
don't think he'll hesitate to do it again. When we're
done with him, our friend Agent Walker here is going
to get us on a plane somehow, and we're going to find
a way to kill the Mogadorian in charge before his

invasion goes any further."

"You trying to scare me off?" Daniela asks, hands on her hips.

"I just want you to know what you're in for," I reply. "Along the way, I can try to help you with your tele-kinesis. Maybe figure out what else you can do. But you've gotta be up for it . . ."

Daniela looks over her shoulder. I realize that, more than anything, she wants to get out of here. She wants to keep busy and avoid confronting the very real pos-sibility that she lost her entire family during the attack on New York.

"I'm in," she says. "Let's save the world and shit."

Sam grins and I can't help but smile a little bit too, especially when I notice Agent Walker rolling her eyes. With Daniela incorporated into our little bubble of secret agents, we continue on to the pier.

"Hey," Sam says to Daniela, keeping his voice low. "Just so you know, the Mogs were taking prisoners in New York. They weren't, like, killing everything that moved."

"Yeah, I saw them pull that shit in my neighbor-hood," Daniela replies. "So what?"

"So, just because she's not here doesn't mean your mom's . . . you know."

"Yeah. Thanks." Daniela says this gruffly, but I think she actually means it.

The coast guard boat is ready and waiting for us, a chain-smoking captain in a wrinkled uniform prepared to take us wherever we need to go. I let Walker fill him in and a few minutes later we're off, bouncing hard over the waves. Across the water, I can see flashing lights from the New Jersey side, helicopters bobbing in and out of view. Looks like the military set up a perimeter over there too, really trying to make sure the Mogadorians stay contained in Manhattan. I look towards the city and find the place frighteningly calm. There are still Mogs there, I'm sure, patrolling the streets and maybe setting up a stronghold. I hope most of the residents managed to make it across the bridge and, if not, then I hope Sam's right about the Mogs keeping them as prisoners instead of killing them. That means they can still be saved.

As Liberty Island grows larger in front of us, Daniela nudges me in the ribs.

"You're meeting this dude at the Statue of Liberty?" she asks.

"Yeah."

"Man, that's some real tourist shit."

Pretty soon, we pull up at the Liberty Island docks. A half dozen ferry boats float there, empty, one of them with scorch marks along its side. The entire place is deserted; no one's spending the invasion checking out the Statue of Liberty. It's almost peaceful here. As we hop out of the boat, I try to get the lay of the land. I force myself to think like Five, wondering where the best place for an ambush would be.

I have to tilt my head up to take in the statue. We're coming at her from the side holding the book. The gold-plated torch gleams in what's left of the daylight. The big green lady sits atop a huge granite pedestal that in turn sits atop an even bigger stone base that takes up almost half the island. To the right, there's a small park that looks perfectly maintained. He won't be hiding in the park—that's just not how Five operates.

The boat captain stays behind, but the rest of us stride along the dock towards the statue. I think about when I first met Five, how he picked some creepy monster monument in the backwoods to reveal himself. I guess the guy has a thing for landmarks. Or maybe that crummy wooden monster statue was a clue, a stand-in for the monster hiding inside Five. If that's the case, I wonder what his choice of the Statue of Liberty means. Probably nothing, I think, reminding myself that Five's a total nutcase.

Next to me, Daniela snickers. "You know, I've never actually been here. Lived in the city my whole life."

"Yeah, it's like a field trip," Sam says. "A field trip where at the end a dude made of solid steel tries to stab you to death."

"No one's getting stabbed to death," I say.

As we enter the plaza that stretches around the statue's base, I keep my gaze centered on the upper pedestal. That's where I've decided Five is most likely to be. He can fly, so it'd be easy for him to reach that area, and it would allow him to keep an eye out for our arrival. I don't see any movement up there, though. Maybe he isn't here yet. Or maybe he's hiding inside the statue. I crane my neck more, trying to glimpse inside the statue's crown, but it's impossible. We'll have to go inside to make sure the statue is clear.

"Look," Sam says, lowering his voice. "Over there."

I turn my head to the left, towards the perfectly sculpted lawn that stretches out from the statue's foundation. There's movement. A glittering shape slowly stands up from the grass and takes a faltering step in our direction. I was looking in the wrong place.

"You're early," Five calls. "Good."

To say Five looks messed up would be an understatement. His clothes look like they've gone through a thresher—ripped, bloodstained and caked with dirt and ash. His skin is a silvery steel, making me think that he's ready to fight, even though it looks like he can barely stand up. His features look swollen and out of place despite their metallic coating, his nose crooked, and there are visible dents in the side of his shaved head. He's hunched over, one arm dangling uselessly at his side. His other arm wears that wrist-mounted blade of his. The day's fading sunlight glints off his skin.

Immediately, Walker and her team fan out, flanking Five. They've got their guns leveled at him. Daniela goes the opposite way, taking a step behind me.

"Uh, you should've described this rogue dude better," she says.

Five takes a look at Walker's agents and sneers. Even though he looks worn-out, having a bunch of guns pointed at him seems to rekindle his intense temper. His remaining eye tweaks open wider and he stands up straighter.

"Don't make me laugh with this shit," Five says to Walker, then turns towards Agent Murray when the man chambers a round. "I'm bulletproof, bitch. Come on, I dare you."

There's something weird about Five's voice. It sounds tinny and raspy, almost like he's having trouble breathing.

The agents are smart enough not to get too close. I know how fast Five is, though. If he wanted to come at one of them, he'd be able to close the gap in a second or two with his flight. I stride forward onto the grass, hoping to get his attention on me before he does anything crazy. Sam stays right at my side, Daniela a few steps behind. That's when I notice the lumpy shape in the grass next to Five. It's one of those blue plastic construction tarps wrapped around what is obviously a body, all of that tightly bound together by thick coils of industrial-strength chain.

That must be Nine.

"Give him to me," I say to Five, not wasting any time.

Five looks down at the body and it's almost like he'd forgotten it was there.

"Sure, John," Five replies.

Five bends down and hooks his hands through the chains. He hoists up Nine's body and grimaces. He's hurt and tired, and I can tell this show is taxing him more than he counted on. With an animal grunt, Five tosses the body across the thirty yards that separates us. I catch Nine in midair with my telekinesis and lower him gently to the ground. Immediately, I rip off the chains and unroll the tarp.

Nine lies unconscious in the grass in front of me. His clothes are in as bad a condition as Five's and his injuries are similarly gruesome. There are blaster burns on his arms and chest, one of his hands is broken like something crushed it and there's a bad gash on his head. It's that last thing that really worries me. Blood soaks through Nine's mane of dark hair—a lot of it— and his eyes don't open when I gently slap his cheek.

Sam puts a hand on my shoulder. "Is he . . . ?"

"Oh, he's fine," Five groans, answering Sam's question for me. "I had to hit him pretty hard to knock him out, though. You'll probably want to get on that, doc."

I place my hands on the side of Nine's head, but pause before I start healing him. It's going to require my concentration and that means I won't be able to keep an eye on Five. I look up at him.

"You going to do anything stupid?" I ask him.

Five holds up his hands, palms out, even though one of his arms won't go as high as the other. Then, he flops backwards into a sitting position. "Don't worry, John. I'm not going to hurt any of your little friends." All the same, his one eye scans over my crew, sizing each of them up. Five's gaze lingers on Daniela. "You're no cop," he says. "What's your deal?"

"Don't talk to me, creep," she replies.

"Don't egg him on," Sam says quietly.

Five snorts and shakes his head, more amused than anything. He pinches a handful of grass in front of him, rips it up and tosses the tuft away with a sigh. "Get on with it, John. I don't have all day."

I'm still wary this is some kind of trap, but I can't put off healing Nine any longer. I press my hands to the side of his head and let my healing energies flow into him. First, the gash on his head closes up. That's just the superficial injury, though. Intuitively, I can feel the deeper, more serious traumas affecting Nine. His skull is fractured and there's some swelling in his brain. I focus my Legacy there, although I'm careful not to push in more energy than I need. The brain's a delicate thing and I don't want to scramble Nine's any more than it was before he got his head smashed in. He might still have a concussion when I'm done with him, but at least the most serious damage will be reversed.

It takes me a couple of minutes of just concentrating on Nine. I'm vaguely aware of the tense silence around me. When I'm finished, I take my hands off his head. The other injuries can wait until we're not in the presence of a total lunatic.

"Nine? Nine, wake up," I say, shaking him.

After a moment, Nine's eyes flutter open. His body tenses and his eyes dart around wildly. It's like he's expecting to be attacked again. When he recognizes me and Sam, he calms down and his expression becomes dreamy and out-of-it. He grabs my arm.

"Johnny! I got that son of a bitch. I put one right through him," he mumbles.

"Got who?" I ask, and get no response. Nine's head is already lolling away from me. I can and did heal his injuries, but I can't make him not exhausted from fighting for the last twenty-four hours straight. He's way out of it. We're probably going to have to carry him.

I look up from Nine to see Five still seated in the grass, watching us. Seeing that Nine's out of the woods, Five begins a slow, sarcastic clap.

"Bravo, John. Always the hero," he says. "What about me?"

"What *about* you?" I say through clenched teeth.

"No, actually, I'd like an answer to that question, too," Walker says, her gun still trained on Five. "He attacked our soldiers and helped the Mogadorians. He's basically a war criminal. You just want to leave him here?"

"Don't you have some kind of top secret space prison for evil metal guys?" Daniela whispers to me.

"Hell with him," Sam says. He's the only one who gets that we have more important things to deal with. He waves dismissively at Five and bends down over Nine, trying to help him up. "Come on, John. We gotta get out of here."

I'm about to help Sam when Five speaks up again. "That's it?" he asks, sounding almost sullen. "You're just going to leave?"

I straighten up and glare at him. "What the hell do you want, Five? Do you know how much of our time you've already wasted with your stupid theatrics?" I gesture towards Manhattan, plumes of smoke still rising into the air there. "You're not a priority right now, man. You noticed we're at war, right? You're not so far gone that you missed your old Mog friends killing thousands of people, did you?"

Five actually looks towards the city, contemplating the destruction there. His bottom lip juts out. "They aren't my friends," he says quietly.

"Yeah, no shit," I reply. "Too bad you're only figuring that out now. They used you, Five, and now they don't want you anymore. And neither do we. You're lucky I don't come over there and finish what Nine started."

My temper flares as I remember all the crap Five has pulled in the short time I've known him. In spite of my words, I take a sudden step towards him. Sam puts a hand on my shoulder.

"Don't," he says. "Let's just go."

I nod, knowing Sam's right. I still have to get a few last shots in, though. I need to get this stuff off my chest. "I guess you can be alone now," I say to Five. "That's kinda what you wanted all along, isn't it? So, go run back to one of your tropical islands and hide, or whatever it is you want to do. Just stay out of our way and stop wasting our time."

Five looks down at the grass in front of him. "You didn't have to come," he says bitterly.

That actually makes me laugh. The sheer insanity of this guy. "You made us come here. You said you'd kill Nine if we didn't."

Five's forehead makes a metal clinking noise when he knocks against it, like he's trying to remember something. "That's not what I told those army losers when they found me," he says. "I told them *you'd* get a new scar."

"Why are we still talking to him?" Sam asks, his

voice rising a bit in bewilderment. He leans back down over Nine, loops Nine's arm over his shoulders and grunts as he tries to lift him up.

Five's single eye holds mine. He's locked in on me, totally ignoring everyone else. I know he's baiting me into something, I just don't know what. Sam's right that we shouldn't be wasting time here, but I can't help myself.

"What're you saying?" I ask him grudgingly, knowing that it's exactly what he wants.

In response, Five takes off his shirt.

The simple action seems to take a lot of effort, like it's hard for Five to lift his arms. The shirt snags on something as Five pulls it over his head and he yelps. It takes me a moment of looking at his chest, metal-plated just like the rest of him, to realize there's something wrong.

Five has a piece of steel sticking out of his sternum. It looks like a broken-off pole from a street sign. He turns to the side slightly so that I can see the jagged other end poking out through his back. Each end comes out only a few inches, and both are twisted and warped like Five had to shorten the pole by ripping it with his hands. It's straight through and, at the very least, has to be puncturing one of Five's lungs and part of his spine. The steel pole could even be right up against his heart.

"I was already in my metal form when he drove

it through me. That didn't stop him, though," Five explains, wheezing his words a bit. He looks at Nine with something close to admiration. "My instincts kicked in. I used my Externa in a way I hadn't before, made the metal part of me. I can feel it cold inside me, Four. It's weird."

Five seems almost casual about this. I take a tentative step towards him and he smiles.

"I'm tired and I can't hold my Externa forever," Five says. "So I wanted it to be up to you. You're the good one, John. The reasonable one. And you were always right in front of me in the order, keeping me alive all those years, whether you knew me or not. So what's it going to be?"

I take another cautious step towards him. "Five . . ."

"Live or die?" Five asks, and then, without warning, he turns himself back into flesh.

CHAPTER
SEVENTEEN

FIVE CHOKES ON THE NEXT BREATH HE TAKES. A bubble of blood spews from his mouth. His skin, no longer covered by a layer of steel, goes pale in a hurry. His remaining eye goes wide and, in that moment before I watch it roll back in his head, I see fear there. Maybe Five thought he wanted this. But now, looking death in the face, he is scared.

Five collapses backwards into the grass, seizing and struggling to pull in painful-sounding breaths. Ten seconds. Impaled by a sign pole, that's how long I'd guess Five has left to live.

He betrayed us. He told the Mogs where they could find us and got Nine's safe house blown up. Because of Five, Setrákus Ra was able to kidnap Ella, and Sam's dad was almost killed. He murdered Eight. With that needle-shaped blade that even now tears up chunks of dirt as Five spasms in the grass, Five executed one of his own people. He deserves this.

But I'm not like him. I can't just watch him die.

"Goddamn you, Five," I say through gritted teeth as I run forward and slide into the grass next to him. I press both my hands to his chest and use my healing Legacy, putting enough energy into him to at least stanch some of the internal bleeding, buying myself time to do the bigger healing. Five comes back to himself a little, his one eye finds mine and I think I catch the corner of his mouth twist into a knowing smile. Then, he passes out from pain and shock.

I need to get this metal pole out of him. Obviously I haven't read a whole lot of medical textbooks, but I'm pretty sure removing it will further damage Five's insides. Therefore, I should be healing him at the same time that metal is removed, hopefully to minimize the damage. I wrestle Five's limp body into a sitting position, propping him up against me. Then, I wave Sam over.

"I need you to use your telekinesis to push the metal out of him," I tell Sam quickly. "That way I can concentrate on the healing."

"I . . ." Sam hesitates. He stares at Five's mortally wounded frame and swallows hard. "I don't think so, John."

"What do you mean?"

"I mean, I don't think you should save him," Sam

replies, his voice more resolute now. He glances over his shoulder at Nine's unconscious body. "Nine, uh . . . I think Nine was right with how he handled this."

My hand is on the back of Five's neck. I can feel his pulse getting slower. I stabilized him, but it won't last long. He's fading. I'm not sure it'll work if I try using my telekinesis at the same time as my healing.

"He's *dying*, Sam."

"I know."

"This has gone too far," I say. "We're not killing each other, not anymore. Help me save him, Sam."

"No," Sam replies, shaking his head. "He's too—look, I'm not going to stop you. I know I couldn't even if I tried. But I'm not helping you. I'm not helping *him*."

"Hell, I'll do it," Daniela says, pushing by Sam and kneeling on the ground next to me.

I stare at Sam for a second longer. I get why he's refusing to help, I really do. I'm sure Nine wouldn't be leaping to my aid if he was conscious either. Still, I'm disappointed.

I turn my attention to Daniela. She's staring at Five's impalement like it's the craziest thing she's ever seen. She reaches out one hand towards where the metal disappears into his chest, but can't quite bring herself to touch it.

"Why?" I ask her. "You don't know Five or what he's done. Why would you—?"

Daniela cuts me off with a shrug. "Because you asked. Now we doing this or not?"

"We're doing this," I say, setting my hands on either side of Five's wound. "Push. Gently. I'll heal him as we go."

Daniela squints at the piece of metal, her hands hovering a few inches away from Five's chest. I wonder if she has the control for this. If she exerts too much telekinetic force she could end up rocketing the steel pole right out of Five and I'm not sure I'll be able to heal his torn-up insides fast enough. We have to go slow and steady, or risk Five bleeding out.

Slowly, Daniela starts to push the metal. Five's breathing quickens when she does and he begins to squirm, although his eyes stay closed. She keeps her focus and has better control than I anticipated. I press my hands to Five's chest, one on each side of the wound, and let my healing energy flow into him.

"Gross, gross, gross," Daniela mutters under her breath.

I keep sending energy into Five, sensing his injuries mending but also feeling my Legacy thwarted by the metal still in his body. That's until I hear a wet thunk in the grass and realize Daniela's successfully pushed the post out of Five. When that happens, I really amp things up, healing his lungs and spine.

When I'm done, Five breathes easier. He's still

unconscious and, for the first time I can remember, looks almost peaceful. Thanks to me, he's going to live. Now that the moment has passed, I'm not sure how I feel about that.

"Damn, man," Daniela says. "We should be surgeons or something."

"I hope we don't regret this," Sam says quietly.

"*We* won't," I say, glancing at Sam. "I did this. He's my responsibility now."

With that in mind, and considering he's still knocked out, I quickly undo the wrist-mounted blade from Five's forearm and toss it into the grass at Sam's feet. Sam picks it up, carefully examines the mechanism and then hits the button to retract the blade. He tucks the weapon into the back of his jeans.

I remind myself that even without his blade Five isn't fully disarmed. I open up both of his hands, looking for the rubber ball and ball bearing that he carries around to trigger his Externa. He isn't holding them, so I start patting him down. When they don't turn up in his pockets, I know there's only one place they can be.

Cringing, I peel back the yellowed gauze pad that covers Five's ruined eye. Jammed into the empty socket is the glinting ball bearing and its rubbery partner. It can't be comfortable to have those two things stuffed inside his head. This is the life I've saved—a guy who sees losing an eye as an opportunity for more efficient storage. I use my telekinesis to scoop the two spheres out of Five's eye socket and chuck them into the grass. He moans, but doesn't come to.

"That's nasty," Daniela says.

"No kidding," I reply. I look over at Agent Walker. She's been watching this whole scene in silence. I know she probably sided with Sam and thinks I should've let Five die. That's how I know I did the right thing. "Get me something to tie him up with," I say to Walker.

Having just watched me scoop out hidden treasures from Five's eye cavity, it takes Walker a moment to react to my request. She reaches behind her, unclips her handcuffs and tosses them to me.

I catch them and immediately toss them back. "You know that's a terrible idea, right? He turns into whatever he touches, Walker. Go get me some rope or something."

"I'm an FBI agent, John. I don't carry rope around with me."

"Check the boat," I say, shaking my head.

Annoyed that I'm giving her orders in front of the other agents, Walker sends Agent Murray jogging off to check if there's any rope on the coast guard boat.

"You're soft, Johnny."

I turn around to see that Nine's regained consciousness. He's sitting up with his forearms braced against his knees, his head hunched a bit like it's still bothering him. He looks from me to Five and back, shaking his head.

"You know how hard it was to shove that signpost through him?" Nine sighs.

I walk over and crouch in front of him. "You mad?"

Nine shrugs his burly shoulders, seeming oddly zen. "Whatever, dude. I'll just kill him again later."

"I really wish you wouldn't."

Nine rolls his eyes. "Yeah, yeah. All right, man. I get that you're against the death penalty and all that shit. Did he beg you to save his life, at least? I would've liked to have seen that."

"He didn't beg," I tell Nine. "In fact, I think he wanted to die."

"Sick," Nine replies.

"I didn't want to give him what he was after."

"Uh-huh. I know we usually lose when the bad guys get their way, John. But, man, I think this one was a win-win."

"I disagree."

Nine rolls his eyes, then looks towards Five. "We can never trust him, though. You know that, right?"

"I know that."

"And if it comes down to it, I'm not gonna hesitate to do it again. You won't be able to stop me."

"You must still be concussed," I say to him with a smile, deflecting the bluster. I gesture to his chest and arms, still covered in scrapes and blaster burns, and his broken hand. "You want me to finish healing all that?"

Nine nods. "Unless you only do work on murderers now," he replies.

While I heal Nine, Daniela comes over and introduces herself. She gets the usual Cheshire grin from the big idiot. We bring him up to speed on everything that happened while he was brawling across the city with Five. When I'm finished, Nine turns to look out at the water and the burning city beyond.

"We should've done better," he says quietly, shaking out his arms and legs, stretching his muscles. "Should've gotten him when we had the chance."

"I know," I reply. "It's all I've been thinking about."

"We'll have more chances," Nine says, then claps his hands and turns to Agent Walker. "So, you bringing us to Mexico or what, lady?"

Walker raises an eyebrow at Nine. Just then, Agent Murray returns, jogging back with his arms full of thick rope he must've freed from the boat. He hands it over to me and I proceed to tie up the still-unconscious Five, binding his wrists and ankles as tightly as possible. The cuffs of his jeans hitch up as I'm yanking closed the knots and I catch a glimpse of his scars. So similar to mine, identifying us as part of the same nearly extinct people. How did Five ever get to this point? And what happens next?

"What're we going to do with him?" Sam asks, reading my mind.

"Prison," I respond, realizing this is what I want only when I say it. "Just because I saved his life doesn't mean there won't be justice. We need a padded room for him, one where he can't touch anything remotely hard."

"That can be arranged," Walker says.

She makes this offer quickly. It makes me wonder if she and the government have already designed places like that for us, prisons capable of holding us in spite of our Legacies. Maybe that was something MogPro was working on.

"Arrange it after you figure out how to get us to Mexico," I tell her. "We're not waiting any longer, Walker."

"What does that mean?"

"It means that if the president or those generals or whoever the hell's in charge over there don't get us on a jet in the next ten minutes, we're just going to take one."

Walker snorts at this. "You can't fly a jet."

"Bet you somebody'll volunteer when I start breaking faces," Nine says, stepping forward to back my play.

Agent Murray unclips his own walkie-talkie from his belt and offers it to Walker.

"Just make the call, Karen," he sighs.

Walker gives Murray an icy look and produces her

own satellite phone and walks a few steps away from us. Despite our history, I'm pretty convinced that Walker really does want to help us. It's the rest of the government that isn't convinced we're a good bet to win this war. She's doing everything she can in the face of that. Our window to be of any help to Six, Sarah and the others is getting smaller and smaller, though. I can't stand around anymore hoping that these people will support us in our fight. We're going to save them, whether they want us to or not. That's all there is to it.

"You guys aren't really going to attack the army now, are you?" Daniela asks, keeping her voice low so the agents don't overhear.

"Shit, I can barely stand up," Nine replies quietly.

"We do need to get down there, though," Sam says, and I know he's thinking about Six as much as I'm thinking about Sarah. "If she can't help us, what're we going to do?"

Nine looks at me. "You'd actually go through with it, wouldn't you?"

"Yeah," I say. "If they won't help, we'll make them."

Daniela whistles through her teeth. "That's intense, man."

I look over at Walker. She's keeping her voice quiet, but is making a lot of emphatic hand gestures.

"She knows what's at stake. Walker will come through." As I say this, I produce my own satellite phone. I should check in with Sarah and Six, see where they're at and make sure they aren't going to try taking on Setrákus Ra by themselves.

Before I can hit the button to dial, there's a strange and loud whooshing sound from the water. We all turn in that direction just in time to see a large metallic cylinder fly out of the river. It soars high into the air, jets of water shooting off it as it spins towards the nearby docks. The thing is big—big enough that when it lands, with a shriek of crumpling metal, bricks go exploding outwards from the impact. I see the captain of our commandeered coast guard boat go diving overboard into the water to avoid the flying debris.

It's the submarine we saw in the harbor earlier.

"What—how is that possible?" Sam exclaims.

Something tossed the submarine right out of the water.

We run towards the docks to check for survivors, although it doesn't look good. The back half of the vessel is crumpled in like a crushed aluminum can and there are jagged trenches clawed in the sub's side paneling. We can see right through the walls as we get closer— the ship definitely took on water. Loose wires from the fried electrical systems spit sparks as we approach.

"Careful," I say. "Don't get too close."

"What the hell could've done this?" Nine asks, his hands braced on his knees as he catches his breath.

As if in answer, the captain of our boat screams. One minute he's treading water and waiting for us to tell him it's all clear, and the next there's a dark shadow growing underneath him. He's sucked beneath the waves with a sharp cry and swallowed whole by the beast that slowly rises from the depths of the Hudson River.

We all take a step back, then another. Two of the agents break off into sprints in the opposite direction, horrified by the size of the creature before us. Water flows off the monster's knobby skin, which is translucent to the point where I can see the black blood pumping through its power-line-sized veins. It is hairless, neckless and hunched. Crooked fangs protrude from its lower jaw and make it impossible for the thing to fully close its mouth, a steady stream of yellowish drool spilling forth. Gills the size of helicopter propellers spasm as the monster takes its first breath of air. It's on all fours, its hind legs bowed, its front legs more like thick gorilla arms, and already it's almost as tall as the Statue of Liberty.

The tough-girl attitude drops pretty quickly for Daniela. She screams and Nine has to clap a hand over her mouth. I don't blame her. The monster is terrifying and I've fought plenty of the Mogadorians' twisted creations before.

"Holy shit," Sam whispers. "It's a freaking tarrasque."

My head whips around to Sam in disbelief. "You've seen one of these before?"

"No, I—I—," he stammers. "It's a D&D thing."

"Nerd," Nine mumbles as he slowly backpedals.

Daniela shoves Nine's hand away, getting it together enough to glare at me. "You didn't tell me they have, uh—freaking *Mogasaurs*!"

This must've been what Setrákus Ra dropped into the water when the *Anubis* left this morning. One last gift for the decimated city of New York. A reminder for the military presence of who's really in charge. I let my Lumen course over my hands. I'll have to generate a lot of fire if I'm going to make a mark on this beast.

"I know you can see this thing!" Walker shouts into her satellite phone, probably blowing out the eardrum of whoever she was having a hushed conversation with just moments ago. "Air support! Get me some goddamn air strikes!"

The Mogasaur tilts its flat face towards the sky. The viscous membranes that I take to be nostrils start to twitch. Then it opens its eyes—each one milky white, arranged in a diamond pattern on the beast's broad forehead. It's hard to make out at this distance, but I could swear I see a glimmer of cobalt blue in each of those eyes. From the center of each eye, where the pupil would be, I can definitely see a ripple of bluish energy firing into the creature.

The color, the energy—it reminds me of our pendants. Could this be the result of what Setrákus Ra was doing when I glimpsed him on board the *Anubis*? But what does that mean? Besides being as big as a building, what can this monster do that the others we've faced can't? Are the stolen pendants powering it somehow? Or are they doing something else entirely?

Still standing just off the shore, the Mogasaur swings its head around and looks directly at us.

"Shit," Nine says, stepping back. "Is it coming this way?"

"Now!" Walker screams into the phone, backing up as well. "It's a goddamn giant!"

"I think it can sense us," I say. "I think—I think Setrákus Ra left this here to hunt us."

"Okay," Daniela replies. "I gotta go."

As if in answer, the Mogasaur lets out a deafening roar in our direction, spraying mist from the river and its rotten-fish breath all over us. Then, it lifts one of its front arms out of the river muck and brings it crashing down on the dock. Wooden beams explode in splinters and the concrete walkway caves in, two of the ferry boats pushed underwater like toys.

It's coming this way.

I lob a fireball at the Mogasaur. Quickly, I realize it's too small to do any damage. The fireball sizzles and leaves a scorch mark in the monster's hide, but it doesn't even notice.

"Run!" I shout. "Fan out! Use the statue as cover!"

Nine, Daniela, Walker and Murray all run back towards the grass and the statue. But Sam stays rooted in place, even as the Mogasaur takes another booming step towards us.

"Sam! Come on!" I shout, grabbing him by the arm.

"John? Do you feel that?"

I stare at Sam. Both of his eyes are changed—filled up with crackling energy. They look almost like two out-of-tune TVs, except the light Sam's eyes gives off is bright azure.

"Sam? What the he—?"

Before I can finish my question, Sam spasms once and collapses. I manage to catch him and try to drag him backwards. Daniela and Nine see this happen and stop in their tracks.

"Johnny, what's wrong with him?" Nine shouts.

"Grab him and run!" Daniela adds.

Boom. Another explosion behind us. The Mogasaur has gotten all its limbs out of the water, practically crushing the entire dock beneath it. The submarine is stuck like a thorn in the palm of its front hand, and the beast is temporarily distracted trying to shake it loose. I don't know what's wrong with Sam, but I don't think the gargantuan brute behind us is the cause. His affliction is something else entirely.

"He passed out!" I yell to Nine. "He—"

I'm cut off as both Daniela and Nine go all herky-jerky, their eyes filling with the same blue light. They slump to the ground at the same time, collapsing on top of each other.

"No!"

And then it happens to me.

A tentacle of vivid blue light rises up from the ground in front of me. For some reason, I'm not afraid. It's almost like I recognize this weird energy formation. I can sense that it runs deep into the earth, and I can also sense that if Agent Walker or the Mogasaur or someone without Legacies was to look where I'm staring right now, they'd see nothing but empty space. This is just for me.

It's my connection. My connection to Lorien.

Faster than my eye can follow, the finger of light attaches to my forehead. Right now, I'm sure my eyes are spilling electric energy just like the others did before they passed out.

I feel it happening. I'm leaving my body.

I recognize this sensation. It's exactly like when Ella pulled me into her vision.

"Ella?" I say, although I'm pretty sure this word doesn't actually come out of my mouth. I'm pretty sure that my body's currently prone on the docks, not all that far from the biggest monster I've ever seen in my life.

Hi, John, Ella replies inside my head. When she does, I can hear her saying other words as well, like she's holding down hundreds of conversations at once.

I don't think to ask how this is possible. Ella's supposed to be thousands of miles away with Setrákus Ra or, hopefully, in the process of getting rescued by Six. She's not this powerful. Her powers don't work like this. I don't think of any of that. I'm more focused on my physical body, not to mention Nine, Sam and Daniela. Whatever Ella's doing to us, she couldn't have picked a worse possible time.

"What the hell is happening? You're going to get us killed!"

Any second, I expect to hear the crunch of my bones as the Mogasaur steps on me. It doesn't come. Instead, shapes begin to form in front of my eyes—blurry, indistinct forms, like a movie projector that's out of focus.

Don't worry, Ella says, and again there's that echo of other voices. *This will only take a second.*

CHAPTER
EIGHTEEN

HOW LONG AM I KNOCKED OUT FOR? IT CAN'T be more than a couple of minutes before I'm awakened by icy pinpricks along the side of my face. It's Marina, pouring her healing Legacy into me. My head's in her lap. I get a strange pulling sensation at my hairline as the tissue there regrows, the gash I took from falling bricks quickly healed up.

Marina's got her non-healing hand clasped over my mouth, I guess in case I woke up screaming. I widen my eyes at her to show her that I'm with it and she takes her hand away. Her face is covered with chalky brown dust from the exploded temple. There are tear streaks running through the grime on Marina's face.

"He destroyed it, Six," she whispers raggedly. "He destroyed the whole thing." I sit up and assess our situation. We're still at the edge of the jungle, hidden behind the fallen tree trunk and now a whole bunch of dislodged chunks of limestone. There are gaps in the canopy above our heads from where the pieces of the Sanctuary came crashing down. Luckily, no one else appears injured, or else Marina already took care of them.

Marina stays next to me as I crawl forward to approach the others. Mark and Adam lie on their stomachs, side by side, just to the right of the fallen log. They've got their blasters pointed out and are using a block of stone for cover. I notice bloodstains on Mark's shirt and remember that he took a piece of shrapnel to the chest right before I got knocked out.

I touch his shoulder. "You okay?"

He shoots a grateful look in Marina's direction. "I'm good. Really don't want to make a habit of that, though. You?"

"Same."

Sarah is right up against the fallen log, peeking out from behind it. Phiri Dun-Ra is shoved in next to her. She wasn't crushed by any of the debris that landed in our area, which just seems unfair. The Mogadorian is still unconscious or, more likely, playing possum. I make sure to check her bonds quickly before sliding in next to Sarah. She gives me a look—tight-lipped, squinty-eyed. It reminds me a lot of John's brave face, actually. The one where he's scared shitless but wants to keep fighting anyway.

"What're we going to do, Six?" Sarah asks.

"Stay within arm's length in case we need to go

invisible," I say, not just to Sarah but to everyone. "We've still got a plan."

Mark snorts at that and his hands shake a little on his blaster's grip. He's got the detonator for our explosives in the dirt next to him.

"There's no Sanctuary to protect," Marina says forlornly.

"We can still take the *Anubis*," I reply. "And there's still Ella."

"Man, I can't see shit from back here," Mark adds.

I turn invisible so that I can poke my head out from behind the log without running any risk of being seen. I get a way better view of the landscape than what Mark and Adam can see from their spots behind cover. The dust from the *Anubis* attack is still settling in the clearing; between that and the sunset, the entire area is cast in a gritty golden haze. Three thick plumes of black smoke curl into the air—booby-trapped Skimmers that had their bombs explode when the *Anubis* discharged its fury. However, even though some of them are flipped over or knocked into distant areas, I still see a bunch of the Skimmers that we set to blow.

So we might still be able to salvage one of our traps to fight off the Mogadorians. But the pit we spent so much effort digging is gone. Or, more accurately, it has gotten a whole lot bigger.

The land where the Sanctuary sat for centuries is now

a smoking crater. It's about sixty feet deep with stubborn chunks of the temple's bricks still rooted in the ground and small fires from the *Anubis*'s cannon blast only now guttering out in the heat-baked dirt. That force field was in place precisely so something like this wouldn't happen. We made it into the Sanctuary and this is the result. Total destruction.

Unless . . .

Still invisible, I climb up onto the log so I can get a better angle on the crater. Sarah flinches at the noise I make and brings her blaster up in my direction.

"Relax, it's just me," I whisper quickly. "I'm trying to get a look at something."

"What do you see?" Marina asks.

I see a mellow blue glow that emanates from the very center of the crater. I see the stone lip of the well where we dropped our Inheritances, the place where the Entity emerged from.

I hop down from the tree trunk and turn visible again. I want Marina to see the hope in my face because it's very real.

"The well is still there," I tell her. "He didn't or maybe couldn't blow it up. The Entity is fine."

"Really?" Marina replies, wiping her hands across her face.

"Seriously," I say. "We've still got an extraterrestrial god to protect."

"Thing should be protecting us," grumbles Mark.

"What if he wasn't trying to blow it up, though?" Sarah wonders. "What if the whole point is to, like, get at it? What if he had to clear the temple away?"

"Shit," I reply, because that theory makes a lot of sense.

"They're coming down," Adam hisses in warning.

The *Anubis* slowly moves closer to the ground. Even with the temple destroyed, the massive warship is still too big to land in the clearing. All the same, the warship hovers so that it's centered right over the crater. Gears clank as two wide metal gangways extend from the sides of the *Anubis*, a couple of sliding doors opening at their tops. From there, ranks of Mogadorians begin exiting the ship. They look to be the usual breed of vatborn warriors, all of them dressed in black body armor and toting blasters. The Mogs exit the ship with speedy efficiency and begin securing the area. We're outnumbered at least ten to one and it won't be long until they either discover our position or find the bombs we've attached to the Skimmers.

"We have to attack now!" I whisper harshly to the others. I reach over and pull Adam close. "We'll go invisible and flank them. You guys detonate the bombs and get them distracted. Marina, are any of the guns we set up still in position?"

Marina narrows her eyes in concentration, then nods once. "Some. I'll make it work."

Mark sets aside his blaster and picks up the detonator, arming our explosives. Three-quarters of the bulbs don't light up at all, indicating that we lost those bombs in the *Anubis* attack.

"Ready," Mark says.

"Remember, if it goes bad, run for Lexa's ship," I remind them.

Adam, peeking out from behind the log, snaps his fingers at us. "There," he says grimly. "There they both are."

Setrákus Ra steps into view at the top of the ramp. He's as intimidating as I remember—nearly eight feet tall, pale, that thick purple scar on his neck visible even at this distance. He's clad in some kind of garish Mogadorian armor made of the same obsidian alloy as his minions', except his juts up into clusters of spikes along the shoulders and attaches to a fur-trimmed leather cape that runs all the way to the ground. He looks every bit the vain intergalactic warlord and he seems to relish it.

He holds hands with Ella, her small fingers clasped gently by his armored ones. Marina gasps when she sees her. I'm not sure I would even recognize Ella if she hadn't been screaming in my head just a few minutes ago. She looks smaller and thinner and paler, like the life has been sucked out of her. No, that's not quite right. She doesn't necessarily look sickly or diseased, I realize.

She looks Mogadorian.

Ella's eyes are empty and her head hangs so that her

chin is pressed against her chest. She doesn't look even remotely aware of her surroundings. Her movements are robotic and dazed. She follows Setrákus Ra onto the ramp with total compliance. The Mogs sweeping the area stop what they're doing to watch their ruler and his heir descend from the *Anubis*, all of them doing this lame fist-on-chest salute.

Setrákus Ra stops about halfway down the ramp. His eyes sweep across the jungle, searching for us.

"I know you're out there!" Setrákus Ra bellows, his voice carrying through the hushed jungled. "I'm glad! I want you to see what happens next!" Setrákus Ra shouts over his shoulder, into the *Anubis*. "Lower it!"

In response to his command, a trapdoor opens on the warship's underbelly. Slowly, a large piece of machinery telescopes out from the *Anubis*. It's like a length of pipe with support struts and scaffolding built around it. The pipe's sides are covered with complicated circuits and gauges. There's more than just Mogadorian tech to Setrákus Ra's steadily lowering device, though. Engraved into the metal sides between all the electronics are strange glyphs that remind me of the symbols scarred into our ankles. Also, and I can't be one hundred percent sure about this, but it looks like those engravings are done in Loralite. Whatever this device is, it looks to be as much a Loric-Mogadorian hybrid as Setrákus Ra.

"I don't like the look of that," I say quietly.

"Nope," Sarah replies.

"We should blow it up," Mark suggests.

"Whatever he intends to use that for, we can't let it happen," Marina agrees.

"All right. So we destroy his toy, rescue Ella and then either take the *Anubis* or hightail it back to Lexa," I say.

"You make it sound so easy," Adam replies.

Even though he can't see us, Setrákus Ra is still on his rant. "For centuries I've worked to harness the power of Lorien, to utilize it in ways more efficient than nature intended. Now, finally . . ."

Blah, blah, blah. Quickly, I gauge the distance between Ella and the nearest wired-to-explode Skimmer. Pretty far. I don't think she'll be in the blast radius. As Setrákus Ra drones on, I glance at the others.

"I've heard enough. What about the rest of you?"

Everyone nods. They're ready.

"Get low," I say, remembering how Mark got struck by shrapnel just a few minutes ago.

Everyone takes cover. This is it.

"Hit it," I say to Mark.

Fingers flying across the controller, Mark flips the detonation switches.

True, some of the Skimmers we wired to explode became disconnected from their fuses when the *Anubis* bombed the Sanctuary. And true, others already exploded during that impact. So we don't get the widespread destruction that we would've if our neatly arranged Skimmer-bombs had all detonated at once as planned.

But it's still pretty freaking effective.

The Mogs are too busy respectfully listening to Setrákus Ra's latest pompous douchebag speech to see it coming. Five Skimmers scattered around the crater explode in blossoms of white-hot fire. I can feel the heat from here and have to shield my eyes. At least thirty Mogs are dusted immediately, their bodies completely engulfed in the flames. More perish when the Skimmers' parts go flying in every direction. I watch one warrior get lopped in half vertically by a cartwheeling windshield and another crushed beneath a flaming seating column.

The best part is the panic. The Mogs don't know what just hit them and so they start firing towards the exploded ships, not certain where the real threat is actually hiding. At least a few go down as a result of friendly fire. And then Marina and I use our telekinesis to fire off some of the blasters we hid in the jungle, confusing them even more.

A twisted wheel strut smashes down on the ramp right in front of Setrákus Ra and Ella. Maybe it was a little reckless of us to blow those ships—I think Setrákus Ra had to deflect that wheel with his telekinesis to keep it from hitting him and Ella. However, it's good to know that he doesn't want to see Ella hurt any more than we do.

I grin. Setrákus Ra actually looks surprised by our

counterattack. His speech ruined, the Mog leader hurriedly walks the rest of the way down the ramp, dragging Ella along with him.

"Find them!" he screams as he starts down the rocky incline of the crater, heading for the Loric well. "Kill them!"

"Let's do this!" I yell, not loud enough to give away our position thanks to the crackling fires coming from the husks of the Skimmers, but loud enough to fire up my allies. It's do-or-die time.

I grab Adam's hand and we go invisible. I take the lead, bringing us in a wide arc around the Mogs that will eventually get us close to the crater and Setrákus Ra's device. Marina keeps up the distracting blaster fire, using guns hidden in different locations to keep the Mogs guessing. I memorized the locations where we hid our extra blasters, so I'm able to avoid the cross fire.

At least, I'm able to avoid it for about the first twenty yards. Then, dumb luck strikes. One of the Mogs, his back on fire from the Skimmer explosions, stumbles towards us, firing wildly. I dive out of the way and so does Adam.

But we dive in separate directions.

Just like that, Adam pops back into the visible world.

"Shit," he says, bringing his own blaster up and gunning down the nearest Mog.

"There!" shouts one of the other warriors.

So much for doing this guerrilla-style.

Seeing Adam in danger, Bernie Kosar is the first one to launch into battle. One second he's a toucan, innocently flying towards the nearest group of Mogadorians, and a blink of an eye later he's in the shape of a muscular lion, slashing and snapping his way through our enemies. A lot of the Mogs are still scrambling from the explosions and haven't even seen Adam yet, so Bernie Kosar easily gets the drop on them. He's faster and more ferocious than the last time I saw him fight, angrier maybe, and I remember that he nearly died back in Chicago. Whenever the Mogs do manage to draw a bead on him, Bernie Kosar shape-shifts into a smaller form—a bug or a bird—making himself an impossible target. Then, when he's in a better position to kill, Bernie Kosar turns back into his predator form. The transitions are so smooth, it's almost beautiful.

Our pet Chimæra has gotten really good at killing Mogs. And so have we.

A pair of Mogs to the left have managed to regroup enough to target Adam. They're easily picked off by blaster fire from our group's actual position. That must be Sarah and Mark, and they don't stop shooting when those first two Mogs are dusted. There are a lot of warriors caught out on the scorched earth of what used to be their runway. It's all empty space and no cover. I see Sarah put down two warriors in quick succession.

Marina runs out of the jungle to Adam's side and then

they're charging straight into the fray. Some of the Mogs are trying to retreat and regroup, but others see them coming. They square up and take aim. Pretty soon the air is buzzing with blaster fire in all directions. The odds are something like twenty to one.

Not bad.

Adam takes the lead, bounding forward with big strides, his every footfall sending shock waves rippling under the Mogadorians' feet. When the ground quakes it makes it nearly impossible for the Mogs to properly aim. Some of them go toppling into each other, blaster fire zig-zagging in every direction but straight. One particular seismic blast results in a loud rending noise as two sections of ground split apart, half a dozen Mogs plummeting into a deep crevasse.

I guess we got our pit trap after all.

Marina takes it a bit slower, but she's no less deadly. She heads towards the Mogs with both of her hands open and cupped at her sides. Spiked chunks of solid ice form above her hands and, when they grow to the size of base-balls, Marina sends them telekinetically sailing towards the Mogs. Screaming and off balance from one of Adam's tremors, one Mog comes charging at Marina with a dagger. She barely looks at him as she raises her hand in a *stop* ges-ture and flash-freezes his face. Marina cuts a frozen swath through the Mogs, making a beeline towards the crater and Setrákus Ra.

Across the battlefield, Setrákus Ra has made it to the bottom of the crater and the Loric well. Ella stands nearby, listless and zombielike, her head lolling from side to side. She looks on as Setrákus Ra guides by hand the ominous device that's attached to the *Anubis*. He positions the cylinder so it's just a few feet above the well. Then, Setrákus Ra steps back and raises his hands like a conductor, telekinetically maneuvering the complicated switches and dials embedded in the sides of the tube. With a hum I can hear all the way back here, the thing begins to power on. That can't be good.

"We have to stop him!" Marina yells.

I know her words are intended for me, but I don't reply. Still invisible, I don't want to give away my position. I wish I could use my weather Legacy and drop some lightning on Setrákus Ra. The *Anubis* is blocking too much of the sky. Instead, I pick up a dropped Mog blaster.

Lately, I've spent so much time maneuvering groups of invisible people through bayous and jungles that I'd almost forgotten how freeing it is to be alone and invisible. Freeing and deadly. I glide easily through the ranks of the Mogadorians. It's almost like a dance, except they don't know we're partnered up. As I go, I raise my invisible blaster and pull the trigger, close range, head shots only. All while moving closer to the crater and Setrákus Ra. The only thing that could give away my position is the brief flash of light from my blaster's muzzle, and that's usually quickly obscured by the exploding ash particles of Mog faces.

I've wiped out more than ten Mogs in no time at all. I take a moment to glance back towards the jungle to make sure Sarah and Mark are hanging in there. Sure enough, they're still shooting away. Bernie Kosar stayed back that way too, keeping any Mogs from getting too close to the humans' position. I realize Bernie Kosar is probably under strict orders from John to keep Sarah safe. That's good.

The Mogs are already beginning to thin out. Some are actually retreating towards the *Anubis*, while others have formed a loose perimeter around the crater to protect their Beloved Leader. Setrákus Ra doesn't seem at all concerned with any of this. He's completely focused on operating that machine of his.

As I fight my way towards the crater, the tube begins to emit a whooshing sound. I can feel the atmosphere around us change—loose rocks are lifted up from the ground, and I feel a vague sense of gravity pulling me towards the crater. Fully powered on, Setrákus Ra's device is starting to suck up the surroundings. I see Ella, still standing idly in the crater, still telepathically silent, her hair whipping towards the cylinder. The well itself begins to crumble, its bricks lifted loose and briefly hoisted towards the sucking machine before they're deflected by a force field that's probably similar to what protects the *Anubis*. This device of Setrákus Ra's isn't interested in the ground and debris;

it filters them away, creating a mini tornado of dirt and brick.

And then it happens. With an ear-piercing shriek like a thousand tea kettles exploding, the cobalt-blue Loric energy shoots up from the ground and is sucked into the cylinder. The entire area is cast in a flickering blue glow that causes even some of the Mogs to look around in wonderment. It's unnatural, the way the energy ripples up from the ground, at first wild and uncontained, but quickly caught and channeled through what I realize is a pipeline, transferring the Loric energy into the *Anubis*. I found the Entity's glow comforting and serene back in the Sanctuary, but now—the air crackles with electricity, the flashes hurt my eyes and the noise . . .

It's like the energy itself is screaming. It's in pain.

"Yes! Yes!" Setrákus Ra bellows with delight, like some kind of mad scientist, his hands raised in rapture towards the energy funnel.

Marina loses it. Caution goes out the window as she sprints towards the crater. Two thick and sharpened icicles manifest over her hands like swords and she uses them to impale three Mogs on her way, spinning through the ranks of the ones guarding the crater. Then, she's sliding down the rocky incline, towards Setrákus Ra and Ella. She's going to take him on by herself. I did that once—it didn't work out so well.

I sprint to catch up. There are other Mogs along the

edge of the crater besides the ones Marina just punched through and they've all turned to take aim on her. She's distracted, an easy target. But to me, still invisible, it's the Mogs that are easy targets. I run behind them in an arc around the crater's edge, dusting each of them as quickly as I can. Before I can kill him, one of them manages to squeeze off a shot that sizzles into the back of Marina's leg. I don't even think she notices.

In fact, Marina doesn't even notice Setrákus Ra. Or doesn't care. She attacks the pipeline directly, bombarding it with spiked orbs of ice. When those are either swallowed by the swirling dust and brick or deflected by the machine's force field, Marina charges forward. She's going to take the thing apart by hand if she has to.

Setrákus Ra catches her by the throat. He moves faster than a creature his size has any right to. As I sprint down the side of the crater, still invisible, Setrákus Ra lifts Marina by the neck so that her feet are dangling off the ground. She tries to kick at him, but he holds her out at a safe distance.

"Hello, girl," Setrákus Ra says, his tone happy and victorious. "Come to watch the show?"

Marina claws at his fingers. She obviously can't breathe. I'm not sure I'm going to make it in time.

From behind him, a wave of rocks and dirt hits Setrákus Ra in the back of the legs. He's surprised and bowled over, losing his grip on Marina as he falls forward and instinctively braces himself with his hands. Marina manages to roll away as Setrákus Ra's lower legs are buried by the rockslide. Ella lurches forward, like her own legs were hit, but she doesn't cry out and her vacant expression doesn't change.

It's Adam that made the save, skidding his way into the crater from the opposite direction as me. There are blaster burns on his shoulders and a long cut on the side of his face from where some Mog scored a hit with its dagger, but he still looks ready to fight.

I end up coming down in the crater right next to Ella. That's when it happens—*pop*—just like that, I'm visible again, and not of my own choosing. Setrákus Ra must be using his Legacy-canceling ability. Marina is on her knees a few yards from him, holding her throat and coughing. Meanwhile, the Mog leader is having a hell of a time dislodging himself from the landslide. At least Adam got him buried above the knees before our Legacies were turned off.

I take the opportunity to grab Ella by her shoulders. Up close, she's even further gone than I expected. Her cheeks are hollow, her face gaunt, and there are dark black veins running beneath her skin like spiderwebs. Her eyes are glazed over and she doesn't react at all when I shake her. The light from the Loric energy—still being sucked up through the pipeline—is reflected in her eyes. She's staring at it.

"Ella! Come on! We're getting you out of here!"

There's no visible reaction, but her voice finally returns to my mind.

Six. It's beautiful, isn't it?

She's lost it. Screw it—I'm going to drag her out of here just like we planned.

"Six!" Marina shouts, her voice raw. "We have to turn it off!"

I glance at the machine, then up at the *Anubis*. There's no telling what Setrákus Ra is going to do with the Loric energy he's capturing, but it obviously can't be good. I wonder if he'll be able to permanently take away our Legacies if he sucks up enough of the Entity's power.

"Do you know how to stop it?" I ask Ella, again getting right in her expressionless face.

This answer takes a moment. *Yes.*

"How? Tell us how!"

She doesn't respond.

With an indignant snarl, Setrákus Ra pulls one of his legs free of the rock slide. As he does, Adam reaches him. Stripped of his Legacy just like us, the younger Mogadorian has his father's sword drawn. The blade is almost too big for him and his arms shake when he holds it. Even so, he puts the tip of the blade right up against Setrákus Ra's throat.

"Stop," Adam commands. "Your time is over, old man. Turn off your machine or I'll kill you."

Setrákus Ra's face actually lights up, even though there's a sword pressed right against that purple scar of his. He laughs. "Adamus Sutekh," he exclaims. "I was hoping we'd have a chance to meet."

"Shut up," Adam warns. "Do what I said."

"Turn off the machine?" Setrákus Ra smiles. He finishes standing up. Adam has to stretch to keep the blade close to his throat. "But it's my greatest achievement. I've tapped into Lorien itself and bent it to my will. No longer shall we be bound by the arbitrary chains of fate. We can forge our own Legacies. You of all people should appreciate that."

"Stop talking."

"You shouldn't be threatening me, boy. You should be thanking me," Setrákus Ra continues, brushing dirt off his armored legs. "That Legacy you used to such great effect was given to you as a result of my research, you understand? The machine Dr. Anu plugged you into was powered by pure Loralite, the leftovers of what I mined on Lorien so long ago. With the body of a Garde that carried a lingering spark of Lorien herself, well . . . the transfer was made possible. You are the glorious result of my science, Adamus Sutekh. Of my control over Lorien. And today, you can help me to pave the way for others like you."

"No," Adam says, his voice nearly inaudible above the roaring energy being pumped upwards into the *Anubis*.

"No what?" Setrákus Ra asks. "What did you think,

boy? That your Legacies came from somewhere else? That this mindless flow of nature chose you? It was science, Adamus. Science, me and your father. We chose you."

"My father is dead!" Adam shouts, jabbing the sword harder into Setrákus Ra's neck. Next to me, Ella gasps. A bead of blood forms on her throat.

"Adam! Be careful!" I yell, taking a step towards him. Marina is on her feet too, glancing uncertainly between the energy pipeline and the two Mogadorians. They ignore us both.

"Hmm," Setrákus Ra replies. "I hadn't heard—"

"I killed him," Adam continues, yelling. "With this sword! Like I'll kill you!"

For a moment, Setrákus Ra seems genuinely taken aback. Then, he reaches up and takes hold of Adam's blade.

"You know what will happen if you try," Setrákus Ra says, and in demonstration he grips the blade tightly. I spin around to see Ella's body clench from the pain as a large gash opens up across her palm, blood dribbling into the dirt. She staggers forward a few steps towards the well, holding herself.

"I don't care. All my life, I was trained to kill them," Adam says through gritted teeth.

"And you could never do it, could you?" Setrákus Ra replies, laughing at Adam's bluff. "I read your father's reports, boy. I know all about you."

Still holding the sword in one hand, Setrákus Ra steps

closer to Adam, towering over the younger Mog. Adam's whole body shakes, but I'm not sure if it's in rage or fear. I inch closer to them, even though I don't know what to do. If Adam swings that sword, will I stop him? Marina draws closer too, her eyes wide. Behind me, I hear Ella's feet shuffling. In her trance state, she's stumbled closer to the Loric well and the surging pillar of energy.

"Ella!" I hiss. "Stay put!"

"I never wanted to kill for you because I never believed your bullshit!" Adam cries out. "But if doing this means ending you—" Adam's eyes dart briefly towards Ella. I see it happen—his eyes go steely with resolve. He's not bluffing, not anymore. "I can live with it," he says, coldly. "I can live with it if you die, too."

It all happens so fast. Adam thrusts the blade through Setrákus Ra's grip, the edge slicing harmlessly across his palm, the point aimed for his throat. Setrákus Ra looks surprised, but he reacts quickly—he's fast, faster than Adam expected. Setrákus Ra ducks to the left, the blade grinding against the side of his neck, not doing any damage. At least not to him.

I whip my head around to see the cut form on the side of Ella's neck. Blood spills down her shoulder and her body heaves, but she doesn't cry out. In fact, she doesn't even seem to notice. She's totally focused on the energy current, her small feet pigeon-toed as they shuffle a little closer.

Before Adam can bring his sword around for another

strike, Setrákus Ra smashes his fist into Adam's face. Setrákus Ra is wearing armored gloves and I can hear bones in Adam's face crunch from the impact. He drops the sword and staggers backwards. Setrákus Ra is about to hit him again when Marina charges in and tackles him out of the way.

With them both on the ground, I've got no choice but to step forward and put myself between them and Setrákus Ra. As I draw close, Setrákus Ra picks up Adam's sword, swinging it in a lazy arc at his side. He smiles at me.

"Hello, Six," he says, and cuts the air in front of him with the blade. "Are you ready for this all to be over?"

I don't respond. Talking just gives him an advantage, lets him get in our heads. Instead, I yell over my shoulder to Marina.

"Fall back!" I tell her. "Get back far enough to heal him!"

Out of the corner of my eye, I can see Marina holding Adam. He's knocked out, and I'm not even sure Marina wants to heal him after the stunt he just pulled. She definitely doesn't want to leave me behind, or retreat while Setrákus Ra's machine is still running.

"Go! I've got this!" I insist, staring down Setrákus Ra, dancing on the balls of my feet. I just have to stall him, stay alive, until—until what? How are we getting out of this one?

Ella was right. Staying meant death.

Setrákus Ra's smile doesn't fade. He knows we're up against the wall. He lunges at me, slashing towards my midsection. I leap back and feel the tip of the blade pass right in front of my abdomen. The rocky ground beneath my feet shifts and I almost stumble over.

Behind me, Marina's managed to drag Adam to where the crater starts going uphill. She stops there and shouts. "Ella! What—!"

Both Setrákus Ra and I turn towards the well, where Ella has climbed up onto the stone rim. She's just inches from the raging wave of Loric energy. Her hair flies out in every direction, almost like a halo. Electric sparks pop all around her, and the dark blood on her neck turns a shade of purple in the vivid blue light. The skin on her face and hands ripples like she's in a wind tunnel, and small debris buffets her. She ignores it all.

Immediately, Setrákus Ra forgets all about me. He takes a halting step towards Ella. "Get down from there!" he bellows. "What are you . . . ?!"

Ella turns in our direction, her eyes on Setrákus Ra. They aren't spaced out anymore. For a moment, I can see the old Ella in there. The shy girl we first met in Spain who blossomed into a brave fighter. Her voice is small, yet somehow amplified by the torrent of energy behind her.

"You don't get to win, Grandfather," she says. "Good-bye."

And then Ella falls backwards into the Loric energy.

Setrákus Ra screams and races forward, but he's too late. There's an almost blinding flash of light. Ella's body, basically a silhouette at this point, hovers in midair, caught between the Loric well and Setrákus Ra's machine. For a moment, her body twists and contorts, arching painfully. Then, a surge of energy flows up from the well, too much for Setrákus Ra's machine to handle. The circuits on its side explode in showers of sparks and the Loralite carvings melt in a searing burst of white-hot heat. Meanwhile, Ella's body seems to disintegrate—I can still see it there, caught up in the energy, but I can also see through it, like every particle in her body has come apart at once.

A moment later, Ella's body is spit out of the energy flow. She's thrown like a smoking rag doll to the side of the crater. Then, the glow from the Loric energy dissipates and retreats back underground, while Setrákus Ra's pipeline makes a metallic creaking noise and falls apart, twisted hunks of metal burying the Loric well.

Setrákus Ra stares at his ruined machine in disbelief. It's the first time I've ever seen the old bastard at a complete loss.

Marina's in motion immediately. She leaves Adam's body behind and dives towards Ella. Her Legacies are still turned off, so when Marina presses her hands to Ella's body, I know nothing will happen. She's too late, anyway.

I don't need to see the tears streaming down Marina's cheeks to know. Ella is dead.

Setrákus Ra stares at the body of his granddaughter, a desolate expression on his face. While he does that, I pick up the biggest chunk of rock I can find.

And then I crack it across the back of Setrákus Ra's head.

A cut opens. He bleeds. The Mogadorian charm is broken.

My attack brings him back to himself. Setrákus Ra roars, spins to face me and lifts the giant sword over his head.

He's about to bring it down on me when his eyes—normally empty black pits—fill with the blue glow of Loric energy. The sword falls from his grasp and Setrákus Ra, the leader of the Mogadorians, killer of my people, destroyer of worlds—faints right at my feet.

I'm stunned. I turn to look for Marina, but find her passed out too. What the hell is going on?

Ella. The glow of Loric energy emanates from her. It spills out of her eyes, mouth, ears—everywhere, just like when the Entity briefly animated Eight's corpse.

From one of her fingertips, a beam of Loric energy shoots towards me. It hits me right in the forehead. I sink down to my knees, feeling myself drift towards uncon-sciousness. I stare at Ella . . . or whatever she is now. There are other bursts of Loric energy zipping away from her body, flying away from her like shooting starts, out of the crater and off to . . . where? I don't know. I don't know what's happening with her, the Entity or any of it.

I just know that this is my chance.

"Not now!" I scream, fighting against the gentle sleep the Loric energy is trying to force upon me. "Ella! Lorien! Stop! I—I can kill him!"

But then I'm out. I'm pulled into the same artificial slumber as Setrákus Ra and Marina.

What I see next, what we all see, is where it all started.

CHAPTER NINETEEN

SO THIS IS WHAT IT'S LIKE TO BE DEAD.

I float above my body and hardly recognize myself. My grandfather—he'd started to turn me into a monster like himself. The broken girl down there, all pale and washed out, I can hardly believe that's me. Or was me. Marina puts her hands on my body, tries to bring me back even though her Legacies are turned off. It's sad to see her distraught like this.

I don't want to go back into that body. It's a relief being out. There's no more pain and for the first time in days I can actually think straight.

Actually, it's kind of weird that I can think at all considering I'm, you know . . . dead. I guess this is just what the afterlife is like.

Below me, the others—Marina, Six, Setrákus Ra—they all move in super-slow motion. I can see so much. Every particle of smashed temple still floating in the air is visible to me. The beads of cold sweat on the back of my grand-father's neck are visible to me. The pulsing glow of Loric energy inside all of them, even Setrákus Ra, that's visible to me too.

How can I see all this?

I only wanted to break Setrákus Ra's hold over me, to shatter his disgusting Mogadorian charm so that he couldn't hold me hostage anymore. I wanted to help my friends. Something told me the best way to do that was to throw myself into that swirl of energy. I figured I would die and I was almost okay with that. I'm glad it isn't just darkness and worms. Whatever this next stage is, though, I hope it isn't all watching people I love fight to the death in slow motion.

Ella.

The voice comes from all around me. Not one voice, many voices. Thousands of voices. Yet somehow, from that chorus, I can pick out ones that I recognize. Crayton. Ade-lina. Eight. They're calling to me.

You have work to do.

I fall towards the ground and my body. For a moment, I'm filled with panic. Am I going back inside my old skin to once again be puppeteered around by my grandfather? But then, suddenly, a feeling of calm washes over me, like I've been wrapped in a warm blanket. Nothing can hurt me, not now.

I should smack into the ground. Instead, I keep right

on going. I pass through the dirt and rocks, and soon I'm submerged in total darkness. It doesn't feel like I'm falling anymore. It feels like I'm floating through space—no gravity, no weight, just endless peaceful drifting. I lose track of which way is up, which way goes back to the world and my friends, my body. It doesn't seem important right now. I should probably be freaking out. Somehow, though, I know that I'm safe.

Slowly, light begins to shine around me. Thousands of bright blue pinpricks float around me, like the way dust motes drift through a beam of sun. It's just like the Loric energy I dove into. The particles expand and contract, reminding me of lungs. Sometimes they blend together into vague shapes, then quickly break apart.

Somehow, I get the feeling that I'm being watched.

There's a net of the energy beneath me and I no longer feel like I'm floating or falling. It's more like I'm being held, cupped in two giant hands. I feel relaxed and comfortable, like I could lounge here forever. It's so much different from the hell the last few days have been, where exerting any bit of my own will caused shooting pains throughout my body. Part of me wants to turn off my mind and just let whatever's happening to me stretch on forever. But another part of me knows my friends are still fighting back in the world of the living. I have to try to help.

"Hello?" I ask, testing if I can talk. I hear my voice, even though it doesn't feel like I have a mouth, lungs or a body anymore. It feels like it does when I have a telepathic conversation, like how some of my thoughts are louder than others and those are the ones I project to the other people.

Hello, Ella, a voice answers. The blobs of energy floating in front of me pulse in sync with the voice. Weirdly, I feel completely comfortable having a conversation with a bunch of neon fireflies.

"Am I dead?" I ask. "Is this, like, heaven or something?"

I feel a not unpleasant tickle against where my skin should be. I guess that's what it feels like when this thing laughs.

No, this is not heaven, child. And your death is only a temporary condition. When the time comes, I will restore you to your physical form. "Oh." I pause. "What if I don't want to go back?"

You will.

Don't be so sure, buddy, I think, but don't say.

"So . . . where's here? What is this?"

You abandoned your body and used your telepathic gifts to retreat into my mind. You merged your consciousness with mine. Did you even know you were capable of that, child?

"Um, no."

I did not think so. It was a dangerous thing to do, young Ella. My mind is vast and stretches across every where and every when that I have existed. I am shielding you from this knowledge, so as not to overwhelm you.

I guess that's why I feel so cozy in this total darkness, bodiless and cradled by pure Loric energy. Because the Loric Entity thingy is taking care of me.

"Thanks for that," I reply.

You are welcome.

It occurs to me that I should probably ask some important questions. It's not every day that you end up sharing a mind with a godly energy.

"What exactly are you, though?"

I am me. I am the source.

"Uh-huh. But what should I call you?"

There's a short pause before the voice answers me. The dots of energy never stop flitting around in front of me.

I have been called many things. Once, I was Lorien. Now, I am Earth. Your friends called me the Entity.

So, this is what was hidden under the Sanctuary, what Setrákus Ra was after. Marina and the others must have talked to it before its hiding place got blown to hell. The Entity, though . . . that seems all formal, alien and cold. That's not the feeling I'm getting now.

"I'm going to call you Legacy," I decide.

As you wish, child.

Legacy seems so calm. It was only a few minutes ago that the *Anubis* was sucking it out of the ground through a big mechanical straw.

"Did my grandfather hurt you when he pulled you out of the Earth?" I ask.

He cannot hurt me, he can only change me. Once changed, I am no longer me, and so the pain is not mine to experience.

"Okay," I reply, not following a bit of that. "Are you, like, trapped aboard the *Anubis* now?"

Only a small part of me, child. I exist in many places. Your grandfather has tried to harvest me before, but I am greater than he even knows. Come. I will show you.

Before I can even ask—*go where?*—a wave of Loric energy sweeps me away. I'm no longer floating along in the peaceful darkness. Instead, I'm inside Earth itself. It's like one of those cross-sections where you can see the different layers of Earth's crust—the tectonic plates, dinosaur bones, hot molten lava near the planet's core. I can visualize it all. I feel tiny in comparison.

Running through every layer of the Earth, intertwined with the core itself, are glowing veins of Loralite. The energy is thin in some places, stronger in others, but there's nowhere on the planet that isn't close to its gentle glow.

"Whoa," I say. "You really made yourself at home."

Yes, Legacy replies. *This is not all.*

We rise up. Once again, the battlefield appears beneath me. My friends and Setrákus Ra are still moving like they're stuck in molasses. Six is in the process of picking up a rock, hopefully to clobber my grandfather with.

In Six's chest, right over her heart, there's a glowing ember of Loric energy. Marina and Adam have it too.

So do I, although my ember looks a little weaker than theirs, probably on account of the whole dying thing. Even Setrákus Ra has a spark of Lorien in him, although his looks partially molded over by some black substance. He's corrupted himself in ways I don't understand. The thought makes me glance up towards the *Anubis*. There, housed in the ship's belly, is a throbbing glow of severed Loralite. It's nothing compared to what I just saw underground, but still . . .

"What is he going to do with it?" I ask Legacy. "I mean, with you?"

I will show you. First, you need to gather the others. I have decided they should all see why they fight.

"What others?"

All of them. I will assist you.

Without warning, my mind begins to stretch. It's like I'm using my telepathy, groping out for familiar minds, except my range is way extended. It actually doesn't feel so great, like my brain is being pulled in all directions by some really strong magnets.

"What . . . what are you doing?"

I am augmenting your abilities, child. It may be a bit uncomfortable at first. I apologize.

"What am I supposed to do?"

Gather up the ones I have marked.

Crazily enough, I actually know what this means. When I reach out with my telepathy, I can actually sense all the

Legacy-touched people out there. I aim for Marina's spar-
kly blue core, snatch it up with my telepathic hand and reel
her in. It's just like how I was able to pull John into my
visions except now it's so much easier. I snap up Adam too,
bringing them into the warmth of Legacy's consciousness.
Then, I hesitate.

"What about him?" I ask, gazing down upon my grandfather.

Even him. It must be all.

Feeling a little grossed out that I have to come into telepathic contact with that twisted brain and his spoiled Loric
heart, I pull in Setrákus Ra. I try to absorb Six next, but
her consciousness fights against mine. Distantly, I'm aware
of her physical body yelling something.

"What's she saying?" I ask Legacy.

She does not yet understand that I do not interfere,
Legacy intones. *All will see, or none. No advantage will
be given.*

I don't know what Legacy means and I don't have time
to think about it because as soon as Six's consciousness
gives way to mine, we're spreading out even farther.

The entire world unfolds before me. Hundreds of little Loralite embers dot the continents. These are the new
Garde, the humans only recently given powers. Legacy
wants them, too. I reach out with my mind, plucking them
up one by one.

A boy in London who stares up at a Mogadorian

warship, his hands clenching and unclenching as he tries to decide what to do. The gravel on the street hops and pops with his every motion, caught in his uncontrolled telekinesis.

A girl in Japan who just days ago was confined to a wheelchair. Now, she finds herself moving through her parents' small apartment with speed she didn't think possible.

A boy in a remote Nigerian village, where they haven't even heard about the invasion yet. His mother and father burst into tears as he floats above them, emanating an angelic glow.

I snatch all their minds up. Wherever Legacy is taking us, they're coming with.

Some of them are scared. Okay, a lot of them are scared. The Legacies were one thing but now this—a sudden, uninvited telepathic experience? I get that it's a little much. I talk to them. Comfort them. I find that my mind is strong enough that I can hold multiple conversations at once while still zipping across the telepathic plane.

I assure them that they're going to be okay. That it's like a dream. I don't tell them that I have no idea what I'm doing.

Then I get to New York. I snap up Sam first, mostly because I'm so excited he's been awarded a Legacy, I just want to hug him. That creep Five, handsome Nine who I would also very much like to hug, some new girl—they all get pulled into my telepathic embrace. And then I get to John. I've had more practice using my telepathy on him than anyone; it should be easy. But like Six, he struggles against me. That's when I notice the biggest and ugliest monster I've ever seen is looming over him and the others. John wants to fight. Or, well, he doesn't want to get stepped on. I can't say I blame him.

"Will this knock him out?" I ask Legacy. "Will he, like, get eaten?"

No. All will pass in the blink of an eye.

"Don't worry, John," I say triumphantly. "It'll only take a second."

I pull in John's consciousness, too. That's everyone. Every Garde on Earth. All their pulsing Loric heartbeats, pulled into my vast consciousness.

"So, what now?" I ask Legacy.

Watch.

CHAPTER
TWENTY

I'M SOMEWHERE ELSE. A PLACE THAT'S BOTH strange to me and familiar. I float through the air, able to see the entire scene around me, but not able to take any action. I can sense the hundreds of other minds along for the ride with me.

This is what Legacy wants to show us.

It is a warm summer night. Two vivid white moons hang in the cloudless dark purple sky, one in the north and one in the south. That means it's a special time for my people. Two weeks out of the year the moons are like that and for those two weeks the Loric would celebrate. That's where we are. Lorien.

I know this because Legacy knows this. What I don't know is how far back in time we've gone.

We're on a beach, the sand dyed flickering orange from the light of a dozen bonfires. There are people everywhere, eating and laughing, drinking and dancing. A band plays music like nothing I've ever heard on Earth. My gaze drifts towards a teenaged girl with a curly mane of auburn hair as she dances to the music, her hands thrown over her head, not a care in the world. Her dress shimmers and twirls, caught occasionally by the warm ocean breeze.

Down the beach, at the edge of the party, two teenaged boys sit in the sand, taking a break from the festivities. One is tall for his age with close-cropped dark hair and sharp features. The other, smaller but more handsome than the first guy, has a shaggy mop of dirty blond hair and a square jaw. The blond is dressed in a loose-fitting white button-down, untucked and casual. His friend is dressed more formally in a dark red shirt, ironed and perfect, the sleeves meticulously rolled up. The two of them, but the taller boy in particular, seem super interested in the dancing girl.

"You should just go for it," says the blond, elbowing his friend. "She likes you. Everyone knows it."

The dark-haired boy frowns, sifting a hand through the sand. "So what? What would be the point?"

"Uh, are you watching her dance? I can think of a lot of reasons, buddy."

"She isn't Garde. She's not like us. We wouldn't be able . . ." The dark-haired boy shakes his head gloomily. "Our worlds are too different."

"She doesn't seem to mind not being Garde," the blond boy counters. "She's having fun anyway. You're the one hung up on it."

"Why do we have Legacies while she doesn't? It doesn't seem fair, that some should be stuck being so . . . normal." The dark-haired boy turns to his friend, an earnest look on his face. "Do you ever think about that stuff?"

In answer, the blond boy holds out an open palm. In it, a tiny ball of fire comes to life and quickly shapes itself into the form of a dancing girl.

"Nope," he says, grinning.

The dark-haired boy concentrates for a moment and the little fire-dancer suddenly winks out of existence. The blond boy frowns.

"Stop it," he complains. "You know I hate when you do that."

The dark-haired boy smiles apologetically at his friend and turns his Legacies back on.

"Stupid Legacy," he says, shaking his head. "What good is something that only works against other Garde?"

The blond boy waves towards the dancer. "See? You're perfect for Celwe. She doesn't have any Legacies, and you've got the crappiest one there is."

The dark-haired boy laughs and punches his friend playfully in the shoulder. "You always know the right things to say."

"That's true," the blond replies, grinning. "You could learn a lot from me."

I don't have eyes in the traditional sense here, but the vision seems to *blink*. In that split second, the boys sitting on the beach appear as the men they'll grow into. The blond guy is handsome, athletic, with kind eyes—and I'm not paying any attention to him. Instead, I'm drawn to the hulking form seated beside him, deathly pale, with a ghastly scar around his neck.

Setrákus Ra.

This scene must be hundreds of years ago. Maybe more than a thousand. It's back before Setrákus Ra joined the Mogadorians, before he became a monster.

A split second later, they're teenagers again. The blond-haired boy pats young Setrákus Ra on the back as they continue to watch the girl dance. I'm shocked by how normal he seems, a young guy sitting on the beach, staring glumly at a girl he likes.

Where did it all go so wrong?

The vision melts away, blending seamlessly into another.

My grandfather and his friend stand in a giant domed room, a map of Lorien stenciled in glowing Loralite across the ceiling. They're not boys anymore, more like young men. How many years later is this? It could be decades with the way we Loric age. If they were human, I'd guess they were in their late twenties, but who knows what that translates to in Loric years. They stand in front of a huge round table that grows right out of the floor, like it's made from a tree no one bothered to cut down. Carved into the center of the table is the Loric symbol for "unity."

I know that because Legacy knows.

Around the table are ten chairs, all of them filled with very serious-looking Loric except for two that sit empty. Stadium seating like in a big movie theater surrounds the round table on all sides. It's packed today, every row at capacity, Garde squeezed in elbow to elbow.

This, I realize, is the chamber of the Elders. It's where the Elders gather in the presence of the Garde to make the big decisions. The whole scene reminds me of senate setups I've seen on Earth, except with a lot more glowing Lora-lite. Currently, all eyes are on a slender Elder with straight white hair and gentle eyes. Aside from the white hair, he doesn't look much older than my grandfather. But the way he carries himself projects an aura of seniority.

He is Loridas. He's an Aeternus, like me, which means he can appear a lot younger than he actually is. Everyone listens respectfully as he begins to speak.

"We gather here today to honor our fallen," Loridas says, his voice carrying through the entire chamber. "Our latest attempt to improve diplomatic relations with the Mogadorians was rebuffed. Violently. It appears the Mogadorians only accepted our delegation onto their world so that they could slaughter them. In the ensuing battle, our Garde were able to cripple their interstellar capabilities, which will keep them confined to their home world for some time. We still believe that there are those among the Mogadorians who value peace above war, but their society must reach this conclusion on its own. We Elders view further engagement with Mogadore to be detrimental to both our species and theirs. Therefore, all contact with Mogadore is forbidden until further notice."

Loridas pauses for a moment. He glances to the two empty chairs at the table and a frown deepens the lines on his face. He suddenly looks much, much older.

"We lost many brothers and sisters during this latest battle, including two Elders," Loridas continues. "Their given names, long ago set aside so that they might become Elders, were Zaniff and Banshevus. They served loyally on this council for many ages, shepherding our people through times of war and times of peace. We will reflect on them in the days to come. However, the chairs of Setrákus Ra and our leader, Pittacus Lore, must not sit empty. We move forward, as we Loric always do, and recognize that we did not only suffer losses on Mogadore. We also made heroes. Come forward, you two."

When Lordias commands it, my grandfather and his friend step up to the table. The blond guy allows himself a grim smile and nods to the many people gathered in the gallery. On the other hand, my grandfather, tall and gaunt as he'd be centuries later, seems hardly aware of what's going on. He looks haunted.

"Your quick action, bravery and powerful Legacies saved many lives on Mogadore," Loridas says. "We, the Elders, have long seen your potential and know well the great things you shall accomplish for our people. Thus, it is on this day that we offer you these empty seats and welcome you as Loric Elders, to serve and protect Lorien, its people and the peace. Do you accept this sacred duty and swear to place the needs of your people above all else?"

The blond man bows his head, knowing his part in the ceremony. "I accept," he says.

My grandfather, lost in his own thoughts, says nothing. After a moment of awkward silence, his friend nudges him.

"Yes," Setrákus Ra says, bowing as well. "I accept."

Years later, the blond man sprints down the hallway of a modest home. Broken glass crunches under his feet. The place is trashed. Tables are overturned, picture frames knocked off the walls, glass vases shattered into millions of pieces.

"Celwe?" he yells. "Are you all right?"

"In here," a woman's shaky voice responds.

He bursts through two bamboo double doors and into a brightly lit bedroom, the beautiful beach from before visible through the room's sprawling windows. This room is as wrecked as the rest of the house. The bed is flipped over completely, bookshelves are toppled and their contents scattered and even the floorboards themselves are uneven. It's like someone had a telekinetic tantrum in here.

Gazing out the window is the auburn-haired woman who many years ago danced away the night on the beach.

Celwe. Hugging herself, she doesn't turn around when the man enters the room.

"I met him right out there," Celwe says, motioning at the beach. "He was so shy at first. Always in his own head. Sometimes I'm still surprised he got up the nerve to marry me."

"What happened here?" he asks as he slowly approaches.

"We had an argument, Pittacus."

"You and Setrákus?"

Celwe snorts and spins to face him. My grandfather's childhood friend, the man who must have become the next Pittacus Lore. Her eyes are red-rimmed from crying but she seems unharmed otherwise. "Oh, don't call him that. That title has brought nothing but trouble."

"It's who he is now," Pittacus replies earnestly. "It's a great honor."

Her eyes narrow. "It was hard enough being married to a Garde. We used to talk about having children, you know. Now, after that trip to Mogadore, after becoming an Elder . . . I hardly see him. When I do, all he talks about is that project, his obsession."

Pittacus tilts his head. "What project?"

Celwe swallows, maybe realizing that she's said too much. She walks away from the window and goes to the bed. She begins to push the wooden frame away from the mattress so that she can flip the thing right side up but thinks better of it, instead looking to Pittacus.

"Help me out, would you?"

Pittacus uses his telekinesis to turn the bed over, straightening the covers at the same time. His eyes never leave Celwe.

"So easy for you," she mutters as she sits down on the newly made bed.

Pittacus sits down next to her. "What is Setrákus working on?"

She takes a deep breath. "It's a dig. Out in the mountains. I shouldn't—I don't know how exactly to explain it. What he does out there . . . he says he does it for me, Pittacus. Like it's a gift." Celwe's voice catches. There are tears in her eyes. "But I don't want it."

"I don't understand," Pittacus replies.

"You should see it for yourself," she says. "Don't . . . don't tell him I told you."

"Are you scared of him?" Pittacus asks, his voice low. "Has he hurt you?"

"He hasn't hurt me. And I'm only scared of what he might become." Celwe reaches out and grasps Pittacus's hand. "Just make him come home, Pittacus. Please. Make him see reason and bring my husband back to me."

"I will."

Pittacus streaks through the sky, flying, slicing through clouds. He dips through a mountain range and then shoots downwards into a deep chasm, like a bigger version of the

Grand Canyon. As he descends, walls the color of sandstone flecked with Loralite gems rising up on all sides, Pittacus notices an array of complicated machinery and heavy-duty construction gear below him. Someone's been digging deeper, as if this chasm wasn't already deep enough.

Pittacus's gaze turns, like mine, to the towering piece of machinery at the dig site's center. Twisted beams of steel augmented with blinking circuits and Loralite symbols— it's like a bulkier, less-refined version of the pipeline Setrákus Ra lowered from the *Anubis*.

So this is what Legacy meant when it said Setrákus Ra had pulled it apart before. This is where it all started, all these centuries ago. The beginning of my grandfather's descent into madness.

When Pittacus lands, a young Loric in a lab coat hustles forward to greet him. His skin is oddly pale for a Loric and he moves in a way that's almost robotic, as if his limbs are no longer quite in sync with his brain. Pittacus seems taken aback by his appearance, but it doesn't put him off his task.

"Where is Setrákus?" he asks.

"He's at the Liberator," the young Loric says, and points towards the giant pipeline. "Is he expecting you, Elder Lore?"

"It doesn't matter," Pittacus replies, and marches towards the so-called Liberator. The pale Loric gets out of his way, but Pittacus hesitates. He turns back to study the kid. "What has he been doing out here? What has he done to you?"

"I . . ." The guy hesitates, like he isn't supposed to say. But then, he holds out his hand, concentrates and levitates a handful of rocks with his telekinesis. It seems like a real strain for him.

Pittacus cocks his head, surprised. "You're Garde? Why don't I know you?"

"That's the thing," the guy replies, "I'm not Garde. I'm nobody."

During his weak telekinesis demonstration, black veins began to pop out on the Loric guy's forehead. Pittacus takes notice of these and reaches out to touch the young man's face. He flinches away.

"It's . . . it's a work in progress," the pale guy says. "I haven't had my augmentation today."

"Augmentation," Pittacus whispers under his breath, then strides purposefully towards the Liberator machine. He passes a handful of other assistants on his way there, all of them similarly pale and skittish. I can feel the anger building inside him, or maybe that's my own rage, or maybe it's both. We're witnessing something truly corrupt.

The Liberator is turned on. It emits the same grinding and shrieking as the pipeline Setrákus Ra lowered from the *Anubis*. There are lumps of Loralite dumped all around the dig site, like the crew here had to rip the bluish rocks out of the earth to get at the current beneath. Loric energy is pulled up from the ground and transferred into big, pill-shaped glass containers. Once in the containers, the energy goes through processing—it's zapped by high-frequency sound waves and blasted with subzero bursts of chemical-filled air, all until the energy somehow becomes solid matter. Then, it is churned by a roller covered in razor-sharp blades before passing through a series of filters.

The result is a black sludge that Setrákus is able to fill a test tube with. He's in the process of doing just that when Pittacus comes upon him.

"Setrákus!"

My grandfather looks up and actually smiles. He's proud. There are black veins running under his skin, too, and his dark hair has begun to thin out. Surprisingly, he's excited to see Pittacus and sets aside his twisted work to greet him.

"Old friend," Setrákus Ra says, approaching with open arms. "How long has it been? If I missed another meeting of the Elder council, tell Loridas I'm sorry but—"

By way of greeting, Pittacus grabs the front of Setrákus Ra's shirt and slams him into one of the Liberator's support beams. Although he's smaller than Setrákus, he manages to take the larger man by surprise.

"What is this, Setrákus? What have you done?"

"What do you mean? Unhand me, Pittacus."

Pittacus checks his temper. I really wish he wouldn't. He takes a deep breath, lets go of Setrákus and takes a step back.

"You're mining Lorien," Pittacus says, clearly trying to

wrap his mind around the dig site. "You're—what did you do to these people?"

"The volunteers? I helped them."

Pittacus shakes his head. "This is wrong, Setrákus. This looks . . . it looks like you've defiled our world."

Setrákus laughs. "Oh, don't be so dramatic. It only frightens you because you don't understand it."

"Explain it to me, then!" Pittacus yells, and small flames erupt from the corners of his eyes.

"Where to begin . . . ," Setrákus says, running a hand over his scalp. "We were together on Mogadore. You saw the hate the Mogs had for us. The savagery. What good could ever come of that place?"

"It will take time," Pittacus replies. "One day, the Mogadorians will choose peace. Loridas believes that, and so do I."

"But what if they don't? They endanger not just our way of life, but the entire galaxy. Why should we simply contain them and wait for their mind-set to improve when we could hasten their evolution? What if the Mogadorians we chose, the ones we see as peaceful and potential allies—what if we could give them Legacies? Make them Garde? Leaders among their people, capable of excising the warlike and dangerous? We could change the fate of an entire species, Pittacus."

"We aren't gods," Pittacus replies.

"Says who?"

A moment of silence follows. Pittacus takes a step away from his old friend.

"It's all I've thought about since we returned from Mogadore," Setrákus continues. "Not just the Mogadorians, either. Us. All of us. The Loric. Why are there Garde and Cêpan? We have peace, yes, but at what expense? A caste system where our leaders are decided by who is and isn't lucky enough to be born with Legacies? We Elders sit around a table that reads 'unity,' but how are we equal?"

"It is as Lorien wills it—"

Setrákus barks a bitter laugh. "Nature, fate, destiny. We are beyond these childish concepts, Pittacus. We control Lorien, not the other way around. You, me, everyone—we could choose our own fate, our own Legacies. My wife, she could—"

"Celwe would be disgusted by this and you know it," Pittacus counters. "She's worried about you."

"You . . . you spoke to her?"

"Yes. And I saw the mess you made of your home."

Setrákus Ra's eyebrows shoot up and his mouth hangs open, almost like he's been slapped. I half expect him to start shouting Pittacus down in the haughty tone he used so often with me on board the *Anubis*. I can see the arrogance that I know so well in his expression, but also something more. He isn't so far gone yet. Competing with my grandfather's delusions of grandeur is a healthy dose of shame.

"I . . . I lost my temper," Setrákus Ra says after a moment.

"You've lost a lot of things and stand to lose more if you don't stop this," Pittacus replies. "Maybe our world isn't perfect. Maybe we could do more, Setrákus. But this—this isn't the answer. You aren't helping anyone. You're making them sick and torturing our natural world."

Setrákus shakes his head. "No. It's not . . . this is *progress*, Pittacus. Sometimes, progress needs to be painful."

Pittacus's expression turns steely. He turns towards the Liberator and watches the steady flow of Loric energy wrestled free from the planet's core. He makes his decision quickly. Fire courses over his hands and arms.

"Go home to Celwe, Setrákus. Try to forget about this madness. I will . . . clean up what you've done here."

For a moment, Setrákus seems to consider this. I root for him, I really do. I wish he would realize that Pittacus is right, turn his back on his machinery and head home to my grandmother. But I already know how it all turns out.

My grandfather's expression darkens and the flames growing in intensity from Pittacus are suddenly extinguished. "I can't let you do that," he says.

The Elders' Chamber is empty now except for Pittacus and Loridas. The younger Garde slumps in his high-backed chair, his face bruised and his knuckles raw. The older Garde stands on the other side of the table, bent over a glowing object, working at whatever it is with his gnarled hands.

"I don't agree with their decision," Pittacus says.

"*Our* decision," Loridas corrects him, gently. "You had a vote. All nine of us did."

"Execution is too far. He doesn't deserve that."

"He was your friend," Loridas replies. "But he is not that man anymore. His experiments would corrupt our very way of life. They pervert everything that is pure about Lorien. It cannot be allowed to continue. He must be removed entirely. Erased from our history. Even his seat on the Elders shall not be filled, he has damaged it so. His malignance cannot be allowed to take root and spread."

"I heard all this when we convened, Loridas."

"If I bore you, then why are you still here?"

Pittacus sighs deeply. He looks down at his hands.

"We grew up together. You named us Elders together. We . . ." His voice trembles and he pauses to steady himself. "I want to be the one to do it."

Loridas locks eyes with Pittacus. Satisfied that the younger man is serious, he nods.

"I thought you might."

Loridas activates his Aeturnus, his features slowly smoothing out until he looks much younger. Pittacus watches this with a raised eyebrow.

"He took your Legacies the last time you met," Loridas says. "Beat you into retreat."

"It won't happen again," Pittacus replies, voice a growl.
"Show me."

Pittacus focuses on Loridas. A moment later, the skin
on Loridas's face turns saggy and wrinkled, his hairline
recedes drastically and his body withers within his cere-
monial Elder robe. He looks even older than before and I
quickly realize this is his true appearance. Somehow, Pittacus just took away his Legacy.

"Good," Loridas says, voice raspy. "Now give an old
man back his dignity."

With a wave of his hand, Pittacus restores Loridas's
Legacies. The Elder changes shape again, still old, but not
disconcertingly so.

"How many Legacies have you mastered with your
Ximic, Elder Lore?"

Pittacus rubs the back of his neck, looking modest.
"Dreynen makes seventy-four. Never bothered learning it
before. Didn't think I'd ever need to use it."

Dreynen, that's my Legacy, one of the few I share with
my grandfather, which lets us take away Legacies by touch
or by charging projectiles.

"Impressive," Loridas replies, turning his attention back
to the object spread out on the table before him. "Ximic is
the rarest of our Legacies, Pittacus. The ability to copy and
master any Legacy that you've observed. It is not a gift to
be taken lightly."

"My Cêpan used to give me lectures about that," Pittacus

replies. "I understand the responsibility that comes with power. I've tried to live my life with that in mind."

"Yes, and we are fortunate that Legacy found you and not someone else. Imagine, Pittacus, if your friend Setrákus found a way to duplicate your power. To make it his own. Or grant it to anyone he chose."

Pittacus grits his teeth. "I won't let that happen."

Loridas holds up the object he's been working on. It looks like a rope, except the braided material isn't similar to anything I've ever seen on Earth. It's thick and sturdy, about twenty feet long, and one end is knotted into a complex noose. The noose portion of the rope has been molded and hardened, one edge razor sharp. Loridas demonstrates tightening the noose and, when he does, the lethal edge makes a *shink* sound.

Pittacus makes a face. "A little old-fashioned, don't you think?"

"It has been centuries and you are young, but this is how we once punished treason. Sometimes, the old ways are best. It is made from the Voron tree, a plant almost as rare as you. The wounds caused by Voron cannot be healed by Legacies." Loridas motions Pittacus over. "Come. Let me borrow that Dreynen of yours."

Pittacus walks around the table and rests his hand on Loridas's shoulder. I can't see it happen but I can sense— *Legacy* can sense—that Pittacus uses a Legacy-transferring power just like Nine has, granting Loridas use of his

Dreynen. Loridas concentrates on the noose. It begins to emit a faint crimson glow, exactly like when I've charged an object with my leeching power.

"You will have this charged with Dreynen now, in case he takes your Legacies before you can take his," Loridas explains, carefully swinging the sharpened edge of the noose. "Collar him with this and—"

"I know how it works," Pittacus interrupts.

"It will be quick, Pittacus."

Pittacus takes the rope from Loridas, careful not to touch the charged noose. He clenches the rope tightly, his expression grim and determined.

"I know what I must do, Loridas."

And we—the ones watching him here in the future—we know that he screws up big time.

Setrákus crawls across the canyon floor, smeared with dirt and ash, his face and head covered in small cuts. In the background, a team of Garde commanding all kinds of different elements lay waste to his Liberator. The machine belches huge plumes of black smoke as it begins to collapse. The bodies of his assistants litter the ground. They weren't killed by the Garde, though. No, something sinister and black seeps from their pores even in death.

"I'm not the one who's crazy . . . ," Setrákus says, spitting blood into the dirt as he drags himself away from his dig site. He doesn't look back when his machine explodes, although a look of almost physical pain does cross his face. "The rest of you, all of you—you're the wrong ones. You don't understand progress."

Pittacus follows along behind Setrákus. The noose dangles from his hands. His strong jaw is set and determined, but his eyes are glistening.

"Please, Setrákus. Stop talking."

Setrákus knows that he can't escape, so he stops trying to crawl away. He rolls over onto his back, flat in the dirt, and looks up at Pittacus.

"How can I be wrong, Pittacus?" Setrákus asks breathlessly. "Lorien itself gave me the power to dominate other Garde, to strip their Legacies as I see fit. That's the planet's way of saying that it wants me in control."

Pittacus shakes his head and stands over his friend. "Listen to yourself. First you decry the way Lorien gives out its gifts at random, and now you claim that your Legacies are destiny. I'm not sure which thought I find more disturbing."

"We could rule together, Pittacus," Setrákus pleads. "Please. You are like a brother to me!"

Pittacus swallows hard. With his telekinesis, he loops the noose around Setrákus's throat. He crouches down so he's straddling his fellow Elder, his hand poised on the thick knot of rope that will tighten the noose.

"You went too far," Pittacus says. "I am sorry, Setrákus. But what you've done . . ."

Pittacus begins to tighten the noose. He should do this quickly, but he can't quite bring himself to end things, not yet. The sharpened edge bites into Setrákus's neck. My grandfather gasps at the pain, yet doesn't fight against it. There's a sudden knowledge in his eyes, a resignation. Setrákus leans back. The noose bites deeper into his flesh. He stares up at the sky.

"There will be two moons tonight," he says. "They'll dance on the beach like we used to, Pittacus."

Blood darkens the ground beneath my grandfather. He begins to weep, so he closes his eyes to hide this.

Pittacus can't go through with it. He pulls the noose from around Setrákus's throat, tosses it aside and stands up. He doesn't make eye contact with Setrákus. Instead, he peers off towards the Liberator and Setrákus's research area, watching as the entire place is put to the torch. He believes in his heart that this means it's over. He believes that Setrákus can come back from this, that he has realized the error in his ways. He still sees his old friend there, lying in the dirt. He doesn't know the monster he will become.

The Liberator is a long way off. No one back there notices when Pittacus uses telekinesis to drag one of Setrákus's already-dead assistants across the dirt towards them. While Setrákus watches, wide-eyed, Pittacus uses his Lumen to set the body on fire until all that remains is a charred and unrecognizable corpse. When it's done, Pittacus looks away.

"You are dead," Pittacus says. "Leave here. Never return. Maybe one day, you can find a way to heal what's been damaged, here and inside you. Until that day comes . . . good-bye, Setrákus."

Pittacus takes the burned body with him and leaves Setrákus there in the dirt. He stays perfectly still, letting his blood pool from the circular wound carved into his pale neck. Eventually, he wipes the tears out of his eyes.

Then, Setrákus smiles.

We linger in that canyon as the years begin to fly by. The ash from the battle is blown away, the scorch marks fading from sunlight. The remains of Setrákus Ra's machine erode, eaten away by the red dust and the winds that whip through the mountains.

Every year, when there are two moons in the sky, Pittacus Lore returns here. He stares at the wreckage of the Liberator and considers what he did. What he almost did. What he didn't do.

How many years go by like this? It's hard to tell. Pittacus never ages thanks to his Aeturnus.

And then, one day, as Pittacus stands in the very spot where he should've killed my grandfather, an ugly insectoid ship cuts across the sunset and zooms down towards him. It looks just like an older version of the Mogadorian Skimmers that I've seen so many times. As the ship lands in front of him, Pittacus lets flames curl over one hand, the other encased in a spiky ball of ice.

The ship opens and Celwe steps out. Unlike Pittacus, she has aged. Her once-auburn hair now gray, her face deeply lined. Pittacus's eyes widen when he sees her.

"Hello, Pittacus," she says, self-consciously tucking strands of hair behind her ears. "You haven't aged a day."

"Celwe," Pittacus breathes, at a loss for words. He takes her in his arms, she hugs him back and they linger for a long moment. Eventually, Pittacus speaks. "I never thought I'd see you again. When Setrákus Ra—when he—I didn't expect you to go into exile with him, Celwe."

"I was raised that we Loric mate for life," Celwe replies, not coldly.

Pittacus raises a skeptical eyebrow at this but says nothing. Instead, he looks past Celwe towards the old-model Skimmer. "That ship. Is it . . . ?"

"Mogadorian," Celwe replies simply.

"Is that where he's been hiding all these years? Where you've been living?"

Celwe nods. "What better place than one the Garde are forbidden to travel to?"

Pittacus shakes his head. "He should come back. It has been decades. The Elders have erased him from the histories, his name forgotten by everyone but us. I truly believe after all these years that his crimes could be forgiven."

"But the crimes have never stopped, Pittacus."

That's when he notices it. The telltale black veins

running along Celwe's neck. Pittacus takes a step back, his expression hardening.

"Why have you returned now, Celwe?"

In answer, Celwe turns back to her Skimmer. "Come here," she says and, a moment later, a timid girl, no more than three years old, peeks out from the Skimmer's entrance. She has Celwe's auburn hair and Setrákus Ra's stern features and suddenly I'm reminded of Crayton's letter. Setrákus Ra may call me his granddaughter, but I'm actually his great-granddaughter. There's no denying it now—not just because Legacy knows, but because I recognize myself in her—this child will grow up and give birth to Raylan, my father.

"This is Parrwyn," Celwe says. "My daughter."

Pittacus stares at the child. "She's beautiful, Celwe. But . . ." He looks at the elderly face before him. "I am sorry, but how is it possible?"

"I know I am old to be a mother," Celwe replies, a distant look in her eyes. "Fertility is Setrákus Ra's speciality now. Fertility and genetics, to help uplift the Mogadorians. They call him Beloved Leader." She scoffs at this, shaking her head. "Yet he wouldn't see his only child raised among them. So here we are."

Parrwyn creeps forward, hiding behind her mother's leg. Pittacus Lore crouches down, waves his hand over the canyon's lifeless rocks and causes a single blue flower to bloom from the sandstone. He plucks it and hands it to

Parrwyn. The girl smiles brightly.

"I will arrange for your protection here," Pittacus says to Celwe, not looking at her but her daughter. "You can live a normal life. Keep her safe. Do not tell her of . . . of *him*."

Celwe nods. "He will come back one day, Pittacus. You know that, right? Except it won't be like you imagine. He won't be seeking forgiveness."

Pittacus touches his throat, running a hand along the place where Setrákus Ra's scar is located.

"I will be ready for him," Pittacus says.

He wasn't.

The vision ends and the darkness returns. There are starbursts of Loric energy all around me. Once again, I'm floating through the warm space that is Legacy.

"What now?" I ask. "Why did you show us that?"

So you would know, its voice replies gently. *And so knowing, now you will meet.*

"Who will meet?"

All.

CHAPTER
TWENTY-ONE

I WAKE UP IN A LIBRARY, FACEDOWN ON A SOFT carpet, surrounded on all sides by comfortable lounge chairs. "Waking up" probably isn't the right term, actually. Everything has a fuzziness at the edges, even my own body. I can tell that I'm still in the dream state that Ella created, except I'm no longer in full-on spectator mode. I can move around and interact with the room, even though I don't know what the hell I'm supposed to do next.

I stand up and look around. The lighting here is mellow and the walls are covered in old leather-bound books, all of the titles written down the spines in Loric. Normally this would be the kind of place I wouldn't mind exploring, except that back in the real world there's one nasty Mogasaur bearing down on me and my friends. Ella assured me that we'd be okay. That doesn't mean I'm cool just sitting around some astral library waiting to see what will happen next.

"Man, somebody break out the violins for that cry-baby Pittacus Lore."

I turn around to find Nine standing in the middle of the room where there was nothing but empty space a moment ago. He nods at me.

"What're you talking about?"

"You saw that too, right? The Setrákus Ra life story?"

I nod. "Yeah. I saw it too."

Nine looks at me like I'm an idiot. "Dude should've killed Setrákus Ra when he had the chance instead of getting all mushy with it. Come on."

"I don't know," I reply quietly. "It's not easy holding someone else's life in your hands. He couldn't have known what would happen."

Nine snorts. "Whatever. I was shouting at him to kill that chump, but he wouldn't listen. Thanks for nothing, Pittacus."

In truth, I'm not at all ready to process that vision, especially not with Nine's commentary. I wish I could replay it back so I could take the time to really examine my home world as it was centuries ago. More than anything, I wish I could see more of Pittacus Lore using that Ximic Legacy. We'd heard stories about how powerful he was, about how he had all the Legacies. I guess that's how he did it. Seeing him use Ximic got me thinking about the time I developed my healing Legacy. It was in a desperate situation when I was trying to save Sarah's life that the Legacy manifested. What if it wasn't a healing Legacy that manifested at all? What if it was my Ximic kicking in when I really needed it, and I've just been unable to figure out how to harness it for anything but healing since?

I shake my head. It's foolish to hope for something like that. I can't will myself to stronger Legacies any more than Nine can will the past to change. We've got to win this war with what we've been given.

"What's done is done," I tell Nine, frowning. "All that matters is that we stop Setrákus Ra. That's the mission."

"Yeah. I'd also like to avoid getting eaten by that big-ass monster back in New York," Nine says, glancing around. He doesn't seem at all weirded out being here in this dream state. He's going with the flow. "Ugh, books. You think any of these talk about how to kill Godzilla back there?"

I look around too, but not at the books. I'm looking for an exit. This room we're in doesn't appear to have any doors. We're stuck here. Ella, the Loric Entity, whoever's doing this—they aren't done with us yet.

"I think we're in some kind of psychic waiting room," I say to Nine. "Not sure why."

"Cool," he replies, and flops down into one of the

lounge chairs. "Maybe they're going to show us another movie."

"What do you think happened to Sam and Daniela? I saw them pass out at the same time we did."

"Beats the hell out of me," Nine says.

"You'd think we would end up in the same place."

"Why?" Nine asks. "You think there's a lot of logic in operating some kind of shared telepathic hallucination?"

"No," I admit. "I guess not."

"So, you think Ella's doing all this, right? I'm picking up a total Ella vibe."

"Yeah," I say, nodding in agreement. Nine's right. I'm not sure how I know that we're in Ella's psychic projection, I just do. It's intuitive.

Nine whistles. "Damn, man. Girl got a serious power upgrade. I kinda feel like we're slacking off. I want to copy some Legacies like your boy Pittacus. Or at least get some sweet razor-edged lasso thing."

I sigh and shake my head, a little embarrassed to hear Nine say out loud what I was just thinking. I change the subject. "We need to find a way out of here."

Nine gives me a funny look, so I turn away and walk over to one of the bookcases. I start pulling books off the shelves, thinking that maybe I'll trigger some kind of secret passage. Nothing happens and Nine just laughs at me.

"We shouldn't be sitting around," I say, glaring at him.

"Dude, what else are we going to do? You know how hard I tried to murder young Setrákus Ra while we were watching that highlight reel? Pretty hard." Nine punches his hand into his open palm, then shrugs. "But, you know, I didn't have any arms or legs. We can't do anything right now. So let's just chill out. I've been brawling my ass off for days and even if this chair is just, like, a figment of my imagination, it's hella comfortable."

I give up pulling books off the wall and return to the center of the room. Ignoring Nine, I tilt my head back and shout at the ceiling. "Ella! Can you hear me?"

"You look so stupid right now," Nine says.

"I don't know why you're just sitting there," I say, staring at him. "Now is not the time to chill out."

"Now is exactly the time to chill out," Nine replies, glancing down at an imaginary watch. "We'll get back to almost dying as soon as Ella's showed us whatever weird prophetic crap she needs to."

"I agree with Nine."

I spin around at the voice to find Five standing a few feet away from me, newly manifested in our little lounge. He purses his lips and shrugs his beefy shoulders at me, like he's not that happy to see us either. Even in this dreamworld, Five is still missing one of his eyes. At least it's covered by a normal-looking eye patch here instead of the grungy pad of gauze he sports in the real world.

"What the hell are you doing he—?"

There's a guttural battle cry from behind me and then Nine is by me in a blur. He drops his shoulder and aims right for Five's gut. For some reason, Five doesn't expect to be attacked on sight and barely has time to brace himself before Nine is on him.

Except, Nine doesn't hit him. He passes right through Five and ends up sliding on his face into the pile of books I tossed off the shelves.

"Son of a bitch!" Nine growls.

"Huh," Five says, looking down at his chest, which sure looks solid enough to hit.

"There can be no violence here."

We all turn to look at the room's far wall, where a doorway just manifested. Standing there is a middle-aged man with a muscular build, his brown hair graying at the temples. He looks exactly the way I remember him.

"Henri?" I exclaim.

At the exact same time, Nine shouts, "Sandor? What the hell?"

Five doesn't say anything. He simply glares at the man in the doorway, his lips curled into a sneer.

Nine and I exchange a quick look. It only takes us a

second to realize that we're all seeing different people. If it's really Ella running this trippy dreamland, she must have plucked someone from our subconscious that we'd feel comfortable with. Except that doesn't really seem to have worked with Five. He keeps balling and relaxing his fists, like he might spring forward at any second. I can't help but smile looking at Henri, even though the moment is definitely bittersweet. "Are you . . . are you real?" I ask, feeling stupid asking this question.

"I'm as real as a memory, John," Henri replies. When he speaks, I see a glow inside his mouth of the same energy that Setrákus Ra was mining from Lorien. It's similar to the way Six described her group's encounter with a briefly reincarnated Eight. I don't think it's just Ella pulling off this telepathic masterpiece anymore. She's got some high-powered support.

"I'm sorry I got the penthouse blown up," Nine says. He pauses for a response, then says, "Yeah, it was totally Five's fault, you're right."

I glance first at Nine and then to Five, who still hasn't said anything but appears to be listening intently, and finally back to Henri. We can't see or hear each other's visitors, only our own.

"What are you . . . ?" I'm about to ask Henri what he's doing here, but I think better of it. Him being here actually makes as much sense as anything. There's a much more important question that needs answering. "What're *we* doing here?" I ask.

"You're here to meet the others," Henri replies, then turns around and walks through the open doorway that wasn't even there a second ago. He motions for us to follow.

"What others?"

"All of them," Henri says, and smiles at me in that same frustratingly knowing way that he used to. "Remember, John. You've only got one chance to make a good first impression. Better make it count."

I don't know what he's talking about, but I follow anyway. He's my Cêpan, after all. Even manifested here in this crazy dream state, he still feels like the real deal. I trust him. Nine heads to the door too, following a version of Sandor I can't see, chatting about the Chicago Bulls. Five begrudgingly follows a few steps behind, still silent.

When I get close to him, Henri puts a hand on my shoulder. He lowers his voice even though the others can't hear him, like he's letting me in on a secret.

"Start with the ones you've felt, John. Those will be easiest. Remember what it was like. Visualize."

I stare at Henri, not sure what the hell he's talking about. In response to my look, he flashes that knowing smile again. Holding back on me, making me work out the details myself. The Henri way. I know it makes me stronger and smarter in the long run, but man does it piss me off.

"I don't get what you're trying to tell me," I say.

Henri pats my shoulder, then starts down the hallway. "You will."

CHAPTER
TWENTY-TWO

I'M IN A BIT OF A DAZE, MOSTLY BECAUSE I'M being led down a long hallway by Katarina, my dead Cêpan. Marina and Adam lag a few steps behind me. We didn't have much to say to each other when we "woke up" in some lavish private library. All of us were either still stunned from what we'd just seen or else in a bit of shock from the vicious battle we were suddenly teleported out of. Anyway, it wasn't long until Katarina came to collect us.

Except, I don't think the others are seeing Katarina. Marina addressed the figure leading us as Adelina and Adam's been keeping his voice purposefully low so we can't hear what he's saying. They're both having separate conversations from me. It's like we're here together, but not really existing on the same wavelength.

Adam's expression has been clouded with guilt since we woke up here. Now, though, he gets a little ahead of me and Marina, moving closer to the figure that I identify as

Katarina. Marina and I exchange a look, both of us getting the urge to eavesdrop. We inch up behind Adam.

"Did I do the right thing?" he asks whatever form the Ella-Entity has taken for him.

I don't hear what response he gets. Whatever it tells him, all Adam does is shake his head.

"That doesn't change what I tried to do, One."

Ah. I know what he's asking about. Adam pretty much tried to kill Ella right before . . . well, right before she basically killed herself. I've got my own guilt about that considering I sure as hell didn't spring forward to stop him. I was planning to let the whole thing go, just chalk it up to being in the heat of battle. Apparently, Adam can't do that.

Neither can Marina. She grabs Adam by the elbow, turning him away from the shape-shifting Katarina-Entity so she can confront him. Knowing her, this anger's probably been stewing for a while now.

"What the hell was that back there?" she asks him. I almost expect Marina to start radiating her icy aura. I guess that doesn't happen here in Ella's headspace, though. Her wide-eyed death stare gets the point across.

"I know . . . ," Adam replies, hanging his head. "I lost control."

"You could've killed Ella," Marina snaps at him. "You *would* have!"

"He didn't, though . . . ," I say, trying to keep things

peaceable. They both ignore me.

"I don't expect you to understand this," Adam says, his voice soft. "I've never—I've never actually met Setrákus Ra before. But I've spent my entire life in his shadow, under his thumb, a prisoner to his words. When I got the chance to kill him, to free myself . . . I just couldn't help it."

"You don't think we want to kill him?" Marina asks incredulously. "He's been hunting us our entire lives. But we knew Ella would've died first so we . . . we stopped ourselves."

"I know," Adam replies, not even trying to defend himself. "And in that same moment I became the thing I've always hated. I'm going to have to live with that, Marina. I'm sorry it happened."

Marina runs a hand through her hair, not sure how to respond to that.

"I just . . . I just can't believe she's gone," Marina says after a moment. "I can't believe she did that to herself."

"I don't think Ella's gone," I tell Marina, waving a hand at the deep blue marble walls of the hallway surrounding us. "I think she's got something to do with our current situation, you know? I saw a bunch of Loric lightning bolts shoot out of Ella's body before we went under."

Marina smiles tightly, looking at me now instead of glaring at Adam. "I hope you're right, Six."

"The charm is broken, though. I tested it before we

came here," I tell them, remembering with no small amount of satisfaction how it felt to crack Setrákus Ra's head with a rock.

Marina pinches the bridge of her nose. It's a lot to take in, going from fighting Setrákus Ra to seeing him as a normal Loric to this.

"Is he . . . ? Could he be killing us right now?"

"No, he went down to whatever Ella did, too. We should make a plan, though, because I've got a feeling once this little trip down memory lane is over, we're going to be right back in the shit."

Adam frowns, looking embarrassed. "I'm in a bad way. I think he broke my whole face."

"I'll heal you," Marina says curtly. "I was about to do it anyway."

"Good, good," I say. "And then you guys can help me kill Setrákus Ra."

Adam and Marina both stare at me.

"What?" I ask. "You think we're ever going to get a better shot at him? We've got his troops on the run, he's hurt, it's three-on-one . . ."

"We don't have our Legacies," Marina says. "He drained them. I'm going to have to drag Adam out of the crater just to heal him."

Adam nods, studying me. I can tell he's not sure if I'm being crazy or if he thinks it's a good plan. Either way, I don't miss the admiration in that look. "It won't be three-on-one right away, Six. It'll be one-on-one."

"I don't care. I'm not wasting this chance," I tell them.
I look around at our surroundings, wishing that I could
figure out a way out of here. "As soon as this is finally
over, I'm going to end him."

Marina forgets about her anger with Adam long enough
to exchange a quick look with him. I guess I might sound
a little crazy. At this point, we've entirely stopped walking
down the hallway to have this discussion. Katarina, or
whoever or whatever has taken her form, notices our delay
and stops, clearing her throat impatiently.

"We don't have much time," she says in that same
stern tone she used to take when I really annoyed her.
"Let's go."

We start walking again. Marina gets close to me,
leaning her shoulder into mine.

"Let's just be careful, okay, Six?" she says quietly. "The
Sanctuary, maybe Ella . . . We've already lost a lot today."

I nod, not replying. Marina was the one who wanted to
stay behind and protect the Sanctuary from Setrákus Ra
in the first place. But now that we have a real chance to
kill him, she's getting gun-shy.

Eventually, the hallway opens up onto a domed room
with a large circular table that grows right out of the floor.
Katarina steps aside to let us enter and when I turn around
to check on her, she's disappeared.

The room is an exact replica of the Elders' Chamber

from the vision we all shared. The only difference is the glowing map that's drawn across the ceiling. Instead of Lorien, it depicts Earth. There are glowing dots on the map in places like Nevada, Stonehenge and India—the locations of the Loralite stones. The gallery is currently empty, but one of the nine seats around the table is already filled.

Lexa looks majorly uncomfortable sitting in one of the high-backed chairs. She drums her hands on the table, the woman obviously not sure what she's supposed to be doing. She looks relieved when we enter the room.

"I don't think I'm supposed to be here," Lexa says, rising to greet us.

"I've got the same feeling," Adam replies, staring at the huge Loric symbol in the table's center.

"I'm not Garde. I'd never even seen one of these meetings until that vision thing. You guys saw that too, right?"

We all nod.

"If you're here, it's for a reason," Marina says.

Lexa looks towards me. "I heard the explosions from the jungle. How's the fighting going?"

Adam touches a hand to his face where Setrákus Ra struck him, then wanders off towards one of the empty seats. I try to figure out the best way to tell Lexa about our current situation.

"We're surviving," I say eventually. "We pushed the Mogs back and I think we've got a real chance to get

Setrákus Ra. If we ever get out of here."

Lexa nods approvingly. "Hell yeah," she says. "I'm keeping the engines warm, though. In case you need to bail."

"We very well might," Marina says, giving me a look.

"You were the one that wanted to stay and fight in the first place, Marina. Now we've got to finish it."

"But don't you get it, Six? The knowledge—it's what we needed. We know what Setrákus Ra is after and we know how to stop him. We broke the charm. Ella wrecked his machine so he can't mine any more of the Entity. Just being here—" Marina gestures around the room. "This is a victory. Adam's hurt, Ella is . . . we don't know, and I'm sure Sarah, Mark and Bernie Kosar won't be able to cover us forever. Maybe retreating is the smart move. Ella did tell us we should run, after all. Run or . . ."

"Oh, now you want to listen to her," I reply, shaking my head. "Look, I don't know what you took away from that vision, but if I learned one thing it's that Pittacus Lore should've manned up and killed Setrákus Ra when he had the chance."

"Boom. See, Johnny? Six agrees with me."

John and Nine enter from a side passageway. In spite of everything, I can't help smiling when I see them. That smile falters quickly, though, when Five trudges in behind them. Marina tenses up immediately and takes a step towards him, but John puts himself between them, widening his eyes like now isn't the time. I put a hand on Marina's arm to keep her calm. To his credit, Five seems to realize that he's a really unwelcome presence. He lingers on the edge of the room, avoiding eye contact.

John and Nine rush over to us and we all hug. We quickly introduce them to Lexa, who John already heard about from Sarah.

"So, you're in the middle of fighting Setrákus Ra and we're about to be swallowed by a giant piken," Nine says, crossing his arms. "Some timing with this shit, huh?"

"How's Sarah?" John asks me.

"She's fine," I tell him, leaving out the part where I haven't actually laid eyes on her for the last few minutes. There's no reason to worry him. His girlfriend can handle herself. "She's gotten to be a pretty good shot."

John smiles and looks relieved. "What about Sam?" I ask him.

John shakes his head. "I don't know. He's got Legacies and I saw him pass out right before I did. He was definitely pulled into Ella's telepathic group chat. I'm not sure where he ended up, though."

"He'll be here in a second."

We all recognize the voice. Ella appears out of thin air, sitting in the same chair Loridas occupied in the vision. Her eyes are overflowing with crackling Loric energy. She rests her hands on the table in front of her and sparks flare out across its surface. Ella's hair floats out from her head, surrounded as she is by static electricity. We all stare at her, stunned to silence.

"Ella . . . ?" Marina is the first to speak. She steps towards Ella. "Are you okay?"

Ella flashes a quick smile, although she never looks in our direction. Her eyes remain focused on the empty space in front of her. Her demeanor reminds me of the Entity. It's like they're sharing a body now.

"I'm fine," Ella answers. There's a ringing quality to her voice, as if she's not the only one speaking, or there are snatches of other conversations coming through. "I can't hold this for much longer, though. We have to get a move on. Don't be scared by what's next."

"Scared of what?" John asks.

In answer, Setrákus Ra appears in the chair next to Ella, wearing the same ornate armor as when he attacked the Sanctuary. All of us flinch backwards. The Mogadorian leader doesn't notice us, though. He can't, on account of his head being covered in a black hood. Chains made from glowing blue Loralite are wrapped around Setrákus Ra's chest and shoulders. They keep him pinned to the chair, even though he struggles.

"What the hell?" Nine asks, taking a cautious step towards Setrákus Ra.

"Why is he here?" I ask Ella.

"I had to pull in everyone who's been touched by Legacy," Ella replies. "It was all or none."

"Legacy . . . you mean?"

"The Entity," she replies. "I gave it a name. It doesn't seem to mind."

Marina chuckles. That makes me smile too, actually. It sounds like the old Ella in there.

"Is this Legacy thing going to come out and introduce itself?" Nine asks. "I want to say what up and ask for new powers."

"It's here, Nine," Ella replies, and I think I see a corner of her mouth perk up in a smile. "It's in me. It is this room. It is all around us."

"Oh, okay," Nine replies.

"Can he hear us?" John asks, staring at the shrouded Setrákus Ra.

"No, but he knows something is happening," Ella says. "He's fighting me. Trying to break through. I'm not sure how long I can hold him. We better do what we're here for."

"What *are* we here for?" I ask.

"Everyone, sit down," Ella replies.

I look around to see if anyone thinks this is as nuts as I do. John and Marina immediately pull up chairs at the table, with Lexa and Adam quickly joining them. Nine catches my eye, flashes me a cock-eyed grin and shrugs like *what the hell*. He sits down next to John and I squeeze in between Marina and Ella. That leaves only one seat, the one next to Setrákus Ra. No one was eager to sit there.

Grudgingly, Five walks over from the room's edge and

sits down next to his former master. He looks like he'd rather be just about anywhere else right now and avoids making eye contact with any of us.

"Perfect," Nine sneers.

While everyone gets settled, I lean over and whisper to Ella. I can't keep my mind off my impending showdown with Setrákus Ra.

"Ella, you said run or die," I begin, not really sure how to approach clarifying a prophecy with my maybe-dead energy-riddled friend. "Is that . . . are those still our only options? If I fight Setrákus Ra will I—will any of us . . . ?"

Veins in Ella's forehead throb. "Six, I can't. I can't tell you what to do. It's all . . . it's all too uncertain."

"Now what?" John asks Ella, breaking up our conversation.

It takes her a moment to answer. There's clear strain on her face. She's concentrating hard on something.

"Now, I'm going to bring in the others."

"What others?" John asks.

In answer, there's a rush of noise from all around us. All of a sudden, it seems like we're in the middle of a crowded party. That's because the gallery surrounding the Elders table is now completely filled with people. They're all our age—some maybe a few years younger—and at first glance seem to come from all over the world. Many of them talk excitedly among themselves, some making introductions, others discussing the vision they just saw, analyzing the details of the Setrákus and Pittacus story. Others sit by themselves, looking nervous or afraid. A tanned boy with dark hair and a beaded necklace won't stop crying into his hands, even though he's being comforted by a pair of blond girls who look like they belong in a commercial for hot cocoa. The way they're acting, it's like these people have been sitting here the whole time and we're the ones who just teleported into view. I guess, from their perspective, that's exactly what happened.

Sam sits in the very first row, a surly-looking girl with a mess of braids sitting next to him. He looks right at me, smiles and mouths *hey*.

Then, the commotion really starts.

"Look!" screams a Japanese girl, and it takes me a second to realize she's pointing at us.

A murmur goes through the crowd as everyone notices us sitting around the table. At first, they all talk at once, peppering us with questions that I can't even distinguish. Slowly, the room goes quiet. A respectful silence eventually falls. These are the human Garde. I can only imagine how bat-shit insane this whole thing is for them.

And now, I realize, they're waiting for us to explain the situation.

I look around our table. Ella is still completely spaced out. Next to her, Setrákus Ra thrashes and struggles. Adam and Five both look like they're about to hide under the table. Even Marina is blushing and looking uncomfortable. Unlike the others, Nine grins, nodding to as many people in the crowd as he can.

"What up," he says. A few people in the audience snicker.

Obviously, one of us needs to say something more substantive than that.

John stands up, his chair scraping loudly against the marble floor. "It's the dude from YouTube," I hear someone whisper, and from the other side of the room someone else says, "It's John Smith." John looks at all the different faces, trying not to appear overwhelmed. I see Sam flash him a thumbs-up. John takes a deep breath, then hesitates. He turns to Ella.

"Do they all, uh, speak English?"

"I'm translating," Ella answers simply, her eyes glowing intensely.

I don't know when the hell she learned to do that. I'm not going to question it, though, and apparently neither is John.

"Hi," John says, holding up his hand. A few people in the crowd mutter greetings. "My name's John Smith. We're what's left of the Loric."

John walks around the table. He ends up standing right next to Setrákus Ra.

"I guess you probably saw what we saw, right? Well, that story ends with Setrákus Ra here coming back to our planet, Lorien, and massacring everyone on it. Everyone except for us." He lets this sink in for a moment before continuing. "If you aren't sure what that has to do with you, well, maybe you've noticed all the alien warships on the news? Setrákus Ra is here. He's going to do to Earth what he did to Lorien. Unless we stop him."

John tries to make eye contact with as many people in the audience as possible. He's really doing the whole leader thing pretty well.

"I don't mean *we* as in my, uh, friends here sitting around the table," John continues. "I mean you and us. Everyone in this room."

That gets the kids in the crowd murmuring. The crying Hawaiian kid has at least stopped sobbing long enough to listen, but now I see his eyes darting around for an exit.

"I know this seems crazy. It also probably doesn't seem fair," John continues. "A few days ago, you were leading normal lives. Now, without warning, there are aliens on your planet and you can move objects with your minds. Right? I mean . . . is there anyone here that *can't* do telekinesis yet?"

A few hands go up, including the crying boy's.

"Oh, wow," John says. "So you guys must be really confused. Try it when you get out of here. Just, uh . . . visualize something in your house moving through the air. Really focus on it. It'll work, I promise. You'll amaze yourself and probably freak out your parents." John thinks for a moment. "Has anyone developed any other powers, besides telekinesis? We call them Legacies, by the way. Anyone else . . . ?"

A guy in one of the middle rows stands up. He's stout with a shock of brown hair and he reminds me of a stuffed animal. When he speaks it's with a slight German accent.

"My name is Bertrand," he says, nervously looking around. "My family, we are beekeepers. Yesterday, I noticed, um, the bees . . . they talk to me. I thought I was going crazy but the swarm goes where I tell them to, so . . ."

"What a nerd," Nine whispers to me. "Beekeeper."

John claps his hands. "That's amazing, Bertrand. That's really quick to develop a Legacy. I promise the rest of you will get them too, and they won't all be talking to insects. We can train you how to use them. We have people that know, people with experience . . ." Here, John glances around the table. I guess we're all going to be Cêpan now. "Anyway, there's a reason you're getting these Legacies, especially now. In case you haven't figured it out yet . . . it's because you're supposed to help us defend the Earth."

That really gets the gallery talking. Some people actually cheer like they're ready to fight, but mostly they murmur uncertainly, talking among themselves.

"John . . . ," Ella says, her teeth now gritted. "Speed it up, please."

I glance at Setrákus Ra. His thrashing is getting more and more forceful.

John raises both his hands for quiet. "I'm not going to lie and say what I'm asking you to do isn't dangerous. It most definitely is. I'm asking you to leave your lives behind, to leave your families behind and join us in a fight that started in an entirely different galaxy."

Something about the way John says all this makes me think he's practiced it before. I notice he glances towards the girl sitting next to Sam. She smirks at him.

"I obviously can't make you join us. In a few minutes, you'll wake up from this little meeting back wherever you were before. Where it's safe, hopefully. And maybe those of us who do fight, maybe the armies of the world, all of us . . . maybe that will be enough. Maybe we can fight off the Mogadorians and save Earth. But if we fail, even if you stay on the sidelines for this battle . . . they *will* come for you. So, I'm asking you all, even though you don't know me, even though we've royally shaken up your lives— stand with us. Help us save the world."

"Hell yeah," Nine says, clapping for John. "You heard him, newbs. Quit being wimps and join the goddamn fight!"

The respectful silence that had mostly held during John's speech breaks when Nine opens his mouth, like we're in a press conference all of a sudden. There are shouted questions from every direction.

"Is that a Mogadorian at the table?"

"Go back to your galaxy, freaks!"

"How do I quit breaking stuff with my telekinesis?"

"I want to go home!"

"How can we stop them?"

"What's with your eye patch, bro?"

"Can that scary guy see us?"

"Why do they want to kill us?"

And then, rising above the cacophony, a lanky guy with a bleached-blond Mohawk in the style of some long-retired punk rocker stands up on his seat and stomps down hard. I guess the sturdiness of his combat boots translates to the dreamworld because the sound is loud enough to shut everyone up.

"You lot are in America, right, mate?" the punk asks John, speaking with a thick English accent. "Let's say I did want to join the fight and take it to these pasty wankers. How the hell am I supposed to get to you? In case you haven't noticed, there's no bloody transatlantic flights on account of the giant spacecrafts."

John rubs the back of his neck, uncertain. "I . . ."

Ella's hands tense on the table. "I can answer that," she says, her voice ringing and melodious, definitely not Ella. This is Legacy speaking through her.

Above us, dots of light on the world map steadily brighten. Everyone turns their attention to the ceiling. I remember the brightest ones as the locations of the Loralite stones we used to teleport, but there are more, dimmer lights taking shape all over the globe.

"These are the locations of Loralite stones," Ella says. "The brightest ones have existed on this planet for a very long time. The others are only now beginning to grow as I bond with the Earth. Soon, they will surface."

Marina speaks up. "We needed . . ." She falters, gathers herself. "We needed a teleporting Legacy to use those before."

"Not anymore. Not now that I have awoken," Legacy intones via Ella. "The Loralite are attuned to your Legacies. When you are close, you will feel their pull. All you need do is touch one of them and picture the location of another stone. The Loralite will do the rest."

"Is that Stonehenge?" the Brit asks, squinting up at the map. "All right, then. That's doable."

"Uh, I think one of those is in Somalia," says someone else.

"There will be more changes to your environment—," Ella continues, but cuts off suddenly, shaking violently. Her hands grip the table and actually melt into the wood, sparks hissing out from her. When she next speaks, it's with her own voice, not Legacy's.

"He's breaking through!" Ella screams.

The glowing chains binding Setrákus Ra to his seat shatter. The broken links clatter across the table yet harmlessly pass right through us. Ella must've lost her telepathic hold on Setrákus Ra's mute button. He's no longer isolated from the rest of us. In one fluid motion, the former Elder and current leader of the Mogadorians stands up, his chair toppling over behind him, and whips off his hood. People in the gallery scream and begin to scramble out of their benches, although there's nowhere for them to go.

First, Setrákus Ra rests a hand on Ella's shoulder. The light in her eyes flares, but otherwise she doesn't move. She maintains her focus. Not getting a reaction from his granddaughter, he turns to look at the closest Garde. That just happens to be Five. Setrákus Ra grins.

"Hello, boy. Would you like to be the first to kneel?"

Five recoils in terror, backing away from the table. The Garde are standing up now. I'm ready to charge but, next to me, Nine doesn't seem all that concerned.

"He can't do anything in here," Nine says to me. "Figured that out when I tried to beat Five's ass."

Setrákus Ra swings his gaze towards the human Garde in the audience. I know what he's doing. He's memorizing faces.

"He *can* do something," I say. "Don't let him see them, Ella! Get us out of here!"

"I don't know what they told you!" Setrákus Ra bellows at the audience. "I assure you, it is foolishness. If you saw what I saw, then you know how the Loric attempted to murder me for the crime of curiosity. Come! Swear allegiance to your Beloved Leader and I will show you how to truly harness your powers."

No one in the crowd rushes out to pledge their allegiance to the psychotic Mogadorian, but many of them look justifiably terrified.

"I'm releasing you," Ella says. "It'll happen quickly. Be ready."

And then, the light in her eyes goes dark. She slumps over. I hope that's not the last time I ever get to speak with her.

"Six . . ." It's John. He is standing right next to me. "We'll be in touch soon. Bring everyone back safe."

Then he and Nine abruptly wink out of existence.

The map on the ceiling begins to fade. The room starts to get dimmer. The vision is ending.

Many of the new Garde have already disappeared, returning to the real world. Sam and that girl next to him are already gone. There are still some left in the gallery, though, and Setrákus Ra zeroes in on them.

"I've seen your faces!" Setrákus Ra shouts at the humans, totally ignoring the rest of us. "I will hunt you! I will kill you! I will—"

Well, I'm not going to let this go on.

I hop up on the table, bound across it and put myself right in Setrákus Ra's face. He stops his rant, his black, empty eyes staring right into mine. I bounce from foot to foot like a prizefighter.

"Hey, fucker," I say. "When we wake up, I'm going to kill you."

"We'll see," Setrákus Ra replies.

I feel it start to happen. My body here becomes transparent. The details of the room become fuzzy. I can smell the smoke from the fires around the Sanctuary, can feel the dust on my skin. I need to move fast. I'm willing my muscles to snap to as soon as I'm able.

"Let's go!" I shout. "LET'S GO!"

It's time to end this.

CHAPTER
TWENTY-THREE

IT HAPPENS FAST. AS REAL AS THE DREAMWORLD felt, it didn't do justice to the physical weight of actually having a body. Shoved unceremoniously back where I belong, all the sensations hit me anew. The heat from the fires, the choking dust, my aching muscles. My knees go weak from the impact of it all. I was unconscious for a moment there and my body went limp as a result. I can't entirely stop myself from falling over.

I crash right into Setrákus Ra as he stumbles, too. The big bastard is as disoriented as I am. I hear a thump at my feet and realize Setrákus Ra has lost his grip on Adam's sword.

With a scream, I shove him away from me with as much force as I can muster. I scrape my hands on the overlapping metal plates of his armor.

Come on, Six. Come on!

I regain my balance before Setrákus Ra does. It only

gives me a second or two of advantage, but that's all I need. I somersault forward, grab Adam's sword and am swinging it for Setrákus Ra's head the instant I pop back to my feet.

At the last second, Setrákus Ra gets his forearm up. The blade sinks into his armor with a metallic shriek. Dark blood spurts out as I pull the sword back. I hoped to at least lop off his arm, but the armor was too strong and I've only cut him. Even so, Setrákus Ra's eyes are wide—I think he knows how close he came. He forces a smile, though, his balance regained, eyes locked onto mine.

"Too slow, girl," he growls. "Now let's see if you can really do what you promised."

I grit my teeth in response and swing with all my might. Setrákus Ra easily deflects the blade aside with one of his armored fists, avoiding the blade's edge this time, and then kicks me right in the stomach. The wind goes out of me and I'm knocked clear off my feet, landing hard in the dirt. I roll to the side immediately to dodge his follow-up stomp, which probably would've caved my whole face in.

The blade gets caught underneath me as I roll, making a shallow slice in my upper thigh. I never really trained with swords before, never saw the point. Definitely wish I had now. Without my Legacies, it's the only weapon I have against Setrákus Ra. He's stronger than me and just as fast. I'm starting to think that I should've listened to Marina.

Speaking of Marina, as I come back to my feet with a few yards between me and Setrákus Ra, I glance around for her. There she is—dragging Adam's unconscious body up the far side of the crater. As I watch, blaster fire bites into the dirt around her and she's forced to take cover behind a pile of limestone bricks right on the crater's lip. From the direction of the shooting, it seems like the Mogs have regrouped around the entrance ramp to the *Anubis*. The massive warship still hovers over us, its gunmetal underbelly our new sky.

I backpedal as Setrákus Ra comes at me, dodging a couple of big overhand strikes from his metal-plated fists. When I dance out of range of his strikes, he uses telekinesis to fling a few loose pieces of brick at me. I bat them away with my sword, hands sweating on the grip.

"Where is your bravado now, child?" he asks. "Why do you run?"

Let him go on thinking that I'm retreating. I mean, I *am* retreating. It's just not *all* that I'm doing. My real goal is to draw Setrákus Ra as far away from Marina's side of the crater as possible. Once she's out of his Legacy-canceling radius and can successfully heal Adam, we might be able to turn the tide.

As I duck under another rock, I see Marina cradle Adam's head and press her hands against his face. Her Legacies must be working! Now I just need to keep playing cat-and-mouse until—

Oof.

The backs of my feet hit an object and I fall over backwards. My landing is cushioned by something soft and it takes me a moment to realize that it's Ella's body I've tripped over. She's pale, completely still, and there's a coagulated trail of black ooze leaking from both her nostrils. She still looks very much dead. I don't have time to check for a pulse. Setrákus Ra stands right over me.

He actually pauses. Ella's body has thrown him off his game. I'm not good at reading that wrinkled face and empty black eyes, but if I had to guess I'd say Setrákus Ra is feeling some creepy mixture of remorse and disappointment. He cared about his granddaughter in the grossest way possible, wanting to turn her into a monster just like him. I hope it eats him up inside to know how badly he failed.

"She hated everything about you," I say, then bring the sword up point-first for Setrákus Ra's groin.

Setrákus Ra tries to pivot away. The blade grazes across the armored cup he's wearing, but then I get lucky. The sword's point grinds to the side, finds a gap in the armor plates and digs deep into the inside of his upper thigh. Setrákus Ra barks in pain as I gash him, viscous black blood spraying down his leg.

"You little bitch!" he bellows. In response, I grab a handful of dirt and sling it into his eyes.

I'm already on my feet, running again, looking for

more gaps in his armor. The spots are mostly around his joints to allow for flexibility—his elbows, his knees and of course, his head and scarred neck. That's where I have to aim for.

"This has gone on long enough!" Setrákus Ra yells, and I don't think he just means this fight right now. Hunting us for years has frustrated the old man, and now we're trying to thwart his carefully laid invasion plans. He's losing his temper. I can use that. It makes him fight stupid.

Setrákus Ra grows. In the space of a few seconds, he goes from an eight-foot-tall behemoth to a twenty-foot-tall giant who completely towers over me. The thing is, his armor grows with him, and that just makes those gaps at his joints look like bigger targets.

Now, I only have to avoid getting crushed to death. No big deal.

I can't run from him anymore. He can cover way too much ground. I turn to face him as he comes barreling in, trying to stay light on the balls of my feet. My plan is to dodge his strike, maybe run under his legs and slice out the back of his knees.

Setrákus Ra's fist is the size of a cinder block. It sails down at me. I'm not sure I can make this dodge.

I don't have to. At the last second, Setrákus Ra recoils and grabs at his face, howling in pain. A lion with the head of an eagle, razor-sharp claws and beautiful feathered wings just flew by and slashed the hell out of him. A griffin. A griffin just came to my rescue.

Bernie Kosar. God bless BK.

Setrákus Ra wheels around to face the Chimæra, who's a much closer match to him in size. Bernie Kosar roars and slashes at Setrákus Ra with his talons. Strong as he is, Setrákus Ra is stronger. He clenches BK's talon in one hand, then pulls him forward, wrestling him into a headlock. Bernie Kosar yelps, obviously in pain. With a feral yell, as much animal as Bernie Kosar if not more so, Setrákus Ra tries to snap the Chimæra's neck.

I don't let that happen. With all my might, I jam the sword into the soft tissue at the back of Setrákus Ra's knee. It slides in easily and he howls with pain, loses his grip on BK and stumbles forward. The sword gets yanked right out of my grasp. He kicks backwards and even though I try to dive out of the way, his big boot glances against my side. I can feel ribs break as a result.

"Get him, BK!" I scream as I land hard in the dirt.

Bernie Kosar's about to pounce when a sharp gasp from behind us catches our attention.

Ella sits up. She takes in another breath that sounds raw and painful. Her eyes are mostly back to normal, except there are still sparks of Loric energy popping out from the corners. That black goop continues to ooze from her nose and she spits some out of her mouth.

Setrákus Ra pulls the sword from the back of his leg like it's a thorn. The weapon looks comically small in his huge hand. He hurls it towards Bernie Kosar, propelling it with his telekinesis. BK manages to dart out of the way at the last second, but the blade still carves a bloody gash in his side. He's hurt and his powerful griffin form begins to revert back to normal. BK whips his head back and forth, snarling, fighting to maintain his form and stay in the battle.

"Granddaughter!" Setrákus Ra bellows, his voice thunderous in his huge form. He limps towards Ella. He actually sounds relieved. "I'm coming for you."

In response, Ella pukes more black soup into the dirt. She's out of it. However, whatever crap Setrákus Ra injected into her, it sure seems like her body is rejecting it now. I can't let him get hold of her again.

"Bernie Kosar!" I shout. "Get her out of here!"

The wounded Chimæra glances at me with his sharp eagle eyes, but doesn't hesitate. He swoops towards Ella just ahead of Setrákus Ra, gently scoops her up in his talons and flies her towards the jungle.

"No!" Setrákus Ra screams. "She's mine!"

Setrákus Ra gives chase. He pulls at Bernie Kosar with his telekinesis, managing to slow the Chimæra down. Setrákus Ra almost has him when a jackhammer-sized icicle flies down from the crater's rim, gouging the side of Setrákus Ra's face and ripping off a piece of his ear.

Marina. She stands at the crater's edge, already developing another wicked ice projectile to hurl at Setrákus

Ra. Next to her, Adam is on his feet. He stomps and a teeth-clattering wave of seismic energy rolls down the side of the crater, loose bricks and broken ship parts descending with it. If I wasn't already on the ground, the seismic blast would've put me there. Setrákus Ra, with his already wounded legs, goes down hard. Maybe it's just my imagination, but I think he shrinks a little bit when he's knocked off his feet. We've messed with his concentration enough that he's struggling to maintain all his Legacies. I try to use my telekinesis to fling some debris at him, but I'm still too close.

Blaster fire comes from the *Anubis* aimed at Marina and Adam, but it's answered in kind by Mark and Sarah as the two of them race along the edge of the crater. Between their cover fire and the broken rocks of the Sanctuary, we've actually inadvertently managed to cut Setrákus Ra off from the rest of his forces.

At a glance, I see Mark is bleeding from a cut on the top of his head and Sarah has some pretty nasty blaster burns up and down one arm. Otherwise, they look just fine.

They look better, in fact, than Setrákus Ra. His face slashed, ear missing, legs carved up. He struggles onto his knees.

We've got him. We've really got him.

Marina slings another icicle towards Setrákus Ra. He thrusts a fist forward and shatters it in midair.

"I am not dying at the hands of children," he rumbles.

But you know what? He doesn't sound so sure.

Sore as all hell and wheezing, I push myself back to my feet and sprint towards the opposite side of the crater from Marina and Adam. If we can stay separated then there's no way Setrákus Ra can catch us all in the radius of his Legacy-canceling field. We can bombard him from a distance.

Mark and Sarah see me coming, even though they're exchanging fire with the Mogs. They stop running along the edge of the crater about halfway between me and Marina and Adam's position. I see them exchange a few words, and then Sarah doubles back towards me while Mark presses on toward the others.

"You look like you could use a hand!" Sarah says, coming a few steps into the crater to help me the rest of the way up.

"Thanks. You all right?"

"Hanging in," she replies. I can tell she's trying not to look at the blistered burns on her arm.

I've got a much better visual of our situation from up here. The Mogs still holding position in front of the *Anubis* are surprisingly few. The others must have killed a whole lot of them while I was fighting Setrákus Ra. Even while I'm watching, Mark dusts one of them with a head shot. There's only a handful left.

Setrákus Ra doesn't have any reinforcements.

He isn't going down easy, though. The Mogadorian

overlord, still way oversized, clambers up the side of the crater towards Marina and Adam. With his wounded legs, he has to scramble up on his hands. Smartly, the others don't let him get close. Adam keeps unleashing seismic currents that cause Setrákus Ra to stumble backwards. Meanwhile, Marina alternates between freezing the ground beneath his feet and hurling chunks of ice at him. Setrákus Ra is able to absorb most of her volleys with his armor, but it has to be taking a toll. He isn't talking smack anymore. Instead, the Mogadorian leader is looking kind of desperate.

"You covering me?" I ask Sarah.

"You know it."

I nod and shout across the crater to Marina and Adam. "This is it! Throw everything you've got at him!"

I sense the ground shake as Adam amps up his earthquake and Marina redoubles her ice-chucking. Sarah and Mark keep firing steadily at the Mogs on the *Anubis*'s walkway, killing some and keeping the others at bay. I reach up, concentrating on the weather above, and start conjuring the biggest storm I can manage. The atmosphere around us gets heavy and humid as I pull the clouds low, even with the hovering *Anubis*. Pretty soon, the warship is wreathed in thickening fog.

"Whoa," I hear Sarah say. It's not every day you see storm clouds gathering so close to the ground.

Before I can finish, I hear a metallic tearing sound.

Setrákus Ra's given up on climbing out of the crater and getting at Marina and Adam. He was overconfident and bloodthirsty before. Now, he's acting smart. With his telekinesis, he tears what's left of his pipeline loose from the *Anubis*. The massive piece of machinery floats in the air for a second before he hurls it at the others.

"Look out!" Mark screams. He and Adam dive one way, Marina dives the other. The pipeline crashes to the ground in between them. None of them are hurt, but without them peppering him with Legacies, Setrákus Ra is able to start climbing out of the crater, his huge strides covering a lot of ground.

It's my turn to keep him down there.

I twist my hands through the air, conducting the weather. The wind picks up, whipping around debris and dirt. My face gets stung by little rocks and my eyes burn from the dust. I power through. I'm creating a tornado, right on top of Setrákus Ra.

"Die, you son of a—!"

My back explodes in pain. A blaster shot, right between the shoulder blades. I fall forward onto my hands and knees, almost tumbling into the crater. My concentration is shot along with me, the wind immediately beginning to die down.

"Six!" Sarah cries out. She grabs me around the waist and together we roll behind a pile of rubble, just ahead of more blaster fire.

The shooting didn't come from the *Anubis*. It came from the jungle.

"Protect the Beloved Leader!" screams Phiri Dun-Ra as she sprints into view, spraying blaster fire. She leads a small contingent of Mog warriors. They must have gone into the jungle, found and freed the trueborn and come around behind us. Seeing reinforcements, the Mogs on the *Anubis* get bolder. All of a sudden, we're caught in a cross fire. Sarah tries to shoot back, but the blaster fire is too intense. She hunkers down next to me.

"Six, what do we do?"

I poke my head out just in time to see Setrákus Ra reach the top of the crater. He's got Adam's sword again and is using it almost like a cane.

Marina is right in his path.

"Marina! Get out of there!" I scream. She can't hear me. I see it all play out.

Marina thrusts her hands forward, expecting ice to jut out in Setrákus Ra's direction. Nothing happens. Her Legacies are turned off. Setrákus Ra raises a hand in the air and, even though she struggles, Marina's plucked up from the ground. He's got her in his telekinesis.

"Oh God," Sarah says. "Oh no."

Setrákus Ra slams her down against the ground. Picks her up. Slams her down again. I watch as Marina's body goes limp. Each time, he raises her almost twenty feet in the air, then sends her plummeting back down to the hard ground. Over and over.

It's Mark who saves her. He darts around the smashed-up pipeline and shoots Setrákus Ra right in the side of the face, scorching the bloody hole where his ear used to be. The Mogadorian screams in rage and new pain, then returns fire by sending Marina's body hurtling in Mark's direction. They collide and both of them go crashing to the ground. Mark's still moving, though. He gets his arms around Marina and tries to pick her up.

Even at this distance, she looks broken.

I haven't felt a new scar burn into my ankle. Not yet. She's still alive.

Adam runs over to Mark and together they grab Marina's body. Dodging blaster fire, they retreat into the jungle.

Phiri Dun-Ra and the other Mogs have reached Setrákus Ra. They surround him on all sides, although he refuses any help, viciously caving in the skull of one Mog bold enough to touch him. They escort him up the ramp. He's almost back into the *Anubis*.

"Damn it, no," I hiss, forcing myself to stand up despite the searing pain across my back.

"Six!" Sarah grabs for me. "Stop! It's over!"

I don't accept that. We were so damn close. He can't just keep getting away like this.

I can still kill him. We can still win.

I step out from cover and throw my hands into the air,

making the wind kick up again. Bricks from the Sanctuary, twisted metal from the exploded Skimmers, sharp chunks of glass—all of it swirls together in a deadly funnel. Phiri and her Mogs shoot at me. I feel a blaster burn light up my thigh, another on my shoulder. It doesn't stop me.

"This is suicide!" Sarah yells in my ear. She's at my side, returning fire on the Mogs.

"Get back," I tell her. "Run for the jungle."

"I'm not leaving you!" she replies, again trying to grab me. I shrug her off.

Setrákus Ra reaches the top of the ramp. I scream and push forward with all my might, combining my weather Legacy with a wild burst of telekinesis, throwing everything my whipping winds have picked up at Setrákus Ra.

Two of the surviving Mogs get dusted immediately, smashed by my bombardment of debris. Phiri Dun-Ra shrinks back, shielding her face. But, in the doorway to the *Anubis*, Setrákus Ra stands tall. He turns towards me, stones and shrapnel bouncing off his armor, and pushes back. His own telekinesis slams up against mine.

Objects fly in every direction. From the corner of my eye, I see Sarah's blaster get ripped right out of her hands. The dislodged windshield of a Skimmer slices into the ground next to me like a guillotine blade. I'm hit—over and over again—by things I can't even identify. Still, I stand my ground, heels digging into the dirt. I keep pushing.

It happens.

A metal pole with a Loralite symbol carved into it, a piece of Setrákus Ra's destroyed pipeline, flies through the air. The end is sharp. Serrated.

It plunges right into Setrákus Ra's chest. I watch him double over, stumble back from the impact. I can see Phiri Dun-Ra scream.

The force from his telekinesis dies down. I feel him weaken.

I did it.

Tears stream down my cheeks.

I did it.

Phiri Dun-Ra and the others drag Setrákus Ra onto the *Anubis*. The door slams shut behind him. The ramp retracts.

I fall onto my knees. He's dead. He has to be dead. It has to have been worth it.

Sarah wraps her arms around me.

"Get up, Six," she says, her voice strained. She coughs, sucks in a breath. She's hurt. We both are. "We have to go!"

I place my hand on top of Sarah's and turn us invisible. This way, I don't have to see the blood.

So much blood. Too much.

I hope it was worth it.

CHAPTER
TWENTY-FOUR

I MADE A LOT OF PROMISES BACK IN THE Elders' Chamber. I told those new Garde that I'd lead them, that we'd help them train, that together we could save their world. It was pretty amazing, seeing them all there. Yeah, some of them looked scared, a few of them completely confused, and a couple even appeared downright angry to be roped into this. But most of the others . . . they looked ready. Nervous, yeah, but ready and willing to step up and join the fight.

Now, to keep those promises, I just have to survive one seriously pissed-off Mogasaur.

The second that I'm back in my body, I feel a hot gust of the beast's stinky breath as it roars. It's right behind us. I've still got an arm around Sam from when I grabbed him before we all briefly fainted. He's got his wits back too, so we stumble against each other but manage to get it together and run.

"Nice speech!" Sam shouts in my ear. "Are we going to die now?"

"Hell no," I reply.

The gathering of the Garde isn't the only thing that stuck with me from Ella's dream space. I'm still dwelling on watching Pittacus Lore in action. Ximic, that's what Loridas called Pittacus Lore's copycat Legacy. And then there was my brief meeting with Henri.

Visualize, he said. *Visualize and remember.*

Agent Walker pauses from screaming into her satellite phone to eyeball us. She seems just as confused by our awakening as she must have been with our sudden collapse a couple of seconds ago.

"What the hell's happening?" she yells.

"Don't worry about it! Get your people to cover!" I yell, waving my arms.

"How are we supposed to fight that thing?" Sam asks, glancing over his shoulder.

"I don't know," I reply grimly.

"We hit it a lot," Nine barks.

Walker and most of the agents use the Statue of Liberty for cover. I'm not sure how much good that's going to do considering the Mogasaur is almost as large as the statue. One of the agents, I didn't catch his name, trips up in his panic as the behemoth bounds forward. It moves like a gorilla, keeping its weight on its front fists, its clawed back feet churning up furrows of cement as they scrabble for purchase. Lucky for us, the newborn monster is still getting used to walking.

That doesn't save the fallen agent, though. I try to yank him backwards with my telekinesis, but I'm not quick enough. The Mogasaur brings one of its closed fists down and crushes the poor guy. I don't even think the beast notices. Its eyes, each of them dotted with what I'm sure is a stolen Loric pendant, are locked onto us.

It's only a matter of time before it catches us. Suddenly, I find myself thinking about the first night I met Six, back in Paradise. It was also the first time I'd taken on a piken, although it wasn't anywhere near as big as this behemoth. Six used her invisibility to get us out of a lot of jams that night. I remember the way she grabbed my hand. I remember the dizzying feeling of being able to see through my own body.

Remember. Visualize.

"John?" Sam screams as we run. "JOHN?"

"What's wrong?" I yell back, head on a swivel.

"You—" He's staring at me and almost trips over his own feet. "You just disappeared."

I didn't disappear, I realize. I turned invisible.

"Holy shit, I can do it," I say out loud.

"Do what?" Nine asks.

I don't answer. My mind races. I just used Six's invisibility Legacy, if only briefly. It just clicked, like remembering a name that you thought you'd forgotten. I could make us invisible. We could escape. But that would mean abandoning Walker and her people.

All this power, right at my fingertips, always just out of reach. And now—what can I do with it? I need time to practice, to figure things out, to train.

What Legacies can I crack in the next couple of minutes that will help us defeat this monster?

Agent Walker and her group empty their guns into the beast. The bullets are all swallowed by the thing's thick hide, no more effective than my fireball was earlier. Nothing but a swarm of gnats to the Mogasaur. It ignores the agents completely, coming for us.

"Come on!" I yell. "Bring it towards the lawn!" We'll have more space to fight it there and, considering how clumsy the monster seems, it's probably best if we keep it moving. Hopefully, I can figure something out while it chases us.

"Oh man, I don't feel so hot," Daniela says. Normally a graceful and fast runner, Daniela stumbles over her own feet as we sprint towards the lawn. I grab her by the arm and drag her along. "Something happened to me in that vision shit. My head is pounding."

Chunks of cement erupt from the Mogasaur's latest forward step and pelt my shoulders.

"I'm gonna try something, Johnny!" Nine says, and breaks off from us.

"Do your thing," I say, trusting Nine not to get himself killed.

Nine sprints to the edge of the plaza, where there's a row of metal binoculars on poles stuck into the ground, the things meant for tourists to admire the view of Manhattan. He rips two of these out of the ground, holding one in each hand like clubs. Then, he charges right towards the monster. His super speed kicks in and he's a blur streaking across the plaza.

I could use that. I try to focus on Nine, imagine the way his muscles work overtime, how he builds up that speed with his Legacy. But nothing clicks.

The lumbering creature actually seems confused when Nine runs right at it. The thing hesitates, trying to decide whether to go straight at Nine or to keep chasing the rest of us. Then, maybe reasoning in its tiny brain that it's easier to stay stationary, the Mogasaur lets out a welcoming shriek in Nine's direction. It raises up one of its giant hands, preparing to swat Nine as soon as he gets close.

"Does he know what he's doing?" Sam asks.

"Does he ever?" I reply.

We reach the edge of the lawn across from the Statue of Liberty. At that point, Daniela straight up falls to her knees, unable to go any farther.

"Oh man, my head's going to explode," she moans. She curls up into a ball and massages her eyes with the heels of her hands.

"What's wrong with her?" Sam asks me.

"I don't know!"

Our eyes meet and we both realize something at the same time. Together, Sam and I turn towards Daniela.

"She's getting a new Legacy!" Sam says.

I crouch down next to her. "Whatever's happening to you, Daniela—let it happen! Let it out and—" I'm cut off as the Mogasaur swipes at Nine.

The impact is massive. The beast leaves a six-foot-deep hand-shaped indentation in the plaza's concrete. At first, I think there's no way Nine could've survived that. But then I see him, using his antigravity Legacy to run right up the muscled, black-veined forearm of the Mogasaur.

The monster roars, enraged, and swats at Nine with its other hand. Nine runs along to the underside of the creature's forearm at just the right moment, avoiding the impact. He's fast and he's stuck to the Mogasaur, moving farther and farther up his arm like an annoying little bug. I'm not sure what he's going to do when he gets to the beast's head. If I had to guess, I'd bet Nine doesn't know yet either.

"John!" someone shouts from behind me. "John! Release me!"

I turn around to see Five struggling across the grass on his knees. We'd left him there all tied up with the ropes we got from the coast guard boat. He doesn't have his blade weapon or his ball bearing to change his skin to metal, so Five's about as harmless as he'll ever be.

"Oh, hell no," Sam says, glancing at Five.

"I know what that thing is," Five says, reaching us. He sits back on his knees, his hands bound in front of him, and looks up at me. "I know how to kill it. I can help you."

"Tell me," I say.

"Setrákus Ra calls it the Hunter," Five says quickly. "He was building it while I was still on board the *Anubis*. It has Loric pendants in its eyes and can use them to sense the location of any Garde. There's no retreat, we *have* to kill it."

As Five speaks, Nine reaches the crux of the Hunter's shoulder. The beast gives up on trying to swat him off. Now, it tilts its spiny head over and tries to swallow Nine whole. Nine responds by jabbing the broken end of one of the metal poles straight up into the roof of the monster's mouth. The creature whips its head away and howls.

Next to me, Daniela moans. Sam kneels down next to her and rubs her back. "Come on, uh, do what John said," Sam tries, but Daniela's only response is to groan. He looks up at me. "We need to figure something out! If you guys have some new badass powers, now is the time to use them!"

"He needs to go for the eyes, John," Five insists,

ignoring everything but me. "Let me free. I can help you."

"Why the hell should I trust you?" I ask.

Five's expression darkens. I see him strain against his bonds, testing them. He looks up at me, and I can tell he's making a concerted effort to control his anger.

"Because I could break out of these if I really wanted to," Five answers me. "But I won't. You saved my life, John, and no matter what you think, I'm not like *him*."

I know exactly what Five's talking about. Setrákus Ra and Pittacus Lore. Mercy followed by betrayal.

"I want to help," Five growls. "Let me help."

"Screw it," Sam says, making the decision for me. He takes out Five's wrist-mounted blade, extends it and slashes through Five's bonds. "All hands on deck."

I glance back at the monster. Nine jabs his remaining metal pole into the side of the beast's neck over and over. I can see some black blood spilling out, but he's definitely not doing much damage. Then, shrieking, the monster swats at him again. This time, he clips Nine a little, and he's forced to retreat down the monster's back.

Above the Hunter's bellowing, I hear the familiar *whup-whup-whup* of helicopters. A pair of sleek Black Hawks just took off from the Brooklyn Bridge and are on their way. So, Agent Walker's not totally useless after all.

"Can I have that back?" Five asks Sam, holding a

hand out for his weapon.

"No," I say, putting myself in between the two of them. "You said you could help. Go help."

Five sighs. "Fine. I'll do it the hard way." He floats a few feet off the ground, then looks at me. "All right, John. Light me on fire."

"What?"

"Light me on fire!" he shouts.

I don't need much more convincing to hurt Five. I let my Lumen go and lob a small fireball at him. He lets it hit him and immediately his skin is covered in flames.

"Thanks," he says, and streaks off towards the Hunter, our very own flaming missile.

I crouch down next to Daniela and press my hands against her head. I let my healing Legacy flow, hoping that will help ease her pain. It's not really my healing Legacy, though, is it? It's Ximic, and healing is just the one Legacy I've gotten really good at copying. It doesn't help Daniela, but something does happen when the energy flows between us. Suddenly, I can sense exactly what's happening inside her.

I can feel it too. A pressure behind the eyes. A heavy weight that feels like it's trying to punch through my face.

"It's tearing me apart!" Daniela screams.

"Agh, I know! I feel it too!" I reply, holding the sides of my head like my cranium might split apart.

Meanwhile, Five, pure velocity and white-hot heat, flies himself right into one of the Hunter's eyes. There's a sick puckering sound and the monster screams louder than ever. A moment later, a hole explodes through the back of its head and out comes Five. He holds something aloft. It must be one of the Loric pendants.

"Holy shit," Sam says. "That was nasty, but it worked."

The Hunter just took a human bullet through the brain. I bet he feels pretty similar to the way Daniela and I do right now. It doesn't topple over dead like I hope. Instead, it just gets angrier. It flings itself towards Five, who zips away quickly. Still clinging to the beast but now getting the idea of how to really hurt it, Nine starts climbing up towards its remaining eyes.

That's when the Black Hawks arrive. They bombard the Hunter with missile strikes that only annoy the monster further. While I appreciate the help, their weapons aren't going to hurt this thing. There's a good chance those pilots are just going to get themselves killed or hit Nine and Five by accident.

The Hunter thrashes around, smashing through the plaza, and nearly backhanding one of the choppers out of the sky. It makes it extremely hard for Five to line up another strike at the creature's eyes.

When the Hunter tilts its head back and roars, the powerful gust of bad breath is enough to blow Nine right off the monster's face. He flies away from the Hunter's body and plummets the hundred or so feet back towards the concrete ground. I try to reach out with my telekinesis, but the distance is too far and my head is pounding so much that I can't focus.

Five swoops down, flames extinguished. Instead of going in for another strike, Five catches Nine by the wrist in midair. He lowers him gently to the ground. In response, Nine punches him right in the face. Because of course he does.

The chopper pilots are coming in for another pass. Grounded now, Five and Nine are right in the Hunter's path. Things are going south in a hurry.

"If you guys are going to do something, now is the time!" Sam yells.

I don't know what to do. I can feel this Legacy I copied from Daniela building up inside of me, but I have no idea what it does or how to use it. I'm flailing here. All I've got is a splitting headache. There has to be more to it.

With an anguished cry, Daniela springs to her feet. She shoves both of us aside and screams.

"I have to let it out!"

Daniela opens her eyes and a concentrated beam of silver energy shoots towards the Hunter. At first, she's completely out of control, the energy beam seeming painfully large as it rips through her head, and zigzagging all over the monster's body. But, after a few seconds, Daniela gets a grip. The beam becomes narrower and more focused.

The result is better than I could've hoped.

The Hunter makes a confused yelping sound as it looks down at itself and finds its massive body turning into stone.

As soon as I see Daniela do it, I realize that I can do it too. I focus on the weight behind my eyes—like a boulder, aching to roll down a hill—and shove it out. My vision takes on a silvery tint as the beam flows from my eyes. It's difficult at first, I have to control it with my eyes, so it's not easy to be precise, but I get the hang of it pretty quickly. So does Daniela. Soon, we're painting streaks of stone up and down the confused monster's towering frame.

The Hunter tries to lumber forward to get at Nine and Five, but its legs aren't working anymore. They're solid blocks of rock.

It's over a few seconds later. Towering next to the Statue of Liberty is a grayish tombstone of the most formidable Mogadorian creation I've ever seen, its hideous features forever frozen in a mask of confused rage. Nine and Five stare up at the thing, too confused to even fight each other. The helicopters circle around it, obviously detecting that the beast is no longer a threat and merely an eyesore.

"Ow," Daniela responds, and leans against me for support. "That did not feel good at all."

I rub my own face. "No kidding."

"That was amazing!" Sam shouts. "You're like Medusa."

"That is *not* going to be my superhero code name," Daniela responds sharply. "Ugh."

"And you're like—like—" Sam's too excited to even say it.

"Like Pittacus," I finish for him.

"Holy shit, yes! This is big. Do you realize how big this is?"

"It's big."

"Kinda stealing my new Legacy thunder here," Daniela grumbles.

I shake my head and laugh, actually feeling relief for the first time in days. Nine walks towards the monster monument, hands on his hips, and knocks on the stone. While he does that, Five slinks back to the rest of us. I notice that he's hung the Loric pendant ripped out of the monster's skull around his own neck. I wonder if that's his original pendant that he gave up or had taken by Setrákus Ra, or if it belongs to one of the dead Garde. I don't press the issue right now. He holds out his hands.

"Well, I tried," he says. "You can tie me back up if you want."

I exchange a quick look with Sam. I know Five just helped us and I know he said he could've broken those ropes if he needed to, but I still feel more comfortable with him tied up. He's a loose cannon and a murderer. I don't know if I'll ever be able to really trust him.

As I pick up the ropes that Sam just cut through a few minutes ago, Agent Walker and her surviving team walk over to us. She's on her satellite phone in the middle of a hushed conversation. While she isn't paying attention, Agent Murray grins at us and flashes a big double thumbs-up.

The helicopters set down a ways off, on one of the few stretches of plaza that wasn't demolished by the Hunter. I guess they're going to ferry us back to the military encampment. I have to find out what's happened with the other Garde. I don't have any new scars on my ankles, which means the battle is either won or still ongoing. I need to get to them, to Setrákus Ra, and put this new Legacy to good use.

Well, as long as I can figure out how to use it.

"Yes, sir," Agent Walker says into the phone, then holds it away from her face, blinking in shock like she can't believe what's happening. She seems more surprised by her conversation than by the monster statue Daniela and I just made. She covers the mouthpiece of the phone and holds it out for me. "John, uh, I have the president on the line for you."

THE FATE OF TEN

I stare at her. "What? Seriously?"

Walker nods. "He's apparently . . . um, changed his opinion on fully supporting the Loric. He wants you in Washington right away to discuss strategy."

I hand the ropes off to Nine as he saunters over to us. He's all too happy to be the one tying up Five. "Catching me didn't make us even," I hear him mutter to Five.

"No, it doesn't," Five replies quietly.

I ignore them for now. I'm about to talk to the president. I shake my head, eyeing Walker. "This isn't some kind of trick, is it?"

"No," Walker says, shaking the phone at me. "He's for real. It sounds nuts but, apparently, his older daughter just experienced some kind of . . . vision? Where you gave a speech?"

Sam can't hold back the laughter. "Get out!"

Walker looks at both of us. "Did I miss something?"

"No," I say, smiling and reaching for the phone. "I'll explain later."

Before I can take Walker's satellite phone, my own phone begins to vibrate in my back pocket. Only two people in the world have that number—Sarah and Six. The fight with Setrákus Ra must be over if they're calling me. Hell, maybe they even killed the old bastard.

"Sorry," I tell Walker, taking out my own phone. She looks at me like I'm crazy. "Tell the president to hold. I've got to take this."

I answer the phone and immediately my good mood evaporates. I can hear rushing air, distant blaster fire and way too much screaming. I think that's Mark and he sounds absolutely out of his mind, shouting at someone to wake up. My stomach drops.

And then, Sarah starts talking.

"John . . ." Her voice is shaky, weak. "Listen, I don't have much time . . ."

CHAPTER
TWENTY-FIVE

"HOLD ON!" LEXA SHOUTS OVER HER SHOULDER from the pilot's chair, and the ship rocks violently to the side. Blaster fire sizzles through the air outside, close to hitting us. She takes another evasive maneuver and banks us hard to the right.

The *Anubis* chases us, unloading its energy cannons anytime it has anything close to a clear shot. I have faith that Lexa will get us clear, though. Our ship is smaller, faster, and she's a damn good pilot.

"What's going on back there?" she yells, sweat dripping down her face as she dips us lower to the jungle, using trees for cover. "Six? Talk to me, Six!"

I can't talk.

Across the aisle from me, Ella sits with her back against the wall, her knees drawn up tight to her chest. She hugs herself and rocks back and forth, crying. Her face is smeared with that oil-like garbage, but at least it has stopped flowing out of her. There's still the occasional crackle of Loric energy around her head.

"I warned him," she whispers to herself over and over again. "I warned you all what would happen."

Marina lies on a cot towards the back of the ship, unconscious and in a bad way, her body strapped down so as not to be jostled during our hurried escape flight. I don't even want to guess how many of her bones are broken, or if she'll ever wake up again.

That doesn't stop Mark, desperate and crying, from violently shaking her by the shoulders.

"Wake up!" he yells in her face. "You're the healer, goddamn you! You have to wake up and heal her!"

Adam lunges at him. The Mogadorian slams Mark hard against the wall of the ship and presses his forearm right up against his throat. Mark struggles against him, so Adam just slams him against the wall until he stops.

"Stop! You could kill her, shaking her like that," Adam growls.

"I have to—" Mark pleads. Adam shakes his head firmly.

"There's nothing you can do," he says, trying not to sound cold.

Mark presses his forehead against Adam's and screams, "We never should have come here!"

All the chaos doesn't seem to bother Sarah. She looks up at me and smiles peacefully. She's paler than I've ever seen her. A second ago, I gave her my satellite phone to call John.

"John . . . Listen, I don't have much time," she says, her voice thin and weak.

My hands are covered in Sarah's blood. I'm doing my best to stop the bleeding, but the wound is huge. I don't even know what hit her exactly, there were so many objects flying through the air. Something jagged and large. It tore right through her side, above the hip and out. Took a big part of her midsection with it. I took some bad shots during that exchange with Setrákus Ra, but I'm going to make it.

Without Marina, Sarah doesn't have long.

She dragged me away from the landing strip when I was still stunned. I don't know how she did it, bleeding so much. Adrenaline? Her strength faltered when we hit the jungle. I had to carry her the rest of the way to Lexa's ship.

The floor is covered in her blood. So are my clothes. It's all over my hands, in more ways than one.

This happened because of me. Because she wouldn't leave me to face Setrákus Ra alone.

Stupid girl. She probably saved my life.

"Please, John, don't talk, just listen . . . ," Sarah says. "You have to know, from the moment I saw you outside Paradise High, I knew. I knew we were going to fall in love. And I've never regretted even a second of it. Not even now. I love you with all my heart, John. I always will. It was . . . it was all worth it."

The ship banks hard to the left. If I killed Setrákus Ra back there, it hasn't stopped the *Anubis* from trying to chase us down. How am I going to explain this to John? How am I going to live with it?

It should've been me.

"I wish . . . I wish I could've seen you one more time," Sarah says quietly, tears welling up in her eyes. "Maybe I still will. I'll be waiting for you, John, wherever is next. Maybe it'll be . . . it'll be like Lorien. Or like Paradise."

Bernie Kosar lies down next to Sarah. He whines and licks her cheek. She actually laughs a little.

"BK is here," she tells John, sounding increasingly distant, out of it. "He says hi."

Sarah gasps. Coughs. Blood leaks from the corners of her mouth, coming from inside her. I see her try to fight it. She's trying so hard to stay.

"Promise me, John . . . promise me you'll keep fighting. Promise you'll win. Don't let it all be for nothing, my love. Please, just remember, I love you, John. I always . . ."

Sarah stops talking. Her mouth keeps moving for another second, no sound coming out, and then it stops. I keep one hand braced against her stomach and press the other to her neck, even though I already know.

She's gone.

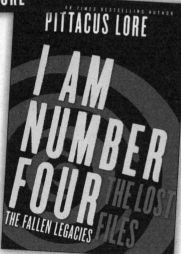

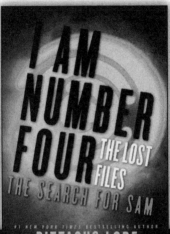
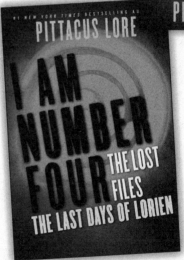
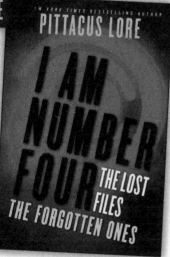

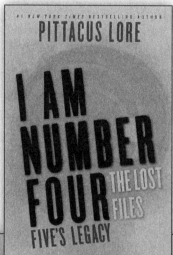
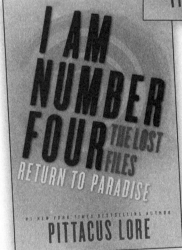
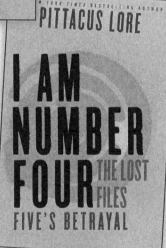

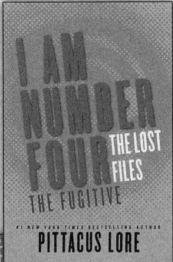

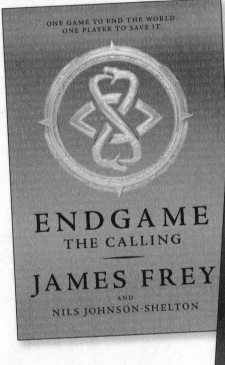
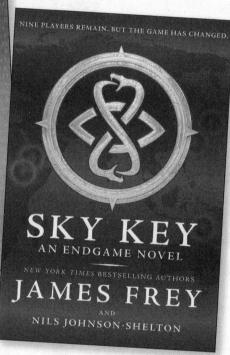

BARRACKS

LABORATORY WING

SETRÁKUS RA'S
QUARTERS

OBSERVATION DECK

CONTROL ROOM

ENGINE ROOM

MAIN CANNON

AUXILIARY WEAPONS

DOCKING BAY

THE ANUBIS: DESTROYER OF WORLDS
THE LEAD WARSHIP AND CROWN JEWEL OF THE MOGADORIAN FLEET.

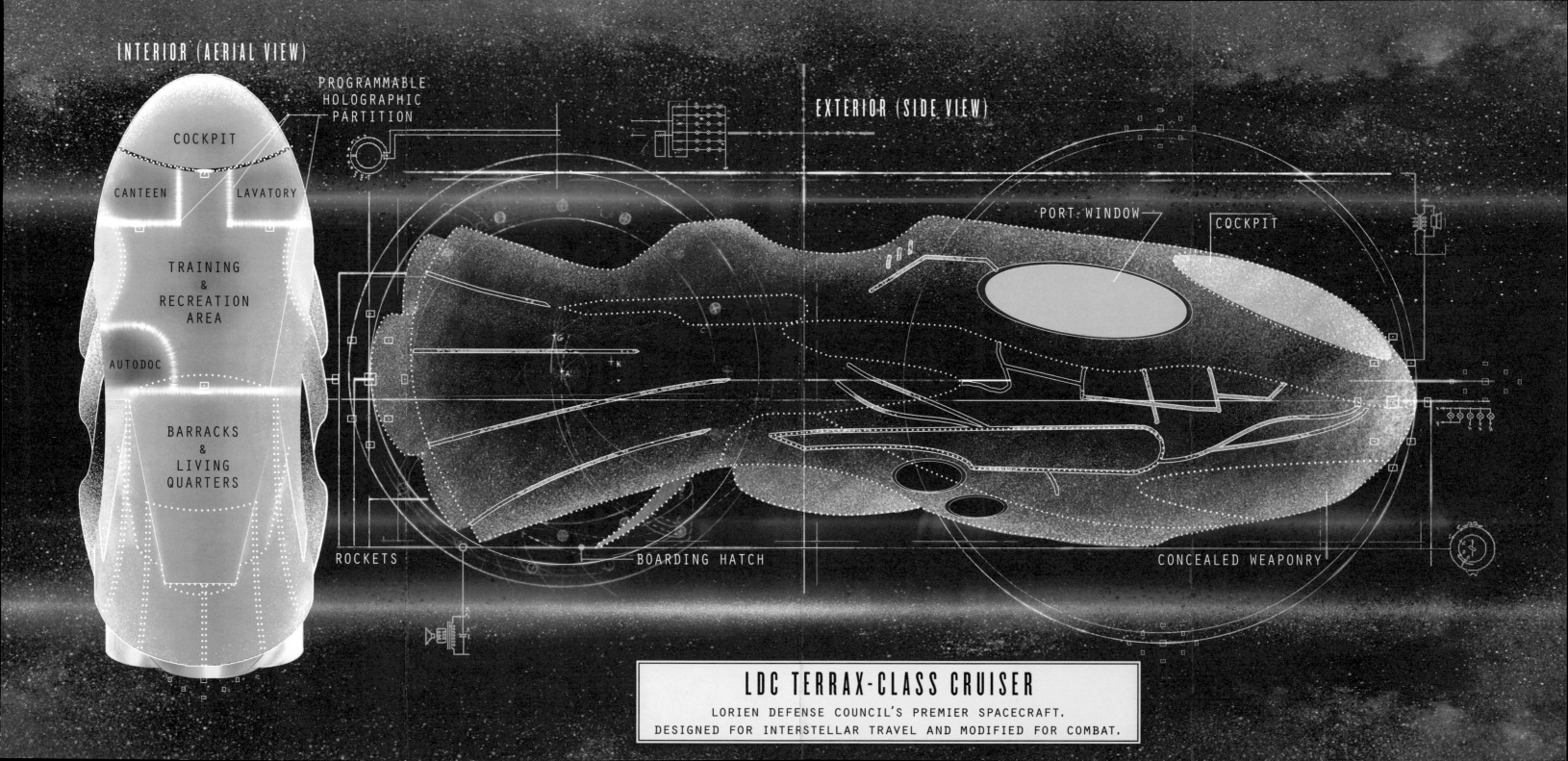

INTERIOR (AERIAL VIEW)

PROGRAMMABLE
HOLOGRAPHIC
PARTITION

COCKPIT

CANTEEN   LAVATORY

TRAINING
&
RECREATION
AREA

AUTODOC

BARRACKS
&
LIVING
QUARTERS

ROCKETS

EXTERIOR (SIDE VIEW)

PORT WINDOW   COCKPIT

BOARDING HATCH   CONCEALED WEAPONRY

LDC TERRAX-CLASS CRUISER

LORIEN DEFENSE COUNCIL'S PREMIER SPACECRAFT.
DESIGNED FOR INTERSTELLAR TRAVEL AND MODIFIED FOR COMBAT.